LUMEN SER

THE ANCIENT CASTLE

MATT SPRUNT

Living Room Adventures

The Ancient Castle
All Rights Reserved.
Copyright © 2016 Matthew Sprunt
v5.0

Cover Photo © 2016 Petur Atli Antonsson. All rights reserved - used with permission.

Living Room Adventures

ISBN: 978-0-578-16641-4

PRINTED IN THE UNITED STATES OF AMERICA

Table of Contents

Chapter One

CastleOne

The air was stifling hot and things were unusually quiet. Except for the soft crunch of his boots, and those in his division, moving through the overgrown brush, there wasn't a noise to be heard. Eric slowly crept to the crest of the hill. If their spies had been correct, the Badgers' camp was just on the other side of the hill they were climbing.

"Slowly," he could hear DeFries whisper. "We don't want to give ourselves away."

Suddenly, out of the corner of his eye, Eric saw a blur of green, followed by the sound of gunfire. Bullets zoomed everywhere. Instinctively, he dropped to the ground and rolled toward a clump of trees. Behind the shelter of a large oak tree, he was better able to survey the situation, and it wasn't pretty. The Badger division had somehow known the Falcons' position and had attacked with lightning speed. They had taken his division by surprise and several of his men were down. Actually, most of them were down. Bullets were still flying from both sides. Eric knew he couldn't just sit there. He had to do something. But before he knew it, the battle was over. His entire division had been slaughtered. The Badgers, rejoicing in their victory, began to cheer and celebrate.

After the initial shock of defeat left him, it dawned on Eric that the Badgers had no idea he was still alive, hiding behind the tree. He waited just long enough for them to let their guard down. Then, whipping out from behind the shelter of the giant oak, he pulled the trigger of his semi-automatic paintball gun. Bullets, which were actually just paintball pellets, sprayed everywhere hitting Badgers right and left. It took at least ten seconds before any members of the opposing division were able to gather their wits about them and register what was happening. Then, before he could react, bullets riddled Eric's body and he dropped.

Eric awoke with a start, beads of sweat running down his forehead. It had just been a dream. He lay there thinking about it for some time, steaming with frustration. The dream had reminded him of his team's loss to the Badgers, a rival team at school. For two years in a row, the Badgers had beaten the Falcons. Actually, the Badgers had beaten the Falcons for five consecutive years, but Eric had only attended CastleOne Military School for two years and was about to start his third. He wanted nothing more than to beat the Badgers at War Games this coming year. The Falcons had done well against the Badgers in basketball and football, the other two sports of interest to Eric, but the school trophy, a cannonball, went to the team that won the War Games. Eric wanted that trophy!

CastleOne was a boarding school for both American military brats and other English-speaking civilians who lived in Europe, but who preferred to attend an English-speaking school. Because of its remote location, students were encouraged to board at school while attending, rather than commuting from their homes. Eric Frontier attended CastleOne not only because his parents were American civilians who worked in Germany, but also because the headmaster, Linus McDougal, was a very good friend of his parents.

CastleOne was a large and ancient castle that sat on an immense expanse of land nestled in the countryside of southern Germany. Converted into a military school many years ago, it was much like any other school, except for the military training each student received.

In addition to English, math, science, and other basic academic courses, each student was required to learn how to shoot a gun, military strategy, hand to hand combat, and of course maintain physical strength and endurance.

Since there were no other schools of this same type to compete against, all competitions took place within the school. Throughout the year, the Falcons and the Badgers, the two divisions in the school, competed against each other in athletic events such as football and basketball. They also trained for a military competition called the War Games, which took place at the end of the year, consisting of a strength and endurance course, shooting competition, hand-to-hand combat, and a military exercise to see which team could capture the other team's flag first. The winner of this military competition was awarded the coveted cannonball—a school trophy. The cannonball was placed in that team's dormitory throughout the following year. In addition, the losing team was required to sing the winner's victory song at the closing awards banquet.

It was the cannonball that Eric was thinking about when his alarm clock went off. He had left his window open the night before to let in the cool night air, and as he lay in bed thinking about his dream, he could hear the faint voice of someone outside.

"Ladies and gentlemen, next up, the one and only, the person you've all been waiting for, wearing his black snake shoes and signature black flexfit hat, Josh Frontier! AHHHH! The crowd goes wild!" Eric slowly lifted his head and peered out the window. He could see his younger brothers, Josh and Scott, outside with their skateboards. Scott was standing to the side while Josh was teetering on the edge of the half pipe their father had built in the backyard. With the sun just peeking over the mountains, Josh shoved off and Eric could hear him talking again.

"A drop in tail drop, followed by an easy axel stall. Drops back down the pipe, up the transition and—whoa! A backside air! This guy is unbelievable! The crowd is on their feet." Eric crept down the stairs and outside to the backyard.

"Yeaaaaaah," he screamed as though he were one of Josh's make-believe fans. Josh was so startled, he just about fell off his board. "How come you guys didn't invite me to the show?" Eric teased.

"Because you are not worthy," Josh haughtily proclaimed.

"I have to admit, you and Scott are getting pretty good. What are you guys doing out here so early?"

"Since they don't allow boards at school, I figured I'd come out for one last run. I wanted to make sure I could still out-board Josh. You, I don't have to worry about," Scott joked.

"Oh yeah? Give me that board."

"Drop the board," their mother yelled. "You've got to eat your breakfast so we can get you boys to CastleOne on time."

This was Eric's third year at CastleOne, while it would be Scott's first. Scott had always followed in Eric's shadow, and everywhere he went, he was known as Eric's little brother, even though in height they were about the same. He would have liked nothing more than for people to refer to Eric as Scott's brother, rather than the other way around. Despite the rivalry between them, they were still the best of friends. They were also as different as night and day.

Eric was built like a freight train with little or no neck, broad shoulders, and thick legs. He had a magnetic personality and was usually found hanging around large groups of people. His big blue eyes and sandy blond hair made him a very good-looking kid. Although Eric was very muscular, he preferred using brains over brawn to solve his problems and was a straight-A student.

Scott, on the other hand, was skinny but muscular. He had dark brown eyes, hair that was so blond it almost bordered on white, and a smile that could melt any girl's heart. He also had a reserved personality, which was the reason he had so few friends. However, the friends he did have were true friends because of his loyalty to them.

Unlike Eric, Scott had a bad temper and did not take teasing very well. As a result, he often ended up fighting, which in turn meant he also spent a significant amount of time in the principal's office. In all fairness, most of his fighting was in defense of others, exposing his tender heart.

As the boys sat down to eat their breakfast, they noticed their youngest brother Josh looking very solemn. "What's wrong with you, runt?" Eric asked.

"What do you think? You guys are going to school and I'm stuck here alone with Mom and Dad for the whole year!" Josh replied grumpily. Joshua was three years younger than Scott and was attending a German school.

"Don't worry. With you here all alone, Mom and Dad will probably spoil you rotten," Scott assured him. He poured himself a bowl of cereal and then reached for his spoon. "Hey, where did my spoon go? It was right here," he mumbled to himself.

"Scott, my bro, you are so careless. Here, let me get it for you," Josh said in a rather disgusted voice. He then materialized a spoon, seemingly out of thin air, right behind Scott's ear and gave it to him.

"Very funny," Scott retorted.

Josh, who was eleven years old, had been practicing magic tricks since he was quite young. He especially loved sleight of hand and levitation tricks. Although he was pretty good at his tricks, he still had plenty of room for improvement.

After finishing breakfast and clearing their dishes, the boys loaded their luggage into the car, and soon the whole family headed off to CastleOne. While on the road, their mother gave them the usual lecture about good manners, getting their homework done, and respecting others. She then turned to Scott. "Scott, promise me that you won't fight. I don't want to become any closer friends with Linus than we already are."

"Mom, you make it sound like fighting is my hobby."

"I wouldn't call it a hobby, but considering how often it happens, it might as well be."

"Mom, it's not like I go out of my way to fight. I only hit those people who deserve it."

"There sure are a lot of deserving kids," Eric piped in. Then, in a more serious tone, he added, "Watch out for Slim Johnson, Scott. He'll be a senior this year, and he's the captain of the Badger division. He seems to find every opportunity he can to harass lower classmen, especially freshmen."

"All I am trying to say, Scott," their mother continued, "is that I would like you to control your temper. Even if there are a few kids who deserve—how do you put it, a good butt kicking?—you don't have to use your fist to do it. Try ignoring them. Will you do that?"

"I'll try, Mom. But I can't promise."

"Look at it this way, Mom," Eric spoke up again. "This is a military school. Either Scott will learn to keep his temper or he'll be in the best shape he's ever been in. I guarantee you the first time Buzz catches Scott fighting, he'll have him doing pushups and running the grounds for days."

Scott pretended to ignore that remark, but inside he was very nervous. He had a kind heart, but he also had an uncontrollable temper, and he wasn't really sure he would be able to keep it in check. He also knew the chances of him not getting into a fight, were slim to nothing. Scott really didn't like to fight, it just seemed to happen.

Before long, they arrived at CastleOne. Scott had been there twice before when they had dropped Eric off the previous two years. He thought the castle, with its large moat, high thick walls, and pointed turrets, looked very majestic. He wondered who had built this great fortress, but not even the German people were sure of its true origin. The beautifully kept grounds were covered with large and majestic oak trees. Scott had often heard Eric talk about the War Games, and he could easily imagine himself running and hiding behind trees to avoid being hit. That thought sent a thrill of excitement coursing through his body.

"It's gone!" Scott said out loud.

"What's gone?" Eric asked.

"The gargoyle that sits on top of the castle. It's no longer there."

Eric looked up. "There was never a gargoyle on top of the castle."

"Yes there was. The last time we came to drop you off, I distinctly remember seeing it. In fact, I stared at it for a long time."

"Scott, I've been going to this school for two years and have never seen a gargoyle on top of the school."

"You don't have to believe me, but I know it was there."

"Come on, let's argue about this some other time. You need to see the castle. You are going to love this place," Eric said enthusiastically.

Scott wasn't so sure about that. Eric made friends easily and his teachers loved him because he was polite, outgoing, and always did his homework. People he didn't even know loved him because he treated everyone as a friend. And despite his great popularity, he never let it go to his head. Scott admired Eric for this, but he hated being compared to him. He was quite the opposite from Eric and always felt as if he were letting people down, especially his parents.

The school grounds were buzzing with excitement. Students were picking up school supplies, purchasing books, registering for classes, and saying good-bye to parents. The most exciting thing about the first day of school, however, was seeing friends again. It didn't take long for a couple of boys to spot Eric and mob him with the "How are you doing?" and "How was your summer vacation?" talk. Scott walked behind Eric feeling glum. He wondered if he would ever make any friends here.

Just then, Eric turned toward Scott. "Hey, I want you guys to meet my *little* brother, Scott."

Eric's friends held out their hands and said, "Hi. How are you?"

and "Welcome to CastleOne." Shaking each of their hands, Scott smiled and said hello to them. The boys soon turned their attention back to Eric and started planning how they were going to beat the Badgers this year.

They arrived at the registration office, where several other freshmen were waiting with their parents. Scott glanced around, looking to see if any of them seemed his type. He caught sight of a couple of girls waiting to pick up their books. They were looking right at him, which made him slightly uncomfortable. He tried to avoid their eyes the best he could, but he couldn't help looking back at them every now and then. As he was scanning the crowd, his eyes wandered back to the two girls, and to his utter embarrassment, they were waving at him. He quickly looked away, but then realizing they knew he had seen them, looked back. Once eye contact was made, he pointed to himself as if to say, "Are you waving to me?" They both nodded, so Scott smiled and waved back and then turned to speak with his parents as if he had something important to say to them. He could hear the two girls laughing and giggling behind him. They weren't exactly what he would call pretty, but they weren't ugly either. At least it gave him hope that he would find friends here, although he wasn't looking for any girlfriends.

After they finished the registration process, picked up their supplies, and received their dorm numbers, Scott noticed he was, not surprisingly, assigned to the Falcons' military unit. He knew his parents had contacted the headmaster ahead of time and requested he be put in the same unit as Eric. This made Scott feel a bit more comfortable, knowing he would have Eric around. The two boys and their parents headed to the dormitory to drop off their belongings before returning to the reception.

When Scott and his family arrived at his dorm, they found his roommate already there. He was unpacking his belongings with his back turned toward them. When they entered the room, he turned around wearing a pair of glasses with the eyes bugging out. "Hi!" he blurted out, as the eyeballs on the glasses bounced up and down on springs.

"Hi," the foursome replied, not quite sure what to think.

"Nice glasses," said Mr. Frontier.

"I know, I get a kick out of them," the boy laughed. He took off the fake glasses and put on his real ones. He was a short, skinny, nerdy-looking kid with blond hair. He turned to Scott. "You must be Scott. I'm Ned, your roommate. I was just unpacking my stuff. You don't mind if I take this side, do you?" Before Scott could answer, he continued. "This is going to be a great place to attend school. I've never lived in a real castle before." He turned to Mr. and Mrs. Frontier and extended his hand towards them. "Hi, Ned Niedermeier."

Obviously, Ned was very outgoing, and this put Scott more at ease. Scott threw his stuff on his bed and was about to unpack when Ned asked him, "Scott, are you going to the orientation?"

"Yeah, I was planning on it."

"Why don't you and I go together? That way your parents can take your brother to his bunk and we'll meet them down in the reception room."

"Sounds good to me." He turned to his parents. "I'll meet you guys downstairs."

Scott and Ned took off down the winding staircase while Eric and his parents left to look for Eric's room. On their way, Ned turned to Scott, saying, "My brother Neil graduated from here last year. He says this place is haunted."

"Haunted?" Scott asked skeptically.

"Yes! He says that when he was here, he and his friend were out after curfew exploring the castle. They walked into this room and some of the chairs were floating in mid-air."

"Floating in the air, huh? Don't you think he was just trying to scare you?"

"No! He was serious. He says it scared them so bad they turned and ran. While running, they knocked a painting of a knight with a golden sword, off the wall. As a result, the headmaster came to investigate the noise. When they heard him coming, Neil and his friend hid so that he walked right past them. He found the painting on the ground and they heard him mumble something they didn't understand. But here's the weird thing. After hanging the picture back up, the headmaster headed down the hall and then walked right through a wall."

"No way!" Scott said. "There is no way the headmaster walked through a wall. If they really saw all this, and I seriously doubt they did, but if they did, there must be some sort of explanation."

"I'm telling you, Scott. He was dead serious. He wasn't joking. He also said he saw shadows once in a while outside his window at night, shadows of something large flying through the air!"

"I'll believe it when I see it," Scott whispered. A little chill ran down his spine, but he was quick not to show it. Soon they arrived at the reception room where the headmaster was speaking to the parents.

The reception was an opportunity for the students to visit with friends, while also giving the parents time to meet with the teachers and discuss any concerns. In addition to the reception, a welcome orientation was given to all freshmen. During the orientation, students were given a tour to show them the layout of the castle. This was a great opportunity for the new students to meet each other and get acquainted.

Scott and Ned headed over to the refreshment table, which was laden with plates of cookies, pies, and cakes just waiting to be eaten. They each wolfed down a piece of pie as the headmaster explained that math, English, science, and history would be taught by grade, while military drill would combine grades, with freshmen and sophomores together and juniors and seniors together. He continued, explaining that all competitive events would take place after school, with football beginning in one week.

"Do you play any sports?" Scott asked Ned.

"Not really. I'm more the brainy sort. I do like basketball, but I'm too short and clumsy to play on any team. How about you?"

"I like both basketball and football, but my real love is swimming. Unfortunately, they don't offer swimming here."

"There's always the moat," Ned joked.

Scott laughed at that. "Yeah, who knows what kinds of creatures are lurking in that water?"

The headmaster finished and parents began saying good-bye to their children, while Ms. Peterson, the English teacher, gathered all the freshmen together for the orientation. Scott looked for his parents and found them across the room talking to the headmaster. He walked over to say good-bye before he headed off to the orientation. When he approached, his mother put her arm around his shoulders. "Scott, this is Linus McDougal, the headmaster."

Headmaster McDougal reached out his hand to shake Scott's. "We met last year, didn't we, Scott?"

"I believe so," Scott replied.

"So, are you excited to start a new year here at CastleOne?"

"I guess so. The castle is pretty cool, but school is never easy to get excited about."

"I bet you'll like it here better than you think," the headmaster said winking at him, as though he knew something that Scott didn't.

Scott gave his parents a good-bye hug and once again shook the headmaster's hand before trotting over to the already large group of freshmen waiting for the orientation tour to begin. He quickly found Ned and sidled up next to him. "Did I miss anything?" he asked.

"No. We're still waiting for the captain of both divisions. I believe each division provides their own tour."

They had only waited for a moment when two older students arrived. They introduced themselves as Ian Karding, captain of the

∽ 11 ∽

Falcons, and Slim Johnson, captain of the Badgers. Ian was of average height with short brown hair and glasses. Eric had mentioned earlier that Ian was nice and personable, but very competitive. Slim was tall and slender and had blond hair, freckles, and a pug nose. His face seemed to have a permanent sneer attached to it. This was the guy Eric had warned Scott about. Slim was the epitome of the word *bully*.

After the two seniors introduced themselves, the freshmen were asked to separate into their respective teams and meet with their captains for the tour. Scott and Ned moved to the spot where Ian was standing. As they approached, Ian moved toward them and held out his hand to Scott. "Hi, Scott, glad to have you on board," he said. He then turned to Ned and the rest of the freshmen, calling them by name and shaking each of their hands.

"How does he know all of our names?" Scott whispered to Ned.

Before Ned could respond, Ian glanced over at Scott. "I know your names because I make it a point to know your names. I know everything about everybody. I know your names, your strengths, your weaknesses, your likes and your dislikes."

Ned leaned over to Scott and whispered, "Do you think he keeps track of when we go to the bathroom?"

"I heard that," Ian said. He then continued in a very important-sounding voice. "A captain must know every one of his soldiers if he is going to win." Then in a more animated voice, "And we are going to win this year, aren't we?"

No one said a word.

"Aren't we?" he said louder.

"No, Sir!" Ned yelled as loud as he could.

The other freshmen looked at him and laughed, but Ian just ignored him.

"AREN'T WE?"

At this point everybody yelled back, "Yes, Sir!"

"That's better. Now that we are clear on that point, let's begin our tour."

They were already near the North Wing, so they started there first. That part of the castle was boring since it was just classrooms. There were two long halls with several rooms branching off on both sides. These rooms didn't look any different than the classrooms Scott had seen in other schools. From there, they moved into the East Wing. That wing housed the cafeteria, exercise room, assembly hall, and several other large halls that were used for big gatherings, such as dances and special receptions. The student dormitories were located in the South Wing. Since most of the students had already been there, Ian didn't waste much time showing them that area.

He continued with the tour, taking the students outside to the military practice range. "This is where you will learn shooting and hand-to-hand combat skills. It's also where mock battles take place. This part of your education is very important. Not only will you learn valuable lessons that could save your life if you ever have to engage in real combat, but most importantly, these skills will be instrumental in winning this year's War Games!" The students laughed.

"This is not a laughing matter!" he barked out. At this, everyone shut up, shocked by his intensity. But then he smiled as if to say, "Gotcha!" Then continuing, "Most important, is that you have fun. Okay, moving on."

The West Wing was occupied by the administrative offices, which also included the private quarters of the staff. Ian took them into Mr. Billock's office, one of the math teachers. "As you can see, their offices are really the front door to their private quarters, so please don't go wandering past those brown doors. Their living areas are off-limits to students. Anyone caught in those areas will be severely punished up to, and including, termination from school. Is that understood?"

"Yes, Sir!" everybody but Ned shouted.

Ned, of course, yelled, "No, Sir!"

Ian just ignored him again. "Good!" he said. He lead them out of the office and on to the next point of interest. As they continued down the hall, Ned suddenly stopped. At first, Scott didn't notice that Ned was no longer beside him. When he finally realized Ned was missing, he walked back and found him studying a painting on the wall.

"What are you looking at?" he asked.

"Look at this painting. What do you see?" Ned questioned him.

"Umm... oh! It's the painting of the knight with the golden sword."

"It's the painting my brother told me about that night they almost got caught."

"Just because the painting exists, doesn't mean your brother was telling the truth. Come on, we're getting left behind," Scott said, tugging on Ned's arm.

"Wait. There's one more thing. Don't you see it?" Ned asked, holding him back.

"See what?"

"The knight in this painting looks remarkably... like you."

Scott studied the painting for a second. "Just because he has blond hair and brown eyes? He's also a lot older than I am. Even if he does look a little like me, what does it matter?" Scott asked, walking off. But as he continued down the hall he couldn't help but shudder at the resemblance.

Ned shook his head as he followed Scott. The two of them ran to catch up with the others. When they couldn't find their group, they decided to walk back the way they had come. This would be the shortest way back to the dorms. They turned around and when they came upon the painting once again, Ned remarked, "He's not that much older. I still say he looks like you."

"So what if he does?" snorted Scott, trying not to show his disconcertment.

"Hey, if this is the painting that fell, which wall do you suppose the headmaster walked through?" Ned asked, remembering the rest of the story.

"Ooooh…that must mean the room with the floating chairs is nearby," Scott said in a spooky voice.

"You mean a room like that one?" Ned said, pointing to a door just around the corner.

"That's more like a closet, Ned. The door and the hallway are much too skinny to lead to a room of any size."

Ned cautiously walked towards the door. "Look! The door's open. Let's just take a peek."

"How do you know the door is open?"

"From this angle I can see it. Come on, let's take a look." The hallway was dark and skinny, which would explain why they hadn't seen it before. They crept slowly forward. Ned stretched out his arm and placed his hand on the doorknob, slowly pushing the door open wider. Suddenly a loud moan echoed through the hall.

Ned jerked his hand and jumped back. "Aaahh!"

Scott, who had let out the moan, was laughing hysterically.

When Ned realized the noise had come from Scott, he turned on him. "You idiot! I almost wet my pants," he jokingly said.

"Why are you creeping toward the door like you're about to find a ghost inside?"

"Well, you never know what you're going to find," Ned answered sheepishly.

Scott brushed past Ned and threw open the door. It was pitch-black inside. He felt along the inside wall until he found a light switch and flipped it on. The room was actually bigger than Scott thought it would be. Standing in the center of the room was a massive oval table, with three large chairs placed at the head. Hanging above was a huge chandelier with diamond-like crystals strung from one arm to the next. At the end of each arm were candleholders with wax melted down like raindrops frozen in time. It looked as if candles had been used quite frequently at one time, but of course, there were none in the chandelier now.

Ned stared at the room in awe. "Wow! Except for the lights on the walls, this room looks like it hasn't changed since the day it was built. Look," he pointed out. "All three of these chairs have the same crest engraved on their backs."

"Hey, you're right," Scott remarked. "It kind of reminds me of King Arthur's round table, except there are only three chairs."

"Maybe it is!" Ned replied.

"Give me a break. King Arthur took place in Great Britain. We are in Germany. Besides, King Arthur is just fiction."

"I was just kidding!" Ned said.

Scott rolled his eyes. "Sure you were. Come on. We better get out of here before Sir Lancelot finds us."

After dinner, Ned and Scott spent the rest of the evening in their room, unpacking and comparing school schedules. Scott was glad to have found a friend so soon. He was beginning to think he might like it here after all. After helping Scott unpack his bags, Ned opened one of his own drawers and showed Scott all the things he had brought from home. He had all kinds of candy and gag gifts. Things like buzzers, whoopee cushions, smoke bombs, and several other objects Scott had never seen before.

"Why did you bring all those?" Scott asked.

"I don't know. I guess I thought they would be fun. We might play some pretty good jokes."

"Yeah, and get kicked out of school at the same time." Ned ignored that comment and began closing the curtains. "What are you doing?" Scott asked.

"The thought of ghosts flying past my window at night gives me the willies."

"You see? Your brother's plan is scaring you already. He's probably at home laughing to himself right now, thinking of his little brother with all the curtains closed and shaking in his bed."

"I am not shaking!" Ned emphatically replied.

"You would be better off to keep them open," Scott pointed out. "At least that way you could actually prove to yourself whether or not there really are ghosts." Just then someone knocked and rattled on the doorknob. Ned gave out a yelp. "It's just my brother," Scott informed him. "Come in, Eric!"

Eric opened the door. "I just thought I'd come and see how you two guys are getting along."

"What you mean," Scott said, "is that Mom asked you to check in on me to make sure I haven't gone AWOL or something."

"Or something," Eric said with a grin. He walked over to the window and opened the curtains. "You really should keep these open. On this side of the castle, you have one of the best views of the moon, and it can be quite a sight sometimes. If you're lucky, you might see it fly past your window."

"See what fly past our window?" Scott questioned.

"I'm not exactly sure, but there were several students last year who swore they saw something with wings, as large as you and I, fly past their window. There was a boy who said he actually came face to face with it. It frightened him so much that he left school and never returned."

"Very funny, ha ha, Eric. Nice try, but your silly stories aren't going to frightened us."

"I know it sounds out of this world, but there was more than one person who claims they saw it," Eric replied as he turned and left the room.

Chapter Two

The Dream

That night as Scott slept, he dreamt he was in a different world full of strange people and unusual animals. It was a beautiful land with high snow-capped mountains and lush valleys, full of streams and flowers. He was sitting on a low wall looking at the turrets of a castle. The highest turret had no windows and was at least twenty feet higher than the rest. The roof was very steep and he wondered how such a tall structure had been built. It must have been very dangerous. As he was studying the spire at the top of the turret, it began to glow so that he could now see through it. Inside, there was a golden sword shining very bright. It seemed to call to him, wanting him to free it. He desperately wanted to, but had no idea how to get up there.

He looked down and saw a pair of boots next to him. At first they looked as though they were made of glass, but when he took hold of them, the material bent and folded like any other boot. The boots had little wings attached on the back, as though they were meant to fly. They reminded him of the golden winged boots Hermes wore in the Greek mythology books he had read.

"Could these make me fly?" he asked himself. He slipped the boots on over his shoes and they disappeared. Or did they? He couldn't see them anymore, but he knew they were still on his feet because he could feel them gripping his ankles. He stood up and walked around as though he were at the shoe store trying on a new pair of sneakers. The boots had molded to his feet, and except for the snugness around his ankles, there was no other indication he was wearing any boots at all.

He walked around a bit more, and then started to run. The feeling was incredible! He seemed to float on air, like a puck floats on an air-hockey table. The more he ran, the faster he went. He ran around the castle grounds getting used to the floating sensation, and then, approaching the wall, he leapt over it. Actually, he leapt *high* over the wall, almost as if, just for a second, he had flown. It was exhilarating. He tried it again, and this time he ran with the intention of springing hard off the wall to see how high he could actually go. But the first step off the ground had already catapulted him too high into the air for his second foot to hit the wall and he continued to soar higher and higher. Before he knew it, he was above the trees. The view was incredible and the feeling indescribable. He was flying! He was thoroughly enjoying himself until he realized that he didn't know how to get down. He continued to soar higher and higher and panic soon settled in. How was he supposed to direct the boots downward? Would he eventually fall or would he simply continue to ascend into the sky?

He began screaming, "Help me! Someone help me!" and then awoke with a start.

"You're not dreaming! You're not dreaming! Run for your life!" Ned was yelling while shaking his shoulders. When Scott finally realized it had only been a dream and he was actually still in his bed, he turned red with embarrassment.

"Very funny, Ned," Scott grumbled.

Ned laughed. "Are you okay?"

"Yeah, I'm fine."

"What in the world were you dreaming about?"

"I dreamed I was flying and was headed higher and higher into the sky and couldn't get down," Scott replied.

"You are definitely not normal," Ned analyzed. "Normal people have dreams where they are falling and falling and can't stop themselves."

Scott thought back on the dream. "It felt so real, like it wasn't really a dream at all."

"Well, next time you decide to go flying, bring me along. Unlike you, I love to fly."

"Go back to bed or I'll send you flying out the window," Scott jokingly growled.

Ned went back to sleep, but Scott couldn't stop thinking about his dream. It had been so awesome and so real. He had never felt anything like it. His mind kept going over the events of the dream all night long, and he had barely fallen back asleep when his alarm clock went off. His head felt like a freight train had run over it. Despite the pounding headache that caused him to groan when he sat up, he climbed out of bed and headed for the showers. Afterward he felt much better, and he and Ned headed down to breakfast where they met Eric and a few of his friends. When they had dished up their food they all sat down together.

"Ned, did you sleep all right last night?" Eric asked.

"Yeah, except for Scott's yelling," Ned replied.

"Yelling?" Eric turned quizzically to his younger brother.

"I just had a bad dream, that's all," Scott cut in. Actually the dream had been a good one, but he didn't want to explain it.

"Well, according to my schedule," Eric said, changing the subject, "the freshmen and the sophomores have military drill in the morning this year, while the juniors and seniors have it in the afternoon. Don't be too alarmed by Buzz," he warned. "He has a rough bark, but inside he's a teddy bear."

"I hope we get to shoot guns today," Scott said, as he and Ned headed out to the practice range.

"Yeah, maybe we could bag ourselves a couple of chicks at the same time," Ned said in reply.

"Dream on, lover boy."

"Are they hard to shoot?" Ned asked.

"No, chicks are easy to shoot, but I wouldn't recommend it."

"I meant the guns themselves, stupid."

"You've never shot a gun before?" Scott asked, looking at Ned in surprise.

"Nope. The closest I've come to shooting is a water pistol."

"Well, I guess if you're going to learn to shoot, a paintball gun is probably the safest thing to learn with," Scott replied.

When they arrived at the shooting range, there were several other freshmen and sophomores waiting for class to start. None of them minded the wait. It was a beautiful late summer day and the temperature was perfect. As Scott and Ned exchanged small talk, Scott looked around trying to take everything in.

There was the gun range and next to it a large building, which Scott assumed must be the hand-to-hand combat area, judging from the mural of two men poised for a fight painted on the outside. There was also an obstacle course with four lanes. All of the lanes were identical, beginning with a group of tires that a runner had to step in and out of. Next there were ropes to crawl—or more like slither under—and then a wall to climb over that Scott figured was probably about six feet tall. A balance beam about fifteen feet long was next, followed by a jungle gym that had to be crossed hand over hand. Noticing the mud hole below, Scott made a mental note to never mess up on that part. The last leg of the course was the part that caught Scott's attention and looked the most challenging. There were five stumps rising about four feet in the air, where, he guessed, you had to jump from stump to stump until you got to the other side. What made it interesting were the large sandbags hanging from ropes. These were obviously used to swing back and forth at the person trying to jump from stump to stump. They looked heavy, and Scott was certain they had enough power in them to knock a person off.

This was the kind of stuff Scott loved. As he observed the grounds, his eyes caught sight of two girls breaking away from the crowd and heading towards him. They were laughing and giggling and waving at him. One of them even winked at him. They were the same two girls he had seen when he was registering for school with his parents. Pretending not to see them, he quickly turned his attention back to Ned. Ned was talking about how hard Buzz had been on Neil and how much he was dreading this part of school. Scott wasn't hearing any of this. His focus was on the two girls getting closer and closer.

Please don't come over here, he prayed silently. Scott liked girls, but he felt awkward around them, especially around girls as flirtatious as these. He felt a tap on the shoulder. *No!* He thought, while at the same time, politely turning around.

"Hi. Remember us?" one of them asked, trying to stifle a laugh. By now, Ned had stopped talking to see what was happening.

"Yeah, I saw you the first day of school, right?" Scott asked.

"Yes, and we couldn't help noticing how cute you are," the same girl answered.

Embarrassed, Scott went red in the face. He didn't know what to say to that, so he said nothing. The girls also stood there in silence, just smiling, not knowing what else to say. After a long awkward moment, Ned finally stepped in. "Hi. My name is Ned. I'm Scott's bodyguard."

The two girls laughed and he held out his hand to shake theirs. They each took his extended hand, but the second girl didn't let go after she had given it a shake. "So what's your last name, Ned?" she asked.

"Bond. Ned Bond," he replied.

"'Cornball' is more like it," Scott said, butting in. They turned to Scott.

"So, your name is Scott. What's your last name?" asked the girl who still had a hold of Ned's hand.

"Scott Frontier," he said.

The girls stood there looking at Scott and he knew they expected him to ask their names, but he wasn't sure he wanted to know. They were way too forward for his liking and it made him very uncomfortable. When he failed to ask for their names, they simply volunteered them. The sandy-brown-haired girl introduced herself as Nancy Shoemake. She was short, and a bit on the heavy side, but not bad looking. The second girl introduced herself as Tina Bottom. She was skinny and a little taller than Nancy. She had long dark hair, which she had pulled back into a ponytail.

"Let's see here, Tina Bottom, Tina Bottom, I know that name from somewhere," Ned said. "Oh, yes, are you related to Rosie and Harry Bottom?" he asked with a totally serious expression. Scott started to laugh and then both Ned and Nancy joined him.

"Ha, ha, very funny," Tina said and slugged Ned on the shoulder.

"Ouch," Ned hollered. He turned to Scott, "watch out for her, she bites."

Tina ignored him and continued with the introductions, explaining that they were both sophomores and members of the Badger division. Scott was only half listening, because he was trying to figure out how he and Ned could politely excuse themselves. He didn't have to wonder for long, however, because a shrill whistle interrupted their conversation. It was Buzz.

Some of the students had been getting wild and Buzz lit into them, yelling at the top of his lungs. Scott wondered if Buzz had purposely been late, knowing all too well the students would act up, giving him a chance to make his grand entrance. It also let each student know, in no uncertain terms, that he was the boss and they had better not forget it. After reprimanding them for their behavior, Buzz ordered the students to line up by division. This was a relief to Scott, since it meant Nancy and Tina had to go to the other side.

As the girls turned to leave, Tina winked at Scott. "Maybe you and that hunk of a bodyguard would like to do something some time?"

Again, at a loss for words, Scott was grateful when Buzz's voice boomed out again, eliminating the need to reply.

"My name is Buzz," the big man thundered. "It's the name I have always gone by and it's the only name you need to know. Today, we are going to start off by running the obstacle course. However, before we start class each day, each and every one of you must run the loop. If you will look to my right, you will see a dirt path that heads into the forest. This path makes a loop and comes out there behind you. You must stay on the path. If I catch any of you trying to cut through the forest, you won't like the consequences, especially if you get lost and I have to come looking for you. I want the Falcons to start off first and then the Badgers will follow. Now get going!"

A few of the Falcons took off towards the path, but most just stood there, wondering if he meant right now. "Move it!" he yelled again. This time they all started running.

Ned and Scott took off and about a minute later they heard Buzz signal the Badgers to start moving. "I wonder how long this is. I'm not much of a runner," Ned said in a worried voice.

Scott, on the other hand, was a great runner and loved to do it. He wanted to sprint ahead but he told himself he needed to stick by Ned. "Just take it easy," he coached. "Maintain an easy pace and you'll be fine."

However, it soon became apparent that Ned was in worse shape than Scott had figured. Halfway through the run, all of the Falcons and most of the Badgers had passed them. Scott was sure they would be the last ones. He kept his eye out for Nancy and Tina; he didn't want to be passed by them.

As they ran along the path deep, a voice from inside the woods started yelling, "Funny legs! Funny legs!" Scott stopped to see who it was. He walked over to the edge of the path and stepped into the woods.

"Scott, what are you doing?" Ned yelled. "Buzz told us not to leave the path."

"I just want to see who's yelling at us."

"What are you talking about? No one's yelling at us."

"You didn't hear them?"

"Hear who?"

"Whoever was yelling that we have funny legs."

Ned gave Scott a funny look. "I didn't hear anyone say that."

Scott took a closer look, but no one was visible. He shrugged his shoulders and stepped back onto the path to continue their run. They finally finished, and to Scott's relief, before Tina and Nancy, who exited the woods about five minutes later. By the beads of sweat pouring down Nancy's head, she was in at least the same or worse shape as Ned. Tina, on the other hand, looked as though she had just taken a leisurely stroll through the park.

Moving over to the obstacle course, Buzz instructed each division to fill up two lanes. "Today I want you to get used to running the obstacle course. This is just a practice run, so it's not a race and you are not being timed. However, eventually you will race. The division with the fastest time will receive an award at the awards ceremony. The individual with the fastest time will earn a small scholarship. The school record was set last year by a freshman, who now is a sophomore, and who stands today in your midst. His name is Tyson Turner." Turner raised his hand and waved as though he had just won a gold medal in the Olympics. "Okay," Buzz continued, "I am going to run the course first to show you how it's done. Once I've finished, I will expect each of you to do it correctly, so please pay attention."

Buzz walked over to the starting line of one of the lanes and then proceeded to run the course in slow motion. "First, you run the tires," he yelled over to the group. "You must place a foot in every tire. Next, you crawl under the ropes, which are set at a height of two feet. You will definitely need to crawl on your belly." He got down on his belly and crawled like a lizard running on a rock. "Next is the wall climb. Grab the rope and hoist yourself up and over the wall." He did this without any real effort, all the while continuing with his narration. "Once you are on the other side, there is a beam you must run across. This beam is three inches wide and if you fall off, you must go back to the beginning of the beam and do it all over again. From here, you must cross over the water hole on the jungle gym. This is something that every playground has, so this shouldn't be a problem for any of you." He crossed the puddle, hand over hand, to the other side. "Last, you must jump from stump to stump without getting knocked off by the sandbags. Like the balance beam, if you do happen to get knocked off, or simply fall off, you must go back to the beginning." He jumped the stumps and finished the course. Then with a smile of satisfaction, he walked back over to the group.

"All right, it's your turn now," he said. "On my signal the first group will run. While they are running, the next set of runners will line up and be ready for my signal. Any questions?" No hands were raised, so Buzz put his whistle to his lips and blew. The first group took off.

The sophomores had obviously done this before because they ran the course with fewer problems than the freshmen. Some of the freshmen tripped on the tires and got caught in the ropes, but the hardest obstacle by far was climbing the wall.

When Scott's turn came, he noticed he was lined up to race against a girl named Susan DeVice, who was also a Falcon, another boy named Don Simons from the Badgers, and Turner. *Great*, he thought to himself. *My first time on the course and I have to run against Wonder Boy*.

Don was big and awkward looking, while Susan was thin and skinny, so Scott was pretty sure he could beat them. Buzz gave the signal and they took off. Although he knew this was just practice, Scott's competitive nature got the best of him and he took off running as fast as he could. At the third tire, his foot caught and he stumbled and fell. Picking himself up, he noticed Turner and Susan halfway under the ropes. Susan was giving Turner a better race than Scott was.

He started running again and made it under the ropes and to the wall. Don had gotten caught under the ropes and Susan was struggling with the wall, but she made it over and was at the beam before Scott hit the ground on the other side of the wall. He flew over the balance beam and came close to catching Susan on the jungle gym. By the time he got to the stumps, Turner was done and Susan was halfway across. He jumped up just in time to see Susan get nailed by one of the sandbags. In the meantime, he almost got hit himself, paying more attention to her than to the bag. However, he made his way across and finished.

Scott had beat Susan only because of the bag. Otherwise she would have come in second. He walked around to where Ned was still waiting for his turn, and as he did so, ran into Turner. The older boy glanced at him, winked, and pointed to Scott. "Maybe next time, big guy." Scott wanted to throw up right there. This guy already made him sick to his stomach.

When Ned's turn came, he didn't try to race. He concentrated mostly on the course and his technique. He came in last place in his heat, but he didn't seem to care. Buzz had the students run the course two more times, and each time Scott purposely lined himself up with someone other than Turner. He didn't want to compete. He wanted to concentrate on the course and technique as Ned had done. He felt good about his performance on the last two runs. He hadn't won either one, but he hadn't fallen either.

After military drill, Ned and Scott headed back inside for lunch. "Did you see the bulletins for the Halloween dance coming up?" Ned asked.

"Yeah, I saw them. Are you planning on going?"

"Of course! Aren't you?"

"I guess so," Scott answered reluctantly. "I've never been any good at dancing though."

"Well, here's your chance to learn to boogie, straight from the master himself."

"Oh goody!" Scott replied sarcastically. "I'm sure you're a real dancing machine."

They picked up their lunch and found an empty table. While they were eating, Nancy plopped her tray down next to Scott and Tina set hers down on the other side by Ned. "Hi, guys!" Tina said as she sat down. "What did you think of drill today?"

"I loved it. But next time I'm not going so easy on everybody," Ned replied.

Tina and Nancy laughed. "Yeah, I'm sure Scott was embarrassed when his bodyguard had to be given a boost over the wall," Tina joked.

"You were awesome, Scott," Nancy said, patting Scott's back.

"Thanks. But I had my share of mistakes also."

"Didn't we all," she replied.

"Are you guys going to the Halloween dance?" Tina asked excitedly.

"Sure we are!" Ned answered, with a determined emphasis in his voice. "Maybe we could dance together."

Scott choked and spewed his mashed potatoes all over his plate. *If these girls are this forward after just meeting us, what will they be like on the dance floor?* he thought.

"Are you okay, Scott?" Nancy asked.

"Yeah, I think so. I guess something got caught in my throat," he mumbled as he cleaned up the mess. He gave Nancy a false smile and then kicked Ned in the shin under the table. Ned gave out a yelp and grabbed his leg. The two girls now looked at Ned in surprise.

"What's wrong?" Tina asked.

"I... I...I have shin splints and...they're hurting," Ned lied.

"Oh, those can be so painful," Tina replied.

"Yes, very painful!" Ned replied, giving Scott a very pointed look.

"Well," Scott said, picking up his tray, "Ned and I have to head back to the dorms before class, so we'll see you around."

"I'm looking forward to the dance," Tina said, smiling at Ned.

"Me too!" Scott heard Nancy say as he walked away. The two boys put their trays away and walked outside the cafeteria.

"What was that for?" Ned demanded.

"Listen! If you want to dance with them, that's fine, but don't start volunteering me. I don't want to dance with them."

"It's just a dance, Scott. You don't have to marry them. You don't even have to dance with them the whole night, just once or twice. The whole idea is to just have fun."

"Don't you think they are just a little too forward?"

"Scott, listen to the way they talk and act. It's all a game to them. They do what they do because they know it makes you nervous. That's why it's so much fun for them. Why shouldn't we have some fun back?"

"Because I don't want to give them the wrong idea," Scott emphatically replied.

"Well, we already told them we'd save them a dance."

"No," Scott pointed out, "you told them we'd save them a dance."

"No girl is going to think you are going steady with her from a dance or two. Besides, if you dance with a couple of other girls after that, she'll know that you're just friends. It's okay to be friends, isn't it?" Ned asked sarcastically.

"Yeah, I guess so."

"So will you dance with her a couple of times?"

"Okay, fine. I'll give her two dances," Scott said with a kidding smile on his face.

"You're a good man, Scotty boy!" Ned said, slapping him on the back.

The two boys headed up to their dorms to get their books, but on the way they ran into two seniors from the Badger division; Kim Hardman and Dan Henry. Kim was a tall, heavy kid who played nose tackle for the Badgers. Dan wasn't quite as large as Kim, but still very muscular and just a bit taller than Scott.

"Look at the Falcon chicklets. Aren't they cute?" Dan said, teasing the two boys.

The seniors' intentions were harmless enough and they would have simply passed by the two freshmen without a second thought. But in the spirit of rivalry, Ned replied in a loud enough voice so they could hear, "I didn't know Abbott and Costello went to school here. Did you, Scott?"

Dan whirled around and quickly headed back. He grabbed Ned by the waist, picked him up, and turned him upside down. "One thing little freshmen need to learn is that they don't talk back to their superiors," he snarled.

"Leave him alone. He was just having fun," Scott said, more as an order than a request.

"Shut up or you'll be next," Dan growled at Scott as he started to shake Ned up and down. Ned's glasses fell off and some of the change in his pockets came out. When Dan dropped him, Ned was quick enough to catch himself before he hit his head.

"Look at what we have here," Dan taunted, picking up the items that Ned had dropped—or rather that had dropped from Ned. "A pair of glasses and some spare change."

"You can have the change, but I need my glasses," Ned said.

"You should've thought about that before you shot off your big mouth," Dan replied.

"He was just kidding. Give back his glasses," Scott said.

Dan walked up to Scott with a scowl on his face. "I thought I told you to shut up!" he yelled. More as a reaction than anything else, Scott sent a fist smashing into Dan's nose, which resulted in him whirling to the floor. Scott quickly picked up Ned's glasses, which Dan had dropped, and handed them over to Ned. Just then, Scott felt a hand on his shoulder and a second later the lights went out. He fell to the floor reeling with pain. He had never been hit like that before. He could hear commotion around him, other people talking, but he was so dazed he couldn't make any sense of it. That sensation lasted only a few seconds before he mercifully fell unconscious.

When Scott woke up, he was lying on a bench in the nurse's office. He tried to sit up, but intense streaks of pain immediately rushed over him, causing him to moan and lie back down. As he lay there thinking about what had happened, the nurse came in.

"How are you feeling?" she asked.

"Not too good," he said, as gently as he could.

"You were hit pretty hard. We had to give you a few stitches around your eye and your nose."

"Do you have a mirror?" he asked.

"Are you sure you want to look at yourself right now?"

He nodded and she brought him a small hand mirror. He had a bandage over one eye and could see some stitches on the side of his nose. "That doesn't look too bad," he said, only half joking.

"Wait until we take the bandage off," she informed him. "The good news is it won't hurt as bad as it will look. Your buddy, on the other hand, will feel his pain a lot longer than you will."

"What happened to Ned?" Scott asked.

"Nothing happened to Ned," she replied. "I'm referring to Dan Henry."

"Oh. What happened to Dan?" Scott asked hesitantly.

"You broke his nose. And believe me, it's going to be tender for quite some time. They had to take him to a hospital to fix him up."

Scott felt sick. His mother was sure to find out about this and he might even get kicked out of school. He also felt bad about Dan. He hadn't meant to break his nose. In fact, he really hadn't meant to hit him in the first place. It was more of a reflex to Dan's attack on him.

Scott was ordered to remain in the nurse's office for the remainder of the day. While he was eating his dinner, Ned, Tina, and Nancy came to visit him. "How are you doing?" Ned asked.

"Pretty good," he answered. "It looks a lot worse than it really is."

"It looks really ugly," Ned said with a tone of jest in his voice.

"It doesn't look that bad, Scott," Nancy reassured him. "I'll tell you what. I'll wear an eye patch to the Halloween dance, and we'll go together as a pair of pirates. That way we'll look alike and no one will notice." There was no teasing in her voice this time. In fact, she sounded like they had a date.

"Thanks, Nancy, but I'm sure it will heal quickly."

"Whatever possessed you to hit him?" Ned questioned.

"I don't know, he had your glasses and he was being a jerk. It just sort of happened, I guess."

"Yeah, but he's a senior and he had that big ape with him."

"I obviously didn't consider the big ape. Boy, he hits hard!"

"You should have seen Dan run off crying."

"He ran off crying?" Scott asked dubiously.

"Not really crying, but you would've thought he was going to die or something. Yep, he'll think twice about messing with us again," Ned bragged.

"Us?" Tina questioned, looking at Ned.

"Sure. After all, it was Ned's big mouth that got us into this mess in the first place," Scott replied.

"Some bodyguard you got there, Scott," Tina joked.

"I'm sorry about that, Scott," Ned apologized. "It was only meant as a joke. I didn't think they would take it so seriously."

"It's all right, Ned. I'm just teasing you."

Just then Eric and Zack Madsen came through the door. They walked over and sat down on the bed. "I love you, Scott." Eric said as he gave him a big hug.

"Why?" Scott asked, knowing something was up.

"Why? Can't a guy love his brother for no reason?"

"Sure. But why do I have a feeling there is a reason?"

"Because," Eric said with a big grin on his face, "I bet Mom twenty dollars you couldn't last one week without getting into a fight."

At the mention of their mother, Scott got worried again. "Have you talked with Mom?" he asked. "Does she know?"

"I haven't talked with her yet, but she knows. They had to call her in order to give you stitches."

"Ugh. She's going to kill me."

Eric sat there with a hint of a smile on his face, slowly shaking his head. "So why, of all the students in the school, did you have to pick on Yogi?" he finally asked. "I thought you were smarter than that."

"Yogi?" Scott asked.

"The Badgers call him Bear, but we call him Yogi."

"How did Dan get the nickname of Bear?"

"Not Dan, stupid, Kim Hardman."

"Oh. Well…I didn't pick a fight with Kim, the fight was with Dan." Then rubbing his jaw, he said, "You tell him, Ned. My jaw hurts." Ned told them the story and as he finished, the nurse came in and shooed them all out the door so Scott could rest. She informed Ned that Scott would be staying the night and would return to his classes the next morning if all looked well.

Scott lay awake for a few hours, wondering what his punishment was going to be from both the school and his mother. Every so often the nurse came in and asked him if he needed anything, but he was fine. Around ten o'clock he finally fell asleep.

Around midnight, he was awakened by a nurse coming through the door, but instead of walking, she was flying or floating. After a moment, he realized that it wasn't a nurse at all, but a beautiful young girl about his age. *Am I dreaming?* Scott asked himself. She had long curly blonde hair, milky white skin, and deep dark brown eyes, which created a sharp, beautiful contrast in her features. She looked down at him and smiled. Scott was sure he had died and gone to heaven. *She must be an angel. This has got to be a dream,* he thought.

She began to remove his bandage, but stopped after having unwrapped it only halfway. She pulled out a flask of white liquid and proceeded to apply it to his bruise and stitches. It felt hot, almost burning, and he winced at its touch, but he could feel its healing power surging through his body. The angel, or whoever it was, put the bandage back, smiled, and left the room. *Does she have to leave?* he thought as he fell back into unconsciousness.

The next morning Scott awoke feeling remarkably well, considering how tender his face had felt just the day before. The nurse came into the room carrying a breakfast tray, which she placed in front of him. "Eat this," she urged, "and then we'll check your stitches."

Scott ate his breakfast and then called for the nurse. "I feel really good today. Will I be able to attend drill this morning?" he asked.

"I can let you go, but I don't want you to participate," she warned. "Your wounds need some time to heal."

"All right," he agreed.

She removed the plate from his lap and instructed him to lie down. He did as he was told and surprise registered across her face as she realized the stitches had fallen out. She began to remove the bandage, and let out a gasp. She just sat there and stared.

"What's wrong?" he asked.

"I don't know how to explain this, but your bruise is gone and the stitches have fallen out," she said in disbelief. "I can't see that you've been injured at all."

Scott began to wonder about his "dream" the night before. Had it not been a dream? Had an angel really come to him and healed him? The idea was absurd, but how else could he explain it?

"I guess you're free to leave," the nurse said, still shaking her head in disbelief. Scott thanked her, got dressed, and left the room, leaving her still in wonderment.

Scott walked to his dorm, wanting to take a hot shower and put on some clean clothes. As he entered his room, he ran into Ned, who was just leaving for drill. "Scott, they let you go. That's great!" Ned congratulated him. It was then that he noticed Scott's face. "Wow! You look pretty good for having been hit by a six-foot-four, three-hundred-pound gorilla. I thought the nurse said you were going to have a pretty ugly-looking bruise when you got out?"

"She did, but as you can see...she was wrong," Scott replied. He didn't dare say anything about the dream, because he wasn't quite sure about it himself.

"It doesn't make sense," Ned said in amazement. "The guy pretty much knocks you unconscious, cuts you open bad enough to have stitches, and you come out of it looking like nothing happened at all."

"Yeah, kind of weird I guess." Then, not wanting to talk about it any longer, he said, "Listen, I really have to get ready for drill. Tell Buzz I'll be there as soon as I can."

Scott hurried and showered, put on a new set of clothes, and ran down to drill. He was really feeling good and wanted to run the courses. When he entered the drill range, everyone stopped to look at him, including Buzz. Ned had obviously told them about his miraculous healing and they all wanted a look at his face. Even Buzz came over to take a look. "The nurse sent me a note asking me to excuse you from drill today," Buzz informed him, "but I'm not sure why. You don't look like you're hurt."

"Actually, I feel pretty good," Scott said. "If it's all right with you, I'd like to run the courses today."

"It's your choice, but if anything happens to you, I'm going to insist you did it on your own," Buzz replied.

Scott got in line, and unfortunately ended up next to Turner, who was also staring at him. "I can't believe it. You got hit by Bear, square in the face, and you've got nothing to show for it? He's not going to like it. I can tell you that," Turner said.

"What do you mean, he's not going to like it?" asked Ned.

"No one crosses Bear and gets away with it that easy," Turner replied.

"I wouldn't call getting knocked out and spending a day in the infirmary, easy," Scott countered. "And I didn't cross Bear, the fight was with Dan."

Turner shook his head, then noticing they were next, he said to Scott in a cocky voice, "Okay, tough guy, it's our turn. Let's see if you've got anything left in you."

They lined up, Buzz blew his whistle, and the two took off as fast as they could. Scott did pretty well until he got to the wall. He slipped a couple of times trying to get to the top, while Turner flew over it as if he had wings. Scott did worse this time than he had the first time.

"Maybe next time, when you're a bit more rested, you'll come close enough to get a taste of my dust," Turner laughed. He walked off and Scott had to fight the urge to chase him down and pound him. But he knew that would be stupid. He couldn't afford to have another incident on his record. He decided instead that he needed to work on his technique, and eventually he'd be able to give Turner a taste of his own medicine. As a result, during his next two turns, he worked more on his footing and movements and was less concerned with the time it took him to complete the course.

After military drill, Ned and Scott hit the showers and then headed for the cafeteria. They met Eric and his friends already sitting down. By this time, the story of Scott's miraculously healed wounds had spread throughout the school, and they all wanted to get a good look. They were crowded around him, searching for battle scars, when Scott heard a loud voice from behind.

"Out of my way! Make room! Coming forward!" Scott looked around to see Bear coming towards him.

"Uh oh," Ned whispered to Scott. "He doesn't look too happy."

Bear continued to push his way through until he was right in Scott's face. Scott didn't budge. He just looked at Bear. There was no use running.

"Leave him alone, Bear," Eric warned.

"What's it to you, Frontier?"

"He's my brother and he's already been through enough."

"From where I'm standing, it doesn't look like he's been through anything at all," Bear replied. He stared at Scott's face. Scott knew that Eric and Zack were right behind him, ready to help if Bear were to cause any trouble, which gave him some measure of confidence. Still, he remembered the pain he had felt when Bear hit him and he didn't want to experience that again. Finally Bear spoke again. "You're the toughest kid I've ever met," he said, shaking his head. "I don't care if you are a freshman or a Falcon, I respect that." He held out his hand. "Friends?"

"Friends," Scott tentatively replied and shook his hand.

"You must get it from your brother," Bear said, still looking at Scott. "Eric is a pretty mean football player." Then looking at Eric, "Don't quote me on that, Frontier, or I'll deny every word of it." He glanced one more time at Scott and then walked away.

Scott was feeling pretty good about things until later that day, when he received a notice of disciplinary action from the headmaster and a phone call from his mother. The notice of disciplinary action informed Scott that he would not be allowed to attend the Halloween dance. This was actually a relief. He hadn't wanted to go anyway, and now he had the perfect excuse. The phone call from his mother was a different story. She scolded him for fighting, and when he tried to explain how it had happened she wasn't interested in his reasons.

Reprimanding him for getting into the situation in the first place, she reminded him of the talk they'd had earlier. Scott was feeling pretty dejected by the end of their conversation, but when they finally hung up, he was also relieved. He knew he had come through the whole thing better than expected.

The rest of the day was uneventful. In fact, the next couple of weeks passed by without any incidents occurring, other than a few threats from Dan Henry. He kept challenging Scott to a fight in the sparring ring, calling him names to egg him on. Dan's injury was obvious to anyone who happened to glance his way. He had to wear a big ugly bandage over his broken nose, but even more embarrassing was the fact that a freshman had done this to him, and everyone at the school knew it. His pride was hurt the most, but to add injury to insult, Bear and Scott had become good friends. Bear seemed to go out of his way to talk to Scott, and every once in a while even sat with him at lunch. As for Scott, the taunting he received from Dan surprisingly didn't bother him.

Chapter Three

The Witch

Halloween day began like any other. Scott showered, dressed, and headed down to breakfast with Ned. In the spirit of the holiday, the cooks had colored the eggs black and the milk orange. Halloween decorations hung all around the dining hall, and some of the students had even dressed up in costumes. Scott and Ned found Eric and sat next to him and his friends. Trevor Carson, one of Eric's friends, had dressed up as a hideous-looking woman wearing a Badger's sweatshirt. That got a good laugh out of the Falcons. The Badgers, on the other hand, hadn't found it quite as amusing. Slim Johnson made several threats, but Bear told him to calm down and not take things so personally.

"Are you guys going to the dance tonight?" Ned asked the group as a whole. Some nodded, and others mumbled something about not having anything better to do. Ned continued, "Have you guys ever seen these before?" He held out three balls that looked like they were made of glass.

"Those are flash balls!" Scott said excitedly. "My brother Josh uses them sometimes when he puts on his magic shows for us."

"What are flash balls?" asked Zack.

"You throw them on the ground and they create a flash of light and a ton of smoke. Magicians use these to make their grand entrances," Ned explained. "We could use them tonight at the dance to make ours."

"Better yet, we could use them to make a grand exit," Eric suggested.

"What do you mean?" Ned asked.

"It's just about time for class, but let's meet after school in the dorm and I'll explain." They all agreed and headed off to class.

Ned and Scott walked through the dorm entrance and then outside to the drill range. "Where did you get those flash balls?" Scott asked.

"Through a mail-order catalogue. They looked cool so I thought I'd get a few."

"Have you ever used them before?" Scott asked.

"I threw one of them and watched it explode, but that's about it," Ned replied.

"Just be careful. The first time my brother Josh used one, he burned himself and almost choked to death. I guess there's a trick to using them."

"Eric sounded excited about them."

"I'm sure he's dreaming up something extravagant right now," Scott replied.

Just then, Tina and Nancy showed up. "Are you guys ready for the big bash tonight?" Tina asked.

"We sure are," Ned replied.

"Remember, you guys promised to dance with us," Tina said with a wink and a smile.

Ned looked at Scott and then back to Tina. "I'll be sure to save you a dance, but Scott won't be able to," Ned informed them.

Nancy looked disappointed.

"Why not?" Tina asked, looking at Scott like he was some sort of worm.

"As part of my punishment, I'm not allowed to go," Scott said in a voice that sounded much more regretful than he actually felt.

"We don't have to go to the dance. Maybe we could do something else together," Nancy suggested lightly, but very serious.

"But I want to go to the dance," Tina said, turning to Nancy.

"Besides, we're planning a surprise for the dance," Ned interjected.

"Who's 'we'? I thought Scott couldn't go," Nancy asked, looking at him.

"I can't. My brother and his friends are the ones planning the surprise," Scott explained, "and Ned is just in on it with them."

"Okay, I've got an idea then," Nancy said. "The three of us will go to the dance, and once we've danced a couple of times, and seen your surprise, whatever that is, we'll leave early, pick up Scott, and go do something else." Ned looked at Scott. He knew what Scott was thinking but he didn't know what to say. The girls were now looking at Scott too, as though he was the one to seal the deal. What could he say? If he said no, it would be obvious he didn't want to, and that might hurt their feelings. Besides, he knew that Ned really wanted to spend time with Tina.

"You guys don't need to leave the dance on my account," Scott started. "It was my fault for getting in the fight."

"Nonsense," Tina replied. "We want to do something with you. Don't we, Nancy?" Nancy shook her head up and down with that teasing look on her face.

"Okay. I'll be in my room when you're done," Scott reluctantly agreed.

Having made that decision, they turned their conversation to the costumes they were going to wear and what they would do afterwards.

A few moments later, Buzz blew his whistle and called everyone to attention. "Today, we are going to run the courses, but this time you will be timed. Each division will be competing for best individual time and best team time. Since we have four lanes, each division will split themselves into two teams and race against each other. The final time of each team will be added together to determine each division's final time. So I want you all to get in your divisions, split into teams, and determine in which order each member will run."

Tom Jones, a Falcon sophomore, called everyone together, appointing himself as the captain. No one seemed to mind as he continued splitting the Falcon members into two teams and placing them in position as though he had some great strategy for doing so. The Badgers were busy at the other end doing the same. Of course, Turner was acting as their captain and had lined up himself and Roy Hansen to run first. Scott didn't know Roy, but he knew he was a pretty good runner.

Scott was grateful not to be racing against Turner. A freshman girl named Tanya Waters and a sophomore boy named Dave Streeter had that privilege. This was a good idea on Tom's part. Tanya and Dave weren't exceptionally fast and wouldn't feel any pressure from Turner. At the same time, they also wouldn't give Turner any motivation to move faster. Buzz had a couple of seniors tracking individual times, and he himself was tracking the teams' times. Once a runner finished, they would hold up a color-coded flag, signaling the next runner in their lane to start.

When everybody was lined up and ready to go, Buzz gave the signal and blew his whistle. The Badger runners shot out as fast as they could. Tom had told Tanya and Dave to concentrate on simply making it through the course without slipping or falling, and to not worry about beating the others. Again, his wisdom paid off. As the teams hit the tires, Roy tripped and fell. Tanya and Dave passed him and actually made pretty good time. However, Roy quickly recovered and passed them up. Turner's performance, of course, was flawless, and gave the Badgers a huge lead. Tanya and Dave came in last, but to their credit they weren't too far behind.

Toward the end of the race, one of the runners on the Badger division slipped on the balance beam. Not only did he have to go back to the beginning, but he had hurt his shin and couldn't run very well. Although they still managed to maintain their position in first place, that mishap caused the Badgers to lose the large lead they had gained from Turner and Roy's performance. When the injured Badger finally crossed the line, it was Nancy's turn. Nancy hurried the best she could, but she wasn't a good runner and by the time she finished, the two Falcon team members had passed her, putting the Badgers in last place. It wasn't entirely Nancy's fault that the Falcons had passed her. It was the runner ahead of her who had lost the lead for them, but Turner took his anger out on Nancy and started yelling at her.

Scott's blood began to boil. Nancy had done the best she could, and it wasn't fair for Turner to treat her this way. This, combined with the fact that he really didn't like the guy very much, caused him to lose his cool, and he ran over and shoved him away from Nancy. "Lay off, Turner. She did the best she could," he said in a calm but menacing voice.

Turner shoved him back. "Take a hike, Frontier. This is none of your business."

Buzz was immediately on the scene. "Back off, Frontier. The last thing you need is to get into another fight. You can't go shoving and punching every Tom, Dick, and Harry that looks at you wrong. I suggest you learn that right now before you learn it the hard way. Do you understand me?" he yelled.

"You sound like my mother," Scott mumbled, not meaning for Buzz to hear. But he heard it anyway.

"If I were your mother, you'd have a really sore bottom by now," he chirped back. Turner laughed out loud to rub it in even more.

Scott ignored him and walked over to Nancy, who was now softly crying. "Don't pay any attention to him, Nancy." Then in a louder voice so Turner could hear, "He's just a sore loser!"

Turner gave him a dirty look but left it at that.

After classes, Scott and Ned met with Eric and his friends in their dorm to discuss how they were going to use the flash balls at the dance. "I've got a great idea," Eric stated, "but we need to find some Badger sweatshirts. Zack already has one, so we need four more. Anyone know how we can get ahold of some?"

"I'll bet Tina Bottom could get us some. I know she has at least one, and Nancy probably has one too," Ned answered.

"Okay, Ned, why don't you go get them? But hurry back. We have a lot to do to get prepared."

"Why don't I go?" Scott said, stopping Ned as he stood up to leave. "I can't go to the dance anyway, so let me get them while you guys get ready."

"Good idea. Thanks, Scott," said Eric.

Scott took off down the stairs, feeling a bit glum. He was now wishing he could go to the dance, even if it meant dancing with Tina and Nancy. He arrived at the Badgers' dorm and quickly headed for the girls' section. It suddenly occurred to him that it wasn't a very good idea for him to be alone in front of the Badgers'-dorm. After all, he wasn't exceptionally popular with them right now. At the same moment, another dilemma hit him. He couldn't very well just walk into the girls' dorm, so he would have to wait for someone to come by who could get Tina for him. As it turned out, while he was debating what he should do, a red-headed girl came out and Scott grabbed her before she could go anywhere.

"Do you know Tina Bottom?" he asked.

"Sure. Do you need me to get her?"

"Yes, if you wouldn't mind."

"No problem." The girl went back inside, leaving Scott in the hall to wait again. It seemed like an eternity and he was beginning to get a little edgy.

Finally Tina came out. "Hi, Scott. What are you doing here?"

"Do you, by chance, have a Badger sweatshirt I could borrow?" he asked, getting right to the point.

She looked at him strangely for a second. "Yes. Are you going to sneak into the dance tonight disguised as a Badger?" she asked with a smirk on her face.

"Actually, I need you to get me four sweatshirts, as large as you can find them," he said, ignoring her question.

"What do you need them for?" she asked more seriously now.

"I don't know. Ned asked me to come ask you. It's part of his surprise."

"In that case, I'll do my best. I'll be back as soon as I can."

"Thanks," Scott called as she disappeared back into the dorm.

She had been gone about five minutes when Turner walked out of the boys' dorm. He stopped when he saw Scott standing there in the hall. "Well, if it isn't Tough Guy!" Turner said with a snide expression on his face. "Why are you hanging around the girls' dorm, Frontier? Are you hoping to join them some day?"

"Actually, I thought this was where you were staying, Turner. I was hoping to get a look at you in your ballerina costume." Scott knew it wasn't smart to be antagonizing Turner like this, but it just slipped out before he had a chance to think about it.

Turner was shaking his head. "You know, Frontier, you're not making any friends around here. I'd be careful where you hang out if I were you, especially when you're all by your lonesome little self." He turned around and walked back inside the dorm. This made Scott even more nervous. He half expected to see Turner, Dan Henry, and a bunch of other Badgers come pouring out ready to pound him.

What is taking Tina so long? he wondered. He waited another minute or so and then his worst fears were confirmed.

He heard someone yell, "Henry's going to kick some butt and we're going to help," followed by another loud, "Shhh!" Just then the door to the boys' dorm opened. At the same moment, the girls' dorm door opened, and not caring who had opened it, Scott jumped inside, knocking Nancy to the floor.

"What...?" she started to say. Scott quickly dropped to the floor and put one arm around her with his hand over her mouth. He then took his other hand and put it to his lips.

"Shhh," he whispered. She could hear a number of boys out in the hall, and it didn't take long for her to realize what was happening and why Scott had risked entering an area that was completely off-limits to any boy. But that didn't stop her from taking advantage of the situation.

"Really, Scott," she whispered once Scott had removed his hand. "Most boys wait until the end of the evening to try and kiss their dates. What makes you think I'm that kind of girl anyway?" she said with a smile.

He glanced at her with a confused look on his face. He had been listening intently to what was going on outside, and it had taken a moment for Nancy's words to register. When it finally clicked in his brain, he growled, "Very funny." Then even surprising himself, he added, "If I wanted to kiss you that badly, I wouldn't do it right here, on the floor of a well-lit girls' dormitory entryway."

"Where would you do it?" she asked, grinning.

Scott paused for a moment, actually imagining himself kissing her, which caused him to forget about the boys outside who wanted to pummel him. The thought of kissing a girl was quite exciting, but it also scared him to death. Yet, here was a girl practically begging him to do so—or so it seemed.

"Scott, to earth!" she said, widening her eyes.

He must have been staring at her, and now that he was focused back on their conversation, he was embarrassed. "I'm sorry. I was trying to hear if they had left or not," he said, hoping she would believe his little lie.

"I can't believe it! I...," but she was cut off by Tina, who had just entered the hallway. The two of them were still on the ground, Scott kneeling over Nancy with one arm around her back.

"Scott Frontier!" she said loudly, but joking. "What kind of boy are you? I leave you alone for one second with Nancy and you attack her."

"I...I...wasn't...," he stammered, caught totally off guard by the whole thing.

She smiled and walked over to them. "Here are your sweatshirts. I'm dying to know what Ned is going to do with them. Oh... I also need you to promise not to tell anyone that I gave these to you. You know, to protect the innocent."

"You have my word," Scott said. He got up and pulled Nancy to her feet. He took the sweatshirts and put his ear to the door. "It sounds like they're gone. Thanks a lot for your help and I'll see you later tonight." He opened the door and peeked out. The coast was clear.

When he entered the Falcons' dorm, he found his friends sitting around laughing hysterically while Eric was furiously writing something down on a piece of paper. "What took you so long?" Zack asked.

"It's a long story that I'd rather not go into right now. What did you guys come up with?"

"It's going to be awesome!" Ned blurted out. He began to divulge their plans, when Ian came in and told Scott the headmaster wanted to see him in his office right away.

"I guess you'll have to explain when I get back," Scott told Ned as he left with Ian.

"Do you have any idea why he wants to see me?" Scott asked, as Ian and Scott walked down the hallway.

"Not really. He mumbled something about torture treatment for fighting in school. Something about poking your eyes out, and branding you with a hot iron."

"Very funny," Scott said, laughing. "Seriously, what's this all about?"

"I'm sure it has something to do with your fighting, but what's weird is that he asked me to escort you back to his office."

"Escort me?"

"Yeah. Maybe he's afraid you'll get jumped or something if you come alone. I don't know." They walked down the castle halls until they came to the administrative wing and arrived at the headmaster's office. "Here he is, Sir," Ian stated as they both entered.

"Thank you, Ian. You may leave now."

Scott sat down, not saying a word. The headmaster didn't say anything either for a while.

"I guess you probably know...," he started to say, but was interrupted by the door opening. In walked Bear and Dan.

Bear came in and sat down by Scott. "Hey, dude," he said, slugging him on the shoulder.

"Hey," Scott replied, not daring to talk too much. Dan, whose nose had almost healed by now, sat down next to Bear.

"I'm sure you probably know why I called you here?" the headmaster said, starting over. "As you know, we do not tolerate fighting here. As your punishment—and I think I'm being very lenient—I am not allowing any of you to attend the Halloween dance tonight. I expect you to abide by this, or it will get worse. But of more concern to me is your continued animosity towards one another. You need to forgive and forget, all right?"

Scott was okay with that. He didn't want any enemies, and what Turner had said earlier hit home harder than Scott could have imagined. He stood up to shake Bear's hand. Bear stood up, and grabbing him in a big bear hug, cried in a false voice, "I love ya, man. I love ya." He then gave Scott a big slobbery kiss on the cheek.

"Uggh!" Scott yelled as he pushed Bear away, wiping his cheek.

Dan was out of his chair and standing by now, shaking his head at Bear. Scott stepped forward. "Sorry, Dan," he said, holding out his hand.

"Yeah, sorry," Dan said very insincerely as he quickly shook Scott's hand. It was obvious Dan was still very sore about the whole thing.

"Scott," the headmaster said, "you may leave now. I would like you two to stay a moment longer," he added, looking at Bear and Dan.

Without saying a word, Scott walked out of the room. As he headed down the hall, he had a sudden urge to go back to the room he and Ned had discovered by the painting of the knight. He turned the corner, walked down the narrow hallway, and opened the door. It was pitch-black inside. He flicked on the light and looked inside. There were no floating chairs and no ghosts. It was just the same as it had been before, except there was now a fourth chair in addition to the original three he and Ned had seen earlier. This new chair was set against one of the walls. It wasn't as large as the other three and it had a different crest on the back.

That's weird, Scott thought. *I've got to show this to Ned.* He turned off the light and shut the door. He started walking back down the hall, but heard voices. Dan and Bear were just now coming out of the headmaster's office.

"Forgive and forget," Dan mimicked.

"Give it a break!" he heard Bear say. "The kid said he was sorry."

"Why do you all of a sudden like him so much?"

"The kid's got guts. There's not another freshman or sophomore in this whole school who has the guts to do what he did. I respect him for that. Plus, he was only reacting to your *I'm King* attitude. You threatened him for heaven's sake!"

"Maybe I went too far, but he hit me, and he's not going to get away with it so easily."

"I'm telling you, Dan, leave it alone, or it'll come back to bite you later on."

The two continued to discuss it as they walked down the hall. Scott already regretted the entire episode. He didn't want to be looking over his shoulder all the time. He just wanted to go to school, meet friends, and have fun, but his stupid temper always seemed to get the better of him. He was feeling glum at the moment and decided not to return to the dorms. He wanted to find a place where he could be by himself and think, so he headed outside to the gardens, where he sat for some time thinking about things. He finally got up and started to walk.

"Boy! Boy!" a voice rang out in the night.

Scott stopped, wondering who it was. "Who's there?" he called out. No one answered. "Hello?" he called out again and still no one answered. He decided to walk through the maze of tall hedges and he eventually found himself out by the drill range. Running had always made him feel good, so he decided to run the loop.

It was dark by now, but there was a full moon so it was light enough for him to see where he was going. About halfway through the loop, he thought he saw a shadow of sorts fly overhead, but wasn't sure. He stopped to look up, but couldn't see anything, so he started moving again. As he ran he heard something behind him, so he stopped and whirled around, but nothing was there. He started running again, slowly this time, but kept his eyes and ears open. He ran for another minute or so and it happened again, and this time he was sure he had seen something large fly overhead. The hairs on the back of his neck stood up, so he picked up the pace, hoping to make it back to the dormitory as soon as possible. He had just gotten started when in front of him he heard some cackling.

"Hee, hee, hee, heeee!" He was so startled that he stumbled and almost ran into what appeared to be a witch with a broom standing in front of him. He came to a screeching halt and slipped on the dirt, and ultimately landed on his butt. The witch, or whatever it was, began to laugh and giggle so hard, Scott thought she was going to start crying. He stood up looking at her, not knowing what to say.

She finally got her laughter under control just long enough to say, "You should have seen the look on your face!" She then broke out in a fit of giggles all over again.

Normally, Scott would have been embarrassed, which would have made him mad, but her laugh and her voice were musical, almost mesmerizing, and it intrigued him. "Who are you?" he finally asked.

"I am the Wicked Witch of the North. Or was it the South? I can't quite remember," she replied.

"No, I don't want to know who you are dressed as. I want to know who you are!" he said.

"Who says I'm dressed as anyone. Maybe I'm a real witch."

"You look like a witch dressed for the prom and witches don't go to proms," Scott pointed out.

"The prom? What do you mean?" she asked.

He walked closer to her until he was standing next to her. "Your black hair isn't matted and messy like a witch's, but...well...it's beautiful the way it curls and flows around your face. Your eyes, dark as they are, sparkle like water being touched by the rays of a full moon. And your voice is like soothing music. No witch could ever talk like that. And..." Scott stopped in mid-sentence. What was he saying? Why was he talking like this, and especially to a girl he didn't even know? It was almost as if he was under some sort of spell. What would she think of him? Embarrassed, he was glad it was dark or she would have seen how red his face was. He glanced back at her, into her dark eyes. She looked expectantly at him, not saying a word.

"On the other hand," he started, "maybe you are a witch and you've cast a spell on me. Normally I would never say such things to a girl." She stood there for a moment staring at him and he continued to stare right back at her. He didn't know what else to say. He was embarrassed and somewhat uncomfortable now, but he didn't want to leave. There was something about her. Her smile, her eyes, the way she talked—everything about her was so enchanting.

"Thank you," she finally responded. "I have no doubt that came sincerely from your heart." Scott nodded. He was glad she appreciated it, but he was still very embarrassed. "Do you want to walk for a little bit?" she asked.

"Sure. Where do you want to walk?"

"Does it matter?"

"Not to me it doesn't," he said enthusiastically. She looked at him and smiled. Scott figured he must have said that a little too eagerly, but he didn't care. He was just happy she wanted to be with him. They continued walking around the loop, not saying a word. Scott was desperately trying to think up conversation, but he was so tongue-tied he couldn't come up with anything that didn't sound stupid. "How come you're not at the dance?" he finally asked.

"My original intentions were to go. I was out here debating what I should do, when I saw you. Scaring you sounded like much more fun than going to the dance," she teased.

"I'm glad I could provide you with such entertainment." By this time they had almost completed the loop and Scott was thinking they should head over to the gardens. "I'm sorry," he said, "but I don't recognize you in that costume. Who are you?"

She was about to answer when they heard voices. Ned was calling out Scott's name. Scott turned to her and was surprised by the scared, almost panicked, look on her face.

"I told my friends I would meet them in my room. When they didn't find me there, they must have come looking for me out here," Scott explained.

"Quick!" she whispered. "We have to go back the way we came." They turned around and started back, but their feet on the path made too much noise.

"Scott, is that you?" they heard Ned call out. They also heard other feet heading in their direction. He stopped and turned to face Ned. He couldn't very well run away from them, but how was he going to explain his being with another girl? He turned back to face her, but she was gone; vanished into thin air. He sucked in a deep breath. *There is no way she could have run away so quickly. I would have heard her and I would have seen her*, he thought. Just then Ned, Tina, and Nancy came running around the corner.

"Scott?"

He spun back around to face them, his eyes wide with disbelief from the strange encounter.

"Scott, you look like you've just seen a ghost," Tina exclaimed.

"I...I think I might have," he replied.

"Very funny, Scott. You're just trying to scare us, right?" Nancy said. But Scott just stood there staring into nothing.

"You are just trying to scare us, Scott, aren't you?" Tina asked.

"Uh, yeah. I...I was going to scare you, but you guys came out too soon. Anyway, how was the dance?" he asked. The girls launched into a discussion about the decorations and about how crazy everyone was getting. While Ned, on the other hand, was staring at Scott. He knew something had happened, but couldn't figure out what.

"You tell him, Ned. You were one of them," Tina said, bringing Ned back to the conversation.

"Tell him what?" he asked.

"Tell him about what you guys did tonight at the dance. Haven't you been listening?"

"Oh... yeah," Ned replied. "Scott, you should have seen it. It was so great. After you left, we all dressed up as Badger women, except we looked like total dogs as you can imagine. Then we had Jason Bell ask the DJ if some of the guys could do a karaoke number. So we had him play "Like a Sturgeon" or something like that, except we changed the words. The DJ announced that he had a special number and asked everybody to stop dancing. He put on the music and we all jumped out from behind the curtains and started singing. The chorus went like this:

I'm a loser, playing football for the very first time.
I'm a looooser, oops I fumbled, and I broke a naiiiil.

We didn't get much further than that, because half the Badger division charged the stage. But all the other students were laughing their heads off. So anyway, just as the Badgers were jumping onto the stage, we threw down our flash balls, which exploded, making a large blinding light, not to mention a ton of smoke. We darted behind stage, out the back door, and headed for the dorm. It was awesome!"

"Sounds like fun," Scott Sighed. "I wish I could have been there." That wasn't entirely untrue. He really would have liked to have seen the song.

"Well, what should we do now?" asked Ned.

"Do you guys want to go hot-tubbing?" Tina questioned.

"Hot-tubbing?" both Scott and Ned asked simultaneously.

"Yeah. Last year we went exploring in the woods. There are some hot springs a little ways away from here. There is also a cold pond that feels great once you've been in a little too long."

"That sounds like fun," Ned said excitedly, "but I don't have a swimsuit."

"Neither do I," Scott chimed in.

"We don't need swimsuits. We're out in the middle of the forest," Tina exclaimed.

"You mean...go...in...our underwear?" Ned replied, trying to understand what she really meant.

The girls started laughing hysterically. "No, you idiot, don't you guys have any shorts, you know for when it gets hot?" Nancy asked.

"Sure," they both replied.

"Well, go get those on. We'll get ours and meet you back here in ten minutes."

"Okay," Ned answered.

Before Scott had time to object, the girls had already left and Ned was pulling him toward the dorm. "Isn't it kind of late to go swimming?" Scott asked Ned.

"Tomorrow is Saturday, we get to sleep in. Plus, this sounds like a riot."

"Yeah, but are you sure you want to be alone with Nancy and Tina in the middle of the woods in the middle of the night?" Scott asked.

Ned looked at him incredulously. "Oh my, you're right, especially on Halloween night. They might actually try and suck our blood," Ned said seriously, but teasing.

"Funny, funny," Scott replied. "What if we get in trouble, isn't it almost curfew?"

"Since when did that ever stop you? You're the one who hauled off and hit Henry right in the nose without blinking an eye."

"That's different," Scott replied.

"Are you still scared those two girls will attack you or something?"

"I don't know."

"Scott, we are just friends. Tonight I danced with both Nancy and Tina and we had fun, nothing else."

"All right," Scott agreed. He and Ned changed into their shorts and a T-shirt, grabbed a towel, and took off. When they arrived outside, Nancy and Tina were both waiting for them.

"This way, gentlemen," Tina said as she turned and headed in the direction of the gardens. They walked past the garden and into the forest.

"Funny legs. Funny legs," a voice in the forest rang out. It was the same voice Scott had heard the first day he and Ned had run the loop.

Scott hit Ned on the shoulder. "Did you hear that?"

"Hear what?"

"Funny legs. There is someone in the forest again saying we have funny legs."

The other three stopped and were looking at Scott with questioning looks. He turned to the girls. "You guys didn't hear anything?"

"No. Did you, Nancy?" asked Tina.

"I didn't either," Nancy replied.

Scott shook his head. "Okay, maybe I'm going crazy."

"Are they still saying it?" Ned asked.

"No, it's stopped now."

"Well, funny legs or not, I'm still going swimming," Tina commented and continued towards the hot springs.

There wasn't a trail, but both Tina and Nancy seemed to know where they were going. They walked for some time and Scott began to wonder how far the hot springs were. After about twenty minutes, they came around a bend and he could see steam rising from the ground.

"There she is, boys," Tina exclaimed and took off running. When she got to the edge, she stopped suddenly and screamed.

"What's wrong?" Ned called back.

"There...there's a dead body in here!" she stammered. Ned and Nancy stopped right where they were, their faces pale.

Scott's knees went weak. *Could it be the girl I met tonight?* he thought. He didn't want to see the body, but he had to know and took off running. When he arrived at the hot spring, he looked in but couldn't see anything.

"Where?" he asked, leaning over to get a better look.

Tina grabbed his towel and yelled, "There!" as she pushed him in.

Scott yelped as he tried his hardest not to fall in, but it was too late. He had been leaning over and it didn't take much effort on her part to push him in. The thought of falling in the water with a dead body was freaking him out. He hit the water and the warmth engulfed him. He thrashed about trying to feel for the body, but found nothing. He soon realized there wasn't a dead body and that the whole thing was just a joke. Tina was still laughing when Scott looked at her and said in a very serious voice, "What happened to your leg?"

She looked down and started rubbing her hand up and down her leg to see if she could feel anything. Scott leaped halfway out of the water, grabbed her arm, and pulled her in. She came up sputtering and started splashing him with the water. Ned and Nancy soon joined them after they realized what was going on.

They spent the rest of the evening jumping from the hot spring to the pond and back again, splashing each other, talking, and having a good time. They had just climbed out of the cold pond and settled into the hot spring when Scott heard the voice again.

"Man coming. Man coming."

Scott paused only for a second and then spoke. "Let's get out and hide. Follow me."

"What are you talking about?" Ned exclaimed.

"Come on, you guys!" he urgently whispered to them.

The others looked at each other curiously, but did as he asked. They climbed out, grabbed their towels, and walked several yards into the forest and hid. They waited for several minutes but nothing happened.

Tina leaned over to Scott. "What are we doing?"

"We're hiding," Scott replied.

"From what?"

"From the man. I don't want to get caught, do you?"

"What man?" she asked.

"How should I know," he replied.

"How do you know a man is coming?"

He was about to answer when a figure appeared in the clearing by the hot spring. Sure enough, it was a large man, which the group easily recognized as Buzz. He looked around as though he was looking for something or someone. When he was convinced that no one was there, he turned and walked away. The group waited a little longer just to make sure he was gone before coming out from their hiding place.

"Wow. That was a close one." Nancy breathed a sigh of relief.

"Scott," Tina asked once again, "how did you know he was coming?"

"Yeah," Ned chimed in, "how did you know?"

"I don't believe it! You guys really didn't hear someone warn us that a man was coming?" Scott asked, exasperated.

"This is getting a little weird for me," Nancy remarked.

"Weird for you? What about me? I'm the one hearing voices that no one else is hearing," Scott sputtered back.

"Weird or not, we had better get back," Ned said to the group.

By the time they decided to go back, it was past midnight and past their curfew. It was a cool autumn night and with no dry clothes to change into, they practically froze on their way back. When they finally arrived, Ned grabbed the door, but it wouldn't open. "It's locked. How are we going to get in?" he asked.

"Why don't you two walk around the castle and see if you can find an open window?" Tina suggested. Ned nodded and started heading off.

"Ned," Scott called, "all the castle windows have bars on them."

Ned looked back sheepishly and could see Tina chuckling. "You shouldn't have stopped him," she said. "I wanted to see how many he'd check before he realized it."

"We may be stupid enough to return after curfew without a way back in, but I know you're not," Scott said to the two girls.

"How do you know?" Tina asked.

"Because, you'd be freaking out by now too," Scott replied with a smile.

"I guess we can't fool you." Tina reached around her neck and pulled a gold chain out from underneath her shirt. Hanging from the chain was a key to the door. "They hide a spare key in the linen closet. Last year we got locked out and had to knock. Ms. Peterson came to the door and let us in. Boy, did we get in trouble! Anyway, we saw where she put the key and have used it ever since." She inserted it into the lock and soon they were all inside.

"We'll see you girls later. Thanks, it was fun," Ned said as they turned and went in opposite directions.

"Yeah, thanks," Scott echoed.

"See? You had fun, didn't you?" Ned quickly pointed out.

"Yes, I did. I have to admit, it was fun."

"And see, they didn't even bite you," Ned said slugging him on the shoulder.

"That Tina is a real stinker. One of these days, I'm going to get her good."

"Like what?" Ned asked.

"I don't know. Nothing mean, just a trick I can play on her. Something to give her a bit of her own medicine."

The two reached their door, and Scott decided to take a hot shower to get rid of the chill. Ned followed, and as they were basking in the warmth of the water, Eric walked in. "Where in the world have you two been?" he asked. "I've been looking for you everywhere. I even went to Buzz to see if he knew where you were. I almost went to Headmaster McDougal. And why are you taking a shower in your clothes?"

Ned and Scott looked at each other and laughed. "We could tell you, but then we'd have to kill you," Ned replied.

"You guys went to the hot springs, didn't you?" Eric accused them.

"You know about the hot springs?"

"Of course. It's not a big secret, just very much against the rules," he replied. "What I don't understand is why you just didn't go in your underwear. You're in the middle of the forest. Nobody's going to see you. Besides, if you had done that, you would've had dry clothes to walk home in."

"Well, Tina did suggest something like that, but Scott wouldn't hear of it," Ned replied.

"You went with girls, Scott?" Eric asked, somewhat surprised. "Why, you little devil, you. I never knew you had it in you. What else did you do with your girlfriends?"

"Nothing else," Scott quickly blurted out. "And they are not our girlfriends. They are just friends."

Sensing that this girlfriend thing was more sensitive than he'd first thought, and not wanting to push Scott too far, Eric changed the subject. "You missed our great Halloween surprise," he said as they both shut off the water. They walked to their room as Eric once again retold the event to Scott.

After Eric finished, Ned grew very serious and turned to Scott. "Scott, tell me what happened tonight before we found you. I've never seen you looking so scared." Eric looked curiously over at Scott, not saying anything. Scott didn't want to tell them. The whole thing was weird.

"Did something happen, Scott?" Eric asked, wanting to know more.

"Sort of, I guess. I'll tell you if you promise not to say anything to anyone about this."

"We promise," they both said in unison.

"And no teasing either."

"No teasing," they promised.

Scott told them about his visit to the headmaster's office and how he had gone to the room with the chairs afterwards. He told them about the extra chair he had seen, which Ned found particularly interesting. He went on to tell them that he'd decided to go outside and run the loop, and had the weirdest sensation that something was following him. He couldn't see anything, so he assumed it was probably just his imagination. He continued the story with the girl dressed as a witch who had jumped out of the bushes. He left out the mushy stuff, and ended by telling them how baffled he was about her sudden disappearance without a single sound.

"You say you spoke with this girl?" Ned asked.

"Yes."

"And she spoke back to you?"

"Yes."

"And did you understand what she was saying?"

"Yes," he said, thinking these questions were starting to get dumb.

"Did she speak good English?" Ned asked.

"Yes!" he said, now getting irritated. "Why are you asking me all these dumb questions?"

Eric turned to Ned. "Why are you asking all these questions?"

"I think it could have been a girl named Azinine."

"Who is Azinine?" Scott asked.

"Oh, just a local girl that comes around once in a while causing trouble. If you ever meet her, stay away. She is nothing but trouble," Ned warned.

"And how do you know her?" Scott asked Ned, knowing this was his first year at the school too.

"Who? Me? Oh…she grew up in my town."

"So you're from around here?" Eric asked.

"Yes. Can't you tell by my accent?"

"Well, I knew you weren't American, but your English is good enough that I thought maybe you were from England."

Scott yawned, feeling too tired to care anymore. "Well, I'm exhausted, guys. I'm going to bed."

"All right, see you in the morning," Eric said. He left the room as Scott and Ned climbed into bed.

"You're positive she had black hair?" Ned asked.

"Yes! Now go to sleep!" Scott said, annoyed.

Chapter Four
Winged Boots

The next morning Scott woke up later than usual. Ned was not in bed, but that was typical. Ned usually woke up early. Scott figured this would be a good day to catch up on his homework. He had several assignments that were due soon and he hadn't even started on them. He got out of bed, took a shower to fully wake himself up, and sat down at his desk. He spent a considerable amount of time catching up on math assignments and reading his history chapters. After a few hours, his mind started wandering and he decided to take a small break. He stood up and walked over to the window. It was a beautiful day outside, but despite the sunshine, he knew it was a bit on the cold side. Fall was leaving and winter was making its way into the picture. As he sat there looking down at the gardens, his thoughts returned to the girl he had met the night before. Who was she? Could she be the girl from Ned's village? If not, could she be a student here? If so, what division did she belong to? Would he recognize her if he saw her without her costume on? Would she recognize him? Why had she run? He tried to think of all the girls with long, curly black hair he had seen around school. There were a few that came to mind, but not many. He decided that from now on, he was going to pay more attention to the girls around him. He would try and find her, or maybe she would find him. Either way he didn't care.

He walked back to his desk and began writing an English paper. He was having a hard time concentrating and decided to go to the library where he could work on a computer. As he headed down, he ran into Ned. "Hey, Ned. How's it going?" he greeted.

"Pretty good. Did you get enough sleep?"

"Yeah. I guess I crashed pretty good. What time did you get up?"

"I got up around nine and decided to go for a walk. Hey, I ended up walking past that room by the headmaster's office, and decided to check out that chair you told me about, but it wasn't there. Are you sure you saw one there?"

"Positive. It was smaller than the three we saw, but it was there against one of the walls."

"Did it have a different crest on it?" continued Ned.

"Yes, as a matter of fact it did."

"Do you remember what it looked like?"

"Not really. I didn't pay that much attention to it. Just enough to notice it wasn't the same."

Ned merely nodded.

Tired of this same line of questioning, Scott decided to change the subject. "I'm headed down to the library to work on my English paper."

"Maybe I'll join you in a bit," Ned replied.

"Okay," Scott said as he started down the stairs.

When Scott entered the library he ran into Bear. "Hey, Scott. How's it going?"

"Pretty good. Sorry about getting you banned from the dance."

"Ahh, don't worry about it. I needed the time to study anyway. How about you? What did you do last night?"

"I spent some time in my room and then went running. I needed to get rid of some extra energy."

"Did you hear about what happened at the dance last night?" Bear asked.

Scott was pretty sure he knew what Bear was referring to, but he didn't want to admit to it. So he pretended ignorance. "No, what happened?"

Bear proceeded to tell Scott the version he had been told. "Turner is sure it was you and some of your friends and has started planning his revenge against you. I guess he saw you hanging out at the girl's dorm. It took me a while to convince him that you weren't allowed to go to the dance. By the way," he asked as an afterthought, "what were you doing by the dorm anyway?"

Scott wasn't sure what to say at first, but a thought quickly came to him. "I'd told Nancy Shoemake that I'd meet her at the dance, so I went to tell her I couldn't make it."

"Are you and Nancy an item?" Bear asked.

"No! Just friends," he quickly replied, tired of everyone jumping to the same conclusion.

"Hey, Nancy seems cool."

"She's way cool, but I'm just not interested."

"I understand. Listen, I gotta go, maybe I'll see you at the movie tonight. Are you going?" Since there wasn't much opportunity to leave the grounds, the school brought in as many activities as possible for the students, movies being one of those.

"Probably, but it depends on how much homework I get done," Scott replied.

Bear said good-bye and Scott walked over to the computers and started working on his paper.

On Monday morning when they arrived on the drill grounds, Buzz announced it was time to start practicing their skills at the gun range. "You will still run the courses throughout the year, but we need to start practicing our shooting skills," he explained.

Although they only used high-powered paintball guns for practice at the school, Buzz used a real gun to explain the basics of gun safety, how to clean a gun and sight it for accuracy. He then explained how to do this with the paintball guns for practical reasons. Then he set up targets on the gun range about thirty yards away. Since there were six targets, only six students could shoot at a time. Each division was given three bays to shoot from.

"The object," Buzz explained, "is to quickly fire off as many rounds as possible, in the least amount of time, and come as close as possible to the target. Each round contains ten bullets and each student will be given three rounds. Points are given based on speed and accuracy." After Buzz personally sighted every gun's scope, the students got ready to begin shooting.

Ned was up first. He took the gun and aimed as best he could. Buzz blew the whistle and guns started blazing. After the second round, Ned looked like he was just pulling the trigger as fast as he could and praying they would hit the target. A few bullets found their mark, but most missed.

"Not bad for your first try, Ned," Scott said, trying to encourage him.

Tina, who had been shooting next to Ned, had done considerably better. She hadn't ever hit the bull's-eye, but most of her bullets had come close. This made Scott nervous. What if he didn't do as well?

Scott waited for Buzz to change the targets. Buzz had been very adamant that all guns be placed upright while he changed the targets. This was to ensure no one shot while he was up there. Once he returned, Scott picked up the gun, took aim, and waited for the signal. Scott heard the whistle and started firing. When he was finished, he was astonished to discover he had done worse than Ned. He couldn't believe it.

"Frontier, you're as bad a shot as your roommate!" Buzz boomed out in front of everybody. "You two couldn't hit the broad side of a barn!"

I wasn't the only one who did poorly. Why is he picking on me? Scott thought bitterly.

"Hey, Frontier, you should take a few lessons from your girlfriend, Tina," Scott heard Turner's voice laughing next to him. He looked at Turner, who had been shooting in the next bay, and was mortified to see that Turner had done exceptionally well. Scott was baffled by his own performance. He and Eric had gone hunting with their dad many times, and he had always been a pretty good shot.

The other Falcons in Scott's bay took their turns. After a few more rounds, Scott started getting suspicious. Every member of his division in his bay had done just as poorly or worse than he had. What he noticed, however, was that they were all off to the left. *The gun's scope must be off, but how could that be?* he wondered. *Buzz sighted each division's gun before we shot.* When class ended, Scott and Ned headed back towards the dorms.

"Didn't you find it odd that we all missed to the left of the target?" Scott asked Ned as they were walking back to get lunch.

"I hadn't really noticed, but now that you mention it, you're right. The odds of that happening are probably a thousand to one."

"Exactly," Scott mused. "The scope on our gun must have been off, but I can't figure out how. Buzz sighted our gun right before we shot."

As they reached the lunch line, they ran into Eric. "Hey Scott, how was the gun range?" he asked.

"Humiliating!" Scott complained. "Everyone in our bay shot horribly. Somehow, I think our scope was off, because we all shot to the left of the target. What's weird, though, is that I saw Buzz sight our gun right before we shot."

"I'm guessing you fell victim to the Switcherooo."

"The what?" Scott and Ned both blurted out.

Whoever shot first in your line, must have given their gun to a Badger member. The Badger then switched his gun, which he had already tampered with, and gave it to you. It's a common trick."

"Ned," Scott turned accusingly to his friend, "did you give your gun to anyone?"

Ned had a sheepish look on his face. "He only said he wanted to look at it. I didn't think there was any real harm in that."

"Who?" Scott asked.

"Turner. Right before we started to shoot, Turner asked if he could see our gun. He wanted to compare to theirs to ours. He only had the gun for a second before he gave it back, but he must have switched theirs with ours."

"Do you really think he would stoop that low?" Scott asked.

"Easily. The rivalry between the Falcons and the Badgers runs pretty deep. Both sides are always looking for ways to make the other look bad," Eric explained. "And in your case, there's even more motivation."

"You have to admit, it was a pretty good trick," Ned pointed out.

"A good trick, my foot," Scott retorted. "It made us look like idiots."

"It's a trick that's played on freshmen all the time. It was played on us our first year, and it may have been Turner we did it to last year," Eric replied.

The next day at drill Scott made sure he was in line beside Turner as they shot. He also had Ned get in line behind him. "Ned, when I scratch the back of my head, I want you to pinch me on my arm. All right?" he ordered.

"Why?"

"You'll see, just do it."

"Okay."

Scott waited while two Falcons in front of him shot. After the one in front of him finished, he placed the gun on the counter while Buzz changed the targets. Once Buzz had returned, Scott picked his gun up and pointed it towards the ground, waiting for Buzz to give the signal. He used his other hand to scratch the back of his head. Ned of course saw this as the signal and pinched Scott's arm as he had been instructed. As he did so, Scott's gun fired and Turner let out a yelp, dropping his gun and grabbing his foot; cursing Scott and his stupidity.

"Are you okay?" Scott asked sincerely.

"Are you stupid?" Turner yelled back. "You just shot my foot!"

Just then Buzz walked over, looking very unhappy. "Frontier! Did you do this?" he barked out.

"I'm sorry, Sir. Someone pinched my arm and I was so startled by it that I accidentally pulled the trigger."

"What if that had been a real gun? You could have severely injured him. We cannot afford these kinds of mistakes! Who pinched you?"

"Someone behind me, I guess."

Ned was still standing behind Scott looking guilty as ever. He also looked as though he wanted to shoot Scott at that moment. Scott had put him in a horrible position and Ned was sure Buzz was going to come down on him.

"Niedermeier! Do you make it a habit of pinching people with loaded guns?"

"Excuse me, Sir"—Tina came forward—"but I was the one who pinched him. I realize now that it was a dumb thing to do, but at the time it seemed harmless enough." She spoke calmly, as though she were talking about her pet hamster or something. Scott and Ned both looked at her in complete shock.

"My apologies, Niedermeier," Buzz grunted. "I shouldn't have jumped to conclusions. All right, I want everybody back in their lines and ready to shoot, and this time no more funny business."

The students all turned back to their lines except Turner, who was now sitting on the ground with his shoe off. Even though it was just a paintball gun, it was a high-powered paintball gun and it had made a nice welt on his foot.

After class, Ned lit into Scott. "Next time you pull a stunt like that and decide to involve me, I would appreciate it if you would at least let me know what you're about to do. I'll make up my own mind whether or not I want to be a part of it."

"Sorry, Ned," Scott replied apologetically.

"Hey guys, wait up for us," Tina called. They stopped and waited for both Tina and Nancy to catch up.

"Whatever possessed you to take the blame like that?" Ned asked, glaring at Scott. "You didn't need to do that."

"I know. But I also know that Buzz is a male chauvinistic pig and thinks all girls are airheads. He expects something like that from a girl. If you had taken the blame, you'd probably be running the loop and still have six more laps to go. Besides, it was just an accident. There's no reason for you to get in trouble over an accident."

Scott and Ned looked at each other as though they were debating whether or not they should tell her the truth. Tina picked up on this. "It was just an accident, wasn't it?" she asked.

"Well...," Scott started.

"You did that on purpose!" she sputtered out loud, laughing. Unfortunately, she said it too loud and a few of Turner's friends walking by heard her. Scott shushed her, but it was too late—the damage was already done.

That evening while Scott was in his dorm, a boy knocked on his door and delivered a note. "What's this?" Scott asked, recognizing the fellow Falcon, but not able to place a name with the face. The kid just shrugged his shoulders, saying someone had asked him to deliver it to Scott Frontier. Scott opened the letter and read:

> Scott, I hear your trigger finger isn't as happy as you make it out to be. If you really have a burning desire to shoot me, then I'm going to give you a chance. We'll have our own private little War Games—if you dare. If you've got

*the guts, meet me out on the drill range just after dusk, at
7:40. We'll discuss the terms then. Keep this quiet and bring
only one friend with you. We don't want the whole school
showing up.*

Turner

After reading the note, Scott handed it to Ned with a grin. "It
looks like Turner is challenging me to a duel, and you get to act as my
second."

"You're actually going to go?" Ned asked.

"Of course! I wouldn't miss this chance for anything."

"You may get caught."

"I'll get in just as much trouble as he will," Scott replied.

"And you want me to come with you?"

"If you don't want to, I can find someone else."

"No, I'll come," Ned reluctantly agreed. "Someone's got to watch
out for you."

Scott and Ned arrived at the drill range exactly at 7:40 on the
dot. Turner and Slim had arrived earlier and were waiting for them.
They were holding two guns, along with two helmets and two jackets
for protection. "All right, here's the deal," Slim began. "Turner will
start down one side of the loop and Scott, you'll start down the opposite side. The object is to hit your opponent before he hits you. The
winner then gets the pleasure of firing one round at the loser. The
loser will only have the boundaries of the gun range to move about
and dodge bullets. Any questions?"

"What if we both get a shot off?" Scott asked. "How will you know
who hit first?"

"I'm assuming you are both honorable men. But in the event
neither of you will admit to being shot first, you will both have the
opportunity of firing at each other in the gun range. Fair?"

"Fair," Scott replied.

"All right, then. Scott, you and Ned head over to the back side of the loop. Make your way about thirty yards inside to avoid being seen. At that point, put on your helmet and jacket. I'll give you a few minutes to get used to them. When you hear my whistle, that will be the signal for you to go."

Scott and Ned did as Slim instructed and made their way down the back side of the loop. Scott put on the jacket and was surprised at how heavy it was. He had never worn one of these, and it weighed much more than he had expected. He then placed the helmet on top of his head. The face shield was scratched, making it difficult to see clearly. After a few moments, however, he got used to it and was able to look beyond the scratches.

"How is it?" Ned asked.

"It definitely takes some getting used to," Scott replied.

"Leave! Get out of here! We don't want you here!" several voices from the forest rang out.

Scott turned to Ned. "I have half a mind to shoot them. We have just as much right to be out here as they do."

"As who?" Ned asked.

"How should I know? It's too dark out here. I can't see them."

"See who?" Ned asked.

"You know, those voices I keep hearing, that you supposedly can't hear?"

"Scott, you're really starting to scare me. Maybe we should take you to a shrink."

"Ha!" Scott laughed nervously. "Maybe you're right. It's starting to scare me a little too."

Slim had not blown the whistle yet, so Scott took advantage of the time to run around a bit and even fired off a few bullets. The voices continued, but Scott ignored them the best he could. Once in a while he'd fire a few shots in the direction of the voices. About ten or fifteen minutes later, Slim blew the whistle. Scott took off down the track, trying to run as quietly as possible, staying as much as possible to the inside. Every few seconds he stopped to listen for any sound of Turner coming.

This whole adventure was actually quite stimulating, and Scott could easily understand why everyone liked the War Games so much. He stopped once more to listen, and this time he could hear Turner loud and clear, coming just around the bend. He was surprised at how quickly he had made it around the loop and how careless Turner was being. He knelt down and with his finger on the trigger, he took aim. It didn't take long for Turner to come into sight, and when he did, Scott blasted him.

Bang! Bang! Bang! He fired off his gun one bullet after the other. It wasn't until he had shot off at least five bullets that Scott realized, with horror, it wasn't Turner at all. It was Buzz. To make matters worse, every bullet he shot had hit its target, and Buzz was now on the ground rolling into the brush. Scott was horrified. He debated between running to avoid being identified or facing up to what he had done and apologizing. Either way, he was doomed.

"Who are you and why are you shooting at me?" Buzz yelled through the trees.

Scott still didn't say anything, because quite frankly, he didn't know what to say. Finally he had an idea. "Turner, you know exactly who I am. I won. So come out and admit defeat," Scott yelled, pretending to believe that Buzz was Turner.

"Is that you, Frontier?" Buzz yelled back.

"Of course it's me," Scott replied.

"Frontier, you idiot! What are you doing out here with a gun? And why in the world are you shooting at me?" Buzz yelled back as he emerged from the bushes.

"Buzz? I...I thought you were Turner," Scott stammered.

"I don't care if you thought I was Benedict Arnold, you shouldn't be out here with that gun."

"I'm sorry, Sir. Turner challenged me to a mini War Game. I was supposed to start at one end of the loop and he was to start at the other. When we met, the first one to hit the other would win."

"Didn't you see Turner and Johnson on your way around?" Ned asked, coming up on the scene.

Seeing the whole picture now, Buzz uncharacteristically laughed, much to Scott's relief. "I believe you've been conned, son. Slim knows I run this course every night at this time. They knew you would run into me, and thinking I was Turner, pelt me with the bullets. The whole thing was a setup."

Scott's temper started to rise. In his mind he could see Turner and Johnson sitting somewhere laughing their heads off, telling all the other Badgers about their little victory. How they had tricked him and made a fool out of him. Just thinking about it made Scott's blood boil. At the moment, however, he still had to deal with Buzz. "I'm sorry, Sir," Scott apologized. Then, noticing the dirt, debris, and of course the paint on his instructor's running suit, he added, "I'll pay for the cleaning bill, Sir."

"I appreciate that, Frontier, but you are missing the point. You know very well it's against the rules to engage in any unsupervised combat. Had you obeyed that rule, none of this would have happened in the first place. One lesson you should learn, Scott, is that you can choose your own actions, but you can't choose the consequences. Therefore, I will take you up on your cleaning offer, but I still have to turn you over to the headmaster who will determine your punishment."

"I understand," Scott said glumly.

"Well, Sir, at least now you know Scott can hit the broad side of a barn," Ned said with a slight grin on his face.

"Careful, Niedermeier, I might decide to report you also," Buzz grumbled as he walked off with Scott's gun and gear.

The next morning Scott was summoned to the headmaster's office. While he was making his way there, he ran into Headmaster McDougal. "Scott," he said, "I have to attend to one more item. Please continue to my office and I'll meet you there in a moment."

"Yes, Sir," Scott replied.

He found the headmaster's office, walked in, and sat down. Taking in his surroundings, he noticed there were shelves covered with books and little trinkets all over the place. There were also several closets and dressers, which seemed unusual for an office. These things normally belonged in someone's living quarters. As he was looking around, something glinted, just slightly, in the rays of the sun shining through the window and caught his eye. He couldn't quite tell what it was, so he got up and walked closer. What he saw made him freeze. He couldn't believe his eyes. *It can't be*, he thought. But it was. Placed right there, on the shelf before him, was a pair of boots. The same boots he had seen in his dream. They even had the wings attached. He picked them up and examined them. He had never felt or seen such material. Scott desperately wanted to put them on, remembering how they had actually made him fly in his dream. But knowing the headmaster was sure to walk through his door any minute, he put them back and sat down in his chair staring at the shoes. "I can't believe it!" he said out loud. "How could I have dreamed about them, and now here they are? It's just not possible."

At that moment, Headmaster McDougal entered the room. "Scott, do you want to explain what happened yesterday?" he asked in a calm voice.

Scott sat there, thinking for a moment. As much as he didn't like Turner, he also didn't want to be known as a tattletale. On the other hand, Buzz had most likely already given Headmaster McDougal all the details.

"I received a combat challenge from another student, Sir. Even though I knew it was against the rules, my pride got the best of me and

I accepted. Mistaking Buzz for the student, I...fired on him."

The headmaster sat down at his desk and looked at Scott for what seemed an eternity. "Scott," he finally stated, "the usual punishment for something like this is dismissal from school. However, since I know this is not completely all your doing, I am going to let you remain here at CastleOne. However, you will not go unpunished. You will be required to run the loop each day before dinner for the next three weeks. That was Buzz's request. As far as I am concerned, for the next week, after dinner, I would like you to clean the administrative offices and a few of the halls, as directed. You will be expected to empty wastepaper baskets, vacuum floors, and other similar tasks. Agreed?"

"Agreed," Scott replied.

"All right then, you are dismissed."

News of what happened spread quickly around the school. Everywhere he went, Scott heard the students laughing as he walked by. Some just thought it was funny, but others, mostly Badgers, called out various snide remarks. It was all Scott could do to keep himself from punching most of them, but he knew that would only make things worse at this point. The hardest part of all was facing Turner at drill that day. Turner didn't say anything, but he didn't have to. The smirk on his face said it all.

That evening, after running the loop and eating dinner, Scott headed over to the headmaster's office to report for cleaning duty. This, he was actually looking forward to. Maybe it would give him a chance to try on the boots. He approached the office, but as he did so, he could hear the headmaster and someone else talking inside. The other voice sounded young, so Scott guessed it must be another student. He waited for a while so as to not disturb them, but there was no sign of them wrapping up their conversation anytime soon. Finally, Scott decided it would be best to knock and get his assignments. After all, he didn't want to be up all night. He stepped up to the door and knocked. The voices dropped to whispers. "Who's there?" called the headmaster.

"It's Scott. I'm here to do the cleaning."

"I'll be there in a moment," Scott heard Headmaster McDougal's voice answer. A minute later, the headmaster opened the door and asked Scott to come in. "Take a seat, Scott," he invited, "and I'll be with you in a moment."

Scott sat down and the headmaster walked into the back room where his living quarters were. Scott immediately looked over to where the boots had been earlier that day. At first glance, he thought they were gone, but after a closer examination, he realized they were still there. Just then, the headmaster walked back into the office and asked Scott to follow him. Scott hesitated long enough to take one last look at the boots and then headed down the hall. Noticing his shoelaces had become untied, he bent down to tie them. Headmaster McDougal's stride was quick and when Scott looked up from his shoes, he found himself considerably behind. The headmaster had walked about thirty feet down the hall in front of him. This was a part of the castle Scott had never seen before. Suddenly, the headmaster stopped, turned right, and walked right through the wall. Scott stopped, eyes almost bulging out. "Where...?" Scott gasped. Just then the headmaster poked his head out of the wall.

"Are you coming?" he asked.

"Uh... yeah. But...uh...how do I do that?" he asked.

"Do what?" the headmaster asked.

"Walk through the wall like you just did?"

Headmaster McDougal chuckled. "Have you ever been to a magic show before, Scott?" he asked.

"My brother, Josh, does a lot of magic tricks, but you can't really call that a show. I've seen several on TV, if that counts."

"When they make an airplane disappear or cause a lady to levitate, they are simply creating an illusion. This staircase here is something like an illusion, I suppose. Come closer and you'll see."

Scott walked to where the headmaster was standing. From here, he could see a three-foot gap in the wall and a spiral staircase going down.

"Ah, I see," Scott said. "Where does this staircase go?"

"It leads down to the boiler room where the janitorial equipment is kept. Which is exactly where we are headed, seeing as how you will need this equipment to complete your task. Tonight, I would like you to empty all the wastepaper baskets, vacuum the hallways, the offices, and the Great Hall. That should be enough for tonight."

Enough? Scott lamented to himself. *It will take me all night just to get that done.* He grabbed the vacuum and headed upstairs with the headmaster, who had picked up a couple of large garbage bags.

"I'll be in my quarters if you need me," Headmaster McDougal informed him. "When you are done, please put the vacuum back. No need to check back with me."

"Yes, Sir," Scott said.

He plugged the vacuum into the wall and began vacuuming the rugs. As he cleaned the hallway and the Great Hall, his mind was occupied with thoughts of how the headmaster appeared to have walked through the wall. Suddenly he stopped. *Ned's brother said they had seen the headmaster walk through a wall,* he thought. *It wasn't a story at all. Neil had been telling the truth. He most likely had seen the headmaster appear to walk through that very wall. And if that story wasn't a hoax, then had they really seen floating chairs? If that story was true, was there a logical explanation for it?* The thought of seeing chairs floating gave Scott the willies and he started vacuuming even faster.

When he finished the Great Hall, he started on the offices, emptying the wastepaper baskets as he went. He purposely saved the headmaster's office for last with the intention of trying on those boots, and he wanted to be done with all his chores before he did that. As he approached Headmaster McDougal's office, he thought he heard voices once again. He wasn't about to wait around this time. He had heard a student's voice the first time, yet Headmaster McDougal had been the only one in the room when Scott entered. He knew students weren't allowed in the living quarters of the administration, so whoever Headmaster McDougal had been talking to wouldn't have gone back there. He figured he'd surprise them this time. He quickly opened the door and walked in, but found the room empty.

"That's weird," he muttered. "I could have sworn I heard voices." He quickly vacuumed and emptied the trash. When he finally finished, he walked over to where the boots had been, excited about the prospect of trying them on. As he approached the cabinet, however, he noticed they were gone. Hoping he just wasn't seeing them, he knelt down and felt around the shelves with his hands. The boots truly were gone. Wondering where they were and why the headmaster had taken them, he slowly stood up. Disappointment stabbed through him. He had really wanted to try the boots on, if only just for a second.

Dejectedly, he put the vacuum back in the boiler room, and put it where the headmaster had told him. He then headed back to the dormitory to finish up some last-minute homework. When he came upon the painting of the knight with the golden sword, he stopped and studied it for a second. *He does look a lot like me*, he thought. His eyes roamed over to the narrow hallway and the door to the room he and Ned had discovered their first day of school. He thought about taking another look in there, but when images of floating chairs crossed his mind, he decided against it.

He found Ned reading a book when he entered their room. "Guess what I saw tonight?" Scott said enthusiastically.

"What?" Ned asked without looking up from his book.

"I saw the headmaster walk through a wall."

Ned's head shot up. "Are you being serious?" he demanded.

"Yes. And… he taught me how to do it too."

"Very funny, Scott. Why are you all of a sudden bringing this up again?"

"I'm bringing it up because it may mean the story your brother told you might actually be true."

Ned looked at him for a second before speaking. "You really saw him walk through a wall?"

"Well, he didn't really walk through the wall. The way the castle is built, it makes it look like he walked through the wall. It's kind of an illusion, but your brother probably wouldn't have known that."

"So my brother's story is true!"

"Maybe. But we still haven't seen any floating chairs or ghosts outside our window yet, have we?" Scott pointed out. "Plus, Eric said it was just a story rumored by upperclassmen to scare freshmen. Perhaps someone saw the headmaster walk through the wall, like I did, and the rumor started from there."

"Well, I guess we'll have to find out then if it's just a rumor or if it's really true," Ned replied.

Scott woke up the next morning earlier than usual. He glanced over at Ned's bed, and sure enough, his roommate was already up and long gone. *Doesn't that guy ever sleep in?* he wondered. He walked over to the window, which overlooked one of the castle gardens, and noticed the sun was just rising. The scene before him was absolutely beautiful. He was about to open the window to let in some fresh air, when he spotted Ned and Tina below sitting on a bench under one of the apple trees. *They're in love*, he smiled to himself.

After a quick shower, he hurriedly dressed and headed downstairs. On his way down, he ran into Ned. "Are you ready for breakfast?" he asked.

"You bet!"

"So, you've been out walking with your girlfriend again?" Scott said, smiling.

"She is not my girlfriend!" Ned insisted.

"She's a girl and she is your friend, isn't she?"

"In that respect, she is my girl...friend," Ned replied.

"So then, it's settled. She's your girlfriend."

"Oh, brother!" Ned puffed.

Just then Tina walked into view. "Hey, Tina," Scott yelled. "Would you like to eat breakfast with me and your boyfriend?" At this, both Tina and Ned turned slightly red in the face. Ned elbowed Scott, trying to do it so no one would notice, but Scott immediately doubled over, moaning and groaning as if in pain. This made Ned's already red face go a shade darker.

Impulsively, Tina did something that surprised them both. She grabbed Ned's hand in hers and turned to Scott with a devilish smile, saying, "You're just jealous you don't have a girlfriend."

Not expecting this reaction, Scott stared at Tina and then at Ned. Both of them had huge grins on their faces. "I guess so," he said, somewhat still taken aback by this sudden announcement. As they continued towards the dining hall, Scott was silent.

As they entered the large room, Ned leaned over to Tina, whispering, "You sure shut him up." She smiled.

The truth was, Scott was thinking about what Tina just said. She had said it in jest, but she was right. Secretly he was starting to like girls and he really liked the one he had met on Halloween. The trouble was, he hadn't seen anyone that even closely resembled her.

Chapter Five

Azinine

The next few weeks flew by uneventfully. Drill was the only course the students took that was held outdoors, and they spent most of their time on the gun range. Once in a while, mostly on sunny days, Buzz would have them run the courses. Although snow hadn't fallen yet, it was getting quite cold outside. Buzz usually liked to save the warmer weather for the courses and the colder weather for the gun range and hand-to-hand combat practice.

It was now the third week in November. Scott had finished his janitorial punishment, as well as his sentence of running the loop, and had returned to a normal routine. The holiday season was just around the corner. This meant an awesome Thanksgiving dinner and a couple of days off. Although the school was located in Germany with a few students from England and other English-speaking countries attending, the majority were American and so Thanksgiving was celebrated. Christmas vacation was right on the heels of Thanksgiving, and that meant the annual Christmas Ball. This was the only dance the school held where students went as couples. Ned had already asked Tina if she would go with him, and Tina had been dropping several not-so-subtle hints that Scott should ask Nancy.

Scott knew Nancy wanted to go with him, and he told himself he would probably end up asking her, but inside he was still hopeful of finding the unknown girl. He had searched and searched, but the only girl that even came close was a senior named Clara Rasmussen. She was cute and had beautiful black curly hair, but her voice and eyes weren't the same. Added to that, she also acted like she'd never seen Scott before in her life. Scott told Ned he would probably ask Nancy, but he wanted to wait a little longer. As a result, being around the girls was a little awkward, and Nancy began acting cold towards Scott. His hesitation obviously gave Nancy the impression he didn't want to go with her. He knew if he didn't ask her soon, she might turn him down just to spite him and he wouldn't have anyone to go with. Yet, he still wanted to hold off.

"So are you or aren't you going to ask her?" Ned asked.

"Yes, I...I...am going to ask her," Scott replied hesitantly.

"But you don't really want to go with her. Do you?"

"She's not my first choice, Ned. You know that. But she is a lot of fun and since I can't find my first choice, I guess I'll ask her."

"Good. But don't wait too much longer. Now come on," he said, changing the subject. "Let's go get some dinner."

"I have a lot of work to catch up on. Would you mind grabbing me something when you head back up?" Scott asked.

"Sure," Ned answered. He walked out of the room while Scott picked up his homework and began to read. Ned walked down to the cafeteria, picked up his food, and walked over to where Eric and his friends were sitting.

"Hi, Ned. Where's your other half?" Eric asked.

"You mean that yellow-belly, Chicken-Little brother of yours?"

"Yeah, I guess. Why are you calling him that?"

"When it comes to girls, he's as chicken as they come. He keeps telling me he's going to ask Nancy to the dance, but he won't do it. Every dance is like some sort of major event, and he won't go until his princess comes along. He doesn't think you can go out with a girl and just be friends. To him, asking a girl on a date is the same as asking her to go steady with you," Ned said exasperatingly.

The other guys laughed, but Eric gave him a serious look. "I think

I'll ask Nancy," he stated.

"You want to go with her?" Ned asked curiously.

"Scott may not be a lady's man, but he's not as chicken as you think. If he really wanted to go with Nancy, he would have asked her by now. He'll ask her only after he knows for sure that he doesn't have a princess to ask. Besides, even if he really didn't want to go with Nancy, he still might ask her out of obligation. Scott's the kind of guy who'll pass up silver for gold even if there isn't any gold to be had. I like Nancy. She seems like a lot of fun. She deserves to go to the dance with someone who wants to go with her. Plus, it'll put Scott out of his misery."

"She's right over there," Ned said, nodding in Nancy's direction, daring Eric to do it. Without hesitation, he got up and walked over to her. She was sitting by herself so he sat down across from her. "Hi."

She looked at him and gave him a smile. "Hi," she replied. "And to what do I owe the honor of such a visit?"

"I know this is a long shot, but are you, by any chance, still free for the Christmas ball?"

Nancy's mouth dropped open. She hadn't expected this at all. "You want to go to the dance with me?" she asked in a bit of a daze.

"I do. Scott and Ned tell me you're a lot of fun to be with."

"Does Scott know you're asking me?" she asked suspiciously.

"No, and I thought I'd try and beat him to it," Eric replied.

"Will he be mad?" she asked.

"Probably, but it will serve him right for waiting so long. Is that a 'yes'?"

"Yeah. It sounds like fun."

"Okay, I'll see you later then." He gave her a genuine smile and walked back over to the others.

"Did she say 'yes'?" Ned asked.

"Yep," Eric replied.

Ned was stunned by the whole turn of events. "Aren't you even a little bit concerned that Scott will be angry?" he asked.

"I would be very surprised if Scott got angry. He'll be bummed he doesn't have anyone to take to the dance, but I don't think he'll be upset about Nancy."

Ned nodded. "He asked me to bring some food up to him. I think I'll do that and break the news to him at the same time. Are you okay with that?" Ned asked.

"Sure," Eric shrugged.

Scott started to read, but his mind turned to the girl he had met Halloween night. "This is crazy," he said to himself. "I am ruining my friendship with Nancy because of a girl I don't even know and can't even find." He was staring out the window watching the moon as it began to ascend into the sky. As he watched, he suddenly jumped backwards. Something large flew right in front of him. It was too large to be a bird, yet it definitely had wings. Scott jumped back towards the window straining his eyes to get a better look, but it was gone. Just then the door opened and Scott whirled around. "Hi," he said, breathing hard as Ned entered the room. "Thanks for bringing up the food."

"You're welcome," Ned replied, noticing the flushed look on Scott's face. "Are you okay? You look a little pale."

"Yeah, I...I'm fine. Did you see Tina and Nancy down there?"

"I saw Nancy. I don't know where Tina is."

"Well, I've decided I'll ask her tomorrow," Scott said.

"You're a dollar short and a day late, my friend," Ned replied.

"What do you mean?"

"Somebody already asked her. She's going with someone else."

"Really? Who?"

"Your brother."

"Eric? Eric asked Nancy to the dance?"

"Yep," Ned replied. He could see a sort of sadness, but definite relief spread across Scott's face.

"That's just like him," Scott said softly. "He probably thinks he's doing me some sort of favor and now I should be indebted to him. And Nancy, I think by now, hates my guts. She's probably relieved to have been asked by someone else."

"Scott, you should've just asked her. It's only a dance. You're not asking her to marry you."

"I know," he sighed, "but I was hoping..."

"You were hoping that you'd find your princess!" Ned interrupted sarcastically. "Well, I've got news for you, Scott. You're living in a dream world!" Ned said this with surprised emotion. Apparently his disappointment was much more than he had thought. He was really looking forward to the both of them going to the dance together, and now he would probably spend the night with Eric and his buddies. "Do you have anyone else to ask?" he questioned, calming down a bit.

"No," Scott said softly. Scott, too, was feeling sad and a bit silly. Ned was right. Because of his feelings for a girl he didn't even know, he probably wouldn't go to the dance at all. Most of the other girls he would consider asking already had dates. "I need to get some fresh air," he said, needing to get away. "I'll be back in a bit."

"Scott...I'm sorry. I didn't mean to act like that. I just really wanted us to go together, that's all."

"It's okay, Ned," Scott said as he grabbed his coat and walked out the door. He needed to clear his head so he headed down through the dorms and outside to the loop, where he started jogging. He and the loop were becoming good friends, and there was something about it that gave him solace.

The night air was cold, and several times he had to slow to a walk to keep the crisp air from burning his lungs. Since the winter air had arrived and a little snow had fallen, Scott hadn't heard any more strange voices, and for that he was glad. The sky was clear, making it easy to see the bright stars shining overhead. Scott stopped for a minute to catch his breath, gazing up at the stars admiring them. After a few moments he continued his run, and when he finished he walked over to the gardens and sat down.

"Hello," came a voice to the side of him, making him jump. He settled down when he saw it was Nancy. "Did I scare you?" she asked.

"Yeah, a little," he chuckled.

"I guess I'm just a scary person," she said. Then softly added, "Can I sit with you?"

"Are you sure you want to?"

"Scott, I'm sorry for being less than friendly lately."

"It's okay. I deserve it."

"You do?" she asked. "Why?"

He hesitated answering her question. He wasn't sure he wanted to say what he was feeling, but decided to anyway. She deserved an honest answer. "Ned told me you wanted me to ask you to the dance. Is that true?" he asked.

"Yes."

"It's not that I didn't want to ask you, Nancy. I like you and consider you a good friend. So I hope you won't be offended by what I am about to say. I also hope you won't think I'm silly." He stopped and thought about the best way to say what was on his mind.

"Go ahead," she encouraged him. "I promise I won't be offended, but I might think you're silly." Scott looked at her in surprise. "I'm just kidding," she teased.

"The night of the Halloween dance," Scott continued. "Remember when you guys came looking for me?"

"Yes, you tried to ditch us."

"I met a girl that night. She was dressed as a witch so I couldn't really tell what she looked like, but I think I…well, I fell in…. I came to really like her," he finally blurted out.

Nancy sat there for a minute without saying anything. "You fell in love with a girl you don't even know?" she finally asked.

"I know it sounds crazy," Scott replied, "but there was something about her, something...well it's hard to explain. Anyway, I was with her when you guys found me. She didn't want you to see her, so we ran back the other way. Finally I stopped and explained to her that you were my friends and I couldn't keep running. I turned to wait for you, and then looked back towards her, but she was gone. She'd disappeared into thin air."

"That's kind of spooky," Nancy said, looking at him. "Are you... really...being serious? This isn't some kind of joke, is it?"

"No, it isn't," Scott replied. "I'm telling you this, because it's why I postponed asking you. I wanted to find her and learn more about her. The dance would have given me a good excuse."

"Oh, I get it. I was your backup plan. If nothing better comes along, there's always Nancy. Is that it?" she asked, somewhat perturbed.

Scott looked down at the ground. He hadn't looked at it that way before, but she was right. He was only going to ask her as a last resort. "That's not quite how I considered it, but I guess that's how it looks. The fact is, Nancy, I consider you a good friend, but that's all, just friends. Because of that friendship, I know we'd have fun at the dance and for that reason I wanted to ask you. However, I also knew this dance may be the only excuse I'd find to get to know this other girl. In any case, I know it wasn't fair to you. It was selfish of me and I'm sorry."

Nancy considered this and neither of them spoke for what seemed like an eternity. "Scott," she finally broke the silence, "I appreciate you being honest with me. Yes, I feel rejected, but I can't really blame you. And yes, I was hurt at first, but I'm over that now, thanks to your brother."

"My brother?"

"Scott, as long as we're being honest, you should know that I like you a lot too, but also just as friends. I simply wanted to go to the dance, and I figured it would be fun for the four of us to go together.

When your brother asked me, I was shocked, but excited. Now that I know the reason why you didn't ask me, I'm okay with it. Can we still be friends?"

"Yes!" Scott quickly said, feeling relieved. He wanted to continue his friendship with Nancy, and now that they both knew each other's feelings, it would be a comfortable friendship.

"Okay, then," Nancy said. "I need to get to bed. I'll see you in the morning."

"Sure thing," Scott replied. Nancy stood up and headed back inside, leaving Scott feeling relieved about how things turned out. He still didn't have a date for the dance, but dances really weren't his thing anyway. The school was showing another movie that night for those students not attending the dance. Maybe he would watch that.

When Thanksgiving arrived, Scott and Eric went home for the weekend to celebrate the holiday with their family. It was nice to be home, and the boys enjoyed being with their parents and Josh again. Scott's mother had a few choice words directed towards him regarding his fight with Dan Henry and the shooting incident involving Buzz. It bothered Scott that his mother brought up the subject again, but he soon calmed down when she admitted that, overall, she was pleased with how well he was doing. Only one fight during a two-month period was a record for him. They enjoyed a great feast and for entertainment, Josh performed his newest magic tricks.

"Ladies and germs," he began, "I, Zandor the Magnificent, will begin to dazzle and amaze you."

"That's not very original. Don't you have anything better?" Eric teased.

"Sure. Ladies and nerds!" he yelled out. The family chuckled, but said nothing. "Today you will be stunned and amazed, not to mention thrilled and stumped. I, Zandor the Magnificent, am going to take these completely solid rings and hook them together." He showed them the rings and gave one of them to his mother. "Please examine the ring to ensure it is solid, containing no gaps." She checked it over and gave it back, nodding.

"Okay, on the count of three. One! Two! Three! He took the ring and slid it into another one, but it didn't quite make it and got stuck, revealing that the other ring in his hand wasn't quite as solid as the one he had given his mother. He pushed harder and it slid through. "Tadum!" he exclaimed. Everyone clapped despite the obvious blunder.

"For my next trick, I'm going to saw someone in half. Do I have any volunteers?" Everyone laughed. "What? I'm serious."

"I think it's time for more pumpkin pie," their father recommended.

"I second that," Eric chimed in.

The holiday went by quickly and the boys soon found themselves headed back to CastleOne.

When they arrived at school, the sky was dark and threatening to snow. Mrs. Frontier didn't want to be caught in a snowstorm on the way home, so they quickly helped Eric and Scott take their bags up to their rooms, paid a hasty visit to the headmaster, said their good-byes, and headed back home.

The boys had gone outside to see their parents off. While waving, Eric turned to Scott. "Did you notice whether Ned was back or not?"

"I don't think he is," Scott replied. "How about Zack?"

"He wasn't in the room, but his stuff was on his bed. He's around here somewhere," Eric answered.

"Why did you want to know if Ned was back?"

Eric paused for a moment before answering. "I guess you know that I asked Nancy to the dance, right?"

"Yeah."

"You haven't said anything about that. Are you mad at me?"

"No. You actually did me a favor. If you hadn't asked her, she would have killed me for being such a numskull. I was going to mention it to you, but every time I thought about it, either you weren't around or it wasn't a good time."

"Do you have someone you're going to ask?" Eric asked.

"No, I'll probably just watch the movie."

"If you want, I'll ask her if she wouldn't mind going with you?"

"Thanks, but I think she's really looking forward to going with you. She might be insulted if you asked her to go with me. Then she'd think all Frontiers are jerks."

"You're right. That would be dumb. Let's go inside, I'm getting cold."

"Wait," Scott said.

"What?"

"Look up to the top of the castle," Scott said, pointing.

Eric looked up. "No way!...I can't believe it."

"I told you I saw a gargoyle up there once before," Scott said triumphantly.

"It wasn't there before. I wonder who put it up there?" Eric asked.

"A better question is why did they put it up there and why do they take it down sometimes?" Scott proposed.

"Hmm, good question," Eric said.

They walked inside and headed back up to their rooms. "Maybe I could ask around and see if I could find someone for you to go with," Eric suggested.

"Thanks, but no thanks. Dancing and me are like oil and water. I'll probably do better just going to the movie."

"All right, it's up to you. But if you change your mind, let me know." Reaching the upper stairs, they each turned towards their room. Eric stopped for a moment. "If you see Ned, tell him I need to talk to him."

"Okay," Scott replied.

When Scott entered his room, he noticed Ned still had not returned. It was still early in the evening, and some of the students had long distances to travel. Although he didn't know exactly where Ned lived, he had mentioned he lived close by, so Scott figured it wouldn't be too much longer before he arrived. Scott unpacked his bags and lay down on his bed. It felt good to just lie down and relax.

The next thing he knew, it was morning. Scott woke up still wearing the same clothes he had worn the day before. He glanced over at Ned's bed and could see that Ned had arrived, but was not in bed at the moment. Scott looked at the clock to see that it was 5:45 A.M. "Where would Ned be at this time in the morning?" he asked himself. He got up, showered, and dressed, and still Ned was not back. By now it was 6:30 A.M. Scott pulled out his history book and began reading, figuring this would be a good time to get ahead rather than play catch-up. Just as he opened the book, Ned walked in looking surprised.

"Wow, you're up early," Ned remarked.

"You're up even earlier," Scott pointed out. "Where have you been?"

"I had to talk with Headmaster McDougal about a few things. This is the only time he's ever available. Did you have a good holiday?" he asked, changing the subject.

"Sure, it was good to be home for a little while. How about you?"

"Yeah, it was good. Do you want to go down and get some breakfast?"

"Right now?" Scott replied. "We'd be the first ones there. They probably don't even start serving this early."

"Yes they do. Maybe if you got up a little earlier than the crack of noon, you'd know that," Ned teased. "Besides, this time of morning it's warm and tastes like real food."

Scott chuckled at that and stood up. "Sounds good. I can always come back and finish up my reading afterwards."

The two boys went downstairs and entered the cafeteria. Ned was correct, the cafeteria was empty, and the cooks were ready; the food actually smelled pretty good. They picked up their food and sat down. A few moments later, Nancy and Tina walked in. Scott and Ned waved and motioned for them to sit with them.

"Nancy seems to be in a better mood. She at least looks like she's no longer eating raw meat," Ned remarked to Scott.

"Raw meat?" Scott questioned.

"Haven't you ever seen a wolf with raw meat? Go near one of them and they'll bite your head off just for trying."

"She never wanted to bite my head off. We've always been good friends," Scott replied, purposely leaving out the conversation he'd had with Nancy.

"Are you blind?" asked Ned. "Haven't you noticed her icy looks lately. If looks could kill, you'd have been dead weeks ago."

Scott laughed. "I think you're overreacting a little," he shot back. They both abruptly stopped the conversation when they saw the girls approaching.

"Hi," Scott said in a cheerful voice as they both sat down.

"Hi," they both replied.

Scott put his arm around Nancy's shoulders. "It's sure good to see your happy smiling face again, Nancy."

Nancy put her arm around Scott and gave him a hug. "Your's too," she said in just as friendly a voice, and then just to top that, she kissed him on the cheek. This took Scott completely off guard, but he did a good job playing along. Ned and Tina, on the other hand, both looked dumfounded. Ned's jaw was open so wide it about hit the table.

"So, how was your holiday?" Scott asked, posing the question to both of the girls.

"Oh, it was great to see my family again. I had a really good time," said Nancy.

Tina, on the other hand, said nothing. She was still in a state of shock, even more so than Ned. It was obvious that Nancy hadn't told Tina about their conversation. The group talked about this and that while they ate, once again as good friends.

"Well, I gotta get in some last-minute reading before classes start. I'll see you girls at drill," Scott said as he started putting items on his tray.

Ned followed him. When they were out of earshot of the girls, Ned turned to Scott. "What was that?"

"What was what?"

"You know darn well what I'm talking about."

"Come on, Ned, the food wasn't that bad."

"No, no, I'm talking about you and Nancy being all buddy-buddy with each other."

"Okay, okay," Scott laughed. "Nancy and I had a talk before the holiday and everything is fine between us. We're friends and we both know it's nothing more than that. To tell you the truth, I'm relieved. Now I can be myself without having to worry about what she might read into it."

"Does this mean no more worries about a so-called date?" Ned asked.

"Yep," answered Scott.

"And no more whining about dancing with the girls?"

"Yep."

"And no more barfing if a girl so much as looks at you?"

"Oh come on! I wasn't that bad. But yes, no more worries," Scott assured him.

"Good," Ned said.

They both did as much studying as they could and then headed out to drill. The door to the combat building was open, and since the other students were headed in that direction, Scott and Ned turned that way too.

"I guess we must be starting combat training today," Ned said casually.

"Awesome!" Scott replied. "This is the kind of stuff I like."

"Yeah, we'll see how you like it when you get your butt kicked all over the ring. You at least have a little height. I'm short and skinny," complained Ned.

"Ned, there is usually an advantage in everything: tall, skinny, fat, short. You just have to know how to use it *and* use it better than the advantages of your opponent."

"Okay, tell me how I use short and skinny against tall and strong."

"Well, whenever you're the underdog," Scott explained, "you almost always want to use the element of surprise. When I hit Dan, I hit him at a time when he didn't expect it, and I'm sure he also didn't expect a freshman to hit him. So timing and expectations were the key, although that time it wasn't on purpose. Of course, I should have considered Bear as part of the picture. That was my mistake. But you can do the same. For example, someone bigger and stronger than you will already believe he has the advantage and will be overconfident. You can use other techniques to make him even more overconfident. This will, in turn, increase your element of surprise."

"Like what?" Ned asked doubtfully.

"Act like you're afraid. It's..."

Ned cut him off. "What if I'm not acting? Will it still work?"

Scott didn't pay much attention to that. "It's only natural for someone smaller to be afraid of someone bigger. Once they believe they have things in the bag, search for a time to attack when they least expect it. And then when you do attack, do it with fury. Hit them with all you've got and don't let them recover."

"What if they recover?"

"You're toast."

"Gee, thanks. I'll be sure to remember that," Ned said as they entered the building, finding several students already there. Inside were two sparring rings, a large open area where mats were spread out under the kicking bags hanging from the ceiling, and two sets of bleachers, one on each side. Most of the students were sitting in the bleachers, but there were a few who had wandered over to one of the rings where two students from the Badger division were pretending to duke it out. Scott and Ned sat down on the bleachers to wait for class to begin.

"Scott, how do you know so much about fighting?" Ned asked.

"Much to the chagrin of my mother, I've spent my whole life fighting," Scott replied. "My parents put Eric and me in karate lessons when we were younger. My mother took me out after a while because she thought it was the karate that was encouraging me to fight, which was quite the opposite. It's not something I've meant to do or something I'm even proud of. I guess trouble just finds me and I react to it. There always seems to be some kid in the neighborhood or at school who deserves a good butt kicking, and I always seem to get the honors. I've been here three months now, and I've only been in one fight. Believe it or not, that's a record for me."

Ned shook his head. "I wish I knew how to fight."

"No, you don't. Whether you win or lose, there's no glory in fighting. If you win, you usually end up feeling bad for what you did and the person you did it to. It never brings you friends, and you are the one who usually gets in the most trouble. If I had my way, I'd never get in another fight again, but my temper always makes sure that doesn't happen. The only good reason for learning to fight is for self-defense."

Just then Buzz entered the building. Noticing the boys goofing off in the ring, he blew his whistle and yelled at them to sit down on the bleachers along with the other students. While everybody was settling in, getting ready for Buzz's instructions, Slim Johnson entered the room and walked over to stand next to Buzz.

Buzz blew his whistle again, indicating it was time for everybody to be quiet so they could get started. "For those of you who don't know," he began, "this is Slim Johnson, the division leader for the

Badgers. I have asked him to help me demonstrate some of the moves I'll be teaching you. I'll be working with half of you in one ring, and I've asked Slim to serve as an instructor and to help out in the other ring. Slim can only be here the first part of class, so I need you all to be attentive and not goof around. We need to maximize his time with us. Now, the sophomores have already heard my beginning combat lecture, so I want all sophomores to go with Slim, while all freshmen stay here with me."

Slim motioned for his group to follow him over to the mats. Buzz waited until they were all gone before he continued. "There are several forms of martial arts, and too many for us to practice them all. We are going to focus mainly on kickboxing, with a bit of jujitsu mixed in. The first thing I want you to remember is that we train you in combat, not as killers, but rather to protect yourself from killers."

Buzz continued to talk about the history and philosophy of martial arts. Once he was finished with his speech, he took his group over to the mats to join Slim and the other students. There he explained the importance of stretching and warming up and then proceeded to show how this should properly be done. After everyone had warmed up and stretched out, Buzz continued with a demonstration of a few basic punches and kicks, asking the students to follow along with him as he performed them in slow motion. They spent the rest of the class time practicing these basic movements, which quickly became monotonous and boring to a few of the students. Scott, on the other hand, loved every minute of it. Finally, when class was almost at an end, Buzz had everybody run the loop and head for the showers.

"I have to admit, I really feel good," Ned remarked. "I think I'm really going to like this kick-boxing stuff."

"Really?" Scott asked. "Why don't we come back after school and we can practice against the bags?" he suggested.

"Okay," Ned replied.

The two boys headed to the showers followed by a trip to the cafeteria for lunch. There, they saw Eric and his friends sitting at a table, so they joined them.

"Hey, runt," Eric said, greeting him.

"You better watch what you say to him, he's a martial arts expert now," Ned joked.

"Did you guys start combat today?" Eric asked.

"Yeah."

"Who did he pick as his aid?"

"Slim Johnson!" Scott said, speaking for the first time since they'd joined the group.

"Buzz sure knows how to pick 'em," Zack remarked.

"I've already warned you about him, Scott," Eric said. "He's good and nothing would give him more pleasure than to humiliate a Falcon division member, especially a freshman."

"I don't plan on giving him that pleasure," Scott replied.

"We're going back to the combat arena later tonight to practice. Any of you juniors want to come show us a thing a two?" Ned asked.

"No, we're going to the gym to play basketball. You guys should come play with us," Eric suggested.

"What's wrong? Are you chicken?" Ned asked. "Are you afraid I'll kick your booty?"

Several of them laughed. "Ned, one flick of my finger and I'd knock you out," bragged Trevor Carson. Trevor was a fairly big kid who looked like a giant compared to Ned.

"All right," continued Ned, "if you're so confident, come on over and this old boy will give ya some learnin'." The others laughed again, but Scott just shook his head. He knew Ned was just kidding, but Trevor looked like he might just take him up on it.

The day passed by slowly for Scott, but when it was finally over, he and Ned ate a quick dinner and headed back to the arena. They warmed up like they had been taught and then walked over to the kicking bags to practice the basic punches and kicks they had worked on that morning.

"Why don't we go get some gear and do some sparring in the ring?" Scott suggested after they had worked on their moves for a while. "This is the perfect time to do it while no one else is here."

"Sounds good, as long as you take it easy on me," Ned cautioned. They walked over to the supply cage and picked out some gloves and helmets. They put the gear on and climbed into the ring. At first, they danced around each other, taking a few punches here and there.

After a few punches Ned looked at the entrance, pointing, "Oh no! Look!"

Scott looked over. Seeing no one there, he turned back around and felt a fist pound him across the jaw.

"I can't believe you fell for that!" Ned chuckled.

"I can't believe you'd stoop that low," Scott replied. "By the way, you really should do more laundry. You still have food stains on your shirt." Ned bent over to look. *Whomp!* Scott dealt a blow to Ned's head, sending him reeling to the floor.

Ned was back on his feet surprisingly fast. "Touché," he muttered. He then threw himself at Scott, leg high, heading right for Scott's chest. Scott saw it coming, grabbed Ned's leg, and was about to shove him off when Ned pulled his leg forward bringing Scott with him. Now within range, Ned sent a surprisingly hard punch square into Scott's face. Had it not been for the headgear, it would have hurt something fierce. Scott shoved Ned's leg upwards, throwing him to the ground, but Ned was quick to get back up and shot towards Scott with amazing speed. By pure reflex, Scott dropped to the floor, landing on his back, catching Ned with his feet and sent him flying into the ropes. Scott quickly jumped up, but Ned got up quickly also, and was once again hurtling towards him. Scott was amazed not only at Ned's ability to recover, but also at his tenacity. As Ned came towards him, Scott positioned himself to dodge his friend's attack and send him once again into the ropes. However, just as Ned reached Scott, he suddenly stopped, throwing Scott off balance, and then dealt another hard blow across the side of Scott's head. He immediately placed a leg behind Scott and threw him to the floor. Scott, now on the floor, threw his leg out as hard as he could into Ned's legs, tripping him and sending him to the floor.

This time neither got up. They both lay there laughing and gasping for breath. "I thought you said you didn't know how to fight," Scott panted.

"I simply did what you told me to do. I used the element of surprise and then kept attacking," Ned stated. Scott eyed him suspiciously. Even using Scott's advice, he found it hard to believe that a beginner could have fought like Ned just did.

At that moment the door opened and Slim Johnson and some of his buddies walked in, dropping their gym bags on the floor. "Beat it, losers," Slim yelled in their direction. Scott and Ned sat there looking first at each other and then back at Slim. "I said, 'beat it'!" Slim barked out.

Scott was looking at Slim and Ned could tell he was getting angry. "Last time I remember, this gym...," Scott started.

"Scott, no!" Ned quickly interrupted. "Remember what your brother said?"

"I'm not going to fight him," Scott whispered.

"You are still challenging him. You know how things will end up."

"What was that?" Slim asked, coming closer now.

"Nothing. He was talking to me," Ned replied. "We were just leaving."

"That's a good little boy," Slim sneered.

"No, let the two little lovebirds join us," another voice sang out from the corner of the building. Scott glanced over to see Dan Henry standing there. His heart sunk. He thought his troubles with Dan were over. Dan had pretty much left him alone, but now Scott was right where Dan wanted him. This was the perfect opportunity for Dan to get his revenge.

"Yeah, I guess we could let them join our practice," Slim said with a grin on his face. "You can never get enough practice, you know," he continued as he looked at Scott and Ned.

Then Scott said something that completely surprised Ned. "Right now, you guys would kill us. Before we spar with anybody at your level, we'd need a lot more practice. At this point, we've only learned the basic punches and kicks. I've seen you fight, Slim, and neither of us would have a chance against you. We'll catch you later in the year, once we have more experience." Slim appeared to be pleased with Scott's words and Ned thought he saw him soften a bit.

"Well, there's no time like the present," Dan countered, trying to sound sincere. "We'd be glad to teach you two some new moves."

"That would be great!" Scott said. "Why don't you and Slim demonstrate and we'll watch."

"Fine," Dan replied, "and then we'll pair off and see how well you learned."

"Oh that sounds like a great plan," Scott responded.

Ned was speechless and apparently so were Slim and Dan, because no one said anything for a second. *Surely any idiot could see their intentions*, Ned thought. *Scott has to see what they are up to, so why is he being so agreeable?*

Finally Slim spoke up. "All right then, let's get going," he said in a cheerful voice. Then turning to another member of the Badger division, he continued, "Ron, please shut and lock the door. We want this to be our practice and no one else's." This was obviously Slim's way of calling Scott's bluff and letting Scott know there was no way out now. Interestingly enough, Scott still showed no sign of nervousness and eagerly looked on as though everything was all right. Slim, Dan, and the other four students all started to warm up.

"I hope you have a plan," Ned whispered to Scott.

"I have to admit, I wasn't planning on them locking the door," Scott whispered back.

"So what do we do?"

"Just remember the element of surprise. Plus, it will be good practice."

"Practice! More like baptism by fire. I feel like mother bird is just about to push me out of the nest."

"You'll be fine," Scott reassured. "It's me they hate, not you. You pair up with Slim and act like he really is your teacher. If you pump up his ego, you'll come out of this unharmed. I, on the other hand, could be in real trouble. I'm just hoping to last long enough to break Dan's nose again."

"What?" Ned whispered loudly. "Dude, you're a freakin' lunatic."

"Sometimes in life, Ned, you just have to act without thinking about the consequences."

"I take that back. You're a dumb lunatic."

"What I mean is that you can't let fear keep you from trying. Otherwise, you'll fail anyway. These guys are not going to let us out of here without a fight. So we might as well make the best of it. Let's turn this into a real learning experience. Rather than letting Dan have his way with me, I'm going to fight back. And if I do have to fight back, I might as well have the element of surprise on my side."

"Scott, don't do this," Ned pleaded.

"I'm not really going to try and break his nose, I'm just going to spar with him. You know, see how well I can do against him. It really could be a good learning experience."

"I've got a bad feeling about this," Ned whispered with a sigh.

Slim and his gang finished stretching out and he and Dan hopped into the ring. "For your first lesson, we will teach you a kick from Kang Fa." Slim turned and bowed to Dan and Dan did likewise. They positioned themselves and before Dan knew it, Slim slammed a foot into his chest, sending him reeling to the floor. Ned winced as he imagined Slim doing that to him.

Dan got back up and looked at Scott and Ned. "All right," he said, "now it's our turn to show you."

"Already?" Ned asked nervously. "You guys just got started."

"That's right, one step at a time." Slim smiled and motioned for Ned to follow him to the other ring.

Dan turned back to Scott. "Okay. Are you ready, Frontier?"

Scott took in a deep breath. "As ready as I'll ever be."

Dan started dancing around so Scott followed suit and did the same. They moved around each other for a bit and then Dan sent a punch flying in Scott's direction. Scott went to block it, but realized it was a decoy a second too late. Dan sent a foot slamming into his chest, knocking him to the floor. It hurt much worse than Scott thought it would, but he did his best to hide any pain and jumped back up.

"Excellent move! And thanks for taking it easy on me. A move like that could really hurt," Scott said, trying his best to make Dan think it hadn't really hurt. Dan took it as the insult Scott intended, but Scott continued to act as though it was a well-intended comment. They started to dance around some more.

In the other ring, Slim and Ned were dancing around too. In reality, Slim was doing the dancing and Ned was simply doing his best to keep out of reach. It would have been amusing to watch, but Scott didn't dare take his eyes off his own opponent. He had to concentrate on Dan, who was now dancing and moving a little bit faster. Scott figured Dan was doing this to intimidate him, but he realized a second later this wasn't the case. Dan sent a foot his direction again. This time, however, it didn't have the same power and meaning the first one had. It was meant only as a distraction. Scott saw it coming and easily dodged it. But before he could recover, Dan fell to the floor and in a circular motion swept Scott off his feet, landing him on his back. This hurt worse than the first kick and Scott was beginning to regret this whole thing.

He got up, breathing heavily. "Another nice display of technique. We'll have to keep practicing that one. Perhaps I could take a turn now," he said, once again acting as though none of Dan's blows had any impact on him. Out of the corner of his eye he could see Ned still running around dodging Slim. Scott decided he had to try a different approach. He needed to do something that would distract Dan's concentration. He jumped up and leaped into a mock karate stance, yelling, "Whaa!" as though he was some kung fu expert and meant business. He then began to throw all kinds of dumb karate moves at some invisible opponent, all the while yelling things like "Ya! Ha! Whaa!" This, of course, did exactly what he had hoped. Dan stopped and looked at him incredulously. What Scott didn't know was that it also worked on Slim. Amused by Scott's antics, Slim had stopped focusing on Ned and was watching what was happening in the other ring.

Ned, taking advantage of the distraction, did the most unexpected thing Scott had ever imagined. Ned slammed a fist directly into Slim's gut, causing him to double over in pain. He then sent an uppercut fist hard into Slim's face. Slim howled out in pain and hit the floor. Ned could see blood coming from his nose. Slim, being the cocky person he was, had decided that wearing head gear wasn't necessary. After all, Ned was a freshman punk half his size.

"Are you okay?" Ned asked Slim, genuinely concerned. Hearing this, Dan stopped to see what had happened and Scott, in turn, didn't waste any time. He slammed a fist into the side of Dan's head, sending him flying to the ground. Dan, of course, was wearing head gear and quickly recovered. Dan sent his leg in a circular motion as he had done seconds ago. Scott had anticipated that move this time and jumped, but Dan's leg still caught him enough to throw him off balance and knock him to the floor. However, this time he landed on Dan's leg and it was Dan who let out a scream. Scott wasn't hurt and he immediately jumped to his feet. Dan, on the other hand, was still down on the mat holding his leg, making Scott wonder if he had broken it.

Slim's nose was definitely broken and Ned wasn't quite sure what to do now. They could both run, but that would look cowardly. On the other hand, Ned was sure that once Slim recovered, broken nose or not, he was going to mutilate him. To his immense relief, however, he heard someone at the door trying to open it, which of course they couldn't since the Badgers had locked it. Seconds later, however, it opened and in walked Ian Karding and several other Falcons. Because Ian was the Falcon division leader, he had a key to the building and had used it to unlock the door.

What they found shocked them. Two of their freshmen were in the rings standing over two Badger seniors, who were both obviously hurt. No one said a word at first, and then Ian walked quickly over to the ring Slim was in, sizing up the situation. "Trevor," he said, talking to one of the Falcons with him, "go get the school nurse. Tell her we may have another broken nose and possibly a broken leg. We may also need a doctor." Trevor quickly left as the other Falcons walked over to see what had happened.

"What is going on here?" Ian demanded of Ned. Ned explained that Slim and his group had offered to give him and Scott some lessons and that they were just sparring. Ian glared at Slim. "It's a darn good thing it's you and Dan that are hurt instead of these freshmen. Otherwise I would have your butt in the headmaster's office quicker than you could count to ten. You know perfectly well this is against school rules." He then turned to Scott and Ned. "You two, gather your gear and meet me in my dorm in twenty minutes. Now move it!"

Scott and Ned didn't need any further prodding. They quickly gathered their stuff and exited the combat building. As they walked toward the dorms, they ran into Trevor and the school nurse, along with the headmaster, who were all heading in the direction of the building.

Headmaster McDougal stopped in front of them blocking their

way. Scott and Ned stopped also, but didn't say anything. He stood and looked at both of them, and then looked at Scott.

"Really?" he said, exasperated. "Why am I not surprised," he said, looking at Scott.

"Hey, don't look at me," Scott said. "Ned's the one that broke his nose."

He eyed Ned suspiciously, but to Scott's relief he just shook his head and continued walking.

"Do you think we'll get in trouble for this?" Ned asked.

"I hope not. After all, it's not like we had any choice in the matter," Scott reasoned. They walked a little further before they spoke again. "You surprise me, Ned," Scott started. "You act like you're scared, like you're this little wimp or something, and the next moment you haul off and break Goliath's nose. That sort of thing takes guts."

"Why, thank you, Scott. I'll take that as a compliment. I really owe my courage to you, though. After all, didn't you say sometimes in life you just have to act without thinking about the consequences?"

"That's what I said, but I didn't mean act blindly. You don't jump off a cliff without first making sure that there's water below and that it's deep enough. You don't declare war on a country without having an army to back you up, and you don't break the nose of the Badgers' division leader, who just happens to be twice your size, if you have any consideration for your own life."

"Oh, you're a fine one to be talking. Who's the one who hauled off and broke Dan's nose for no apparent reason?"

"Dan Henry is not the Badgers' division leader and he is not twice my size. And if I had known then what I know now, I wouldn't have hit him."

"What do you mean by that?"

"He's good! If you hadn't distracted him, I'm pretty sure I'd be the one with a broken nose right now."

"I doubt that," Ned replied. "You would have found a way."

"Thanks for the vote of confidence, but I'm not so sure. Things are a lot different here. Where I used to go to school, the kids were just that...kids. Beating them in a fight was easy. Here, they are trained to fight and they're much bigger. I feel like a little fish in a big pond, instead of a big fish in a little pond. I'm just out of my league here."

By this time they had reached their dorm. After a quick shower, they dressed and headed over to Ian's dorm. There was a huge crowd consisting mostly of juniors and seniors talking outside Ian's door. When they saw Scott and Ned come around the corner, they all began to cheer and give Scott and Ned high fives. Ned thoroughly enjoyed the attention and joined in quite vigorously. Scott, on the other hand, wasn't sure they should be celebrating. Making his way to the door, he could see Eric standing against one of the walls. He was watching Scott with mock disappointment on his face. Looking back at him, Scott mouthed that it wasn't his fault, but Eric just raised his eyebrows.

They entered Ian's room and found him sitting in a chair at a desk. He had a room to himself, which was much bigger than the room Scott and Ned shared. "Nice place," Scott heard himself say as they sat down.

"Thanks. I guess leadership does have its privileges," Ian said. Then for a long moment he sat there and stared at them. "One half of me wants to strangle both of you," he finally blurted out, "and the other half wants to shake your hands and pat you on the back. Since congratulating you wouldn't look too good in my position, I guess I'll have to strangle you." Scott was relieved to hear that Ian was back to his normal joking self. "Ned," their division leader continued, "I want you to start from the beginning and tell me exactly what happened tonight. I need to know everything. Otherwise you two could be in a lot of trouble."

Ned started from the beginning and explained how they had gone to the arena to practice the moves they had been taught that day. He then went on about Slim and Dan and how they pretty much forced him and Scott to spar with them.

"If you were just sparring, then why in the world did you punch Slim in the nose, knowing full well he wasn't wearing any head gear?" Ian asked.

"To be honest, I think they wanted to do more than just spar. Otherwise, why would they have locked the door? Dan had already knocked Scott to the floor twice, and he was just warming up. We had to do something before things got really ugly. So when the opportunity opened up, I took it. I thought if I could really make Slim hurt, maybe he would call things off."

"Or really beat you to a pulp!" Ian exclaimed. "You guys need to be more careful. You two have pretty much single-handedly humiliated the whole Badger division by what you just did. Don't you dare repeat this, but, between you and I, it was great to see. But I am also worried about you. This could come back to bite you. Slim won't rest until he gets revenge, you can pretty much count on that. And I'm pretty sure Dan will want his also. This is the second time you've humiliated him," he pointed out, looking at Scott, "so be careful. I will need to discuss this with the headmaster, but for now you can go. During school hours, I want both of you to always be together and with others if possible. If you want to take part in activities after school, do it with some of the other Falcons, preferably juniors and seniors. Is that understood?"

"Yes," they both answered together.

"All right then, get out of here. If you suspect any foul intentions from the Badgers, I want you to notify me immediately," Ian further instructed them. Scott and Ned nodded their agreement and walked out. Again there were cheers from the group of students hanging outside the dorm, which by now had grown even larger. Scott looked around, but there was no sign of Eric anywhere. He and Ned walked back to their room. When they entered the room, they found Eric and his friends sitting inside.

"You've done it now, little brother," Eric stated as Scott walked in.

"We had no choice," Scott replied.

"I know. But you would have been better off letting them beat up on you for a bit. At least that way they would have had a good laugh and no more bad feelings. Now they'll have to do something to save face, and whatever they come up with isn't going to be pretty."

"Yeah, Ian already warned us of that."

"So, we've decided to be your bodyguards for a while. From now on, you'll eat meals with us, we'll walk you to your classes, and you will hang with us during your spare time. You will pretty much spend every living moment with us when you're not in class. Okay?"

"You betcha!" Ned replied in a voice of relief. The other boys in the room laughed.

"All right then, we'll see you outside your door tomorrow morning," Eric said as he stood up and headed for the door.

During the next week, either Eric or one of his friends was with Scott and Ned at all times, with the exception of class time. When class was over, however, there was always someone outside their door waiting for them. For the most part, Scott thought all this protection was going a bit overboard. There were no further altercations with any of the Badgers. In fact, it seemed like the whole thing had been forgotten. There were a few times when Scott and Ned ran into Dan or Slim, but for the most part all they received were dirty looks. Surprisingly, Dan didn't seem half as upset this time as he had the first time he and Scott had crossed paths. Dan's leg wasn't actually broken but only had a minor fracture, and Eric surmised that Dan took some consolation in the fact that it was Slim this time with the broken nose. Slim, on the other hand, seemed to be in a worse mood than normal, which caused Eric some concern. He cautioned Scott and Ned to continue to stay together and to wait for a Falcon escort.

The Falcons, on the other hand, were still gloating over the victory. When Falcon members walked by Scott and Ned, they gave the two of them either a thumbs-up or a high five. The rivalry between the two divisions was an escalating rivalry, and the Falcons had definitely come out on top in this one.

On Friday morning, Ned was up bright and early. It was the day of the Christmas Dance and he wanted to pick up his suit from the cleaners as early as possible. The school had a rather large laundry facility for the students to use, but they also had a dry-cleaning service available for delicate clothing. When Ned returned to the dorm with his suit, Scott was still in bed, but he was awake.

Ned held up his suit against his body. "Don't I look goood!" Ned said in a cocky, confident voice.

"Not to me, you don't," Scott remarked.

"You're just jealous because you're not coming. You could be going, but nooo, you had to wait for your princess," Ned said only half joking. He was still miffed with Scott for being so picky.

Throughout the week, Scott had thought a lot about his decision to not go to the dance, and he was beginning to regret it. Ned's teasing didn't help any. Ignoring Ned's further remarks, he got out of bed and headed for the showers without saying anything more.

When he got back to his room, Trevor was waiting by the door to take them to breakfast. Scott was beginning to get tired of this constant babysitting, but he understood the need. "Sorry I'm late," he said to Trevor as he walked by. "I'll hurry." He walked inside to dress and found Ned at his desk reading a book. "Our bodyguard is waiting outside," Scott informed Ned.

"I thought so," Ned answered. "But I figured there was no reason for me to leave until Prince Charming was ready." Making a face at him, Scott quickly put some clothes on and combed his hair. Once he was finished, they both walked out and headed for breakfast with

Trevor at their side.

"Trevor," Scott began, "is this really necessary? Slim and Dan haven't shown any signs of revenge."

"No sign? Didn't Eric tell you?"

"Tell us what?"

"We've heard rumors that Slim has been planning something and we expect him to try it soon."

"Like what?" Ned asked.

"We're not sure, but our sources heard something about attacking you from behind and ripping your eyeballs out."

"Wow, I'm sure glad I wasn't the one who hit him," Scott jokingly remarked.

"Really, what have you heard?" Ned continued. "This could be a matter of life or death."

"Ned, we just hear rumors, nothing more. It's probably nothing, just a lot of talk," Trevor assured them.

"Maybe he'll try something tonight at the dance?"

"I doubt it, too many people. As long as you stay with Eric, you should be fine. Scott, you should stay in your room and keep the door locked."

"I know, I've already received the lecture from Eric."

Scott and Ned attended their combat class and were actually feeling pretty good about some of the moves they had learned. Since the incident with Slim and Dan, Buzz had decided to use Don Grealey as an instructor instead of Slim. Don was a senior on the Badger division who also had a pretty good knowledge of the combat moves. After drill, the boys, with their escort, headed off to their academic classes. History and English were boring as usual, but science was pretty interesting since they were able to use the lab. When the day finally ended, Ned was all bubbles. Scott had never seen him so excited and it was starting to bug him. Scott knew Ned liked Tina, but he couldn't believe how excited he was for the dance.

While Ned was getting ready, Scott decided to do his homework. He didn't really have any pressing assignments, but there wasn't much else to do. Almost everybody was getting ready for the dance. He had decided he would go to the movie even though Eric had told him to stay in his room. Eric was worried that since everybody else was going to the dance, there wouldn't be any bodyguards available. However, Scott figured that Slim and Dan would also be going to the dance, so he wouldn't be in too much danger.

A bit later, Eric came for Ned so they could pick up the girls together. Once again, he warned Scott to stay in his room. Scott nodded, but didn't say anything. After they left, Scott hung around for another hour just to make sure everybody else would be at the dance, and besides, the movie didn't start until later anyway. He lay on his bed thinking about the dance, wishing he had asked Nancy. When the band started playing (he could hear the music even in his room) another wave of self-pity washed over him, making him feel even more dejected.

At seven thirty, he got up and headed down to the activity room where the movie was being shown. The movie hadn't started and the room was still well lit. There were only three other students in the room, two of whom he recognized as boys from the Falcon division. The other must have been a Badger. He sat down and waited for the movie to begin. When the lights eventually dimmed and the movie started running, only two other students had arrived, each sitting in their own solitary spots.

What a bunch of losers, Scott thought. *Have you ever seen a more pathetic group of people?* Disgusted with himself, he almost got up to leave, thinking it would be nice to run the loop again. That always gave him some comfort. He started to get out of his chair, but the thought of the snow on the ground and how cold it was outside made him change his mind again. Sitting back down, he noticed, out of the corner of his eye, a figure enter the room and sit down behind him. Immediately on guard, Scott wondered if this was one of Slim's goons.

Scott decided to ignore him and acted as though nothing was wrong. This was much harder than he thought it would be. Visions of someone putting a cord around his neck and strangling him in the dark, or a knife being pressed against his throat, kept popping into his head. Finally, he decided to get up and move down the row a few chairs. As he did this, so did the unknown person. Next he decided to move up three rows, but the figure also moved up three rows.

Who is this, he thought, *and what does he want? Was he part of Slim's plan to get revenge?* Fearing something was up, Scott wondered what he should do. He was about to get up again when he felt a hand on his shoulder. He whirled around, fist cocked, ready to knock the living daylights out of his stalker. What he saw, however, completely threw him off guard. Sitting there behind him was a girl.

"Remember me?" she asked. Scott froze. The voice was unmistakably the same as the girl he had met on Halloween night, but her hair was now blonde, not black like it had been those few months earlier.

"Are you her…I mean, did we meet on Halloween?" he asked in a whisper.

"Yes! You do remember."

"I remember a girl with black hair and dark eyes, but your voice is definitely the same."

"I changed my hair to black that night to go with my costume," she explained, "but my eyes are still the same. You just can't see them. Do you want to get out of here and do something?" she continued. She didn't have to ask that question twice. The movie was the last thing on his mind right now. For weeks, he had been looking for this girl, and now here she was, right in back of him.

"You bet," Scott replied. As they walked out, Scott couldn't help but stare at her. She had long blonde hair, brown eyes that were so dark they almost looked black, and a smile that melted his heart. He couldn't believe she was right here by his side and that she actually wanted to be with him. He had almost given up hope of ever finding her again.

"Is everything all right?" she asked Scott hesitantly.

"Yes. Why do you ask?"

"You're looking at me kind of weird."

"Oh, I…guess I'm just getting used to seeing you with blonde hair," he stammered. It was lame, but the best excuse he could come up with. He hadn't realized he was staring and was embarrassed that she had noticed.

"So what do you want to do?" she asked.

Scott knew exactly what he wanted to do, but he wasn't sure he dared ask her. He paused, but finally mustered enough courage. "There's a dance going on right now. Would you like to go?"

She looked at him for a second, opened her mouth to say something, but then shut it. She paused, opened her mouth once more and then shut it again. Scott could tell she was hesitating but wasn't sure why. "We don't have to go if you don't want to," he reassured her.

"No! I want to go. I'm just not sure I should."

"Why?"

She was deep in thought and didn't answer him. "Why don't we do something else?" Scott suggested.

"No! I do want to go. Let's go, okay?"

"Are you sure?"

"Yes. Absolutely."

"All right!" Scott said with a grin a mile wide. "I need to shower and change my clothes. I don't think jeans would cut it at a formal dance. Why don't we meet back by the dormitory stairs in twenty minutes? Does that give you enough time to get ready?"

"That will be great," she replied. Scott ran upstairs, feeling like he was on top of the world. He couldn't wait to see the look on Ned's face when he showed up at the dance with "his princess." Then another thought hit him while he was taking his shower. He still didn't know her name. For that matter, he didn't even know who she was, and why hadn't she been asked to the dance? However, at this point, he decided he didn't really care, he was just happy to see her again and to be going to the dance.

When he was finally ready, he began to grow nervous. He walked down the stairs, and seeing that she hadn't arrived yet, sat down on the bottom step to wait for her. Ten minutes went by and she still hadn't shown up. He began to wonder if she had disappeared again and wasn't coming back.

"Well, well, well. If it isn't tough guy Frontier all dressed up and no one to go with," Scott heard a voice say. He looked up to see three large Badgers standing over him. Scott could tell this wasn't a friendly visit. The three of them had on Santa hats and makeup that covered their faces to keep from being identified.

Whatever possessed him to say what he said next, he would never know. Perhaps it was just his personality.

"Wow, you guys must really be desperate, but I'm going to have to decline your invitation. I already have a date for the dance."

"Ah, he has a sense of humor, but not for long. Moose, would you like to do the pleasures?"

A large, heavy fellow moved forward and lifted Scott up by the lapels of his jacket.

"I know I haven't been good, Santa, but is this really necessary? Couldn't you just give me a lump of coal or something?" Scott once again joked.

"How about a lump on the head?" the one called Moose replied. He slammed Scott against the wall and cocked his fist. Scott tried to turn his head and brace for the impact. *Whack!* Scott heard the crunch of Moose's fist against the brick wall. Moose let out a howl.

He missed! Scott thought. *How could he have missed at that distance?*

"You idiot! You missed!" the first Badger yelled. Moose was on the ground writhing in agony. It looked like his hand was broken. Scott jumped away from the wall in an effort to get away, but the third Badger grabbed him from behind and held him. The first Badger grabbed Scott by the shoulder, cocked his fist, and propelled his arm forward with the intent to punch Scott. At that same moment, a large, hairy spider, about the size of small dinner plate raced up the arm of the badger holding Scott. He screamed and let go of Scott, trying to brush it off.

Scott saw the punch coming and ducked. The first Badger's punch sailed past Scott and slammed into the other Badger's face, knocking him to the floor.

Scott put up his fist. "Now it's your turn," he growled.

But before his assailant could respond, a voice sounded down the hall, "Hi, Scott. What are you doing?" The two boys turned and saw a girl coming down the hallway. Both of their jaws dropped as she approached. She had on a white dress with black trim, which matched the black ribbon she had tied in her long blonde hair. Scott drew in a breath as he gazed on her. She looked like something out of a storybook.

"Hi. Are you ready?" he asked as though nothing was happening.

"Yes, but you look a little busy at the moment."

"Oh, we were just finishing up. Weren't we, boys?" Scott said, still amazed he had escaped unscathed. The Badgers, two of whom were still sitting on the ground nursing their wounds, were looking at the girl, just as stunned as Scott. Scott grabbed her hand and they quickly walked to the dance hall and entered the doorway. The actual dance floor was a level below the entrance and a person had to descend the stairs to get down to the floor. When they entered the room, Scott stopped on the staircase to scan the crowd, hoping to find Ned and Eric. When he finally spotted them, he noticed that several couples were staring at them, especially the boys. His eyes landed on Eric and he waved as he headed in their direction. Eric waved back, but the expression on his face was that of complete astonishment.

Quickly making his way over to Ned, Eric grabbed his arm. "Ned," he said, pointing in Scott's direction, "look who the cat dragged in."

"The mystery girl," Ned replied in a distant voice.

"What?" Eric asked.

"I'm gonna kill her!" Ned replied, now in a much livelier and louder voice.

Scott was approaching them by now and realized once again that he didn't know her name. "I'm embarrassed to ask you this," he said, turning towards her, "but you've never told me your name."

"It's Azinine."

"Azinine? Oh, Azinine!" Scott repeated, remembering that Ned had spoken of her earlier as someone whom he should avoid. 'A local girl who is nothing but trouble' was how Ned had described her. Thinking all this through in one quick moment, Scott wasn't quite sure how Ned would react, but it was too late now.

"Hi, guys. This is Azinine," he said as he introduced her to Tina and Nancy. Smiling, they both said hello to her while giving her their names. Azinine smiled and waved back, but didn't say anything.

"I think you already know her," Scott said, looking at Ned. He waved at Azinine with a fake smile on his face and she waved back. Scott could tell she was nervous, but she had reassured him earlier that she wanted to do this and was determined to stick it out.

"Come on, let's dance," he said, hoping to relieve some of the tension. They danced for a while and it did help. Everyone seemed to be having fun. Ned kept glancing over at them, but Scott just ignored him. The next song was a slow dance and Scott wasn't sure whether he should put his arms around her or not. He was afraid she might disappear like she had the first time they met out on the loop. As it turned out, she had no reservations and quickly put her arms around him. Scott had never enjoyed dancing before because he had always been so nervous around girls. So he was surprised when he found himself thoroughly enjoying this dance with Azinine.

"I'm glad we came," she said. Scott was about to agree when he felt a tap on his shoulder.

"Cutting in," he heard Ned say. Scott dropped his arms from Azinine's waist, and was about to tell his friend to buzz off when Ned grabbed her arm and whirled her away, leaving Tina standing there. Feeling awkward, Scott walked over to Tina and asked her to dance with him. He was more than a little perturbed with Ned for pulling a stunt like that, but he soon felt relief wash over him when he noticed that Azinine had only put her hands on his shoulders and was not giving him the same affection she had given Scott.

"What are you doing here?" Ned whispered angrily to Azinine.

"I had to drop off a message to Magus McDougal," she explained. "I heard the school was showing a movie and I wanted to watch it before I returned. I noticed Scott there, so I sat down by him. He asked me if I wanted to go to the dance, and I did, so here we are. I don't see what the big deal is."

"A message, huh? And I suppose you just happened to be wearing this dress when you delivered your message."

Azinine glared at him. "Something like that," she responded curtly.

"Azinine, there are lots of things you don't understand and I don't have time to explain them to you right now. You know you're not supposed to..." He broke off and looked at her for a moment. "Did you say he asked you to go the dance with him?"

"That's right."

"How did he ask you?"

Azinine looked at him a bit exasperated. "What do you mean, how did he ask me? He turned to me and asked me to go."

"I didn't think you understood English that well, let alone speak it."

"He didn't ask me in English, he asked me in Lumen."

"How could he do that? Scott doesn't speak Lumen."

"Yes he does," she argued. "He speaks it as well as you and I do!"

Ned stopped dancing. He was stunned, but intrigued, by this bit of information. "So Scott speaks Lumen," he wondered aloud.

By this time the song had ended. Scott thanked Tina for the dance and headed back over to Azinine. "Can I have my date back?" Scott said, not really asking. Ned didn't say a word. He was still puzzling over what Azinine had just told him.

The night passed by like a dream for Scott. He and Azinine had a great time. When the dance was over, the two of them decided to walk outside in the garden to cool off before saying good night. Scott couldn't bear the thought of not seeing her again so he quickly asked, "At the risk of sounding a bit anxious, I was wondering if I could see you tomorrow?"

Azinine contemplated that for a second or two, and then agreed. "On two conditions," she said. "One, you meet me in the council room early in the morning, and two, you can't tell anyone, not even Axtar, where you are going."

"Axtar?" Scott questioned.

"Oh, I mean Ned."

"Why did you call him Axtar?"

"It's...a...nickname I have for him."

"Where is the council room?" Scott asked.

"You haven't seen the council room?"

"I don't know, maybe I have. I just haven't heard that name before."

"The council room is down a narrow hall just around the corner from Magus McDougal's office. There is a big round table inside with a large chandelier hanging over it."

"Magus McDougal? Don't you mean Headmaster McDougal?"

"Yes, of course that's what I meant."

"Okay," Scott agreed. "I know the room you are talking about. I'll meet you there as early as I can."

"Sounds good, I can't wait," she said.

"Me too," Scott replied. They both stood there for a bit in silence until it started to get awkward.

"Well," Azinine finally said, "I guess I better be going. It's getting quite late."

"Yeah, I guess so," Scott said but made no move to leave. Azinine noticed a perplexed look on his face.

"Is everything okay?" she asked.

"Well, yeah, I guess. I was going to offer to walk you to your dorm, but I've never seen you here before. Are you a student?"

"No, I'm just visiting."

"Visiting who?" Scott asked.

"A...um...Mag...I mean Headmaster McDougal. He's a friend of the family."

"Really? He's a friend of my family also," Scott replied. Then with a curious look on his face, he asked, "Are you here with your parents?"

"My parents?" Azinine replied, taken off guard.

"Yeah, I mean he's kind of old for you to be visiting alone. I just wondered if you had come with someone else, like your parents?"

"I guess that does look kind of weird, but I really just came here to deliver a message to him from my father."

"Your father made you come all the way out here just to deliver a message? Hasn't he heard of e-mail or a phone?"

Azinine let out an uncomfortable chuckle. She knew what he said was supposed to be sort of a joke just by the way he had said it, but the term *e-mail* wasn't familiar to her, and she had heard about phones but didn't really understand them.

"To be truthful, I really like coming here. Plus, I knew the dance was tonight and was hoping to go if the opportunity arose, and it did, and so here we are," she said with a smile on her face. She kept on talking before Scott could reply. "Well, Headmaster McDougal is going to take me home, so I better go, but I'll see you tomorrow."

"Can I walk you to his office?" Scott said.

"No, no, I know the way, please don't trouble yourself," she said quickly. She stood up on her toes and gave him a kiss on the cheek, then quickly backed up and headed for the doors, waving her hand in the air. "Good-bye, Scott. I really had a great time tonight," she said one last time as she disappeared inside the castle doors. Scott didn't make a move to follow her because he was so taken off guard by the kiss on the cheek.

When he finally got over it, he figured he'd better get to bed also. As he entered the building, words she had used crossed his mind that puzzled him. Words like *Magus McDougal? Axtar? Council room?* He determined he would ask her about them tomorrow.

Chapter Six

Lumen

Scott entered his dorm room to find Ned in a chair reading a book, apparently waiting for his return. "So, you found your princess after all. Did you have a good time?" Ned asked.

"Yeah, it was great! I don't know why you're so down on her. She's a lot of fun!"

"Sometimes she can be a little too much fun," muttered Ned.

"What do you mean by that?"

"Never mind. So, what are your plans for tomorrow?"

"I'm not sure," Scott said, hoping that would be the end of their conversation. He didn't want to discuss this, but he knew Ned had something on his mind.

"Tina and Nancy want to go to the hot springs tomorrow. Do you want to come?"

Scott groaned inwardly. He wasn't sure what to say. If he said no, Ned and the girls would want to know why. If he said yes and didn't show up, they would be angry, and rightfully so. "It sounds like fun," he answered, "but I've got a ton of laundry to do and some homework I need to finish up. I better make sure I get everything done before I commit." Ned nodded and seemed satisfied with that answer.

Ned was tying his shoelace when he heard Scott's alarm go off. He glanced at the clock next to his bed where it flashed a bright red "six o'clock." He was surprised to see Scott getting up this early on a Saturday morning. His astonishment quickly turned to amusement when he watched Scott turn off the alarm and bury his head beneath his pillow. Ned quickly left the room, hoping to be back before Scott woke up. As he hurried down the dorm stairs making his way to the administrative wing, Ned kept going over in his mind the discovery he had made during his conversation with Scott last night. When he arrived at the headmaster's door he knocked loudly three times. It seemed like an eternity before Headmaster McDougal finally answered his door.

"Ned, I didn't expect to see you this early on a Saturday morning. Is something wrong?" the headmaster asked. Ned stepped inside and shut the door.

"No, nothing is wrong. But I have discovered something I know you'll be interested in."

"Oh? And what is that?"

"I think Scott is lingual."

The headmaster looked at Ned with raised eyebrows. "Really? And just what makes you think this?"

"He showed up at the dance last night with Azinine. They were talking and laughing with each other like they were the best of friends. At first, I thought Azinine must have really improved her English, but when I asked her about it, she said they were speaking Lumen. Obviously, Scott doesn't know how to speak Lumen. After the dance, I spoke to him in Lumen and he spoke it right back perfectly—or at least that's how I heard it."

"Hmmm, interesting," Headmaster McDougal pondered. "His older brother isn't lingual, but he is. This is very encouraging. If Scott is indeed lingual, we must be very careful he does not enter Lumen. If anyone noticed him and his ability, he would be in grave danger. We must also find a way to test the amulet on him."

"Do you think he could be the one?" Ned asked.

"I would never have guessed it. But if you are correct, it's very possible. I need you to go back and keep your eye on him. And," he added as an afterthought, "do not let Azinine get him alone, she is too reckless."

"What did she do this time?" Ned asked, rolling his eyes.

"Based on the story of a couple of students who ended up in our infirmary last night, I'm pretty sure she used magic in the castle."

"Why would she do that? She knows that's against the rules," Ned replied.

"I'm not exactly sure. I don't think the students were telling the entire truth about what happened, but she was with Scott, so that should explain part of it."

"You think Scott got in another fight?"

"From the broken bones in their hands, yes, I think there's a pretty good chance, and by the size of those students, the odds weren't in Scott's favor. So I'm guessing she helped him out. In any case, if you do see her, tell her I must talk to her immediately. I must question her about this."

"Sure thing. I'll keep an eye out for her," Ned replied.

He got up and walked out the door, heading back to the dorms. When he returned, he was surprised to discover that Scott wasn't there. Figuring his friend must be getting an early start on the day, he didn't think much about his absence.

After Ned left their dorm room, Scott jumped out of bed and got ready as fast as possible to meet Azinine. He headed for the council room, stopping at the cafeteria just long enough to grab a doughnut. He was grateful Ned hadn't questioned him about his alarm going off. He hadn't wanted to come up with more excuses, so he had merely acted as though his alarm was an accident, rolled back in bed, and pretended to go back to sleep. He was a bit curious about Ned's early departure, but then it wasn't uncommon for Ned to get up early and do whatever it was he did at this time of day.

Scott hurried down the halls until he came to the administrative wing of the castle. It wouldn't look good if he were caught in this part of the castle on a Saturday, especially so early in the morning. He knew coming up with more excuses wouldn't be easy. But he figured everyone would still be asleep, and so the risk wasn't too high. As he passed Headmaster McDougal's office, he was surprised to hear voices behind the door. He was tempted to stop and listen, but if he were caught, he could get into serious trouble, so he kept walking. Besides, he was just being curious, and right now he was more excited at the prospect of meeting up with Azinine. Hopefully, she was waiting for him in the council room. He walked down the narrow hall until he found the room and opened the door. No lights were on and Scott felt a stab of disappointment. He had expected Azinine to be there, just as excited as he was. He entered the room but opted to keep the lights off. He didn't want anyone to discover him in there. He held out his hand and felt his way toward a far wall. Upon finding one, he leaned back and waited.

No more than two minutes had passed when the strangest thing happened. While standing against the wall, something touched him on the cheek. Startled, he swung out trying to hit whatever it was that had touched him, but all he encountered was air. He figured he must have imagined it, so he settled back against the wall. Seconds later it happened again and once more he swung out at nothing. This time he headed directly toward the light switch, found it, and turned it on. Nothing! The room was empty, but Scott knew he hadn't imagined it. Something had touched him.

"Aaaaah!" he suddenly screamed. Out of thin air, only inches in front of his face, a large creature loomed at him. He leapt backwards, trying to take in what it was. Further away, it became obvious what it was—or rather who it was. It was Azinine. She was upside down as if hanging from a rope, but there was no rope. She was laughing hysterically. Scott was still in shock and stood there in amazement. Then, as if it were the most natural thing in the world, she floated down to the floor and landed on her feet, still laughing of course.

"How...how did you do that?" he stammered.

"I promise I'll show you, but first we have to get out of here. You probably woke up the whole castle with your screaming. See that chair over there?" she asked, pointing. Scott looked over and sure enough, along with the three that had always been there, was another chair. The same one he had seen the last time he looked in here.

"Yeah, I see it."

"Go sit down and I'll meet you there as soon as I turn off the light."

Confused, Scott walked over and sat down, wondering what was going on. She turned the light off and within just a few seconds, she landed in his lap. "Now put your arms around me and whatever you do, don't let go of me until I say so. Okay?" she said, very seriously this time.

"Okay," he answered.

"This is probably going to feel very weird to you at first, but do not let go!" Azinine warned him again.

"I promise!" he said, wondering what could possibly happen sitting in a chair.

"Cylindhall!" she cried out.

Weird is not the way Scott would have described it. Terrifying was more like it. He felt like his whole body had been blasted into a million pieces. Things all of a sudden became very bright and he found himself shooting very quickly through a conduit of light. He became dizzy and had to concentrate heavily to stay conscious and keep his hold on Azinine. What he couldn't figure out was what had a hold of him. What kept him in the chair? It seemed like hours, but was probably more like just a few minutes, before the feeling stopped and they were once again sitting still.

The place where Scott and Azinine ended up was another room, similar to the one they had just left, only much more beautiful. The ceiling was wooden and domed with an amazing assortment of moldings all around. There were cherubim, grapes, flowers, birds, trees, unicorns, other creatures Scott had never seen before, and much, much more all carved out of wood.

On the walls hung huge portraits of distinguished-looking men who were obviously kings because each wore a crown and held a type of scepter in his hand. Scott slowly looked at each one of them until his gaze stopped at one particular portrait. The man in the picture was the same person who had posed for the portrait hanging outside Headmaster McDougal's office. It was the knight with the golden sword, only in this picture, he wasn't carrying the sword.

"Where…are we?" Scott asked, still looking at the picture. "What is this place and how did we get here?"

"This is Cylindhall," Azinine answered, her voice full of reverence. "Cylindhall was once the grandest castle in all our land and someday will be so once again. The High King used to hold balls, fantastic fairs, and great tournaments here."

"I've never heard of Cylindhall," Scott replied, still in a daze. "What just happened?"

"Ahh…it's a bit difficult to explain. Let's get out of here and I'll try and do my best to clarify things."

They walked out of the room and into a hallway that was even more beautiful than the room they had just left. It looked like it was made entirely of marble, yet it wasn't marble. The stones were letting off a soft light—one of the most remarkable things Scott had ever seen.

"Wow, this is amazing architecture. It must take a lot of light bulbs to light up all these stones," Scott commented.

Azinine began to laugh again. "Scott, this world will be hard to explain, you'll just have to see it for yourself."

"This world?"

"Yes, we are on Lumen now, where I live. On Lumen, the light from these Lumenarty stones comes naturally, no light bulbs are necessary. I am sure there are lots of things about our world you'll find interesting and also difficult to understand."

Scott stopped. "Our world? What do you mean by 'our world'?" he asked.

"Lumen is our world, just like Earth is your world," she tried to explain.

"You mean like a totally different planet?"

"Yes," she said with relief, seeing that Scott seemed to be getting it.

"I...I don't understand, there is no way we could be on another planet."

She paused. "Maybe it was a bad idea to bring you here. I should probably take you back."

"No!" he yelled louder than he had intended. Still not believing he was in another world, he didn't want to go back to his school just yet. That might mean not being able to spend time with her. "I'd like to learn more about this place," he argued.

"CastleOne serves as a gateway between your world and ours. It allows us to travel quickly between the two worlds. You are not in your world anymore. Are you okay with that?"

"Not in my world anymore?" Scott repeated. The thought was so unbelievable it was almost absurd. But what had happened to him in the past few minutes was absurd, so why not this? Scott didn't know what to think. "So what you're saying is that I'm in a different world. No longer on Earth?" he repeated.

"Yes, is that okay?" she asked again.

"Well...I...how could this be possible? Is this some sort of other dimension to our world?" he asked, still very confused.

"No, we are on a completely different planet and universe than yours," she said, exasperated.

"But that's impossible! We couldn't have traveled that far. I mean, we are talking light years to get to another universe."

"Scott, I know it's hard to understand, but you have to believe me. I'm not sure exactly how it works either, but it has something to do with pure energy or light, which in turn allows us to travel faster than the speed of light. The portal uses a process to cheat distance, kind of like taking a long rope and instead of moving along the rope to get from one end to the other, we bend the rope and jump from one end to the other. I know that explanation is probably not completely correct, but it's the best way I can explain it."

Scott nodded slowly, still trying to take it all in. He wasn't sure he believed her. It could be another one of her jokes, but he decided to make the best of things and go along with her. If what she said was true, it could be pretty cool to explore a whole new world.

But then a new fear set in on him. He suddenly realized that he was completely at her mercy. Without her he couldn't get back home, and if they got separated, he'd be lost in a world he didn't understand or know. He almost asked her to take him back, but something made him hold his tongue. He was fascinated by the thought of another world, not to mention the adventure it might bring. It was that thought that pushed him to stay.

"Are you okay?" she asked him.

"Yes, I just wasn't prepared for all this."

"Things will be fine. I just want to show you some stuff and then I'll take you back." Hearing this, Scott felt better and was able to relax a little. They walked down a few more halls and finally outside through two very large doors. To Scott's surprise, the doors opened automatically as they approached.

Once outside, he was surprised again to find the weather warm and the world in full bloom. Everything was so green and beautiful. The castle grounds were huge and well kept. On one side there was a vast forest, and on the other was a meadow that expanded almost as far as the eye could see. At the edge of the meadow rose a hill, blocking any further view.

Looking back, Scott noticed the door they had just walked through had disappeared. "Hey," he exclaimed. "The door is gone."

Without turning around Azinine answered, "Yeah, it does that sometimes. Drives me nuts." Scott shrugged and followed after her. They walked for a few minutes until Azinine stopped. She looked at Scott, smiled, and then began to slowly rise off the ground and hover about three feet in the air. Scott watched her as if nothing strange were happening, although he was actually quite excited. However, he didn't want to let her know that.

"Well? Aren't you going to ask me how I do this?" she asked impatiently.

"I already know how you do that," he replied.

Surprised, she floated over to him. "Okay, smarty-pants," she questioned. "How then?"

"You have winged boots on." Scott smirked. It was a guess, although he was pretty sure that's how she was doing it. He thought of the boots he had seen in the headmaster's office, so he knew they were real. He had also dreamt about the flying boots. Even though that certainly wasn't proof, he made the assumption and as it turned out, he was correct.

"You know about these boots," she said, feeling a little disappointed that her surprise had been ruined, "and you don't know about Lumen?"

"Know of them, yes, but not much else," Scott admitted.

"Would you like to try them?" she asked.

"Yes!" Scott blurted out with enthusiasm.

Azinine seemed pleased with his response. "Okay, follow me," she instructed. She floated down a long flight of large stone stairs, which led into some gardens. She led him through some hedges and out to a small pond. The water was azure blue, and an assortment of flowers grew around the edges. Scott sat down on a marble-looking bench on the pond's edge, but instead of landing on a hard surface, he fell right through the bench and landed on the ground. A buzz of laughter went up from several voices all around him, but all he could see was Azinine standing over him, laughing. He was now lying underneath the bench. He reached out to touch the bench and it was hard as stone. He couldn't figure out how he could have fallen through it. He reached up and grabbed the bench to pull himself up, but as he did so, the bench became like liquid and he fell to the ground again.

"Bogar, be nice! He is my friend," Azinine said, speaking to the bench.

Scott scurried out from beneath the bench. Azinine giggled again. "Scott, this is Bogar. Bogar, I want you to meet my friend Scott."

Scott was still staring at the bench with wide eyes. "This bench is alive?" he asked incredulously.

"Not really alive, as in a living, breathing creature, but it is a magical bench. Go ahead and sit down, it'll be okay." Scott hesitantly bent over, felt the bench to make sure it was hard, and then sat down. This time it felt like a regular bench, but now, Scott felt weird sitting on it.

As he sat there, a bee buzzed around his head and then came to a complete stop in midair right in front of his face. As he took a closer look, he discovered it wasn't a bee at all, but a very tiny woman with wings. She was looking at him with intense curiosity.

"Shoo!" Azinine said with a half-hearted swing of her hand in its direction.

"Wh..what was that?"

"An annoying fleary."

"Are they something I need to worry about?"

"Normally they stick to their own business, but they can be dangerous if you antagonize them. If you leave them alone, they'll leave you alone. Here," she said, handing him the pair of boots she had just taken off her own feet. "These boots are very valuable and are the only pair I own. I don't want them ruined. Do exactly what I say and everything should be okay. Put them on over your shoes, but don't try anything until I get back."

As she walked away, Scott began to put on the boots. As he did so, the fleary came back and once again parked herself right in front of Scott's face. He tried to ignore her, but everywhere he moved, she moved also. He tried to shoo her away with his hand. "Beat it, tiny lady," he muttered. The fleary fell back on her heels at the sound of Scott's voice and then her face took on an angry look, indicating she wasn't at all pleased by his manners. She flew up even closer to his face this time, her arms folded as if to tell him she wasn't going anywhere.

Next he tried to blow her away, which didn't work. Not to mention, by the look on her face, she didn't appreciate. "Beat it or I'll squash you like a fly!" he yelled, trying to swat her at the same time. She let out an obvious squeal of displeasure and took off. But Scott's victory was short-lived as she returned moments later with numerous other flearies. He had just pulled on the second boot when they arrived, and he could tell from the looks on their faces this wasn't a welcoming party. They all gathered around him and in one motion picked him up and threw him into the pond. When he came up out of the water, he could hear them laughing at him.

"Okay, okay, I guess I deserved that," he said out loud even though he didn't think they could understand him. At the sound of his voice they all shut up.

One of them flew over to the fleary who had originally approached Scott. "What have you done?" he demanded, yelling at her. "He speaks our language. Do you want us to all get in trouble?" He then flew over to Scott. "Please excuse our horrible manners. We did not know who you were." Then turning to the others, he gave them a wave and flew off, with the others following him.

Strange that the flearies on this world would speak English, Scott thought.

Just then Azinine showed up carrying a rope that looked like it was made out of the same material as the boots. "Scott," she scolded, "I told you not to try the boots until I got back!"

"I...I...didn't," he defended himself.

"Then what are you doing in the pond?"

"That fleary came back with some of her friends and they threw me in."

"That's odd. They're normally not hostile unless you antagonize them. You didn't antagonize them, did you?" she asked with raised eyebrows.

"Well, I guess that depends on how you define 'antagonize.' She came back so I told her to beat it and then I tried to shoo her away just like you did. She didn't go away, so I tried to swat at her and I guess that made her mad," Scott explained as he dragged himself out of the pond.

"Well, it looks like they're gone." She shrugged. "So, let's get going. You did put the boots on, right?"

"Yep, they're on." Scott was excited, but also a little nervous. Scenes from his dream came flooding back, and he remembered flying upward and upward and not being able to get back down. Azinine tied one end of the rope around his leg and the other end around a nearby tree. His dream apparently wasn't too far off the mark, since the rope was obviously being used to keep him from getting too far away or out of control.

"All right," Azinine said, "the boots respond to your thoughts. You basically command them just as you would your arm or your fingers to perform some sort of task. However, there is one catch. All the laws of gravity still apply. For example, if you ask the boots to thrust upward, but you don't distribute your weight correctly, you could end up falling over. The faster you go horizontally, the more you'll have to lean forward. When you slow down, you'll have to move your body to a more upright position. I would suggest you try getting the feel of the shoes over the pond first. That way you have some cushion."

"Cushion? Am I going to need a cushion?" Scott asked cautiously.

"Of course. Otherwise you might go *splat* all over the ground and then I'd have to clean you up, and that's not something I want to do," she replied as seriously as she could muster. "So I would prefer you first try this over the water."

"I wish you hadn't used the word *splat*," Scott mumbled as he walked over to the pond. Once there, he tried getting the boots to move, but nothing happened. In his mind he thought *up*, and then *upward*, followed by *high*, but nothing worked.

"Well, what are you waiting for?" she asked impatiently. "Go!"

"I'm trying, but nothing is happening. I've tried *up*, and *upward*, and *high*, but nothing happens."

"Didn't you hear what I said? There are no commands. They don't understand commands, they just follow your thoughts or intentions. When you reach out to grab something, you don't first say 'grab.' You just do it. It's the same with the boots. You just do it."

Scott thought about that and then leapt into the air pretending to be Superman. To his utter surprise he shot up at a very rapid rate, and had it not been for the rope tied to his leg, he was sure he would have kept going. The boots were still trying to fly skyward, but the rope continued to tug at his foot keeping him from flying off. He could see Azinine down below, laughing and cheering him on at the same time. When he finally got his wits about him, he willed himself to float slowly back down to the ground. Once again, the boots did as he wanted and he began to descend at a much slower pace. About halfway down, Scott lost his balance, tipped over, and was hanging by his feet upside down, while still descending. "What do I do now?" he yelled.

"You can either do one of two things. The first one is the more difficult, but it's a move you will have to master sooner or later. It involves moving the boots faster to the ground than you could fall, so the boots end up underneath you again. However, once the boots are underneath you, you have to stop them or they'll continue to shoot toward the ground. I would suggest you practice that over the water."

"Right, so I don't go *splat*," Scott said.

"Exactly, you see, you're catching on," she said, giggling a bit.

"Well then, what's the other alternative?" Scott asked.

"You can continue upside down, moving slowly until you reach the ground."

Scott was tempted to do just that, but decided on her first recommendation. He motioned the shoes over the pond—still hanging upside down of course. He could imagine well enough what had to be done, but since he didn't know how fast he would fall, he didn't know how fast to make the shoes move. "Here goes nothing," he muttered, taking a deep breath. In a flash, he willed the boots rapidly toward the ground. The boots responded just as he wanted, but before he could get himself balanced and stopped, he was in the middle of the pond and up to his waist in water.

"See? Better *splash* than *splat*," she called out.

"Yeah, it's a good thing you suggested the pond," Scott yelled over to her, smiling.

She smiled back at him, and then suddenly her face went grave. "Scott!" she yelled. "Watch out for the sea monster behind you!"

Scott whirled around and at the same time shot skyward again, but this time he was able to slow himself down before the rope caught him. He couldn't see any sea monster in the pond. He looked back to see her laughing at him again. He floated about fifteen feet in the air, shaking his head, but also chuckling. He had to admit it was funny. Without warning, he lost his balance again and turned upside down once more. Watching this, Azinine lost it and was rolling on the ground in a fit of laughter. As he had done before, he willed the shoes rapidly toward the water, but this time he caught himself faster so that he was only knee deep in the water. He quickly rose out of the water, hovering just over the surface. He then proceeded to walk toward Azinine, giving the impression he was walking on the water.

"You are getting pretty good on those," Azinine commented when he reached her.

"I'll get the hang of that maneuver sooner or later," Scott vowed.

"Oh, I forgot to tell you. There is one more option you could try that might work just a little bit better."

"Another option?" he replied, giving her the evil eye.

"Yep. When you are hanging upside down, have the shoes give you a quick upwards thrust and then flip over. With a little practice, you'll find yourself about right where you were before you lost your balance."

Scott stood there for a second, and then realized she was playing with him. He was her entertainment. *What a turd*, he thought. Then on an impulse, he swept her up in his arms and thrust upward. The boots took off, but the motion, coupled with the extra weight, just about caused him to drop her. She was screaming as loud as she could, but gave little resistance. He headed over to the pond, where his intentions were to simply tease her. But he wasn't able to compensate for her weight, and once again lost his balance and flipped upside down. He lost his grip on her and she tumbled into the pond. When she surfaced, Scott was still upside down and had a horrified look on his face. He wasn't sure how she'd react to this, but to his relief, she was smiling.

"Come on down, the water is great," she called. "Oh, I forgot! You already know that. But did you also know that those boots work in water too?" Scott allowed the boots to relax and down he went headfirst. When he came up, with the help of the boots, he shot out of the water like a dolphin and then back in again. He headed over to Azinine with the intention of stopping right before he reached her.

However, instead of stopping the shoes, he simply relaxed them and his momentum sent him colliding right into her. It wasn't enough to hurt her, but it was enough to push her underneath him and under the water.

"Are you okay?" he asked once she surfaced.

"Yes, but I think we need to continue your training. You know just enough to be dangerous."

"Okay, what do I need to do next?" he asked.

"You're doing pretty good with the vertical thing. We need to work on moving horizontal, especially speeding up and slowing down. Obviously we can't use the rope for this. However, if you get in trouble, you now know how to stop yourself in midair and upright yourself if you fall over. The pond is too small to be of any use for this stuff, so I would recommend you practice higher up where you can't run into anything and still have plenty of room to fall. Since you won't be doing this over water, you really will go *splat* if you mess up."

The words 'higher up,' 'fall,' and 'splat' did nothing to calm the nervousness that had suddenly overcome Scott, but he was willing to try. He had never had this much fun before and he wanted to continue.

"We should probably do this in the pasture over there," Azinine recommended, pointing in the distance. "Away from the castle and the trees." Scott nodded and they walked over to the clearing she had pointed out. He contemplated picking her up again, but thought better since there was no pond to cushion her fall if he goofed up. He supposed she was thinking the same thing because she kept her distance.

"Okay," she said when they had reached their destination. "What you want to do is take off in a sort of arching movement. Rise off the ground about fifteen feet and then start moving forward as you continue to rise. As you move forward, you will want to start leaning forward to keep yourself from being pushed backward by the wind. If you lean too far forward you will start to fall and you'll need to speed up to compensate. Once you get up there, you'll instinctively feel what I'm saying."

Scott nodded, took a deep breath, rose into the air, and began moving forward. As he did, he leaned forward and immediately started to fall, so he sped up to compensate. However, the boots compensated too much and he flew backwards and fell over before he could slow them down to counteract the move. He found himself moving forward, upside down, as if he were being dragged through the air by a helicopter or something. He quickly got his wits about him and stopped, but he was still hanging upside down. This time there was no pond beneath him and it scared him to upright himself. He was tempted to just slowly descend, but then he remembered the other solution and decided to try it. He made a quick thrust upward and to the left. Amazingly enough it worked and he found himself upright in the air about thirty feet higher than where he had started. He could hear Azinine back on the ground clapping and cheering him on, which made him feel good about his progress.

He started again, but this time he tried it slower and it didn't take long before he got the hang of it and was flying all over the place, diving and rocketing skyward. It was the most exhilarating, unbelievable thing he had ever experienced. He didn't want to stop but he could tell Azinine was getting bored, so he decided to head back to the ground.

"You are doing amazingly well," she said.

"I am quite amazing, aren't I?" Scott half joked, feeling good about himself.

"I'm starving. Let's go get something to eat," Azinine suggested. "I'll show you my home and the city I live in. I think you'll find it fascinating."

"Sounds good to me."

They walked back to the castle, but instead of going inside, they headed towards what looked like some stables. "Are we going to ride back?" Scott asked.

"Of course," she answered. "I'm not going to walk, it's way too far." However, when they arrived at the stables there were no horses anywhere to be seen.

"Where are the horses?" Scott asked.

"Horses? We are not going to ride horses. We are going to ride on my MOC."

"What's a MOC?"

"That's a MOC," she replied, pointing to the ground. "A Motion Oscillating Cruiser."

Scott looked down but all he could see was a large rug or carpet with four crystal balls on each corner. "You mean that rug?" he asked.

"Rug? I guess if that's what you want to call it."

"How does it work?"

"Similar to the boots, except it does respond to special commands and it allows you to carry several people at once without dropping them!"

"Are you telling me this...this carpet flies?" Scott questioned.

"Of course! What did you think?" she asked

"I've heard of flying carpets in storybooks, but I never dreamed I would actually fly on one," Scott commented. "Is it hard to stay on?"

"No, once it begins to fly you'll be lucky if you're able to move at all. We could fly upside down and you wouldn't fall off. Come on, let's go."

They both hopped on and Azinine barked, "Ob!" and the carpet rose slowly into the air. Scott felt himself being sucked onto the carpet. It was like a giant magnet was holding him against it. He also noticed Azinine using her hands like a music conductor conducting an orchestra. "Fort," she spoke, and the carpet moved forward out of the stable. Again she seemed to be using her hands to direct the carpet out of the stable. Once outside, she yelled, "Hieme," and the carpet took off amazingly fast. Scott tried to grip something to keep himself from falling off, but soon realized that the carpet had a better hold on him than he did on it. As they sped along, the air current began to whip around their faces until it became uncomfortable and Scott wondered how long he would have to endure it. He didn't have to wonder long, though, because a few minutes later Azinine raised her hand and an invisible bubble of some type covered them. It was quiet compared to the rushing wind just moments before, and Scott could now only feel a very slight breeze.

"How did you do that?" he asked.

"It's called a wind stopper. It's kind of a funny name, but I guess whoever first conjured it didn't have a better one so he simply called it a wind stopper, because that's what it does."

"What do you mean by 'conjured'?" Scott asked.

"You don't know what 'conjured' means?" she asked, surprised.

"The only definition I know has to do with magical spells," he replied.

"Exactly. So why did you ask what it meant?"

Scott was confused, but he didn't ask any more questions. Azinine was acting like his questions were stupid, and he felt like a fool when she answered him. Instead, he turned his attention toward the ground and admired the beautiful landscape. Below him were farmlands and small villages that dotted the countryside. It looked like he had gone back in time and was now observing 17th century Europe. Off in the distance, on one side, loomed a very large mountain range with white snowcapped peaks. On the other side were rolling hills and more farmland. Further on, he could see what looked like another castle and more mountains rising behind it. He looked ahead and was surprised to see yet another castle. This one had several different flags flying from the turrets. Below this castle, in all directions, he could see smaller dwellings stretching out for miles.

After about an hour, the number of MOCs, and what looked like people riding broomsticks, increased until they appeared to be on some sort of flying highway. "That's my home," she said, pointing towards a very large castle on a hill overlooking the town.

"That castle is your home?" Scott asked incredulously.

"My father is the High Magus and so he gets to live there."

Scott figured the High Magus must be like the mayor or something. As they approached, he could see a huge wall surrounding the castle with several smaller dwellings inside. On the outside of the castle walls was a large gathering of people yelling something that he couldn't make out.

"Who are those people?"

"Protesters."

"They don't look very happy. Why are they protesting?"

"It's a long story," she sighed. "But in a nutshell, they believe the magi council isn't being honest with them. When we have more time, I'll explain it to you better."

They flew over the castle and as they did, Scott noticed another large group of people gathered on one of the castle courtyards. Several waved as Azinine flew over them and she waved back. She lowered the MOC onto a balcony. Once they landed, the MOC released Scott so he was free to move around. Azinine jumped off and headed toward the far corner of the balcony.

"Af," she spoke, and to Scott's surprise a door materialized. "This is where I sleep," she explained as they walked through the doorway.

"Nice," Scott replied. Nice was an understatement. This castle was immense and absolutely beautiful with all the woodworking and trim outside and in. The room they were standing in was rather large and not only had a bed, but several chairs and a couch. Azinine walked across the room and through another door leading out into a large hall, which was illuminated by the same Lumenarty stones Scott had noticed earlier in the first castle. They walked down a set of stairs, through another beautiful room which resembled a sitting room, down another hall, and finally outside to the courtyard where a party was being held.

"My dad holds these gatherings all the time," she explained. "It's great because it also means lots of good food. Tonight's party is the beginning of a three-day magi council. They'll spend tonight socializing and tomorrow they'll remain behind closed doors all day. Pretty boring if you ask me."

As they walked out onto the main area, people began waving to Azinine, but soon several stopped, their hands still in midair, when they noticed Scott. They were looking at him as if he were from another planet. Of course Scott was from another planet, but he was sure they didn't know that. He didn't look any different than they did, except for maybe his clothing, but he really didn't think his clothes would create this much of a stir. Whispers arose among the people in all directions, and more and more were turning to stare at him.

"Why are they all staring at me like that?" Scott nervously muttered to Azinine.

"I'm not sure," she whispered back.

As they turned a corner, they came upon an older gentleman who let out a yelp when he saw Scott, and then a thought occurred to her. "Scott, come here quickly," she said, grabbing his arm. They hurried around another corner and ducked into the kitchen. Passing through, they entered a small viewing room that looked like a museum, with all sorts of artifacts and paintings.

"Look." Azinine pointed to a picture on the wall. It was the same painting that hung on the wall outside Headmaster McDougal's office. The painting of the knight with the golden sword.

"That was the last High King," she explained. "You saw his picture at Cylindhall this morning. The picture at Cylindhall is a picture of the High King just before he was murdered. This picture, the one with the golden sword, is a picture of him when he was much younger, but it's a very well known picture. Most of the people out there also knew him very well. I believe that's why you are causing such a stir," she replied with a kind of giggle.

"But I'm so much younger than him. Certainly they don't think I'm him?" Scott replied.

"Of course not, he's dead. But you look so much like him that you could be his son."

"Did the king have a son?"

"Yes, but he was murdered along with his father."

"Then they should know that I'm not his son."

"The king also had a daughter who disappeared the day the king was murdered."

"Where is she now?"

Just then Azinine's father entered the room. "Hello, Azinine. Who is your guest?"

"This is Scott."

"It's nice to meet you, Scott. I'm Magus Axmeer Polimar," he said, turning to Scott and bowing. Scott bowed back, assuming that was how they greeted each other.

"It's nice to meet you too, Sir," Scott replied.

"Do you live in town?" Magus Polimar asked.

Scott wasn't sure what to say. It felt a little awkward saying he was from another planet. He looked toward Azinine for help.

"Father," she replied, "this is Scott Frontier. You know who he is."

Scott turned to her in surprise, thinking, *Why would her father know who I am?*

"I thought so, but I just wanted to make sure." Magus Polimar nodded. "Follow me," he instructed. "I need to speak with both of you."

They followed him through the castle until he led them up a spiral staircase, and ushered them into a small room at the top. Closing the door behind him, he motioned for them to sit down. "Scott," he began, "Headmaster McDougal and I are very good friends. That's how I know of you, though it is nice to finally meet you. The way you're dressed is also a pretty good clue that you are not from around here. Under different circumstances, I would welcome you to this world and would love to show you around. However, things are not exactly peaceful at this time and I fear for your well-being. As you are already aware, you have created quite a stir down there. Although a much younger version, you look a lot like King Ashta. So you see, to these people you look like a ghost from the past or"—he hesitated, giving Azinine a stern look—"possibly an heir. Because of this, they'll want to know more about you. However, they must not find out who you are and especially that you're not from this world. If anyone asks, tell them you're visiting here with your family. You come from across the sea, from a small farming town called Thunal. Once Azinine takes you back, you should stay in your world until it is safe to visit ours. It's not that you're not welcome, but it could be dangerous. I can't explain now, you'll just have to trust me. Understand?"

"Sure," Scott replied, but his head was spinning. Everything was so weird.

"Azinine," Magus Polimar continued, "there probably isn't any danger at the moment, but I would suggest you both grab some food and eat it somewhere away from the guests. You can take Scott back once you've finished eating."

"Okay," she replied, steering Scott out the door. They headed back to the kitchen, where Azinine told Scott to wait by the stairs while she went to get the food. After what Magus Polimar had just revealed to him, Scott was nervous sitting there alone in this huge castle. While he was waiting for Azinine to return, someone approached him from the hall. He looked back to see a man dressed in robes like those Azinine's father was wearing. He felt butterflies in his stomach. This man was obviously another magus, and Scott was sure he would say something to give himself away.

"Hello," the man said in a soft voice, while bowing. Scott stood up, said hello back, and bowed.

"You created quite a stir out there, young man."

"Yeah, I guess so," Scott replied, trying to say as little as possible. The man said nothing else, but just stared at Scott, almost as if he were trying to pierce him with his eyes. Scott began to feel very uncomfortable and panic started to set in. Knowing that panicking would for sure cause suspicion, he took a deep breath and told himself to relax. "Are you okay?" Scott asked him. It was the only thing he could think of to break the silence.

"Yes. Why do you ask?" the man replied.

"You're staring at me or staring right through me. Either way it's a little disconcerting."

"My apologies. But certainly you must realize that the resemblance you bear to the late High King is uncanny. King Ashta and I were friends from childhood. I knew him all his life. Are you a relation of his?"

"No, I didn't even know who he was until today."

The man's face took on a surprised look, giving Scott the impression he might have made a very big mistake. "You have never heard of King Ashta?" the man asked.

Wondering if everyone should know of King Ashta, he replied, "No, I grew up in a small farm town across the sea. My parents never mentioned him."

The man eyed him closely now, making Scott feel even more uncomfortable, if that were even possible. Much to Scott's relief, Azinine returned at that moment. "Hello, Magus Marda," she said respectfully.

"Hello, Azinine," he replied. "Why do you keep your friend from the party?"

Azinine kept her wits about her. "Father asked us to stay away. I guess he didn't want us disrupting his party any more than we already have. If you'll excuse us, we are both starving."

The man nodded and bowed. Scott and Azinine did likewise and then walked away. They headed outside, down a hill toward some orchards and sat down beneath the trees to eat.

"Oh," Azinine exclaimed, "I forgot drinks. Please feel free to start eating and I'll be right back." She stood up and headed back up towards the castle. While she was gone, Scott decided he would go ahead and start eating. He was starving. There was some meat that was cut into circles that tasted like beef, but looked nothing like the beef he was used to. There was also bread, some sort of food that looked like it might be a vegetable, and lots of cakes. After a minute, Scott turned his attention towards the castle to see if he could spot Azinine. She was nowhere in sight, but he could see people at the gathering still looking down towards him. He didn't like all these people gawking at him, so he looked away and continued eating.

He had just bitten into a cake when something caught his eye. What he saw, or rather thought he saw, surprised him. Just beyond the orchard was a fenced corral with what looked like unicorns inside. Scott loved horses and had ridden several times in his life. He had read about unicorns in books, but they were just mythical creatures. He couldn't believe he was actually looking at real unicorns, if indeed that's what they were. He decided to get a closer look and ran over to the corral. Sure enough, they were horse like creatures with large horns protruding from their foreheads. The only difference from the mythical unicorns was that these were pure black and very large and muscular. The pictures he had seen of unicorns always depicted them as white and smaller than normal horses. The feature that impressed Scott most was their horn. Each horn was about three to four feet long, thick at the base and rising to a very sharp point at the tip.

The corral they were in had an outer fence and then an inner fence about twenty yards in. The outer fence was about twice as tall as the inner one. Scott guessed this was to either keep the unicorns from getting out or to prevent others from getting in. He noticed a gate, but it was heavily locked. He desperately wanted to get a better look, but couldn't see any possible way to get in. Suddenly, he remembered the winged boots were still on his feet. In an instant, he was up and over the taller fence and standing just behind the inner one. He knew better than to actually go in the corral. He just wanted to get a closer look. The unicorns were a fair distance from Scott, but they were all looking at him as a horse or a deer might do when something unexpected has caught their attention.

"He is not our friend. Destroy him," Scott heard a voice say. He looked around to see who had said that. He saw Azinine running down the path.

"Scott, no! Get out of there—now!" she yelled. He turned around and noticed that practically all the castle guests were now looking down at him while Azinine was frantically running towards him. He wondered what could possibly be wrong. Why was she so upset? And why was everyone staring at him again? It was at that moment he heard hooves and whirled around. The unicorns were running at full charge and were headed in his direction. Scott had never seen a more terrifying sight than those horns coming towards him. If they charged the inner fence, Scott was sure it wouldn't hold them. Thoughts of his family flashed through his mind, followed by an image of Azinine.

"Fly!" he could hear her yelling, amidst the shouts coming from the other people at the castle.

Fly? Oh…fly! he thought. Using the winged boots he shot into the air, but forgot about the wooden overhang. *Crash!* His head and body slammed against the wooden braces. Floating in midair, he discovered he was having a hard time focusing. After a second or two, the shoes relaxed and he fell. His head was swimming, but he was conscious enough to know that he had fallen inside the corral with no fence between him and the charging unicorns. They were almost upon him now and he was starting to slip into unconsciousness. With all the energy he could muster he yelled, "Stop! Please don't hurt me!" and then everything went dark.

Chapter Seven

The Amulet

When Scott finally came to, he could hear voices in the room. It was Magus Polimar and the older gentleman he had bumped into at the party.

"We have to get him out of here, now!" he heard Magus Polimar say.

"We can't move him. He must heal first."

"I know, but he is in danger here. We must do something."

"As soon as Azinine gets back with the unicorn serum, we can administer it. Hopefully that will do the trick. In the meantime, can't you place guards over him?"

"Guards, Yorim? If I place guards around him, what sort of message will that send?"

"I think it's too late for that. The incident with the unicorns already sent that message."

"You're probably right. Which means they'll be watching this place very closely." Magus Polimar paced up and down for a bit. "Oh, Azinine," he said more to himself than anyone else, "what have you done?" Then getting worried, he turned to the other man. "Yorim, I need to go see what is keeping Azinine. Will you stay by him?"

"Yes, of course," Yorim replied. Magus Polimar left the room and Yorim walked over to the window, staring outside.

"Do you mind telling me what's going on?" Scott finally dared to ask.

Yorim jumped when Scott spoke, but smiled and walked over to him. "It's very complicated," he explained.

"I seem to have plenty of time."

The older gentleman gave a sigh. "I suppose I could try. About twenty-six years ago, the High King and his son were murdered. It was his only son and hopeful heir to the throne."

"The king didn't have any other heirs that could take the throne?" Scott asked.

"He had a daughter, but she fled to escape from being killed herself."

"Then there's still hope. You do know where she is, don't you?"

"Her whereabouts are known to a few of the magi. They tried the amulet on her, but it didn't choose her."

"Amulet? What do you mean the amulet didn't choose her? I don't understand?"

"A very long time ago when this land was first inhabited, it was ruled by wicked and cruel men who had little regard for their people. The king cared only for himself and his friends and placed harsh burdens upon the people. Then, a great leader named Fabiro, led a revolt and overturned the government. The people made him the High King and he reigned with integrity and kindness for many years. The king, as the story is told, also had a friend who was a very gifted magus named Zandor, who spoke the ancient language very well and made many wonderful things that we are unable to replicate today. Fabiro was not a magus, so he asked Zandor to forge an amulet that would give him certain magical powers to help him, and future kings, rule over this land and keep it peaceful. The amulet was given many great powers. Fabiro knew he wouldn't live forever, and was concerned what an evil king might do with the power of the amulet. One day he expressed his concern to Zandor, and Zandor decided to give the amulet one more power. Zandor took the amulet, and gave it the power of discernment; specifically the power to discern between a good king and a bad king. From that time forth, the amulet has always been used to select the next king. To do so, the amulet is placed around the new High King's neck. Only the one chosen is able to wear it. Anyone else will be badly burned. In most cases the amulet has chosen a High King from the bloodline of the previous High King, though not always the firstborn. In rare cases, the new High King wasn't a blood relative at all, but the people respected the amulet enough to support its choice. It has always served us well."

Yorim stopped for a second, pondering something and then continued. "For several years after the king was murdered, we waited for the amulet to pick a new High King. There were several men who claimed a right to the throne, but the amulet chose differently. It has now been a very long, twenty-six years, and we still have no High King. There are some on the magi council who grow tired of waiting and some say the amulet no longer works. They want to use the vote of the people, and not the amulet, to determine the next king."

"Sounds fair enough," Scott remarked.

"In secret they spread lies to the people about the magi council, telling them the high council has no intention of picking a High King. Telling them the magi council has hidden the amulet so it can't pick a High King, thus giving them power to rule over the people by default. More and more citizens are turning against the council."

"Why not let the people pick a High King?" queried Scott.

"Because, we risk choosing a High King that might be less than honorable to his people. Since the existence of the amulet, it has always picked good kings that have ruled in fairness. It's too risky to let the people choose. But there is also another problem. If we chose a king and later the amulet chooses another, it is very unlikely the reigning High King would stand down. Most likely we would have a civil war on our hands."

"It appears the people are already growing restless. You may have a civil war on your hands if you don't let them pick," Scott observed.

"Of course you are correct, but the high council is adamant that the amulet chooses the next High King. It is in the best interest of everyone, but these dissenters on the magi council are very effective in convincing the people otherwise." Yorim now paused as if in deep thought.

"What does this have to do with me?" Scott asked after several minutes.

"Oh, yes of course," Yorim said, coming out of his reverie. "Most of the High Kings, for what reason I am not sure, have had certain gifts that others haven't possessed. One of those gifts is the ability to speak with unicorns. In the past, High Kings have ridden male unicorns in parades, celebrations, and even into battle. The unicorns have never let anyone else ride them. I took care of the animals while King Ashtar was alive and I take care of them now, and I am the only one they tolerate. The unicorns should have killed you, but they didn't. Because of this, along with your unbelievable likeness to the late High King, many may assume you are of noble birth and possibly a candidate for the throne."

"Me?" Scott sputtered. "But I don't want to be High King."

"It doesn't matter," Yorim patiently explained. "We have reason to believe it was a member, or rather several members, of the magi council that murdered King Ashtar in order to steal the throne. If they believe you could threaten their plans, they will also try to dispose of you. That is why we must get you away from here as soon as possible."

Scott's head was swimming and he felt as though he were going to black out again. All of this information was too much for him. He had come here simply to be with Azinine. Now, he finds out he's a possible candidate for High King and several unknown persons may want him dead. He was having a hard time accepting this. After a few moments processing this new knowledge, he decided to get up and leave. He didn't want to hang around this world any more than was necessary.

"Please lie down," Yorim said gently, pushing him back down on the pillow. "You are in no condition to travel right now. You split your head open when you hit the fence. We have stopped the bleeding, but it is still very delicate. Azinine went to get some unicorn serum, which has amazing healing qualities. Once we apply it, you'll be able to travel."

"If you can't get near those unicorns without them killing you, how do you manage to get this serum from them?" Scott asked.

"We don't get the serum from male unicorns. The male unicorn horn actually contains a very deadly poison, which only the serum from the female's horn can heal. The female unicorn is not deadly and she doesn't use her horn to kill. But they are still very elusive and it is not easy to get serum from them. We can sometimes catch them and physically extract the serum. Mostly, though, we use a little magic— an illusion actually—which tricks them into using their horn on what looks like another injured female unicorn."

"How do you know which unicorns are male and which are female?"

"That's easy. Unlike the males, females are pure white and smaller in stature."

Just then, Magus Polimar and Azinine entered the room. Azinine walked over to the bed and sat down beside Scott, placing her hand on his head. "How are you feeling?" she asked with concern.

"Physically, I think I'm feeling better," he answered. "I'm just not sure I can get my brain wrapped around all this High King and magi council and amulet stuff."

Azinine gave him a reassuring smile while making room for her father at his side.

"We need to apply the serum and get him out of here," Scott heard Magus Polimar say. Yorim moved out of the way and Magus Polimar pulled a small flask out of his robe. He applied several drops on Scott's head where the cut was located. Within seconds of the application,

Scott's head began to feel very hot. It got to the point where he thought his head was on fire. He began to moan while beads of sweat poured down his face. Azinine grabbed his hand and held it tight, whispering words of comfort to him. The pain was growing stronger and Scott fought to get up, to do something to relieve the pain.

"Hold him down," he heard Magus Polimar say. Yorim moved toward Scott, but it was Azinine that kept him from getting up. She put her lips close to his ear. "Scott," she soothed, "just hold on a bit longer. This will only last a couple more minutes. You will be okay. You're going to be okay." She repeated the last phrase several times. After a moment, the pain began to subside just as she had promised. When it was gone, he was amazed at how well he felt.

"Good!" Azinine said. "Now, we need to get you out of here. It's going to be light in a few hours." Scott climbed out of bed and walked towards the door.

Magus Polimar approached him. "Scott, I'm sorry you must leave under these circumstances. I wish I could spend more time explaining things to you, but you'll just have to trust me. Do not come back to Lumen until it is safe. When you get home, make an appointment with Headmaster McDougal. He will answer any questions."

"Thank you," Scott replied, wondering how Headmaster McDougal would know anything about this place.

"I have asked Yorim to take you back to Cylindhall, and Azinine has asked to accompany you. I agreed, but only on the condition that once you arrive at Cylindhall, you proceed home immediately."

Scott nodded and followed Magus Polimar out to a balcony, where Yorim and Azinine were waiting on a MOC. He climbed on next to Azinine and sat down. The MOC took off and once again, Scott felt the carpet suck him down onto it. He felt the warm air blow through his hair as he watched the castle quickly become smaller and smaller as they flew away. He also spotted several other MOCs taking off from the castle, all in different directions. He noticed Yorim was taking their MOC in a different direction from the one he and Azinine had come from—of that he was sure.

Azinine seemed to read his mind. Once Yorim raised the wind-stopper she spoke. "The other MOCs are decoys. Under the cover of night, anyone trying to follow us will not know which one you are on. We are headed toward the Black Mountains. That is the last place they would expect you to go. Once we are out of sight, we'll change course and head toward Cylindhall."

Scott nodded, not saying a word. Although he was sorry to leave Azinine, he was anxious to get home. "I'm sorry things turned out this way, Scott," she continued. "It would have been fun to show you more of this world." She placed a bracelet in his hand and whispered in his ear so Yorim could not hear. "This bracelet is connected to the one I'm wearing. When the blue stone lights up, that means I can see you on Saturday. When the green stone lights up, I'm on my way to CastleOne. When both the green and blue stones are lit up, that means I'm waiting for you in the council room. We may not be able to come back to my house again, but that doesn't mean we can't still see each other. You do still want to see me, don't you?" she asked hesitantly.

"Of Course," Scott reassured her, feeling better.

They sat in silence for a while. He was looking beneath him at all the small lights and thinking about what else might be down there. He felt a burning desire to see more of this world and understand the people. He wanted to learn as much as he possibly could. Far too soon, they reached Cylindhall, and Scott began to wonder if their fears were really warranted. They hadn't encountered any trouble along the way. Even so, when they landed, Yorim hurried them into the big castle, still adamant Scott leave immediately. As Scott entered the castle door, he thought he saw some movement in the trees at the forest edge, but when he stopped for a closer look, he couldn't see anything out of the ordinary. He chalked it up to his imagination and entered the castle. He wondered how they were going to see their way around in the dark, but he soon remembered the lighted stones. Although they weren't extremely bright, they did provide enough light for someone to find their way around. They made their way through the halls and back to the council room where the whole adventure began.

"You first," Azinine said to Scott, pointing at the chair. Scott lowered himself on the seat and Azinine quickly sat down on his lap.

"Remember," Yorim said to Azinine as they were getting ready to leave, "give your message to Magus McDougal right away and then come back immediately."

Azinine nodded and told Scott to hold on. "CastleOne," she commanded, and once again, Scott felt the gut-wrenching feeling he remembered from the first time. The bright light appeared and they sped off. This time, however, was not as bad as the first, mostly because he knew what to expect. Moments later they landed in the council room at CastleOne. At first it was pitch-dark, and then suddenly the room began to glow. Azinine had pulled a Lumenarty stone from her pocket, which was giving off enough light to allow them to see their way to the door. The castle lay in darkness, and Scott was pretty sure that everyone was still asleep.

"Once again, I'm sorry about all this," Azinine said to him.

"Don't be sorry. I was the one who decided to go exploring. And despite everything, I had a great time. Can we meet again next Saturday?" he asked.

"I'll try. Watch the bracelet Friday night. That will tell whether or not I'm coming."

"All right," he said as he followed her to Headmaster McDougal's door.

"Scott," she said, stopping him, "I need to talk with him alone. My father made me promise. I'm sure Headmaster McDougal will want to speak with you in the morning."

Scott didn't want to leave but knew he had to, so he thanked her again and walked back to his dorm. It wasn't until he got to his room that he realized how tired he was. He crept in quietly, careful not to awaken Ned, took off his clothes, and slipped into bed.

Several hours later, in the late afternoon, Scott awoke to find Ned sitting on his own bed staring at him. Scott remembered he was supposed to meet Ned and the girls yesterday. Not quite sure what to say, he turned over and groaned as if he were still tired.

"So did you have fun?" Ned asked.

Scott rolled over and looked at Ned, wondering if his friend knew where he had been. "What do you mean?" he asked.

"You know darn well what I mean. It starts with 'A' and ends with trouble," Ned replied.

"She's not trouble, just a little mischievous I suppose. How did you know I was with her anyway?" Scott asked.

"I spoke with Headmaster McDougal this morning. He asked me to bring you to his office as soon as you woke up. I didn't realize it would be at the crack of noon," Ned joked. "Anyway, hurry up. We need to get going," he added excitedly.

Scott was sure his visit to the headmaster's office couldn't be good, so why was Ned so excited about that? Was he so angry with Scott for not showing up that he wanted to see Scott punished? "Well," Scott yawned, trying to delay the meeting, "I'm not quite awake yet. In fact, I think I need a few more hours of sleep."

"Oh, no you don't! You're getting up right now. I'm not waiting one second longer," Ned said, pulling the blankets off him.

"Waiting for what?" Scott asked, somewhat annoyed now.

Ned wasn't sure how to answer this, but finally decided it was time to tell Scott the truth. He already knew too much anyway so there was no reason to continue to pretend. "Scott, I'm also from

Lumen. My real name is Axtar. I'm here by permission of Headmaster McDougal because I wanted to learn about your world. However, I was told never to reveal this to anyone, and you can certainly imagine why. Since Azinine has already spilled the beans about our world, I don't think there is any reason to continue my charade with you."

Scott sat there with his mouth wide open. After all he had just been through, he now finds out his best friend is also from this other planet. He was too shocked to say anything.

"Scott?" Ned prodded him gently.

It slowly dawned on him that Ned had told him Azinine was a girl from around where he grew up. Of course, Ned was from Lumen! Scott finally spoke up. "You still haven't told me what you are waiting for. Why you are so excited to see me to the headmaster's office?"

"Azinine sent word back from Magus Polimar that you have some unusual talents we shouldn't ignore."

"You want to test the amulet on me, don't you?"

"You know about the amulet?"

"Yes, but I can't see how it would choose me. I'm not from Lumen."

"Well…that's…not exactly true."

"What!" Scott replied, now sitting up wide awake.

"The truth is…" Ned stopped to think things over. "On second thought, I better not say just yet."

"Oh, no you don't. I want to know now."

"Um…okay," Ned conceded. "I probably shouldn't tell you this, but, your mother is from Lumen."

"What?" Scott almost laughed. "My mother is not from Lumen. I guarantee you that."

"I knew you wouldn't believe me, but it's the truth," Ned argued. "She is the daughter of King Ashtar, our High King who was murdered. You have Lumen blood running through your veins. We thought perhaps Eric might be the one, but we've ruled him out. It was disappointing, but we still have hopes for you or Joshua. Will you try the amulet? It's very important to us."

Scott was dumbfounded. "You're telling me that my mother is the king's daughter who escaped when the king was murdered?"

"Yes, she's the one. You sure know a lot for having visited Lumen for just one day."

"My mother never told me this," he said out loud more to himself than to Ned. "Are you sure about this?"

"Positive. But from what I've heard, your mother hasn't even told your father."

"Why?" Scott wondered.

"If you hadn't seen it for yourself, would you have believed her?"

"No, I... guess not."

"Come on. We've got to get to the headmaster's office." Ned got up and started walking toward the door. He turned back to see Scott still sitting there. "Is something wrong?" Ned asked. Scott didn't say a word. "Scott, what is wrong?" Ned asked a little stronger this time.

"Is something wrong?" Scott exploded. "Nothing, except for the fact that I've just been told that my mother and my roommate are Martians. But hey, that's no big deal. I mean it happens all the time, right?"

"You forgot to mention your girlfriend," Ned replied.

"My girlfriend?"

"Yeah. You forgot to mention that your girlfriend is a Martian too."

"And my girlfriend," Scott said, putting his head between his hands. Then looking up again, "She is not my girlfriend," he stated, lowering his head once again between his hands.

"Scott, I wouldn't take it so hard," Ned mockingly comforted him. "After all, you yourself are half-Martian."

At that, Scott jerked his head up once again, his eyes growing wide. "Oh, now you're going too far. I am not a Martian."

"Of course you're not! None of us are. We are all from Lumen, not Mars."

Scott didn't say anything after that. What could he say? He simply sat there trying to absorb it all. Ned could see this was harder on his friend than he thought it would be, so he waited until Scott was ready. After several minutes Scott finally spoke up. "If the amulet chooses me, what then?"

"I don't know. We'll leave that up to Magus McDougal," Ned answered.

"Headmaster McDougal is a magus also?" Scott asked.

"Yes, he's also from Lumen and yes, he's a magus," Ned replied.

"Well, then let's get this over with," Scott sighed. He put some clothes on and the two boys walked out of their room and headed to the administrative offices. As they approached Headmaster McDougal's office, Scott slowed down. He really did not want to do this. He didn't know anything about being a king, especially in a land he knew nothing about. He just wanted to live a normal life like his parents and everyone else he knew, or at least thought he knew.

"Come on, Scott," Ned urged.

Scott took a deep breath and walked over to the door where Ned knocked. The door opened, and there stood Headmaster McDougal. "Good morning, Scott. It's nice to see you," he said.

"Good morning," Scott replied in a less than enthusiastic voice.

"I understand you've been through a lot in the last twenty-four hours. It must have been quite a shock to you. Come in and take a seat."

"That's an understatement, Sir," Scott replied.

The headmaster smiled and chuckled a bit. "I know you must have a lot of questions. Would you like to ask those now?"

Scott sat silently for a while, thinking back on everything that had happened the other day that had turned his life upside down. "Ned tells me you're from Lumen also, correct?" he asked.

"That's correct."

He paused again; he had so many questions. Finally, he decided to ask what had really been bugging him ever since he had accepted the idea of Lumen, and the fact that it was an entirely different world than his own. "I've been to your world, so I know you are not a bunch of aliens taking on human forms, like we see on TV. In fact, you look, talk, eat, and sleep just like we do. If what Ned tells me is true, my mother is an alien like you, so biologically we must be the same. The question I have is why are you here? What are you doing here on earth?"

The headmaster smiled at Scott's intuitiveness. "First of all, let's not use the word *alien*, it sounds so negative and horrible. Second, I want you to imagine in your mind the vast expanse of space and all the planets that exist, not only in your universe, but countless other universes. It's hard to imagine, Scott, but there's no end to space, it goes on and on and on. The earth is but a tiny, tiny speck comparatively. Considering all this, do you really think that life only exists on earth?"

"Well…" Scott thought for a moment. "When you put it that way, I guess not."

"You are here in Germany as an American. In a sense you are an alien here. The German people have different customs, in some cases, wear different clothes, but are generally the same as you. It is much the same on other planets. At one time, people from our world and people from your world moved amongst each other's planets just as you now visit Germany and Germans visit America."

"Really?" Scott was astonished at this piece of information.

"Thousands of years ago, there was a great war on Lumen. There was a king called Zarim, who reigned over a nearby land called Mezantan. He became greedy and wanted to rule over both Mezantan and Shonlante, where our people live now. He incited his people to go to war against us. Many of Zarim's people didn't want to fight and refused to take up their weapons. Zarim had these people killed. There were a few who escaped from his land and came over to ours seeking refuge. King Zarim and his followers were angry and vowed to track these deserters down and kill them.

"About that same time, there was a great magus who discovered that every universe, and the planets within each universe, are all connected. He also learned that each universe has planets that sustain life, and others that don't. The planets that promote life do so from light. In other words, without light, nothing on the planet would survive. There are many different types of light, and we needed a planet that didn't have the light we call magilume. This is the light we use on Lumen to perform spells and other forms of magic. Magilume is very important for us. It is essential for the way we live, but it is also where Zarim, where all of us for that matter, get our powers. If he happened to discover where these people lived, we didn't want him to have power to hurt them. When we found your world, it contained magilume, but not nearly as much as our own world. It would take a magus much more powerful than Zarim to tap into the magilume on your world and use it against these people. It wasn't ideal, but we were running short on time so we sent them to earth."

"Are you saying that your magic doesn't work here?" Scott asked.

"That's right. At least, we haven't been able to use it properly here. There are people who have harnessed the power of magilume on your world and performed magic in the past, but there haven't been many and we aren't sure how they managed it."

"But I saw Azinine use the winged boots. Don't they use magic?"

"Yes, but they only work here at CastleOne. The castle is very closely connected to our world and so magilume is much stronger here. If she were to fly, say a half mile or so, away from the castle, she would drop like a rock."

Scott nodded, beginning to understand. "How are you able to move so quickly between your world and ours?"

"We travel through conduits of light that are sort of like super-highways through space. It's how all the universes are connected. I could go into more detail, but it's very complicated and I'm not sure you would understand." He paused. "Anything else?"

"No, not at the moment," Scott replied, taking a moment to absorb this new information.

Magus McDougal stood up and stepped into his personal quarters. He returned a moment later, carrying a very old box. He opened it and pulled out a glass box containing what looked like a diamond necklace, a very expensive diamond necklace. "Scott, this is the amulet. I think you already know its purpose. Are you willing to take the test?" he asked.

"I guess," Scott replied.

"Okay, I would like you to come over and put your hands on the glass. If the amulet starts to glow red, quickly remove your hands. If the amulet doesn't glow, pull it out and put it around your neck. It's that simple."

Scott stood up and slowly walked across the room. He looked down at the amulet, marveling at how old it must be. He slowly raised his hands and placed them on the glass. Immediately the amulet began to glow red hot. He quickly removed his hands and stepped back a few paces. He could see the disappointment written on Ned's and Headmaster McDougal's faces, but he was extremely relieved. This proved he was not the new king, making him free to go back to Lumen.

"Sorry," he finally said to them with a shrug.

"It's okay, Scott," Headmaster McDougal replied. "We appreciate your willingness to try. You may go if you'd like." Scott nodded and walked towards the door.

Ned glanced at him, saying, "I'll see you back at the room. I want to speak with Headmaster McDougal for a while longer."

"All right," Scott replied as he walked out of the office.

Scott spent the rest of the day in his room, but it wasn't until he was getting ready for dinner that Ned showed up. "Hi, Ned. Are you okay?" he asked.

"Sure," Ned answered, not too enthusiastically. "Do you want to get some dinner? I'm starving."

"Me too," Scott replied. They headed for the door and were just about to leave when Ned realized he had left his dinner card lying on his desk. He reached out his hand and mumbled, "Abtu." Instantly the card shot from the desk and into his hand.

"Whoa! How did you do that?" Scott asked in amazement.

"Oops!" Ned answered sheepishly. "I'm not supposed to do that. I guess I wasn't thinking."

"Well, now you have to show me. Or…I could tell a certain head-master that a certain student was doing things he shouldn't," Scott teased.

"That's blackmail!"

"Yes, at its best. Now that I already know about Lumen, there's no reason you shouldn't tell me how you did it."

What Scott said was true, so Ned figured it wouldn't hurt to show him. "It's a simple command, but you have to set it up in advance," he explained. "Come here and I'll show you."

He and Scott walked back inside the room. "Put your card down on your desk, but keep your hand on it and say, '*hortu.*' Then you simply remove your hand."

Scott put his hand on the card and said, "Hortu." Nothing magical happened. In fact, as far as he could tell, nothing happened at all.

"Okay," Ned instructed him, "now move away from your card. In essence, your card now knows it belongs to you. Hold out your hand and say '*abtu.*'"

Scott held out his hand and said, "Abtu." The card flew from his desk and into his hand. "Wow! That was awesome!" He threw the card down on the ground and said, "Abtu." Once again the card flew from the ground and into his hand. He did this over and over again.

"Come on, Scott. I'm starving," Ned begged, bored by this basic trick.

"Wait a second. I want to do this a few more times," Scott said.

"It's just a simple spell. There are much better spells than that."

"Will you teach them to me?" Scott asked. "My brother Joshua is going to die when he sees this. He's way into magic."

"No way! We are not supposed to use magic here at school. Only when we are in our world."

"Well, then why did you use magic just now?"

"I just wasn't thinking, that's all. We could get in a lot of trouble using it here."

"You mean you could," Scott pointed out. "I was never told by anyone I couldn't use it."

"Oh, come on, Scott. Certainly you realize the commotion you'd create if you performed spells in front of the other students."

"Yeah, I guess you're right. But you could take me to your world and teach me there," Scott suggested.

"We could, except you are still in danger there. Nobody in my world knows you failed the amulet test."

"We could tell them," Scott reasoned.

"We can't tell them," Ned argued. "If they knew we were secretly searching for candidates, it wouldn't go over too well. The amulet test is supposed to be conducted in front of the whole magi council."

"Then let's have me perform the test in front of the whole magi council."

Ned sighed. "It's more complicated than just that. In any case, if they thought there was the slightest possibility the amulet would choose you, they would certainly try to kill you before the test could take place. Can we talk about this later?" he asked. "I need food."

"Okay," Scott relented. As they turned to leave, he purposely dropped his card. "Darn it! I dropped my card," he said out loud.

Once again he yelled "Abtu" and the card flew into his hands. Smiling, he grabbed it, closed the door, and ran after Ned down the stairs.

The next few days passed by for Scott with almost every waking moment consumed with thoughts of Azinine. Eric had talked him into playing basketball for the sophomore-freshman team and that helped to keep his mind off her a little, but he couldn't wait to see her again. Each night he pulled the bracelet out of the dresser drawer to check the stones, but neither was lit. He knew she probably wouldn't contact him until Thursday or Friday, but he checked every night anyway. Thursday evening he was in his room changing into his basketball gear when he heard a sound. It wasn't really a sound, because he hadn't really heard it. Yet that was the best way he could describe it. It was an inaudible sound and it was coming from his drawer. He got up and opened the drawer. The blue stone on the bracelet was shining. Scott leaped into the air shouting, "Yeah, baby!" Quickly shoving the bracelet back in the drawer, he ran off to practice, feeling as though he was on top of the world.

Chapter Eight
Secret Revealed

Early Saturday morning, Scott's alarm went off at five thirty. He shut it off and glanced over at Ned, who was still in bed. Getting out of bed he walked over to his dresser, where he pulled the bracelet out of the drawer. The green stone was still shining, and he was just about to put the bracelet back when the blue stone lit up. "She's there," he said softly to himself. He quickly dressed and left the room.

When he arrived at the council room, it was dark as usual, but he knew she had to be inside waiting for him. He slipped into the room, shutting the door behind him. He began searching for the light switch by moving his hand along the wall. When he finally found it, it was covered with some sort of sticky goop that felt like a spider's web. He switched on the light and then a split-second later screamed, "Aaaah!" This scream was louder than the last time she had scared him.

Right in front of his face, on the wall, was a brown spider about the size of a dinner plate. The spider leaped off the wall towards Scott. He threw out a hand to block it, but the spider went right through it. A few yards away he could see Azinine on the floor, giggling. He looked towards the floor where the spider should have landed, but there was no sign of it. Still breathing heavily from the scare, Scott glared at Azinine, causing her to mellow. He was angry with her and almost left, but she got up off the floor and walked over to him. She put her arms around him and gave him a hug. "You sure are a good sport to put up with me," she said.

That softened Scott's mood and he was able to see things from her side. He also didn't want to ruin this day. He had been looking forward to this all week. "How did you do that?" Scott asked.

"I created the spiderweb, but the spider itself was just an illusion. We should probably get out of here. I think you really did wake the whole castle this time," Azinine said. They sat down in the chair. "Cylindhall," she yelled. Once again Scott felt that strange sensation, saw the bright light, and minutes later landed in Cylindhall.

They walked outside, where the sky was overcast, but the air was warm and felt great. "Does your dad know I'm here?" Scott asked.

"No, and he doesn't need to know. However, Scott, his concerns are valid and we must be careful that no one discovers you," she warned. Scott looked over to the edge of the forest, remembering the shadow he had seen the last time he was here.

Azinine continued, "When we come here, we can't stay at Cylindhall for very long. I don't want anyone to see us here and possibly put two and two together. There are two things we have to do right away whenever we come here. First, we have to disguise you, and second, we have to go somewhere else to hang out."

"What sort of disguise are you thinking about?"

"For starters, we'll change your hair from blond to black," she answered. Before Scott could object, Azinine touched his hair and said, "Vechshartar sharts." Immediately, Scott's hair turned jet black. Azinine giggled a bit and then pulled a black robe out of a sack she had on her back. "Here," she said, handing it to him. "Put this on. It will hide your clothing."

Scott put on the robe and looked back at Azinine. "So do I look authentic?" he asked with a smile.

"I like you with blond hair better, but it will have to do," she answered.

"Do I really have black hair?" Scott asked.

"Yep. And now it's time to have some fun. I've been looking

forward to this all week," she exclaimed quite excitedly. Azinine climbed onto her MOC and motioned for Scott to take a seat. Once they were both on board, she took off in the opposite direction they had flown the last time he was there. After about fifteen minutes they landed in a grove of trees by a small pond.

"So, just what are we going to do? Am I going to need insurance?" asked Scott.

"Insurance?"

"Never mind."

"We are going to play tag," Azinine answered matter-of-factly.

"Tag? Azinine, isn't tag a little kids' game?"

"Oh, I guarantee you're going to like this game of tag. First of all, we are not going to run, we are going to fly. And second, we are not going to use the castle grounds. We are going to use the clouds."

"The clouds," Scott sputtered, looking up at them.

"Yep," she said. She pulled out a pair of winged boots from her bag and handed them to Scott with a big grin on her face.

Scott took them and proceeded to put them on. "I assume you already have a pair on?"

"Of course," she said and lifted herself off the ground, pirouetting as she went.

"Are these boots common among your people?" he asked.

"No, they aren't. They are highly coveted, so do your best not to let anyone know you have them," she cautioned. "And don't remove them where someone could take them. And… watch out for the little people."

"Little people?" Scott questioned.

"You know, like the fleary you saw last time you were here. Above all, don't tell Ned or the headmaster that we've done this. In fact, you must keep this between you and me. Promise?"

"Promise," he replied.

She flew down and touched Scott on the head. "Tag, you're it."

She then shot skyward like a rocket. Scott took off after her, but before he knew it, she had disappeared into the white mass of clouds. He focused on *faster* and the shoes picked up speed. The feeling was exhilarating! It was only a matter of minutes before he reached the clouds and shot through them like a bullet. Seconds later he shot out the other side and quickly slowed himself to a stop. The clouds surrounding him looked like giant piles of cotton balls, while above him was another thin layer that resembled the roof of a gigantic room. He looked around but couldn't see Azinine anywhere, and he didn't have the slightest clue what to do next to find her. *She could be anywhere by now*, he thought.

"Raaaa!" a sound came bellowing out from behind him. Scott whirled around, lost his balance, and fell over, hanging upside down. Azinine started to giggle uncontrollably. Scott quickly righted himself and shot towards her. She shot down feet first, easily eluding him.

"Nice move!" he said to himself. He looked down, but Azinine had disappeared through a large puff of cloud. "Here goes nothing," Scott said, trying to encourage himself. He flew straight down head-first through the cloud, but soon decided he had better slow down to avoid any head-on collisions. He turned right-side-up and slowly entered the cloud. He couldn't see a thing. Azinine could have been ten feet away and he still wouldn't have seen her. Within moments he came out the other side of the cloud and noticed the ground far beneath him. The magnitude of how high he was, with only a pair of boots between him and falling to his death, scared him and he instinctively shot upwards through the clouds, to the other side. At least here he couldn't see the ground and the clouds gave him a false sense of security. He knew it was only an illusion, but it still comforted him.

When he finally came to his wits, he could see Azinine about thirty feet away, kneeling on the cloud as if it were a real floor. She didn't wave, she didn't smile, she didn't say anything. She just sat there looking at him and shaking her head. This made Scott angry, and he no longer cared about being careful. He would have to trust the boots; they hadn't let him down yet.

"Azinine, look!" he yelled, pointing behind her. She turned around and Scott took off as fast as he could towards her. By the time she realized it was a trick, it was too late. Scott blew past her tapping her on the shoulder. "You're it!"

It didn't take her long to begin the chase. Scott looked back and could see her gaining on him quickly. "She must have given me the slow boots," he grumbled to himself. There was no way to outrun her, so he decided to use the clouds. He waited until she was right on him, shot downwards and slammed on the brakes. He stopped to watch while Azinine flew past him like a bullet. That just about cost him dearly, for right as she passed, she quickly threw on her own brakes and was heading back towards him at lightning speed. Slipping down inside the cloud, he reversed direction and moved horizontally.

It was an eerie feeling to be going as fast as he was and not be able to see what was in front of him. However, he was pretty sure, based on his last impression of Azinine's flight direction, that he wouldn't run into her. About thirty seconds later, he peeked above the cloud floor so that only his head was showing. He could see Azinine far off, diving in and out of the clouds like a dolphin playing in the water.

He snickered to himself, "She doesn't have a clue where I am." He soon forgot about the distance of the ground beneath him and was really enjoying this new adventure. However, he soon realized that Azinine had dipped beneath a cloud and had not reappeared for some time.

"Where did she go?" he asked himself.

Smack! Something touched his foot and he saw the vague shadow of Azinine whip past him. He whirled around and took off after her, but she was gone. With no sign of her, he shot upward through the cloud. He immediately spotted her heading the opposite direction with her back to him. Instead of going directly after her, Scott continued skyward, piercing the roof-like cloud covering. This cloud gave him some cover, but the visibility was much greater than the cotton-ball clouds below, allowing him to keep an eye on Azinine. He couldn't see her clearly, but he could see enough to know where she was.

Azinine had slowed down to watch for him, and Scott was tempted to take this time to catch up to her. But he decided any movement might give him away, so he came to a complete stop and waited. Azinine quickly dropped down inside the cloud and stopped. Hanging upside down, Scott dipped his head below the roof to get a better look. She had positioned herself in the cloud so only the top of her head could be seen. Since she had blonde hair, she was not easily visible. Had Scott not watched where she went, he would never have seen her. Suddenly he remembered she had turned his hair black, making it easy for her to see him against the backdrop of white clouds.

"That little sneak," he exclaimed. "Disguise, my foot! She did this on purpose to make things easier for her." He quickly brought his head up to keep from being seen. He had to find a way to sneak up on her, but how? With only the cover of the wispy cloud, any movement would most likely give him away. Then an idea crossed his mind. He quickly removed the robe she had given him and said, "Hortu." Next, he dropped the robe and shot forward at the same time. The black material falling through the clouds distracted Azinine long enough for Scott to get past her. Once behind her, he turned and flew back through the cloud, tapped her on her head, and zoomed past her. "Abtu," he yelled, and the robe changed course from its downward descent to a straight line into his hand. Grabbing it, he noticed out of the corner of his eye that Azinine was rapidly closing in on him. Not having time to put the robe back on, he tucked it under his arm. Knowing Azinine would expect him to head for the clouds, he instead took off in a downward direction. She sped past him and he wasted no time shooting upwards to gain some cover. No sooner had he entered the cloud than he felt the full impact of Azinine colliding with him.

The two drifted backwards several yards and finally came to a stop, with Azinine still holding on to him.

"That was brilliant!" she said, looking at him with awe in her eyes. "You're better at this than most of my friends. And they have spent hours playing this with me."

"Really?" Scott asked.

"Yes. And one more thing," she said with raised eyebrows. "When did you learn to retrieve items?"

"Ned showed me a few days ago."

"I didn't think he was allowed to use magic in the castle."

"He's not. It sort of slipped out of him. I think he really wanted to show me and the temptation got the best of him."

"I can't believe he broke the rules."

"Oh brother, you've broken all kinds of rules since I met you," Scott said.

"Yeah, but Ned would rather die than break any rules."

"He's still quite a stickler to them. I asked him to teach me more, but he said he couldn't do it in the castle and he wouldn't risk bringing me here. However," he said with a mischievous look, "you could teach me. How about it?"

"Of course!" she laughed. "But not until you're ready, that is," she said in a more mellow tone.

"I am ready."

"Oh, no!" she cautioned. "Magic is a very wonderful tool for us, but it's serious stuff. It's kind of like fire. It can be very useful, but if you use it incorrectly it can be very dangerous. I don't mind teaching you; in fact, I think you should learn it. But before I do, you need to become more familiar with our world."

"I don't understand," he replied.

"Race you to the bottom," she yelled, ignoring his plea and taking off. Scott went after her like a bullet heading towards the ground. The trees appeared as though they were getting bigger and bigger and

MATTHEW SPRUNT

the ground seemed to be racing towards him. Butterflies welled up inside him and he wondered if the boots would stop him in time. This was one race he decided he wouldn't mind losing, and he slowed down, making sure he'd land safely. Azinine, of course, didn't have any problem stopping when she needed to, but all the same, he was glad he had been cautious.

They spent the rest of the morning swimming in the small pond. While they were relaxing under the sun, Scott brought up the subject of magic again. "Azinine, I don't understand why it's so important I become familiar with your world before you teach me. Except for the obvious advancements of technology in my world, your world and mine really aren't that much different, are they?" he asked.

"Scott," she began, searching for a way to explain, "this world is similar to yours in some respects, but it is also vastly different in others."

"Can you give me an example?" Scott asked.

"I'm not as familiar with your world as Axt…I mean, Ned is," she sighed. "But I'll try."

She sat there thinking about where to begin and was just about to speak when she saw two magi approaching. She quickly grabbed Scott and softly whispered, "Vechsardgrun." Immediately, the ground around them seemed to swallow them until the grass had completely covered their heads and faces, creating the illusion of a small mound of grass.

"What is…?" Scott began.

"Shhhh," Azinine quietly shushed him.

At that moment, he spotted the two magi. One of them he recognized as Magus Marda, the magus he had met by the kitchen in Azinine's house. Azinine seemed very tense and concerned about the appearance of the two magi. However, they walked past without noticing them. They appeared so caught up in their argument with each other that Scott wondered if they would have noticed them even if Azinine hadn't camouflaged them. Once they were some distance away, Azinine spoke some other word Scott didn't catch and the thin layer of grass dissolved.

"We need to get you back home as quick as possible," Azinine said.

"Azinine, what is going on? How come you're so nervous about those two?" Scott asked her.

"I didn't recognize the guy in the yellow and orange robe, but the one in purple was Magus Marda. Magi like Marda usually don't go on pleasure walks through the country or at least this part of the country. On the few occasions they do head into the country they don't walk, they fly. Unless, of course, they have business nearby."

"So maybe they have business nearby," Scott pointed out. "Why does that concern you?"

"First of all, you are not supposed to be here. If they saw you, who knows what might happen? But it would certainly get back to my father and I would get boiled. Second, this part of the country is not exactly the kind of place respectable magi hang out. That's why I brought us here."

"You say that as though it isn't safe to be here," Scott said.

"It's not, really," she answered. "But it's relatively safer during the day than at night. You wouldn't want to hang out here at night. Since the death of the High King, this forest has become home to all kinds of slimy creatures. I can't think of any good reason why those two would be out here, unless it's to visit some degenerate warlock who is hiding out."

"Warlock? As in witches and warlocks? Why is it so bad for them to visit one?" Scott continued questioning her.

"A warlock is a magician gone bad," she explained. "No respectable magician would have dealings with a warlock. On the other hand, Marda is not a respectable magician; at least I don't like him."

"Well, they're gone now. So why do I have to leave right away?"

"Because," she said a little exasperated, "if there is a warlock hiding out here, he probably saw us playing tag and will certainly inform Marda. We can't risk Marda finding you, especially out here."

"Okay, but how do we get back to the castle without them seeing us. They were heading in the direction of Cylindhall," Scott pointed out.

"I know, I've been thinking about that," Azinine replied with concern showing on her face. "Since flying overhead is not an option, we will fly close to the ground until we reach the woods north of here. Once we reach the woods, we'll fly just above the treetops until we reach the castle, but continue along the treetops until we reach the back side. We should easily beat them there, but I still want to be careful. When we reach the back side, there are about two hundred yards of no cover, but we'll just have to chance that. When we get inside, head directly for the council room. We can't waste any time."

"What about your MOC?"

"I'll come back later for that, it will be easier for us to hide if we don't have it."

Azinine took off in the lead with Scott following her. They darted up to the treetops, flying as close to the tops as they could. Scott found it interesting that all the trees were about the same height. After approximately ten minutes of flying as fast as the winged boots would go, they reached the castle border. They continued along the forest top until they could see the back side. Azinine came to a stop and studied the castle for a bit.

"Okay," she said, taking a deep breath, "I can't see any trace of them at this point. Let's go."

She took off at a rapid speed, and it was hard for Scott to keep up. They were only about twenty yards away from the door when Azinine suddenly changed directions and shot straight up towards a small balcony. Scott followed and landed next to her.

"What's wrong?" he asked.

"Someone is in the castle. Only a few people have access to the castle, mostly magi on the council. It must be Marda."

"How could he have beaten us? They were walking."

"I don't know, maybe their MOC was close by. Who else could it be?"

"Maybe we should go see what he's up to," Scott suggested.

"Are you crazy? No one else knows we're here. If he caught us, who knows what he would do? And no one would know he did it."

"We can fly. How will he catch us?"

"Scott, he is a magus. A very powerful magus. It would take more than a pair of flying boots to escape from him. No, we need to wait here until he leaves. Then we can get you home."

"What if he doesn't leave? Or what if he finds us up here?"

"Unless he plans on staying the night, he'll definitely leave before dark. Not even a great magus like Marda would walk these forests at night. Let's just hope he leaves soon so I can get out of here before dark also."

This new direction in their conversation piqued Scott's curiosity. "We go camping in the forest all the time where I live. What's so different about here?" he asked.

Azinine settled down on the ground, anticipating a long wait before they would be able to move. "All kinds of creatures roam these forests at night. Some are innocent animals that have no evil intentions, like wolves and gargoyles that merely hunt at night."

"Wait," Scott interrupted. "Gargoyles? When I first came to CastleOne, when we dropped Eric off, I could have sworn I saw a gargoyle perched on top of the castle. But when I came to school this year, it was gone. Eric says it was never there, but I know I saw one. Then later on, not too long ago, Eric and I both saw a gargoyle perched on top of the school. We thought it was just a decoration someone was using. Are you telling me that gargoyles are real?"

"Yep, you probably saw Bitterpaw," Azinine said. "He belongs to

Magus McDougal. He's there to help protect the castle at night."

"I knew it!" Scott exclaimed. Then as an afterthought, "So gargoyles are alive? Then how come we don't see it around the school?"

"Well first off, what do you think the students would do if they saw a real gargoyle walking around the school?"

"Ha, good point," Scott said.

"Second, during the day, most gargoyles turn themselves to stone to protect themselves from the sunlight. When the sun goes down, they come alive. Most people here on Lumen use them kind of like watchdogs; they protect their homes while the people sleep."

"A number of kids at school have said they've seen a creature that's as large as a man, but can fly. Is that Bitterpaw?" Scott asked.

"Probably."

"Wow," Scott sighed. Then getting back to their original conversation, "So what other creatures are there that I need to be aware of?"

"Others, like trolls, are the result of dark magic. They don't intentionally go out of their way to harm others, but they can be very dangerous if you happen to cross their path. Last of all are those creatures, like goblins, who are just bad all around. Goblins are one hundred percent pure evil and practice dark magic. Most live under the ground during the day, but come out during the night. Sometimes they even go out of their way to capture Lumens as slaves. "

Scott was fascinated. "Goblins, trolls, gargoyles, warlocks. These are all creatures I've read about in mythical books, but never realized they actually existed," he said.

"Much of the folklore on your world comes from the reality of our world. And it's the same the other way around. Much of the lore on our world comes from the actuality of your world. For example, I would love to see an elephant; we don't have those on our world, but I've seen pictures and they look so cool. Anyways, long ago, the people from our two worlds used to visit each other freely. People from your world came here to experience the wonders and the horrors of our world. Their experiences were told to people on your world. In some cases, people from your world took animals, artifacts, and stuff like that back to your world, perpetuating the myths and legends even more. Although dragons are only legends on your world, they were at one time very real. Your people poached them from our world and took them to your world, hoping to raise and use them as beasts of war, but they were too hard to control. On the other hand, we brought horses and other animals from your world. Now they are as common here as our native animals."

"How come we don't visit each other anymore? What happened?" Scott persisted.

"People from your world took animals, magical objects, and even dark creatures back to your world. They even hunted our animals, like the unicorns. At first, no one cared. But soon it became too frequent and started to upset the balance of our world. Some creatures from our world were difficult to handle in your world without magic. We had to close the doorways between the two worlds. While all of the known doorways were closed, a group of magi secretly opened others because they didn't want to sever ties completely with your world."

Scott was silent for a moment. "There must have been a lot of chairs moving back and forth back then."

Azinine laughed. "They didn't use chairs back then. They used light portals. Some of them still exist in your world, but the only one I know of is the one on the castle grounds. You would have to ask Magus McDougal about the others."

"These goblins and other night creatures, do they ever come out during the day?"

"Some do, but only on rare occasions. They hate the light. Others can't come out during the day. The light will kill them."

"So nobody goes out at night?" Scott asked.

"We do in the city and many of the outlying areas which are protected. Most night creatures won't enter these areas because they're either too well lit or there are too many people. It also helps that the cities are protected by strong magic. However, people that must travel outside the city at night usually go in groups and even then they go well armed."

"Armed with what?"

"Mostly swords, spears, bows, magic of course, and many bring their gargoyles if they are not going too far."

"Why not just use magic?" Scott asked.

"Magic can be used to protect oneself, but it's most effective one on one. It's just too hard to try and use a spell on a group of people. I've been told there are ancient spells created long ago that could be used against a whole army, but they are hidden within the Ancient Book of Magic and must be spoken in the ancient tongue to perform them. Nowadays, when armies go up against armies, weapons are normally more effective. Magic just takes too much…" She stopped in mid-sentence when she heard the castle door open below. She quickly put her finger to her lips, signaling Scott to be quiet. They peered over the edge and soon a single person emerged. It wasn't Marda after all, it was Azinine's father.

"He must be looking for me," Azinine whispered. "Let's hurry and get you home and then I'll deal with him." She reached into her pocket and pulled out a glowing Lumenarty rock. She turned towards the wall, held out the rock, and spoke "af neheime." Within seconds a tiny door materialized. She motioned for Scott to follow her. The room they entered was dusty and filled with cobwebs. It was obvious no one had lived here for years. Nevertheless, Scott was intrigued by the décor. It looked like it had once been a boy's room. As he glanced around, he noticed all kinds of interesting objects. There were several swords, shields, glass balls, and even a couple of glowing rocks similar to the one Azinine was holding.

Scott wanted to look around, but he could tell Azinine had no intention of stopping, so he continued following her. They exited through another door and made their way through several hallways until they found themselves in the large familiar hall leading to and from the council room. From here Scott knew the way and they were soon inside the room. They both jumped on the chair and Azinine gave the word which, once again, sent them whirling through the tunnel of light. Within minutes, they were back at CastleOne. Azinine jumped off Scott's lap, pulled him to his feet, and immediately sat back down, waving good-bye.

"When will I see you again?" he quickly asked.

"Watch the bracelet," she replied. "Oh! One more thing," she added, pointing to his black hair. She jumped up, placed her hand on his head, and said, "Yederharstal," which he assumed was the spell to turn his hair back to its original blond coloring. She sat back down and in an instant she was gone.

Scott poked his head out of the doorway, making sure the coast was clear, before he made his way down the hall towards the cafeteria. He was starving and wanted something to eat. When he arrived, there were only a few students lingering at the tables and the staff had already begun to clear away the food. He was lucky enough to get a couple of rolls, an apple, and a piece of blueberry pie. Sitting down at a table to eat, he contemplated everything he had experienced. He wondered when he would see Azinine again and if he'd ever be able to visit her world without having to hide. Exploring Lumen was something he really wanted to do, but it wasn't likely to happen if he had to keep hiding from everyone and everything.

After dinner, he headed upstairs and found Ned sitting at his desk reading. "Hi, Scott," Ned greeted him enthusiastically. "Did you have fun today?"

"Sure," Scott answered warily.

Ned continued his innocent line of questioning. "What did you do?"

Scott was pretty sure Ned knew he had been with Azinine. Where else would he be unseen for a whole day? But knowing Ned was also from Lumen and that he might possibly send word back to Azinine's father, he decided to play Ned at his game.

"I decided to get away from the castle for a while. I'm starting to feel like a prisoner here. I can't wait for Christmas vacation so I can go home for a few days."

Ned wasn't about to be distracted so easily. "So where exactly, away from the castle, did you go?" he persisted.

"Ned, you are starting to sound like my mother. I suppose you'll want me to start asking permission to leave from now on?"

"Scott, I'm sorry to pry, but you are my friend. Believe it or not, I'm concerned for your safety and it's just not safe for you to visit Lumen right now. Azinine is a very talented witch and can probably take care of herself, but she is also carefree and reckless. Our world has seen better times, and right now there are dark forces building."

"You make it sound so bad, but when I go there, all I see is good. Don't you think everyone is being just a little bit paranoid?" Scott asked.

"Scott, you know nothing about our world. Magus Polimar came here today, and I might add he came because he couldn't find Azinine. Don't worry," he assured his friend, seeing the panicked look on Scott's face. "I didn't tell him you were with her. He told us that some of the magi are looking for you. You are the first person in a long time to show promise. They talk with good intentions, but others are not quite sure. He also told us there were other men in the city looking for you—men with bad reputations."

"You called Azinine a witch," Scott backtracked. "Why?"

Ned chuckled. "Because she is a witch. On our world there are witches and hags, magi and warlocks. Witches and magi are good, hags and warlocks are bad."

"Are you a magus?" Scott asked.

"Not really, I'm considered a magi apprentice I guess. I haven't finished all my training, and quite honestly it's not that important for me to do so, but maybe someday," Ned replied.

"Oh. Are you going home for Christmas?"

"Scott, don't change the subject. This is serious. Promise me you won't go back to Lumen," Ned said solemnly.

"Ned, I can't promise that. Azinine and I have a great time together and I like being with her. Who knows how long it will be before things calm down. It's just something I'm willing to risk."

"What if she were to come here to visit you?" Ned asked.

"Do you think Headmaster McDougal would allow that?" Scott asked hopefully.

"If it kept my numskull roommate here in his own world, he would."

"No, that won't work. I would be too embarrassed to ask him," Scott replied.

"Why?"

"Oh, come on, Ned. What am I going to say? 'Uh, Headmaster McDougal, there's this girl I like. I'm not supposed to visit her world, but the problem is, I really want to do things with her, so I was just wondering if she could come to my world and spend time with me?' Do you realize how dumb that sounds?"

"It did sound pretty pathetic," Ned agreed.

"My point exactly."

"Scott, he already knows you and Azinine are friends. He's not dumb. In fact, I'm pretty sure he knew you were with Azinine today, but he didn't say anything to Magus Polimar either. So he may understand better than you think."

"Do you think she would be willing to spend Christmas with me this year?"

Ned's eyes grew wide with the thought of that and he sat there speechless for a while. "Scott, I don't think that would be a very good idea."

"Why?"

"Let's just say she may not get along with your family as well as you or she would like."

"Why do you say that? Azinine is awesome. Why do you hate her so much?"

"I don't hate Azinine! She...she is like a sister to me. We just don't see eye to eye all the time, that's all."

"Then why don't you think she would get along with my family?"

"Scott, she doesn't speak English—at least not very well," Ned replied.

"What are you talking about? She speaks English just as well as you and I."

"No, she doesn't. One of the reasons we thought you might be chosen as High King is because you have a gift that we call 'lingual.' This gift allows you to speak and understand any language on our world."

"Ned," Scott laughed. "That is the most absurd thing I have ever heard. I spoke English to her and she spoke English right back. I know that for a fact!"

"I'm not going to pretend I understand how it works. I'm not lingual. But I've heard it explained this way. You speak English or your language to a person on Lumen. The Lumen magic or magilume somehow translates the words into the language of the person you are talking to so they hear their own language. It's kind of like you are speaking a translation spell each time you open your mouth. When they speak back to you, the magilume translates it back into your language. The same thing happens when you read. The letters and words may be in a different language, but your eyes will see English, I think; at least you will know what the English translation of it is. When Azinine spoke in Lumen, the magilume took the words and translated them into English."

"Okay, so explain this to me," Scott said, hoping to prove his point. "When I went to a German school, I wasn't able to speak and understand the German language. They spoke German, and my brain did not translate it into English. It remained German and I couldn't understand what they said."

"Didn't you hear what I said? It only works on our world where magilume is strong. It's the magilume that gives you this gift," Ned pointed out. "Scott, don't you find it kind of funny that of all the languages spoken on this world, English would be the language spoken on ours?"

Scott had to think about that for a second. "I guess you have a point there," he conceded. "But I know she spoke English to me!"

"Everyone on my world spoke English to you. Is that what you're saying?" asked Ned.

"Yes!"

"How convenient. That was very considerate of them, considering the language spoken on my world is Lumen," Ned said with a trace of sarcasm.

"Well how come you speak such good English?" Scott asked.

"In order for me to come here, I was required to take part in a very intensive two-year training program. I had to study every part of your language, including your slang. I watched movie after movie, listened to songs, audio books—you name it. I had to practice pronunciation over and over again until I got it right. I read your books, studied your history. Believe me, it was grueling."

"So you're saying that if I took Azinine home for Christmas, she wouldn't understand anything my family says?" asked Scott.

"Scott, she knows some English that she's picked up from her own studies, me and others, but that's it. She not only wouldn't under- stand your family, except for your mother if she spoke Lumen, but she wouldn't understand you and you wouldn't understand her. At least, I don't think you would. You don't speak Lumen, but you were able to speak it and understand it because you were in our world or here on the castle grounds. Once you leave the castle grounds, your gift won't work as well because the magilume is too weak. Besides, even if you could understand her, how would you explain that to your family? Then, imagine if your mother started speaking to her—that would complicate matters even more. How would she explain that to your father?"

"It does sound kind of messy," Scott agreed. "But I'm still having a hard time really comprehending all this." He sat down on his bed and began pulling off his shoes, with the intent of lying down to let it all sink in. It was then that he realized he was still wearing the winged boots. Azinine, in her rush, had forgotten to ask for them back. This was actually a good thing, because Scott knew she would come looking for them and he would see her soon.

When Ned left the room to brush his teeth, he quickly slipped them off and placed them in one of his drawers. He picked up his toothbrush and was about to head for the bathroom when a glint at the window caught his eye. He quickly turned and for a moment, saw two very large eyes staring back at him from outside of the window. It was only for a moment, and then they were gone, but Scott had distinctly seen someone or something looking back at him.

He ran over to the window and looked out. "Bitterpaw!" he yelled, but couldn't see anything. If it had been Bitterpaw, he was gone now.

Two weeks went by, and despite the fact that he still had the boots, Azinine hadn't contacted Scott. He was tempted to go looking for her, but thought better of it. Five days before Christmas, Scott's parents arrived with Joshua to take Scott and Eric home for Christmas vacation.

"Your father and I are going to say hello to Headmaster McDougal. Do you want to come with us or stay here?" their mother asked.

"We'll stay here," Scott replied. He had already seen the headmaster's office more than he wanted to this year. The others also nodded their agreement. Mr. and Mrs. Frontier hurried out of Eric's room, promising to be right back.

Once they were out of sight, Scott quickly turned to Joshua. "Josh, I learned this great magic trick that you will not believe."

"Really?" Josh said, his eyes lighting up.

"Yes, but I have to show you in my room. Eric, we'll be right back," he said, grabbing Josh by the arm and pulling him in the direction of his own room. They made their way over to Scott's room and walked inside, where Scott immediately closed the door. He wanted to make sure nobody saw this but Josh. He pulled out his dinner card and placed it on the desk. "Okay. Now I want you to examine my sleeves. Look, nothing is attached. Go ahead, examine them," he said, trying to imitate a magician-like voice. Josh examined his shirtsleeves and made sure nothing was there.

"Abtu!" Scott yelled dramatically. Instantly the card flew from the desk and into Scott's hands.

"Whoa!" Josh exclaimed, his eyes wide and round. "How did you do that?"

"As you always say, little brother, a magician never reveals his secrets," Scott replied very seriously. "Want to see it again?" he asked, this time more animated.

"Yes!" Josh replied.

Scott put the card back on the desk and walked away a few steps.

"Hold it! I want to examine the card first," Josh demanded. Of course Scott didn't mind. It would only make the trick that much better and more baffling to his younger brother. Josh carefully examined the card and the desk. He even moved the card to a different spot on the desk.

"Put the card on the floor for all I care," Scott said, completely enjoying the moment. Instead, Josh smiled mischievously and held the card in his hand, certain he would foil Scott's trick this time.

"Abtu!" Scott said, and the card flew from Joshua's hand directly into Scott's.

"Impossible!" Josh yelled. "You've got to tell me how you do that! Please tell me, please!" he begged.

"Josh, I told you. A good magician never reveals his secrets. Now let's go."

"That's true," Josh said. "But let's face it, you're not a good magician."

"Okay, let's see you do it," smirked Scott.

"Well, except for that trick, you stink as a magician. So just tell me how you do it."

"Nope. Can't. Will not. See ya, wouldn't want to be ya," Scott said as he headed for the door. Josh spent the next fifteen minutes begging Scott to show him how he did the trick. Finally their father arrived.

"Hi, boys, it's time to go," he said.

"We're coming, Dad," they all said in unison.

The whole family walked to the car and settled in for the two-hour drive home. The conversation during the ride went as usual with all the same questions Scott's mother and father normally asked. It was wonderful to be with his family again, but Scott couldn't help looking at his mother differently. He made up his mind to talk to her about Lumen sometime during his Christmas vacation, but didn't know for sure, when or even how, to bring up the topic.

When they finally arrived home, Eric and Scott put their bags away and headed downstairs to help with dinner. While Scott was setting the table, Josh decided to join him. "Scott, show me how you do that trick and I'll give you some of my Christmas candy," he bribed.

"Nice try, runt."

"Okay, you drive a hard bargain. I'll give you all my Christmas candy."

"Not gonna happen."

That night, they ate one of the best dinners Scott and Eric had eaten in a long time. After the meal was over, the family headed into Munich to see the Weinachtsmarkt, or Christmas Market. From the beginning of Advent until Christmas, booths and stalls were set up in the marketplaces in many German cities. Here, people could buy everything they needed for Christmas, such as Christmas trees, decorations, candles for the tree, crib figures, gingerbread, and presents for Christmas Eve. The lights and the fresh smell of gingerbread made this one of the Frontier family's favorite things to do during the Christmas season. They purchased some gingerbread men to eat later on, some candles for their Christmas tree, and several other knick-knacks. Scott purchased a ceramic white elephant for Azinine, which his family thought was a little odd. When they asked him whom it was for, he simply told them it was for a friend at school who liked elephants.

The next couple of days were spent shopping and getting ready for Christmas. When Christmas Eve arrived they sat down to a wonderful turkey dinner, after which, they sang Christmas carols around the piano while Mrs. Frontier played. When they grew tired of singing, Josh just had to show them his newest tricks.

"For my first trick, I'll make this cup of milk disappear." He picked up a black hat that was sitting on the table, "See, nothing inside, " he said holding the hat up so they could see the inside. He then placed the hat back on the table. Next, he picked up a cup of milk and poured it into the hat. He picked up his wand and tapped it on the hat. "voilà, " he said. Then he lifted the hat and it tipped sideways to show them the milk had disappeared. Everyone started to clap, but it soon turned to laughter as a large, black sponge, filled with milk, fell out of the hat.

"Whoops," Josh muttered.

"Josh, you forgot your own advice," Scott said teasingly. "A magician never reveals his secrets."

"Very funny," Josh replied. "Let's go sleigh riding and I'll make you disappear in my dust."

"Good idea," their father piped in.

By the time they were finished sledding, everyone was cold and exhausted. At home once again, they all enjoyed a cup of hot chocolate and then Mrs. Frontier sent the boys off to bed. While their father was pulling out presents and getting things set up for the next morning, the boys' mother was making her nightly rounds, saying good night to each of them.

When she came to Scott she gave him a hug and a kiss and was about to walk out of the room, but thought better and sat down on the edge of his bed. "It's good to have you back for a while. I understand you've made a new friend." It was a statement, not a question.

"Did Headmaster McDougal tell you that?" Scott asked.

"Yes. He told me she's introduced you to Lumen."

"Then you are from Lumen?" Scott asked curiously.

"Yes, son, I am."

"It's a pretty great place. How come you've kept it a secret all these years?"

"What would you have done if I'd told you that I was from another world? You would have thought I was loony," she said with a smile.

"True, it is strange," Scott agreed. "Even so, I still think you should have tried."

"Perhaps. But you wouldn't have understood while you were young. And once you got older, I wasn't sure how you would handle it, especially if your friends found out."

"Are you ever going to tell Dad?"

"Your father? Oh, he's known about Lumen since before we were married. I've even taken him there before, just once, so he could see for himself. He didn't believe me at first either. He and I agreed it would be best no one else knew about my past, so he has always treated me as though he didn't know."

"Is your real name Hollie?" he continued.

"No. My real name is Valar."

"Lumen is a pretty place. Do you ever want to go back?"

"Not really. There isn't anything there for me now. Thoughts of Lumen just bring back horrible memories of the day my father was killed. I was young when I left, so this world seems more like home than Lumen."

"Mom," Scott sighed, "I want to spend more time there. I want to explore it and learn more about it. But everyone seems to think I'm in danger there. They have this crazy idea that people there are out to get me because I look like the High King."

"It's not crazy," his mother replied. "They won't take any chances. If they feel you might be a candidate, they will try and kill you," she said. She smiled at him and then said, "From what Linus told me, I think you've handled everything much better than most. Someday a High King will be chosen and it will be safe for you to visit Lumen. However, for the time being, I think it would be wise for you to stay in this world."

"But…"

"Good night, Son," she said, cutting him off. He sighed and rolled over, thinking about what she had just said.

He was almost asleep when he heard a noise. "Psst. Scott, you still awake?" Rolling over, he saw Josh standing in his doorway.

"What do you want?"

"I'll do all your chores for the next couple months if you show me the trick."

"You're already doing all my chores."

"All right, name your price then."

"You don't have enough money."

"Show me that trick and I'll be able to earn enough money."

"Go to bed, Josh. If Santa finds you still awake, he won't leave you anything."

"Very funny," Josh mumbled and headed back to his room.

The next morning was spent opening presents and oohing and ahhing over the gifts. After all the gifts had been exchanged, they spent the rest of the day, and the rest of the week, putting puzzles together, sleigh riding, and taking in a movie now and again. Every once in a while, Josh offered to give Scott one of his gifts or something else in return for the secret to his magic trick, but Scott always refused. Scott was enjoying Josh's torment tremendously.

It wasn't long before the Christmas vacation came to a close and they were headed back to school. It had been a wonderful week, and Scott was glad to spend the time with his family and talk openly with his mother about Lumen. However, he was also excited to get back to CastleOne. He missed Azinine and wanted to see her again.

Chapter Nine

Disappearance

When Scott walked into his dorm, he found Ned already there. "Hey, Scott. Did you have a good vacation?" Ned asked him.

"I sure did. How about you?"

"Yeah, it was good to spend some time back home."

Scott put his bags down and quickly opened his drawer to check the bracelet. None of the stones were lit and a wave of disappointment washed over him as he lay down on his bed.

"I saw your girlfriend while I was at home," Ned remarked.

Scott sat back up. "She's not my girlfriend! Did she say anything about me?"

"More than I ever wanted to hear."

"What did she say?"

"She said you were the most handsome guy she had ever met and wants to spend the rest of her life with you. She is miserable when she's not around you and thinks about you all day and all night," Ned said, mimicking a girl's voice.

"She did?" Scott said, feeling better.

"No. But I thought I'd give you something to dream about," laughed Ned.

"You're dead meat!" Scott growled. He jumped up and began pulverizing Ned with his pillow. The two beat up on each other for a while, until they were laughing so hard they couldn't breathe. Scott jumped back onto his own bed. "Ned, you really shouldn't play with a guy's heart like that, it could get you killed."

"You really like her, don't you?" Ned asked.

"We're just friends, but I have to admit I've never met anyone like her before."

"Do you find yourself always thinking about her?"

"Yeah, sometimes."

"Do you find yourself always wanting to be with her?"

"Cut it out, Ned."

"I knew it! You're in love. I guess I should give this to you then." Ned pulled a letter out from under his mattress.

"What's that?" Scott asked.

"It's a letter from your princess."

"Very funny," Scott said as he jumped up and grabbed the letter out of Ned's hand. He opened it and realized that the words on the page were not written in English. Maybe what Ned had told him about being lingual really was true. Despite the fact that the words were written in Lumen, he was still able to read them.

> *Scott — I hope you had a great time with your family. Family is very important. You are also very important to me and it would hurt me if you were ever harmed. For this reason, I can't see you for a while. Things are getting worse here and we must be careful. I know that's very uncharacteristic of me, but that should convince you even more. If I feel things are dangerous, then you can bet they are. I don't know how long it will be before I can see you again, but I will contact you when things get worked out.*
>
> *Sincerely,*
> *Azinine*

Scott's heart sank and soared at the same time. He couldn't bear the thought of not seeing her again, but on the other hand, the letter was proof she cared for him. He lay there thinking about it, a very mellow mood washing over him. He was half tempted to go find her. He didn't care about the danger, he wanted to see her. However, in the end, good judgment won and he decided he would wait. If she did care for him, she would contact him. Ned seemed to sense what the letter had said and kept quiet, leaving his friend to his own thoughts.

Scott must have been tired because he fell asleep in his clothes and didn't wake up until the alarm clock rang the next morning. Ned was gone as usual. Scott crawled out of bed, put on some clean clothes, and headed down to breakfast. He found Eric and his friends already there, seated at a table in the corner. He picked up some food and joined them.

"Hey, Scott," Eric said, along with several others at the table.

"Hi," Scott replied in a less than enthusiastic voice.

"Are you okay?" Eric asked.

"Yeah, I'm just tired," Scott lied. Eric nodded. He didn't believe Scott, but he knew better than to try and pry it out of him. The group chatted about what each other did over Christmas vacation, but Scott wasn't in the mood, so he ate in silence.

Once Scott finished his breakfast, he headed out to drill. He found Tina and Nancy standing outside by the endurance courses, but Ned was not with them. "Hi, Tina. Hi, Nancy. Did you guys have a good holiday?" Scott asked.

"Not me," Tina said with a forced frown on her face. She walked up and put her arms around Scott's neck. "It would have been better if I'd had someone to kiss under the mistletoe," she teased.

Scott knew she was just teasing him, so he decided to play her game. He put his arms around her back and looked into her eyes. "Well maybe we should get some mistletoe then."

"Who needs mistletoe?" she said and laid a big fat kiss on him. Scott jerked away, surprised she had done that.

"Tina!" Ned yelled. Ned had arrived just in time to witness the kiss. His yell also got the attention of everyone else standing around, causing Scott to turn beet red in the face.

Nancy instantly jumped up and took Tina's place. "I'm next. Get in line, girls!" she yelled. Scott wasn't about to play this game any longer. Tina had taken him completely by surprise. By the time he gathered his wits, several other girls had lined up, obviously catching the spirit of the joke and wanting to join in the fun.

"I'm sorry, girls, but my shift is over." He grabbed Ned and stuck him in front of them. "Ned's on duty now."

"Dog pile on Ned!" Tina yelled and tackled him. The other girls joined in and soon Ned was smothered. Tina started to kiss him on the head and the other girls were laughing hysterically. Ned was obviously embarrassed, but Scott was pretty sure he was enjoying himself.

"Georgie Porgie, pudding and pie, kissed the girls and made them cry," Turner mockingly sang as Tina got up. "Now we know who the easy girls are," he said, looking at Tina and laughing. This infuriated Ned, and still on the ground, he whirled his body around and kicked Turner's feet out from underneath him, knocking him flat on his back. Turner landed with a grunt, but got up and lunged forward in an effort to punch Ned, but Scott caught him from behind, jerking him backwards. Turner whirled on Scott, throwing a punch at him. Scott easily dodged it and was about to let Turner have it when a whistle blew. This was a good thing for Scott, because several Badgers were on their way over to assist Turner.

"Break it up!" Buzz yelled. "Frontier, how come every time there's trouble, you seem to be involved?" Scott took in a deep breath but knew better than to say anything. Buzz decided to let this episode slide, so he continued, "All right! Today we're going to run the endurance courses. I want the Badgers in the first two lanes and the Falcons in the last two lanes. Let's line up!" he boomed out. The students obeyed and Scott noticed that Turner had lined up in the same slot as him. Scott shook his head. This was obviously Turner's way of making himself feel superior to Scott.

Buzz's voice boomed out again. "Okay, people. Even though the snow has melted away, the course may still be wet and slippery. So, be careful!" He blew his whistle and off they went. The race was pretty close, and by the time it was Scott's turn, the Falcons were ahead by just a couple of yards. He took off, moving as fast as he could, determined to beat Turner this time.

He did the tires with ease, but the ropes caught him and slowed him down just a little. The wall also gave him trouble, and by the time he reached the balance beam Turner had caught up and was passing him. Frustrated with his performance, he pushed himself harder and in the process, slipped. This allowed Turner to pass him and cross the finish line before he did. Scott crossed the line trying to ignore Turner, but Turner wasn't about to let this opportunity pass. "It's nice to know you still run like a girl, Frontier. It will make the competition that much easier," he taunted.

"Actually, Turner, being the nice, merciful guy that I am, I purposely lost. I didn't want everyone to think you're a total loser. Just call it my charitable act for the day," Scott retorted.

"Purposely lost, huh? That's a good one, Frontier. My five-year old brother uses that sometimes, but I never thought I'd hear it from a loser like you. Oh, that's right, the Falcons always make excuses."

"If you think it's just an excuse," Scott said smiling, "then let's make a wager."

"What sort of a wager?"

"You and I will race alone. If I win, you have to apologize on bended knee to Ned and Tina and then kiss their feet during dinner, in front of everyone."

"And if I win?" Turner asked.

"You name it," Scott replied.

"You have to sing the Badger victory song tonight during dinner, standing on a table."

"You're on. Meet me out here an hour after classes."

"Get ready to sing," Turner replied and walked away.

"Scott, are you crazy?" Ned asked.

"Yeah, Scott," Tina interjected, "it's a very nice gesture, but you haven't been able to beat Turner yet. What makes you think you can beat him tonight?"

Scott hesitated for a moment and then answered with a sly smile on his face, "You guys wait. Turner won't know what hit him. Besides, I don't really have anything to lose. Turner has a lot to lose and I'm betting he's going to choke."

"If those are the kind of bets you make, then I've got a couple I'd like to get in on," Ned replied, shaking his head.

"Where's your faith?" Scott asked them.

"Don't worry. We'll be rooting for you," they both assured him.

After school, Scott was shocked to see a large crowd outside anticipating the event. Turner had even recruited Buzz to start and judge the race. "You've done it now, Frontier," Buzz told him. "But I would rather see this than you two fighting."

Just then Turner walked up. "Well, let's not postpone this any longer. I'm starving and I hear we have some really good entertainment for dinner tonight," he sneered.

"I'm ready when you are," Scott replied.

Buzz ushered them over to the starting line, told them to keep things clean, and put his whistle to his mouth. The crowd went silent with only a whisper here and there. "On your marks, get set," and the whistle blew.

Scott and Turner shot off the line. Scott and Turner both flew across the tires about even. Turner barely beat him under the ropes.

However, Scott overtook Turner at the wall, practically flying over it with a single pull. He looked back to see Turner just climbing over it. He considered slowing down, but decided not to take any chances losing. He practically floated across the balance beam, and handled the jungle gym skipping two bars at a time. He crossed the stumps as though they were simply a hopscotch board. When he finished, he glanced back to see Turner still at the jungle gym.

Most of the Badgers were silent, but the Falcons were going nuts, and Scott could hear Eric and his friends screaming. It didn't take long for them to reach him and tackle him to the ground. Soon, other Falcons were gathered around congratulating him. When Scott finally stood up, he searched the crowd for Turner. What he saw almost made him regret his victory. Turner looked as though he was about to cry. Not only had Scott beat him, but he had done it by at least twenty seconds. Added to that, Turner had let his division down and none of them were speaking to him. Worst of all, Turner knew what was still to come.

Scott and Ned were heading towards the dorms when Buzz approached them. "I don't know how you did it," he said, "but that was the most amazing performance I have ever seen. Do you know you broke the school record?"

"I did?" Scott asked.

"Yes, and I don't think anyone will ever beat it."

"Including Scott," Ned chimed in. "Congratulations!…on a well run, *honest race*," Ned said, emphasizing the last two words as the two of them departed from Buzz.

"Thank you," Scott replied somewhat hesitantly, and the two of them continued towards the dorm.

"I hope you feel good about this," Ned said, looking at Scott in an accusing way.

"Shouldn't I?" Scott questioned.

"No. You know as well as I do, you cheated."

"I don't know what you're talking about," Scott replied with a grin on his face.

"Then sit down and let me check out those shoes of yours," challenged Ned.

"Ned, he needed to be taught a lesson. I simply used the tools I had to teach that lesson," Scott argued.

"I know and the lesson was well taught. But don't you feel a little ashamed of yourself?"

"I don't feel at all bad about Turner. The school record, on the other hand, is obviously undeserved. I hadn't considered that aspect of it."

"Well, I guess there really isn't anything you can do about it now. You'd do more damage if you told the truth," warned Ned.

"Agreed."

"I have to admit, I'm surprised Azinine would lend those to you. There aren't many left. They're pretty valuable, you know."

"So I've heard. Why aren't there more of them?"

"The magus who created them didn't tell anyone else how he did it. Many have tried to duplicate them but haven't quite accomplished it. While he was alive they sold like hotcakes, but when he died his secret died with him. As time went on, they were either lost, stolen, or who knows? You just don't see many people using them anymore. My guess is the trolls have taken them little by little."

"Trolls?" Scott asked.

"Trolls love to collect things. They take, or rather steal, items from people whenever they're given the chance. They have even been known to ransack whole villages before, but not very often. Mostly, they just catch unwary travelers by surprise."

Scott was interested but realized he still had to collect on his bet. "I'd like to know more about this," he said, "but right now I've got to get showered and into the dining hall."

A short while later, the dining hall was packed with students. Scott looked everywhere for Turner, but couldn't find him. He wondered if Turner would even show up. As he waited, Tina and Ned walked in and sat down by him.

"Hi," they both said simultaneously.

"Hi," he replied.

"We saw Turner down by our dorms," Tina said. "He doesn't look too well."

"I still want him to make the apology, but maybe we should let him do it in private. Would you mind?" Scott asked.

"No. We feel kind of silly anyway," Tina said with a trace of relief in her voice.

"Come on, follow me," Scott said.

They walked over to where Eric and his friends were celebrating their own little victory. "Eric," Scott said, "we're going to save Turner the humiliation and do this in private. Give us about five minutes and then announce the ceremony has already taken place."

Eric hesitated for a moment, looking at Scott's face. "You're a good man, little brother," Eric said sincerely.

Scott nodded, and the three of them headed down towards the Badgers' dorm. Along the way, they ran into Turner and Bear heading towards the dining hall. "What's this? Did you get tired of waiting for me? You couldn't wait to humiliate me?" Turner asked in a very disgruntled voice.

Scott was tempted to change his mind, but didn't. "Actually, Turner," he said, "I came to give you a choice. We can either continue back to the dining hall and proceed with our original agreement, or you can sincerely apologize right now and we'll forego the public humiliation and the foot kissing."

Turner stood there in shocked silence, but Scott could see the relief in his face.

"Don't look a gift horse in the mouth," Bear said, slugging him on the shoulder.

"There's no other catch? You really just want an apology for your friends?" Turner asked.

"Turner, Tina was just goofing around, having fun. What you said to her was rude and she deserves an apology."

Turner looked at Tina, hesitated only for a moment, and said sincerely, "Tina, I'm sorry. I didn't really mean what I said. I have a habit of opening my mouth when I shouldn't. Will you forgive me?"

Tina walked closer to Turner. "Apology accepted," she said. "But, I still want you to kiss my feet." Turner hesitated, but slowly moved forward and knelt down to kiss her foot. Just before his lips touched, Tina pulled back. "You were really going to do it, weren't you?" she asked.

"But you said…," Turner began to say, but was cut off.

"You're just as easy as I am," she laughed.

"I was just trying to do what I had to. You know, to apologize," he replied.

By this time everyone was laughing except for Turner. Tina walked up to Turner and gave him a hug, saying, "I know you were, and I'm sorry I did that. It was a mean thing to do. I just wanted to make sure you were sincere. Next time, though, will you do me a favor?"

"Sure. what?"

"Make the apology without someone coercing you. If you really are sorry, it will mean a lot more to the person."

"I'm not very good at apologies, but I'll try."

"Okay!" Bear interjected. "Now that we are all one happy family, can we please go to dinner? I'm starved."

"Bear, if you don't mind, I think I'll pass. If I don't have to show up at dinner tonight, I don't think I want to," Turner replied.

"Do you want us to bring you something?" asked Scott.

"If you don't mind," Turner replied eagerly. "I really could use some food."

"Sure thing. We'll meet you back at your dorm entrance in about ten minutes."

Over the next few weeks, Scott and his friends spent hours and hours after dinner training for some preliminary contests coming up. These contests were trial runs for the competitions taking place at the end of the year. This made getting homework done more difficult, but Scott managed.

Friday afternoon, after classes had let out and he was just hanging out in his room, Scott heard the inaudible sound from the bracelet. He ran over to the drawer and looked inside. He couldn't believe it. Both stones were glowing. Azinine was in the council room at that very moment! Scott had a hard time containing his excitement. He quickly put on the winged boots and headed down to the council room. He walked inside expecting some new trick to besiege him, but this time Azinine was sitting on the chair with a glowing Lumenarty rock in her hand. As Scott entered, she jumped up, ran over to him, and gave him a big hug.

"Hi," he said with a big grin.

"Hello, yourself," she replied as she let go of him. "How are you?"

"Pretty good. How come it's taken you so long to visit?"

"Things are bad, Scott. People are looking for you. Several have tried to question me at my home and once even in the city. I didn't dare risk coming here. I was too afraid someone might follow me and I didn't want to lead them to you."

"Have things calmed down? Is that why you're here now?" Scott asked hopefully.

"No, but I wanted to see you," she answered with a shy smile. "I snuck out early this morning while it was still dark. I hid in the castle for hours, watching to make sure nobody followed me, and when I was absolutely sure no one had, I came. Besides, you still have the winged boots and I need to get them back."

"I have them on right now," Scott said. "Can we play tag one more time before I give them back?"

Azinine had to think about that for a while. "I don't think it would be wise to play in the clouds," she finally answered, "but we could play it in the forest for a little bit."

"Then let's go," Scott said, leading her in the direction of the chair. They both sat down and Azinine gave the word. Once in the council room of Cylindhall, they climbed off the chair and made their way outside.

Before they left the castle, Azinine checked to make sure no one was around. Then she turned back to Scott. "We can't play around here, it's too risky. However, The Great Forest is not too far from here. If we take my MOC, we can probably be there in an hour." The two of them quickly made their way out to the stables, climbed aboard Azinine's MOC, and took off. She rose as high in the sky as she could. She knew they would be easier to spot, but at the same time, it would be harder to recognize them. Besides, MOCs were common-place and no one would take much notice.

"Show me how you fly this thing," Scott asked.

"Okay," she said and began to teach him the various commands. She explained up and down, left and right, and so on. After she was sure he had it down, she let him take control. He practiced flying the MOC, directing it down into a steep dive and then directing it straight up. The MOC itself didn't tip in a downward or upward direction, it just fell and rose but stayed horizontal the whole time, though it did tip slightly sideward when he turned sharply left or right.

This is better than any amusement ride, he thought.

About sixty minutes later, with Azinine coaching him, they dropped down into a thick forest at the foot of a large mountain range. Off to the east, Scott could see a small village not too far away, but other than that it was almost all forest.

"Wow!" he said in awe. "This is some forest. Look at the size of these trees."

"Yeah, it's easy to get lost. I come here sometimes when I want to be alone," Azinine confided.

"I can see why," Scott replied.

"Did you see that tall Iker tree as we came in? The one that's taller than all the others?"

"Iker tree?"

"Yes, that's what it's called. We use that as a marker to ensure we stay in this area. Don't stray much farther than three or four hundred yards from that tree, okay?"

"Okay," he agreed.

Azinine smiled at him. "I'll be 'it' first, you go ahead and hide."

Scott nodded and took off into the trees and eventually rose above them. He could see the Iker tree she had mentioned. He decided to change directions and head back the way he had come and then dip down just below the tree line. When he reached an area he felt had lots of cover, he slowly let himself down into the trees. As he did so, he could see Azinine some way off still waiting. Finally she took off in the direction he had originally gone and disappeared from his sight. This was what he was hoping she would do. He now peered upward out of the trees, waiting for her to rise above them, but she never appeared.

"This is my home! leave!" a voice yelled at Scott from below. He looked down, but didn't see anyone. "Oh no, it's happening again," he muttered. "I'm starting to hear voices. Just ignore them, just ignore them," he repeated to himself. Scott looked for Azinine, but she had disappeared.

She must be up to something, Scott thought. *If she isn't above the trees, then she is obviously below them, but where?* Not knowing where she was made him uncomfortable. He was getting fidgety and wanted to find out. Besides, that voice kept telling him to leave. He decided to slowly fly just above the tree line. This way he could look down and try to assess her location. As he floated along, he looked backwards every once in a while to make sure she didn't come up behind him.

The trees were pretty thick and it wasn't easy to see the ground clearly. As he neared the Iker tree, his eye caught something just below the tree line, but he couldn't quite tell what it was. It looked like some sort of bird. He was straining to see when something from just below the tree line grabbed his foot. It was Azinine. She had waited there very patiently for him to stumble across her and then nailed him.

"Gotcha! You're it," she yelled and then disappeared toward the ground. Scott felt like a fool. He had stumbled right into her trap. Rather than chase directly after her, he decided to fly above the trees in her direction and then dive below. Perhaps he'd be able to cut her off. He darted towards her as quickly as possible, found a gap in the trees, and dove. Halfway down he stopped, hoping to see any movement at all, but everything was still. This was much harder than playing tag in the clouds. There were more places to hide and a lot more objects, like branches, to avoid. He landed on a branch, trying to come up with a strategy to flush her out. In the end, he decided to hide and scream really loud. Azinine would think he was in trouble and come to find him.

"Ahhhhhhhhh!" he screamed.

Sure enough, Azinine appeared within seconds. "Scott! Are you okay?" she yelled out. When she looked away from his direction, he shot out and darted towards her, slapping her on the back. "You're it!" he hollered.

"Oh, that was cheap!" she protested and shot after him. They flew around trees, up through branches, over the treetops, back down again, and around more trees. They looked like a couple of squirrels chasing each other. He flew up to a branch and looked around, but Azinine wasn't behind him. *Where did she go?* he wondered. He couldn't see her below the tree line, so either she was hiding or she was above the tree line. Scott decided to fly lower to the ground and hide. He'd waited there for about five minutes when he heard a blood-curdling scream coming from above the trees.

"Does she think I'm stupid? I'm not falling for my own trick," Scott snorted to himself.

"Help!" he heard her yell, her voice sounding a bit more distant this time. But Scott wasn't going to be fooled.

This is Azinine's world, she's a skilled witch and can fly. It has to be a trick, he thought. But he couldn't help wondering if she really was in trouble. Her scream had sounded real enough. After hiding for another minute or so, he decided he would rather look like a fool than risk Azinine getting hurt. He shot up through the trees and above the tree line. He looked everywhere, but Azinine couldn't be seen.

Thinking she might be down on the forest floor, he headed back down to the ground and landed. Still, he couldn't see Azinine anywhere. He made himself as visible as possible, hoping she would come after him, but she never did. "Azinine!" he yelled. "Come out!" He waited for her to appear, but she never did. He wondered if perhaps she'd hit a branch and was lying unconscious somewhere. He spent several hours looking for her, but to no avail.

About this time, Scott noticed it was almost dark and he became fearful. Azinine had said the woods could be dangerous at night and he didn't know the way back. Even more frightening was being all alone in a world he knew little about. After yelling for Azinine several more times and getting no reaction, he realized she really wasn't nearby. He decided to head for the village he had seen when they first arrived; at least there he would be safe…maybe. He was about to take off when he noticed her MOC still sitting where they had left it. Walking over to it, he rolled it up and lifted it off the ground. To his surprise, it was extremely light. Using the boots, he rose into the air and landed on a large branch of an Iker tree. He set the MOC down and after making sure it was secure, he shot into the air. *Crack!* In the darkness he had not seen the branch above him and had slammed into it. Scott felt a searing pain move through his body. *Not again* he thought. He started to slowly fall, glancing off a branch here and a branch there. He was starting to feel dizzy and he struggled to keep conscious. He hit another branch and finally slammed onto the ground. He tried to get up, but lost his balance and then lost consciousness.

Chapter Ten

Churp

A hot breeze blew across his face, waking Scott up. He was sure it was morning even though his eyes were still shut. When he opened them, he let out a startled yelp. There were two eyes staring directly into his own, only inches from his face. At the sound of his scream the other pair of eyes quickly retreated. When he finally focused, he saw a girl who looked about nine or ten years old sitting next to him. Just then a door opened and in walked a woman.

"Fia, shame on you! Please move away from our guest," she scolded. Then, turning to Scott, "How are you feeling?"

Scott noticed he was in a bedroom, but had no recollection of how he got there. "Where am I?" he asked.

"You are in Churp."

"Churp?"

"Our village is called Churp. We found you unconscious in the forest, and, I might add, you're lucky we did. You were badly hurt, and who knows what might have happened to you?" she said in a motherly tone. "My name is Glora, and this is my daughter Fia. May we have the pleasure of knowing your name?"

Scott opened his mouth to speak and then realized he didn't know. "I'm not sure," he replied. "I can't really remember anything."

"You hit your head pretty hard," Glora said. "It may take a few days for you to regain your memory. In the meantime, we'll let you rest and I'll get some breakfast." With that, she ushered Fia out the door and closed it behind her.

Scott tried as hard as he could to recall anything about himself. He had no idea who he was, or where he was, or anything else for that matter. He lay there for several minutes trying over and over again, but to no avail.

As he looked around, Scott noticed the house was lit with the glowing Lumenarty rocks. "Azinine!" he said out loud, remembering a girl named Azinine. Somewhere in the back of his mind, he vaguely remembered seeing Azinine with a glowing rock just like the ones in the room. Deciding that he was hungry and that lying there wasn't helping any, he got out of bed and made his way into the kitchen.

"I see you can at least walk. That's a good sign. Now let's see if you can eat," Glora commented as she bustled around the kitchen.

"I'm sure I can eat, but are you sure this isn't too much trouble?" Scott asked.

"Of course not," she replied. She set a bowl of porridge and a slice of bread in front of him. Scott quickly discovered just how hungry he was as he dug into the food, and soon had a second bowl of porridge placed in front of him. After filling his stomach, he began to wonder again about himself and his surroundings. "How long have I been here?" he asked.

Glora answered with a smile. "Almost two days. We were wondering if you were ever going to wake up."

Wow, two days, he thought to himself. "Thank you for caring for me and thank you for this food, it was wonderful."

His head began to ache again and he decided to lie back down and rest. He slept most of the day and woke that evening to the sound of voices.

"As long as he's here sleeping in our bed and eating our food, I don't think it's wrong to ask him to lend a hand around here. I could certainly use the help," he heard a man's voice say.

"I still think it's taking advantage. The poor boy doesn't even know who he is." He recognized Glora's voice.

"Then he doesn't really have anywhere to go, does he?" the man argued.

"I suppose not," Glora sighed. "But I don't want you to be angry if he's not up to it. He's had a bad accident, and I don't think he should do any work for a while."

"We'll let him determine how he feels. If he doesn't feel up to it, then I won't ask him to help."

"Agreed," he heard Glora say.

The kitchen became quiet except for the clanking of dishes, and Scott knew they must be eating dinner. He was feeling hungry again, but wasn't sure he wanted to join them just yet. He felt guilty being in their home, using one of their beds and eating their food. He wanted to repay them and the man was right. He didn't have anywhere else to go that he knew of. He lay there for about thirty minutes and then decided his hunger was greater than his guilt. He got up and walked into the kitchen.

Only Glora was there and she greeted him with a smile. "Are you feeling better?" she asked.

"Yes, thank you," Scott replied. His head was still hurting, but he wanted to help and knew Glora wouldn't allow it if she knew.

"So, where's Fia?" Scott asked.

"My husband owns a guesthouse down the street. He and Fia are there taking care of our customers. They'll be back soon."

"What's a guesthouse?" Scott asked.

Glora gave him a strange look, and then remembering he had amnesia she explained, "A guesthouse is a place where travelers can stay the night and get food while they are away."

"Oh, that makes sense," Scott replied.

Glora walked over to him with a plate in her hands. "While you are waiting for the stew to warm up, here's some bread you can eat."

"Are you sure I'm not being too much trouble?" Scott asked.

"I'm positive," she reassured him.

As Scott was eating, the door opened and in walked Fia and, Scott assumed, her father. The man strode over, his hand extended in friendship. Halfway across the room, he froze and stared at Scott. Scott stood up, waiting expectantly for some sort of welcome.

Finally the man spoke. "I apologize for my actions, but you bear an amazing likeness to the late High King. Please sit down. My name is Amalic," he introduced himself while gesturing towards Scott's chair.

Scott remembered other people saying that same thing to him before. The name Polimar suddenly came to him, but he couldn't remember who this Polimar was. "Did you know the High King?" Scott asked.

"Yes. He visited our village several times. I even had the privilege of serving him food and giving him lodging," Amalic boasted.

"Do you know a man named Polimar?" Scott asked.

"I know of a magus named Polimar," Amalic replied. "Why do you ask?"

Scott creased his forehead, trying to think. "I remember he also told me I looked like the High King, but I can't remember who he is."

"He lives in the city Lux, not too far from here. Perhaps I should take you to him. Maybe he could help you remember who you are."

"Yes, perhaps," Scott replied.

"I'm heading to a city near Lux in five days. I could take you to him, if you would like?"

"I guess it wouldn't hurt," shrugged Scott.

Scott woke up the next morning feeling much better. His head was healing quickly and it no longer thumped like it had the day before. In the kitchen he found Glora, once again bustling around fixing breakfast. She served him some food and while he ate, he listened to Amalic and Fia argue over a trip Amalic was planning. Fia was set on going with him and Amalic was determined that it was too dangerous.

"We'll talk about this later, Fia. The trip isn't for some time yet," Amalic finally said, trying to end the argument. They ate in silence until Amalic turned to Scott. "How are you feeling today, young man?"

"I'm feeling much better, thanks to all of you. I don't know how I can thank you," Scott answered.

"Actually, there is something you could do," Amalic began.

"Remember, Amalic. He is our guest and has no obligations to us," Glora quickly interrupted.

"Scott!" Scott suddenly yelled out.

"What was that?" Glora asked.

"My name is Scott. It just came to me." Then glancing around sheepishly, he said, "I'm sorry, you were saying you needed some help?"

"Yes, Scott. I have several barrels of ale I need to move down to the cellar of my store. I could use some help moving them," Amalic said, ignoring the frown on Glora's face.

"I would love to help," Scott replied. "Would you like to do that now?"

"Just let me gather a few things and we can be on our way." Amalic grabbed a leather rucksack and his jacket and then waved Scott towards the door.

"Glora, thank you for the breakfast," Scott said as he headed out into the sunshine.

Scott and Amalic walked outside into the crisp morning air. The sun was rising and Scott could hear birds singing. He thought about how peaceful the village was and what a wonderful life the villagers must live. They walked about ten minutes and soon arrived at the guesthouse. They walked inside to find several people eating and making simple conversation with each other.

"Before we start moving the barrels, I want to introduce you to one of my cooks. Her name is Moranda. She knew the High King better than most because she used to cook for him. I'm dying to see the look on her face when she sees you," Amalic chuckled.

Scott wondered if this might have been the main reason Amalic wanted his help, but he didn't mind. They walked into the kitchen, where Scott could see a woman washing dishes with her back to them.

"Moranda, look who I've brought back from the dead," Amalic announced.

Moranda turned and gave a small cry, dropping her scrub brush.

"Hello, Moranda. It's so good to see you again," Scott said, playing along.

"Impossible! What sort of wizardry is this?" she cried out, her eyes wide.

Amalic started to laugh. "Calm down, Moranda. His name is Scott and he's here to help me. His likeness to the High King is uncanny, isn't it?"

"Yes, though a much younger version," she replied, still staring at Scott in unbelief.

"It's nice to meet you," Scott said. "Sorry for the scare."

Scott spent the rest of the week helping Amalic with various chores around the guesthouse and around the house. With each passing day, Scott was slowly getting his memory back. Images of his own family and their names were becoming clearer. He didn't mention his recall to Glora or Amalic, simply because it was a good excuse to avoid questions he didn't have the answers to. By the fifth day he could remember just about everything, including the incident in the forest and the disappearance of Azinine. This memory caused him great anxiety. He needed to find out what had happened to her.

He decided it was time to leave. As he was preparing, he suddenly remembered the winged boots and realized they were no longer on his feet and nowhere in sight. He determined he would get some break-fast and ask Glora if she knew where they were. When he walked into the eating room, Glora, Amalic, and Fia were all sitting down just about ready to eat.

"Good morning, Scott," Glora said. "Did you sleep well?"

"Yes, thank you. I slept better than I have in a long time," he replied. He sat down and Glora handed him some breakfast. While he ate, he rehearsed in his mind how he would tell them he was leaving, but he couldn't quite find the right words. In the end, he decided it would be best if he just came right out and said it.

"Thank you so much for everything," Scott began as he finished the last of his food. "You have all been so kind. I wish I could do something in return and perhaps someday I will. However, I feel I must find out who I am and I think Magus Polimar may have those answers." He turned to Amalic, asking, "Isn't this the day you are heading that way?"

"Yes, but are you sure you know Magus Polimar?" Amalic asked. "He's a very important man and may not see you unless there's a good reason."

"I'll have to take that risk," Scott replied, continuing his act of amnesia. "Something tells me I must speak with him."

"Okay," Amalic agreed. "I'll be happy to take you there. But first, we must stop off at the guesthouse and pick up some supplies."

"One more thing," Scott added. "When you brought me here and removed my shoes, did you find a pair of..."

"Socks?" Glora quickly interrupted. "Yes, let me show you where they are."

"No, not...," Scott began again.

"I know exactly where they are. Don't you worry," Glora said, once again interrupting him and leading him out of the kitchen. Scott was a little perplexed by her actions. He wasn't missing a pair of socks, he was missing the winged boots.

They entered the room where Scott had been staying. Once inside, Glora shut the door and turned to him. "I have your boots, but did not tell Amalic you had them. He's a good man. But these boots are rare and worth a lot of money. I feared he would take them and not give them back."

"Oh, thank you," Scott said, breathing a sigh of relief. "They actually don't belong to me. I would feel terrible if I lost them."

Scott slipped the boots on over his shoes and they both walked out of the room. Scott met Amalic outside, and the two of them walked down the road towards the guesthouse. On their way there, they passed two rough-looking men who seemed to watch Scott with more interest than Scott liked.

Amalic had apparently noticed it also. "Do you know those men?" he asked.

"No, not that I know."

"Good. You don't want to either."

"Why? Who are they?"

"They'd never admit it, but I'm almost certain they belong to the band of Lardior."

"The band of Lardior?"

"I forgot, you have amnesia. The band of Lardior was originally established by a group of outlaw robbers who would secretly rob and plunder to get riches. Their leader is a warlock by the name of Lardior, thus the name of the band. Since then, men wanted for all sorts of crimes have joined the band for protection. They have grown very strong. These men are all outlaws and anyone caught professing to belong to the band is prosecuted."

"How do you know they are part of the Lardior band?"

"Owning a guesthouse, you hear more than you should and you get used to seeing all kinds of folks. Members of Lardior's band all have a similar look and use secret signs to identify themselves to each other. I'm not positive those two men are part of the band, but they sure look the part."

Scott nodded and looked back as they continued their way towards the guesthouse. The two men had stopped and were looking at Scott. Once they arrived at the guesthouse, they found Moranda in the kitchen preparing some food for them to take on their journey.

She placed the food in two sacks, one for each of them. The sacks she used looked like normal burlap bags Scott had seen before, but they were, in fact, quite different. They held their shape, like a solid object does, yet at the same time, you could mold them to whatever shape you desired.

"Have a safe trip and we'll see you tomorrow," she said, handing each of them a sack. "It was nice to meet you," she added, turning to Scott.

"Thank you for the food, Moranda. Whatever would I do without you?" Amalic said as he headed for the door.

Moranda smiled. The two of them walked out of the kitchen and into the eating area. Scott noticed the two men were now inside the guesthouse sitting at one of the tables.

"Just ignore them," Amalic told him.

Once outside, Scott looked at how much food he and Amalic were carrying and turned to Amalic, asking, "How far is it to Magus Polimar's house? Are you staying overnight?"

"I don't have a MOC, just a horse and a cart. It will take us about eight hours to reach the city. I won't have enough time to get back before dark, so, yes, I will need to stay the night."

Scott started to feel bad about putting Amalic out like this. "Amalic, you don't really need to do this. Just give me some directions and I can make it by myself."

"Nonsense," Amalic replied. "It is way too far for you to walk. Besides, you'd have to pass by the Black Mountains just north of here. It's a very dangerous place. Who knows what you might run into? That, combined with those two lugs following you, you may never make it." He put their bags in a cart and headed over to some stables, where he soon returned with a horse. Amalic hitched up the horse and they both climbed aboard.

They were almost to the end of town when Amalic suddenly stopped, his body very ridged. "Oh, no! No, it can't be," he said, looking skyward. "Hurry, Scott! Jump out and take cover in those woods over there. I must warn the others."

"Warn the others of what?" Scott asked.

"Go! Take cover!" Amalic yelled once again, only this time much more forcibly. Scott grabbed his sack of food and jumped. Amalic turned the cart around and headed back to town.

"What am I hiding from?" Scott yelled as Amalic turned around.

"Dragon!" Amalic yelled as he took off towards town.

"Did he say 'dragon'?" Scott asked himself. A chill ran down his spine. In his mind, a dragon would be worse than meeting a Tyrannosaurus Rex. Not only did they have sharp claws and teeth like a T-Rex, but if the stories were true, they could fly and breathe fire as well. Scott searched the sky, but couldn't see anything. He must have misunderstood Amalic. There was no dragon.

He was about to turn around and head back towards town when he heard screams from the village. He whirled around to see one of the most horrifying, but majestic, creatures he had ever seen. About fifty yards away was an actual dragon gradually descending to the ground. It was blowing fire in huge long streams, setting houses on fire every-where in its path. It looked more like a giant snake with wings, except it had four legs and a very large head. Its scales were like huge shields glistening in the sun and its feet had talons like those of an eagle, only much larger. Scott could see several women and children taking cover in the forest. He noticed a man in the middle of the main street, quickly leading a cow toward the dragon. As he got closer to the fire-breathing monster, the cow became spooked and pulled away. The dragon leapt into the air, pounced on the cow, and flew off with it clutched in its claws. It blew another fifteen-foot-long stream of fire, lifted higher into the sky, and was gone.

Several of the village folk left their hiding places, and soon a strange contraption was brought out that quickly doused the fires. The entire incident was handled as though this was a regular occurrence. Once the fires were out, Scott went looking for Amalic. Not finding him, he decided to go back to the house to see how Glora and Fia fared. He found them both sitting at the table eating their lunch as though nothing had happened.

"Scott, what are you doing here?" Glora asked him in surprise as he walked inside.

"Are you both okay?" he asked, ignoring her question.

"Sure, we're doing fine. How about you?" she answered.

"I suppose I should be more shaken up. I've never seen a dragon before."

"This is your first time seeing a dragon?" Fia asked skeptically.

Realizing he had just made a blunder, Scott began to backpedal. "Well, I don't think I have. But my mind is still a bit foggy, so maybe that's why I don't remember them. Do they come here often?"

"Not that often, maybe once or twice a year," Fia continued. "Usually they come looking for food, in which case, we offer them a cow or a llama and they leave. However, there have been rare times when they have been known to pillage, and burn whole villages, even eat people."

"Why don't you fight back?"

"That just makes them mad," explained Glora. "It's hard to kill a dragon. Their scales are very thick and our arrows just bounce off them. Some men have tried to fight the dragons, but most of them are dead, as you can imagine."

"So you've found it's easier just to give them a cow and hope they go away?" Scott asked incredulously.

"We don't have any magi in this village to help protect us, so we offer them a cow," Glora said.

"It's worked pretty good so far," Fia added, shrugging her shoulders.

Just then Amalic walked through the door. "Oh, Scott, there you are! I'm glad to see you are okay," he said.

"I'm doing fine," Scott replied.

"Unfortunately, I will not be able to take you today. My cart was broken in my rush back to warn the others, I'll need to repair it first."

"That's okay. If you could just give me some directions, I think I can manage on my own."

"You are welcome to stay with us for a few more days. It won't take too long to fix it and then I can take you. It really is far too dangerous to walk, especially alone."

Scott was getting more and more anxious about Azinine and he didn't want to wait. He had to find out where she was. So he smiled and said, "I appreciate your offer, but I feel I really must go today."

"All right," Amalic conceded. "If you must, but be very careful and watch out for those goons."

He gave Scott the directions and wished him well. Scott thanked them all again for their hospitality and then headed out of town on foot. He walked along the road for several minutes until he was sure he was out of sight of the village. He sat down on a rock to rest and took a look around. He wanted to make sure no one had followed him and that nobody was around to see him take flight.

He waited for several minutes and was about to stand up when he noticed his bag was moving. His first thought was that some rodent must have climbed inside while he wasn't looking, so he quickly snatched up the bag and closed it shut. He was about to take a peek inside when he heard a voice from within yell, "Let me out or I'll lepitimize you!"

Scott just about dropped the sack in his surprise. However, he managed to keep it firm in his grasp as he wondered what to do next. Whatever was inside did not sound very friendly and he wasn't sure letting it out was the best thing to do. On the other hand, he couldn't exactly take it along with him. "Who are you and what are you doing in my food sack?" Scott asked, not knowing what else to say.

The voice yelled back, "I'm a leppy. My name is Lino, and I was hungry. Now let me out!"

"Well, I'm not sure I should let you out. After all, you threatened to lipotize me or something like that," Scott pointed out.

"Ohhhh…all right! You win. If you let me out, I'll grant you your favor."

"My favor?" Scott asked curiously.

"That's right. Your favor."

"What exactly is a 'favor'?" Scott asked, not quite sure if a favor meant the same thing he knew it to mean.

"Oi! Do you mean to tell me you don't know what a favor is?"

"Sure I do. I just want to make sure your definition is the same as mine."

"Aye, you're a smart one, you are. You let me out and I'll give you my token," the leppy promised.

"What's a token?" Scott asked.

"Do you play me for a fool? Everyone knows what a leppy's token is."

Scott was starting to get tired of this. He didn't know what a token was, but he decided to pretend he did. "All right. You throw out your token first, then I'll let you go." No sooner had he said this than a gold coin flipped out of the bag—or rather through the bag. Scott picked up the coin, and carefully laying the sack down, opened it and jumped away, ready to fly if the leppy inside tried anything funny.

Nothing happened at first, and then a little man no taller than a foot high walked out. "How dare you keep me locked away in that bag!" the leppy yelled, shaking his fist at Scott.

"I'm sorry, but it was you who climbed into my food sack. I didn't put you there," Scott replied.

"True, but you kept me in there against my will," he yelled again.

"You threatened to…to…lidostick me or whatever you said," Scott yelled back.

"Ha, ha! Ho, ho!" The little man laughed hysterically.

"Why are you laughing?" Scott asked.

"Lidostick? Ha, ha, ho, ho!" Lino laughed so hard he slipped and tumbled off the rock.

Now it was Scott's turn to laugh, and he laughed extra hard just to rub it in. Lino picked himself up and smiled. Scott stopped laughing and said, "I guess I should be going now. By the way, my name is Scott. Thanks for your token."

"You're welcome," Lino replied in a most regrettable voice.

"I don't need the food," Scott said. "You may have all you want."

"Why thank ya, lad. That's most kind of you. I wish you well on your journey."

Chapter Eleven

Kidnapped

Scott was about ready to leave when he saw the two goons approaching, "Hey!" they yelled, "we want a word with you."

Scott wasn't about to do that. "Sorry, but I have a really important appointment I must get to," he replied. The two men took off running towards him as fast as they could. Using the boots, Scott raised himself into the air and waved. He saw a bit of surprise cross Lino's face, but didn't wait for any questions. He flew over to the Iker tree where he had stashed Azinine's MOC. Unrolling it, he climbed aboard and rose into the sky heading north, keeping the Black Mountains to his left. He rose as high as he could, hoping to see any large cities. It took a while, but he was finally able to catch a glint of a large city, which he hoped was Lux, just to the east. He dropped down where the air was warmer and easier to breathe. Flying this low, he was able to fly faster and make better time. When he finally reached the city, it wasn't hard to find Azinine's house.

He flew over to the same terrace where the party had been held. It was now empty and Scott wasn't sure where the front door was. For that matter, he wasn't even sure if there was a front door. Did a person even knock or ring a doorbell in this world? Finally, he decided to knock on the kitchen door—at least it was a start. He walked over and rapped on the door. A few minutes later a lady appeared, looking at Scott quite strangely. He guessed the kitchen staff most likely didn't get many people knocking on their door.

"Hi, is Azinine here?" he asked, before she had a chance to question him. "I need to speak with her."

The look she gave him made him nervous, but she told him to wait there and she would be right back. Scott waited a good ten minutes before she returned with Magus Polimar right behind her. Magus Polimar thanked her and stepped outside to speak with Scott, closing the door behind him.

"Hello, Scott," Magus Polimar began. "You are taking a great risk by coming here."

"I know, but I must speak with Azinine," he replied.

"When was the last time you saw Azinine?"

"I'm not sure, a week ago maybe."

"Have you been here that long on Lumen or are you just now getting here?"

"I've been here that long."

"Where?"

"In the village of Churp. But never mind my story right now, can I speak to Azinine?"

Magus Polimar took a deep breath and said, "Scott, Azinine has been taken."

"Taken! By who?"

"Well, we think by dragons."

Scott was stunned. That would explain her scream in the forest, but he never would have thought it. He sat there, shocked by the news, and couldn't help but feel it was partly his fault. Magus Polimar's face was very grave, revealing to Scott just how serious the situation was.

"Why would dragons take Azinine?" Scott asked.

"That's what I keep asking myself. It just doesn't make sense," Magus Polimar sighed. "Dragons normally don't kidnap people, they eat them. The message that was delivered said they were holding Azinine in exchange for the Golden Sword. I guess a dragon would have good reason to want the sword. After all, dragons hoard gold and it's also one of the few weapons that could be used to kill a dragon. But they've never asked for the sword before, so why now? Besides, dragons normally take what they want. I have never known them to kidnap someone to ransom such things."

Scott looked at him in confusion. "You're a magus," he said. "Certainly you could use your magic to get Azinine back, couldn't you?"

"I could certainly try, but it's too risky. It could place Azinine's life in danger, and that's not something I want to gamble with. Besides, it takes some pretty strong magic to control a dragon, and even then it's not easy. However, if I could somehow catch one out in the open, I might be able to use it to get Azinine back. The problem is they spend most of their time deep in their mountain lair and only come out for feeding or plundering."

"Why don't you just take them the Golden Sword then?" Scott asked.

"Humph," Magus Polimar puffed. "When the High King died, the amulet was given to Magus McDougal. The Golden Sword and the Plenum were given to a close councilor to the king, Magus Gephi. Gephi hid them to keep them from whoever killed the king. Two weeks after the king's murder, Gephi was killed. He had been tortured. No doubt to get him to disclose the whereabouts of these two powerful tools of magic, and when he refused to tell them, they killed him."

"So no one knows where the sword is?"

"I'm afraid not. Gephi was the only one who knew."

"You mentioned a...Plenum? What is that and what's so great about it?"

"Magi use staffs to amplify their magic, to make it stronger and to concentrate it at a specific thing or object. A staff is usually made from Iker trees. The wood serves as a medium to funnel and concentrate light into a crystal ball fastened at the top of the staff. The crystal ball is what allows the magi to work powerful magic. The Plenum is a staff that has been handed down from king to king and is capable of very powerful magic. It's been rumored from generation to generation that it was made from the very first Iker tree grown on this world. You could say that specific tree was the father of all Iker trees, and the crystal it holds was formed from the purest crystals, which is why the Plenum is so powerful.

"What about the sword? What's so special about it?" Scott asked.

"The sword is no ordinary sword, though no one really knows everything about it. The blade is not really made of gold but of pure light, and it is capable of piercing almost anything. It also has the ability to reflect or absorb magic. It may have other attributes that I am not aware of. The king himself never had to use it. However, if it or the Plenum came into the wrong hands, it would not be good. Even if I knew where the sword was, I'm not sure I could hand it over."

"So how are you going to get Azinine back?" Scott asked with such intensity that it surprised even him.

"Believe me, Scott, I am not giving up. I have been thinking about every possibility. I haven't come up with a solution yet, but I will. In the meantime, we must get you back home. Magus McDougal is worried and has asked me to watch out for you. It's not safe to take you back right now. We'll wait until early morning when it's dark and everyone is asleep. For now, would you like something to eat?"

Scott realized he was hungry, so he smiled gratefully. "That would be wonderful."

Magus Polimar took him inside and led him to a large dining hall where they found a beautiful woman, who could only be Azinine's mother, sitting at the table. She had dark circles under her eyes and Scott could tell she had been crying. Magus Polimar walked over to her side, saying, "Oline, I want you to meet Scott, Azinine's friend."

She stood up and walked over to where Scott was standing. "Oh, so this is the Scott I have heard so much about," she said with a sad smile.

"It's very nice to meet you," Scott replied.

"It's nice to finally meet you, but I wish it could be under better circumstances. Please sit down."

Scott nodded and sat down. "I'm sorry about Azinine," he said with genuine concern. "I somehow can't help feeling this is partly my fault."

"Nonsense. Do not blame yourself."

"Regardless, one way or another, we'll rescue Azinine," Scott assured her.

Oline smiled, but didn't say anything more. The servants brought out the food and placed it before them. They ate mostly in silence with a few trivial questions here and there. After the meal was over, Magus Polimar turned to Scott. "Scott, I know it's still early, but you may want to get some sleep now. You'll want to be rested when it's time to go."

"Actually," Scott answered, "I'm pretty tired. I could probably sleep without any problem."

Magus Polimar smiled. "Good, I'll show you to our guest quarters."

The two of them stood up and Scott followed Magus Polimar down a long corridor and up a spiral staircase. They came to a dead-end wall. "Af," Magus Polimar said, and immediately a door materialized. They walked into a spacious room where, along with other furnishings, Scott noticed a bed that appeared so comfortable it looked heavenly. He could hardly wait to climb in and go to sleep.

"I will come get you when it's time to go," Magus Polimar said and walked out.

Scott sat down on the bed and took off the winged boots and his shoes. He lay down on the pillow and took a deep breath. He was just about to shut his eyes when he saw something out of the corner of his eye. It was a round glass ball, like those he had seen in the dusty room at Cylindhall. He jumped up and walked over to get a closer look.

The ball had a gray tint to it so that he couldn't see through it.

He reached out to pick it up, but as soon as he placed his hands on it, the gray matter inside began to swirl like liquid air. He immediately removed his hands and the matter, which he guessed was some sort of gas, instantly stopped swirling. He put his hands back on the ball and the gas began to swirl again.

"Could this be a crystal ball?" he asked himself, remembering what Azinine had said about much of the lore in his world coming from the actuality of her world. It was exactly what he had always imagined one would look like. Wondering how it worked, he said, "Show me Azinine," but the gas just continued to swirl. Trying a different approach, he said, "Help," as if some sort of help screen would come up like the one on his computer back home. Again, nothing happened. He took his hands off the ball and the gray gas went solid. He was tempted to ask Magus Polimar, but he wasn't sure he should be playing with the ball in the first place, so he decided against it.

He lay back down on the bed and closed his eyes. His mind started roaming back to when he and Azinine had played tag in the forest. "That's it!" he cried to himself, sitting up. He jumped out of bed and swiftly walked back over to the crystal ball. He laid his hands on it and began to think. He didn't ask anything specific, he simply imagined what he wanted to see. It was the same technique used to operate the flying boots. He pictured Azinine in his mind and the gas inside the ball began to swirl faster and faster. After a minute or so it settled back down.

Disappointment washed over Scott. He had been so sure that was how it worked. On the other hand, perhaps the ball just didn't know where she was. Certainly Magus Polimar would have used it to locate her if it were possible. He put his hands back on the ball and imagined Magus Polimar. Immediately the gray gas cleared and Scott could see the older gentleman sitting in a large study room filled with books. "Wow!" Scott exclaimed. "This is so cool." Next, he thought about Oline. The gray gas came back and then immediately cleared again, revealing Oline sitting on a terrace with what looked like tears in her eyes.

As Scott watched her, a MOC pulled up behind her and two figures in long robes with hooded faces jumped off. Oline whirled around, her face revealing the terror she felt. One of the men pulled out a long stick that had a glass ball attached at the end. It was a magician's staff, just as Magus Polimar had described. Scott watched in horror as the figure held it out and within seconds, hit Oline with a stone spell and turned her into what looked like solid stone. Scott was mortified; he could not believe what he'd just witnessed.

The two men ran inside the castle. Keeping his mind on them, Scott followed their every move.

He watched as they headed toward his room, realization dawning on him that they were coming for him. He let go of the crystal ball and ran over to where his shoes lay. His only chance was to put on the winged boots and fly out of the window. Just as he reached the bed, the window flew open and in jumped two other cloaked figures. Immediately Scott changed directions and headed for the door.

"Af!" he yelled. The door instantly materialized and he ran through. He ran down the spiral staircase three steps at a time. Halfway down he met the two other cloaked figures coming up. One of the figures lifted his staff and started muttering something. Scott leapt from the stair and onto the two figures, sending them and their staffs tumbling down the staircase.

Scott could hear the other two behind him closing in. He picked up a staff, and using it like a baseball bat, turned around and struck the first figure square in the face. The second dove directly for him. Scott ducked and feeling a surge of strength he had never felt before, lunged upwards. He connected with the man and flipped him over his back. Meanwhile, one of the men he had struck coming up the stairs had recovered and was hurtling himself towards him. Scott lifted the staff and swung. The man ducked and the staff smashed against the stone wall, shattering the glass ball. A huge prism of light lit up the room like an explosion.

Scott dropped the staff and ran down the long corridor. He came across a wide pair of steps and realized they were the ones that led into the kitchen. Running through the kitchen, he came out onto the terrace where he had landed earlier and searched in vain for the MOC he'd left there earlier, but it was nowhere to be seen. He ran over to the railing, searching for a way to get down. On the far side, he found a spot where there was a ten-foot drop down to a steep hill covered with small shrubs. Knowing this was his only chance, he vaulted himself over the railing, hit the ground, and rolled for several feet through the shrubs. At the bottom of the hill were several clumps of bushes about three feet tall. He climbed under one, hoping they wouldn't be able to see him in the dark. He lay there as quiet as possible and seconds later heard voices above him on the terrace. Soon, two MOCs appeared and the two people on the terrace jumped on. They scoured the grounds searching for him, but he was well hidden in the cover of the bushes. After what seemed an eternity, they finally gave up and flew off.

Scott desperately wanted to go back to the house and help Oline. He also had bare feet and wanted to get his shoes, as well as the flying boots. He started to get up when another MOC arrived at the castle and two figures jumped off. Knowing they were watching the castle, he realized he couldn't go back now. He lay back down and decided his best chance was to stay hidden right where he was until the excitement died down. Throughout the night, several MOCs came and left. Scott was worried about Magus Polimar and Oline, wondering what these people might be doing to them. At one point, he almost decided to go back in, but quickly changed his mind, knowing he was no match for them. He also knew it wouldn't do any good getting himself captured. He finally decided his best course of action was to try and find a way back to Cylindhall. Headmaster McDougal would know what to do.

After several hours, in the dark before the dawn, Scott crept slowly down the hill and made it to the stables where the unicorns were kept. He ran down the path until he came along the outer wall of the palace, where he crept outside and into the city.

The city was empty. It was still too early for anyone to be about, and Scott didn't have a clue where to go. He needed to find a place to hide until dawn, when he could ask someone for directions. The streets were well lit so he needed to find a hiding place soon, before anyone spotted him. He walked down a few streets, but could not find anything that looked promising. When he came to a crossroads, he stopped for a minute trying to decide which way he should go.

"Hello, Scott," a voice behind him rang out in the silent night. Scott whirled around to see a man cloaked like those he had fought at the castle. This man held a staff in his hand, but at the moment he didn't make any movement toward Scott nor did he try to cast any spell.

"Who are you, and what do you want? I pose no threat to you," Scott said.

"Maybe, maybe not. Either way, we have to be sure," the man said. "You can either come with me willingly or I'll take you by force. I suggest you come willingly," he said in a calm but serious voice.

Scott thought for a moment, weighing his options. Surprisingly, the man did not get angry. He patiently waited for Scott to make his decision. It was obvious to Scott that this man, whoever he was, had no fear of Scott and felt completely in control. Finally Scott decided on a strategy of surprise. "All right," he agreed, "I'll come willingly."

"Good choice," the man replied. "You will walk in front of me and do as I tell you."

Scott walked slowly towards the man. When he was within a few feet of him, Scott kicked swiftly at the man's groin, hoping to disable him long enough to steal his staff and get away. To Scott's surprise the man reacted swiftly, as if he had read Scott's mind and knew what he was going to try. The man whirled the staff in a cross motion, striking Scott's leg, sending him onto his back. Scott jumped up and decided to simply outrun the man.

He hadn't run more than two steps when some sort of invisible force reached in and grabbed his lungs. An immense pressure was sucking the air out of him, crushing his chest. He could hardly breathe. The pain was excruciating and Scott was sure he was going to die at any moment. He fell to the ground, grabbing his chest trying to take in a gulp of air. He glanced at the man, wanting to plead with him for his life, but no words came out. The man continued to stand there, calm, as though nothing were wrong. Once again Scott tried to speak, but with no air the pain was too great and he finally lost consciousness.

It was still dark when Scott awoke to find himself in some sort of stable. He glanced around, and when he tried to sit up, streaks of pain shot through his chest. Uttering a gasp, he lay back down on the ground. A shadow moved from a corner of the room towards him.

"No! Leave me alone. I'll do what you want," he managed to squeak out.

"You don't have to be afraid of me," the figure said. The voice was that of a young girl. "What...what are they... going to do to me?" Scott struggled to ask.

"There is no 'they,' just me and my brother," the girl replied. Scott didn't say anything more. It hurt too bad to breathe, much less speak. He thought about the magus who had done this to him. *What had happened to him and why had he not taken Scott with him? Did he think Scott was dead?* With these questions racing through his mind, he fell back asleep.

He awoke again to the damp wetness of a cloth against his forehead. Opening his eyes, he found the girl sitting next to him wiping the sweat from his head. "How are you feeling?" she asked.

Scott wasn't sure how he was feeling. He took in a deep breath. His chest felt like he had pneumonia, but it didn't hurt like it had before. Looking around the room, he could see daylight outside. He also saw a boy about his own age standing against the wall.

"I suppose I feel better," Scott replied. "Thank you for your kindness." He didn't speak for several seconds and neither did they. Finally he turned back to the girl. "I appreciate all that you are doing, but why are you helping me?"

"That was no doubt a great magus you encountered last night. There aren't many who know how to perform the death grip. We figured you must be someone important. Once you are better, we are hoping you might be able to help us."

"What happened to the magus?" Scott asked her. Inwardly, he shuddered at the name of the spell that had been cast on him.

"My brother and I were sitting behind the wall where the magus was standing. We sat there in silence to keep ourselves from being detected. Originally, our intentions were to wait until both of you left. However, after overhearing your conversation with this magus, Zodi had a different idea. He knew a magus wouldn't concern himself with someone, especially at that time of night, unless that someone were important. We thought if we could rescue you, you might be able to help us. Since the death grip requires immense concentration, Zodi grabbed his stick pole and quietly climbed over the wall, where he whacked the magus over the head. About the same time, you must have blacked out, because we couldn't awaken you. We eventually had to carry you here."

"Did you find out who the magus was?" Scott asked.

"No, we didn't dare. It was risky enough for Zodi to do what he did. Had the magus not been concentrating so intensely on you, he would have no doubt detected Zodi. I tried to stop him, but he was intent on helping you."

Scott looked over at the boy standing against the wall. "Thank you," he said. "I owe you my life."

"Perhaps he would have eventually killed you, but that wasn't his original intent. I think he just wanted to render you immobile," Zodi replied. "Why was he trying to take you? Who are you that someone of his status would concern himself with you?"

"How do you know he was someone of status?" Scott asked.

"As Genin mentioned, there are very few magi who know how to use the death grip, and only those on the magi high council have permission to use it. He could have been a warlock, but my guess is he wasn't. I believe he was a member of the high council. Therefore, either you are a criminal or there is a rotten apple on the high council. Five years ago, I would have guessed you were a criminal. But today, I'm guessing you're not. Now, tell me who you are before I turn you in," he said in a very serious tone.

Scott wondered what he should say. He knew Zodi probably wouldn't believe him if he said he was from another world. He decided to tell only part of the truth. "I am from a small village from across the great sea. I was visiting Magus Polimar, who is a friend of my family. People here tell me that I look like the late High King and some silly rumors started that I might be the next one. Magus Polimar believes there are other magi who want me dead for that reason. He was going to send me home today, but last night the castle was attacked and I barely escaped. I hid on the castle grounds until I thought it was safe to leave. From there I walked into the city where I ran into that magus."

"So you're the guy everyone's searching for," Zodi exclaimed. "There have been magi combing the streets everywhere looking for you. Most appear to have good intentions, but these days you never really know. They are all probably wondering where someone in your condition could have escaped to." Scott could see him grinning now, probably at the thought of having tricked such important and powerful people. "He may be worth more than we thought. We just have to see which side wants him most," he continued, turning to his sister.

"No, Zodi," she firmly stated. "We can't turn him over to those evil magi, no matter how much they are willing to pay."

"It may be our only way to free Mother and Father," Zodi argued.

"We don't even know if they're still alive."

"True, but one way or another, we must find out. A powerful magus might risk doing that for us if the price were right."

"A powerful magus wouldn't bargain with the likes of us," she retorted. Zodi contemplated that for a few minutes.

This turn in the conversation was making Scott rather disconcerted. He didn't like the fact that this kid saw him as nothing else but a tool to be bargained with. "Perhaps I could help you get your parents back," Scott softly chimed in.

Zodi laughed out loud. "Unless you have some great power that I am not aware of, I doubt the goblins would welcome you with open arms, even if you do look like the High King."

"Goblins?" Scott asked. "What do they have to do with your parents?"

"They took our parents," Zodi replied softly.

Scott was beginning to formulate a plan. "I may not be a magus, but I have my own set of tricks. I think I can help you get your parents back."

"Do you really think you can help us?" Zodi asked skeptically.

"I can certainly try. Do you have any better offers?" Scott replied with as much confidence as he could muster.

"No, I guess not," Zodi conceded. "The problem is, we don't know much. Our parents were traveling with a large group of traders to the city of Zaub. One night they were ambushed by goblin raiders, who took several members of the band captive. We were told they were most likely taken to be used as slaves in the goblin mines. Meanwhile, we were sent to live in a children's home. We ran away from the home hoping to find a way to free our parents. Then, when we got to the goblin mines we couldn't find a way in. We've since been told that the entrance is guarded by dark magic and can only be entered at night. We don't know much about the goblins and their caves and we don't dare go at night for fear of being caught ourselves. We've been trying to find someone who could help us, but no one has been willing. Even our parents' friends say it's too risky and won't help."

"Don't you have some sort of military force that could help get your parents back? I can't believe the citizens of this city would tolerate such things," Scott replied.

"The goblins deny anything happened. Forcibly invading their mountain would mean war, and no one is willing to start a war over a few missing people," answered Zodi.

"How would a magus be able to help you?" Scott asked, hoping to get some ideas. Zodi looked at him like he had just asked the dumbest question he had ever heard. "Maybe I should rephrase that," Scott continued. "What sorts of spells would a magus use to get in the caves and free your parents?"

"Possibly some sort of camouflage spell or maybe disguise themselves as a goblin. I'm not a magus, so I'm not sure. But I am sure a magus would know what to do. What sort of tricks do you have?" Zodi asked.

"I am not a magus, but across the sea you don't have to be one to know magic. I've learned some great magic that might just work. At least it's worth a try," Scott replied.

"All right. But you better not be lying to me," warned Zodi.

Scott did intend to help them, but just not how Zodi expected him to help. If he rescued Azinine, maybe Magus Polimar would help Zodi and Genin. He would try and convince them of this plan later, but first he had to get better. Then if they didn't accept his plan, he would simply leave. There was nothing they could do to keep him.

It was several days before Scott was feeling well enough to get up and move around. He wasn't feeling completely one hundred percent, but Zodi and Genin were beginning to get impatient. Scott stood up, and as he did he noticed a bracelet around his arm. He tried pulling it off, but when he did, it sent a very painful shock through his body.

"The bracelet is to make sure you keep your promise," Zodi said, watching Scott's attempt to break free. "Once my parents are back safe and sound, I will release it."

"What happens if we get separated or you end up getting killed?" Scott questioned. "How do I get this thing off?"

"You better hope neither of those things happen," Zodi replied.

Scott didn't quite know what to make of Zodi. He had to be about Scott's age, but he spoke and acted much older. He wondered if the loss of his parents had forced him to grow up quicker than usual.

They left the stable just after dusk and headed toward the outside of town. Zodi had managed to obtain three cloaks and also a pair of boots for Scott, since he had lost his shoes the night of the attack. As they moved along the road, they were careful to keep their faces hidden and to stay out of sight as much as possible. Once outside the city, they removed their hoods and walked briskly down the stone road.

"The goblins dwell in a mountain far away to the left of us. On foot it will take us at least a week to get there. There's a small village about a day's walk from here where a friend of ours lives. We'll ask him to give us a ride to the mountain," Zodi explained.

"Isn't it a bit dangerous to be walking around out here at night?" Scott asked.

"We'll be all right for a while," Zodi said with confidence. "We are still close to the city. As it gets late, we'll have to be more careful, but as long as we stay alert, we should be fine."

"There is another option," Scott began. "Magus Polimar's daughter has been kidnapped by dragons. If we rescue her first, I'm sure he'd be willing to help us get your parents back."

Zodi and Genin both looked at Scott incredulously.

"What?" Scott asked.

"I can't believe you are serious!" Zodi exclaimed. "Our chances are much better with the goblins than against dragons. Let Magus Polimar deal with them."

"Then you've heard about her kidnapping?"

"Of course! The whole town knows about it."

The three of them continued on for several hours. The moon was high in the sky by now, lighting up the tree-lined lane they were walking on. It reminded Scott of the woods he used to go camping in at home. Everything seemed so peaceful, it was hard for him to imagine that these woods could be dangerous. They walked for about another three hours, when suddenly Scott stopped. He couldn't see them, but he could certainly hear them.

"Wait until they get closer," he heard one voice say.

"I can't wait. I'm too hungry," he heard another say.

"If you don't wait, they may get away," the first voice spoke again.

By this time Zodi and Genin had stopped also, but they were looking at Scott, not in the direction of the voices. "What's wrong?" Zodi asked.

"What's wrong?" Scott whispered. "Doesn't it concern you that they want to eat us?"

"What are you talking about? No one wants to eat us," Zodi whispered back.

"Then what, or who, do you suppose they are talking about?" Scott asked.

"Who?" Zodi replied.

"Don't tell me," Scott said in a weary voice, "that you didn't hear those voices up ahead?"

"I didn't hear any voices. Did you, Genin?"

"No, I didn't hear anything," Genin replied.

"Why are they stopping?" the first voice spoke again.

"There! Did you hear that?" Scott asked.

"Hear what?" Zodi said, getting frustrated.

"Someone or something just asked something else why we were stopping."

"You're starting to scare me, Scott," Genin whispered. "Are you really serious about these voices?"

"I am not crazy," Scott said out loud, reassuring himself. "And I'm not joking," he said adamantly. "There is something or some things up ahead and they plan to make us their dinner."

"I don't know why you can hear them and we can't," Zodi said, "but if what you say is true, we'll just fight them off. We have to keep going."

"Fight them!" Genin said in a loud whisper. "We don't know what we're up against."

"I've got another idea," Scott said. "It's a bit risky, but I think it will work."

"All right, let's hear it," Zodi replied.

Scott began to explain his plan. "If they are hungry, they'll follow us. They obviously don't believe we can hear them or they wouldn't be talking like they have been. From the sounds of it, there are only two of them. We could head off into the forest, making them believe we are going another way. You two stay hidden by the road while I lead them into the forest, which should allow you time to pass through. Don't go until I tell you. Since I can hear them, I'll have an advantage and should know where they are. This will also give me the opportunity to slip past them. Once we are all past, we run like the devil and put as much distance between them and us."

"Remember, if this is a trick, I will use the bracelet on you," warned Zodi.

"I promise you, this is not a trick."

"Sounds risky, but I'm willing to try. What's a devil?" asked Zodi.

"Never mind, I'll explain some other time," Scott replied. "By the way, can I take your stick pole? I'd feel more comfortable with some sort of weapon."

Zodi hesitated, but finally gave it to Scott. They started walking again, heading into the woods this time, and just like Scott figured, whatever it was followed.

"Where are they going?" one of the voices asked.

"I'm not sure. This is highly unusual," the other one said. As the two siblings hid, Scott continued into the forest, trying to keep his wits about where the road lay. Finally he stopped and ducked behind a tree. He wanted to see if they knew where he was.

"Where did they go?" he heard one ask.

"They must have stopped."

"Why do they keep stopping? I don't like it."

"Be patient, brother. We'll have our dinner yet."

Scott picked up a small stone and threw it further into the distance. It bounced off a tree and hit the ground.

"What was that?" one asked.

"It must be them," the other voice replied.

"How did they get so far ahead without us detecting them?" Scott threw another rock and then another.

"I'm not sure, but they are getting away. Let's go."

Scott threw more rocks. He was amazed at how silently these creatures moved through the forest. He could hear their voices, but not their feet. Picking up a few more rocks, he threw them even further.

"Hurry, they must not get away," one voice said, and this time Scott also heard what sounded like the beating of wings. This was as good a moment as any to slip away, so he headed back to Zodi and Genin as silently as he could. If he could make it back undetected, they would all be able to make it past together. For the first twenty or thirty yards he did pretty well, but in his effort to move more quickly he stepped on a branch, making a loud cracking sound.

"What was that?" he heard the voices say in unison.

"We've been tricked! They are back at the road," one of them continued.

"Run!" Scott yelled. "Run!" He heard Zodi and Genin crash through the forest but he couldn't see them. Running with all his might, he could hear the creatures behind him. They were yelling also, but Scott couldn't make out what they were saying over the racket he, himself was making. He finally reached the road and could see Zodi and Genin up ahead in the distance. He continued running, but didn't make it more than four steps when out of the woods flew two giant bat-like creatures.

Scott's blood ran cold and he froze. The creatures had wings like a bat, but their bodies were more like a human's. What caught Scott's attention most, however, were the two very large fangs protruding out of their mouths. The bat like creatures didn't hesitate. Screaming, they flew directly at him. Instinctively, as though he had done this a million times before, Scott lifted the stick pole, ready for battle.

A surge of strength coursed through him just like it had during the attack at the castle. His fear left him and he let out a defiant yell while he charged them. Both of the creatures, taken by surprise with this sudden display of courage, hesitated. They tried to retreat, but it was too late. They were already within striking distance of the stick pole, and Scott struck out with all his might. The pole came crashing down on the head of the creature on the left, and as quickly as he could, struck out at the second. The second creature had managed to reverse course, but the pole still struck its wing and it let out a howl. Scott jumped over the first creature, which lay on the ground writhing in pain, while the second one flew into the forest and out of sight.

Not waiting to see if more were coming, Scott ran as fast as he could down the road towards Zodi and Genin. When he caught up to them, they didn't stop to talk but kept running for several more minutes. Finally, when they were out of breath and relatively sure they were safe, they came to a stop. Scott looked back to see if they were being followed, but nothing was there.

"What were those things?" Genin asked.

"I'm not sure. They had wings like a bat and large fangs protruding from their mouths, but bodies like ours. They were horrible looking," Scott said, shuddering.

"Wow! I'll bet those were womvampirs," Zodi exclaimed. "I've never seen a womvampir before, but I've heard stories of them. They are rarely seen because they only come out at night, and those who run into them normally end up dead or sold as slaves to the goblins. The womvampirs are said to spray a paralyzing substance on their victims and then sell them to the goblins in return for Ardfull Worms."

"What are Ardfull Worms?" Scott asked.

"They are huge worms that live deep underground. Supposedly the womvampirs love to eat them, but have a hard time getting them, so they make deals with the goblins. The goblins find the worms in their mines, they gather them up and give them to the womvampirs in exchange for slaves."

"So their intention wasn't to eat us, but capture us in return for dinner," Scott stated.

"Most likely. But I've been told womvampirs will eat almost anything, so who knows? We are lucky to have escaped."

For a moment, Scott began to feel faint. The realization of what he had just done was sinking in. He had fought off two creatures that wanted to either eat him or trade him over to goblins as a slave. Could things get any more bizarre in this world? On the other hand, he began to feel a sense of pride when Genin pointed out that he had beaten two of the most feared creatures on Lumen and hadn't even been wounded in the process. Feeling much better now, they continued on their journey.

They walked for several hours without incident. Genin was getting tired and kept asking when they would be able to lie down and sleep for a while. Zodi, on the other hand, kept insisting it was too dangerous and they must keep going until they reached the village. It wasn't until just before sunrise that they finally arrived at the village where their friend lived. Too tired to wake him up, they crawled into some hay in his barn and went to sleep.

Later that afternoon, they were awakened by the sound of the door being opened. The three of them sat up and at first the man didn't recognize them. He was about to grab a two-headed spear, when Zodi called out and made himself known.

"Zodi? What are you doing here? Why didn't you come inside?" their friend Thomin asked.

"We arrived early this morning before the sun had risen. We didn't want to disturb you."

"How did you get here?" Thomin asked, looking around for a MOC.

"We came through the forest from Lux."

"At night? Are you crazy? You are lucky to be alive. Several folks from our village have disappeared in that forest of late. We've searched for them, but have not had any luck so far."

"They were probably captured by womvampirs," Zodi said.

"Why do you think that?"

"On our way here, we ran into a couple of them. Scott beat them with my stick pole."

Thomin looked at Scott, dumbfounded. After a few seconds he asked, "You actually fought with womvampirs?"

"Well, I wouldn't say I fought with them. We sort of charged each other and I just happened to strike first, I guess."

"Did you injure them?"

"I think so. I smashed one over the head pretty good, but I only clipped the other's wing. It got away into the forest."

"We must go immediately and see if we can find them. Come with me," Thomin said as he ushered them out of the barn. They walked past the house and into the street, where Thomin pulled back his sleeve to reveal a bracelet similar to the one that Azinine had given Scott. He touched one of the stones and then waited. After a minute or two, several other men arrived asking why they had been summoned. Thomin related everything he had learned from Scott. A few left and came back with MOCs. Thomin retrieved his own MOC and Scott, Zodi, and Genin all climbed aboard and led the others back to the place where they had met the womvampirs the night before.

They arrived at the spot where the incident had occurred and scoured the ground for any hint of the womvampirs. It took them several minutes, but one man finally found a pool of black liquid on the road, which they all surmised must be the womvampir's blood. From there they could see the tracks in the dirt where a body had been dragged deeper into the forest. They also noticed a horrible stench coming from that direction. Very cautiously, the group of villagers walked forward with spears held high, ready for a sudden attack. In the end, there was no need for precaution because they found both womvampirs lying dead about twenty feet from the road.

"We've found them," one of the men yelled, "and they are both dead." The others ran over to see. Most of the people in the village had never seen a womvampir and were very curious, despite the horrible stench.

"I don't understand," Scott said. "I only nicked the one's wing. Why would it be dead too?"

"It looks like the healthy one dragged its friend into the forest, but it was too late," Thomin surmised. "The one was too badly injured and didn't survive. My guess is the other stayed too long and died when the sun came up." He turned to the rest of the men, saying, "These womvampirs have haunted this forest for a long time and taken many of our people. We owe our friend Scott here a great deal of gratitude."

"Thank you!" many of them called out. One of the men, an innkeeper, invited everyone back for lunch. News spread like wildfire and many turned up to thank Scott, Zodi, and Genin. Several people even brought gifts. As Scott and his companions ate and chatted with those around them, an elderly woman approached Scott with a package. She studied him for a long moment and then turned and left without presenting him with the gift.

Thomin leaned over to Scott. "That woman lost her husband and son three days ago in the forest, most likely the work of the womvampirs."

"Did I offend her somehow?" Scott asked.

"I don't think so. I'm not sure why she left," Thomin replied.

A while later the woman returned, this time with a different package in her hand. She walked up to Scott without saying a word and looked him straight in the eye, clutching the package very tightly. She paused for what seemed like an eternity before speaking. "Please come with me," she said. Scott looked at Thomin as if to ask for approval. He nodded and told him it was okay.

"I'm very sorry about your husband and your sons," Scott finally said, feeling uncomfortable as he walked beside her. She didn't reply, but kept walking towards a table in the corner of the hall. She sat down and motioned for Scott to sit also.

"This gift is very valuable," she whispered. "Many men have died because of it and many more will try to kill you if they know you have it. Do not open this gift until you are alone and do not tell anyone you have it! Remove all clothing first, slip it on, and then cover it with your regular clothing. Again, I must emphasize, do not tell anyone you have it."

"Why are you giving it to me?"

She paused for only a moment. "I have my reasons." With that, she stood up and walked away. Scott was puzzled and wondered what could possibly be inside that was so valuable. He desperately wanted to open it, but decided he'd better wait and do as she asked.

Chapter Twelve

Goblins

Later that night when he was alone in bed, he opened the package. Inside was a body suit of some type that looked silver one moment and gold the next. It looked like it was made out of light, if that were possible, but it had a definite feel and texture which felt wonderful to the touch. He slipped it on as she had instructed and an incredible warmth engulfed his body. He still wasn't quite sure what value the suit contained, but he knew there was something special about it. He lay down on his bed, and as he did so, he noticed the bracelet Zodi had placed on his arm had fallen to the floor. It was no longer attached. At first Scott thought this was strange, but he surmised that Zodi decided to release him. After the womvampir incident, he must have earned Zodi's trust. The thought of no longer being a prisoner sent a feeling of elation through him; he could finally go home and get Headmaster McDougal's help.

The next morning Scott dressed and walked downstairs to find Thomin and Zodi arguing. When they noticed him they both stopped and greeted him. "Zodi tells me you are going to Goblin Mountain to rescue his parents," Thomin said to Scott.

"That was our intention. Do you think we shouldn't?" Scott asked, hoping Thomin would talk them out of going.

"You'll need an army to free them," Thomin said, trying to reason with them. "There are hundreds, if not thousands, of goblins in those mountains. I don't see how you can possibly hope to free them."

Scott was glad to hear him say this. Perhaps now Zodi would see the futility in their mission and decide not to go.

"Possibly not, but we have to try," Zodi replied emphatically. "We can't just leave them there. We are going whether you help us or not."

"Zodi, your parents are good friends. If I could help them I would, but I can't. There is nothing I could possibly do but get myself captured or killed. If I were to take you and Genin and drop you off at the foot of Goblin Mountain, your parents would never forgive me. Especially if you were captured! I cannot take you."

Zodi let out a deep breath. "I understand," he said glumly.

"Let's get some breakfast. Afterwards, I'll take you wherever you'd like to go, as long as it's safe."

"Okay. Perhaps you could take us back to Lux?" Zodi asked.

Scott was relieved to hear Zodi agree. He planned on asking Thomin to drop him off at Cylindhall where he could get back to Headmaster McDougal. He was sure the headmaster would know how they might find Azinine.

After breakfast they all settled on Thomin's MOC, where they took off toward Lux.

"Wait! I forgot my stick pole," Zodi yelled out. Thomin turned the MOC around and landed on the ground. "It's in your house. Can you get it for me?" Zodi asked.

Thomin was a bit miffed at the request, but he jumped off the MOC and ran inside the house. As soon as he disappeared inside, Zodi jumped up front, gave the command, and the MOC took off.

"Zodi, what are you doing?" Genin yelled.

"I told Thomin we were going to Goblin Mountain whether he helped us or not. I figure Mother and Father can't hold him responsible if we steal his MOC."

"He'll be furious. You're going to get in a lot of trouble."

"If we get out of Goblin Mountain alive, I don't care how much trouble I get in. If not, it won't matter," Zodi said, shrugging his shoulders.

Scott couldn't believe this was happening. He thought he had escaped Goblin Mountain.

The journey took several hours to get there. When they finally arrived, Scott was amazed at the immensity of the mountain. It was like a giant wall rising up to the top of the sky. Along the mountainside, there were large granite-looking rocks and massive trees whose trunk bases were as large as small houses. They stood there in awe. Scott found it hard to accept that goblins, whatever they were, lived inside this mountain and that he might come in contact with them come dark. The thought gave him the chills and he began to think Thomin was right. They had no weapons, and even if they did, there was no way they could fight their way through.

"Where are the doors?" Scott asked.

"All over," Zodi answered. "Just look for the most comfortable spot to sleep or sit down on and it's most likely a door. The goblins use these to attract animals, Lumens, anything they can get their hands on. That way, they don't have to leave the mountain, they only have to open the door and grab their prey."

"Well then, getting in should be easy. Getting out, on the other hand, could be tough," Scott said with a trace of sarcasm.

"You're planning on letting them capture you?" Genin asked with her mouth gaping open.

"It's our only choice," Scott answered. "We have virtually no chance of getting in, finding your parents, and getting them out undiscovered. If we let them catch us, like we're unaware, they'll take us as slaves. We'll at least find out if your parents are down there and still alive. It's getting out that'll be the hard part." Scott said all this as if it was no big deal, but he hoped Zodi and Genin would see the insanity of the whole thing. He had visions of spending the rest of his life trapped inside this mountain working as a slave, and it scared him to death. Zodi's bracelet was no longer attached so he didn't have to do this, but something inside made him feel obligated. Had it not been for Zodi, he might actually be dead right now.

"Okay," replied Zodi. "I don't like the idea of being captured by goblins, but it's probably our only option. Besides, you do have some magic you can use to help us, right?"

"Ah..of course...I do. I said I did, didn't I?" stammered Scott. Then, changing the subject, "Genin, why don't you wait out here for us? You don't have to come," Scott said, noticing the horrified look on her face.

Mustering all the courage she possessed, and then some, she stated, "It scares me, but I think I'd be more scared sitting out here all by myself. No, I'm coming with you."

Scott nodded and the three of them went looking for a comfortable place to wait. It didn't take long before they found a soft grassy spot with no rocks, branches, thorns, or anything else objectionable, so they sat down.

"This must be a door," Zodi said. "It looks too good to be true."

While they waited for darkness to fall, they ate some of the food Thomin had packed for them. They wanted to be at full strength when the goblins came. Scott still could not believe he was actually going through with this. The more he thought about it the more nervous he got. He knew nothing about goblins except they didn't like Lumens, and he didn't really know any magic except that which Ned had taught him.

To take his mind off things, Scott decided to ask Zodi and Genin about their parents. Neither Zodi nor Genin had any problem talking on that subject, and Scott could see why they were so adamant about trying to rescue them. Their love for their parents ran as deep as his love for his own. Talking certainly took their minds off the goblins and dusk came quickly. Just as the sun dropped behind the horizon, the floor of the mountain gave way and the three of them plunged downward, landing on a bed of soft dirt. No sooner had they landed than a pair of grotesquely large hands grabbed each of them and held them tight.

"Lumen children!" a large, ugly goblin exclaimed. The goblins had long, lanky arms and legs, with huge feet and hands. Their heads were also larger than normal with eyes similar to those of a cat, but their pupils were slanted vertically rather than horizontally. "What are these disgusting rats doing on our mountain?" the same goblin continued.

"Lumen children make good slaves," another goblin said. "Shackle them and take them down to the mine. I'll go and inform the lieutenant that we have visitors." As that goblin ambled off, a third goblin with an ugly scar over his eye, pulled three black shackles off a hook hanging on the wall. He proceeded to put them around Genin and Zodi's necks. Zodi attempted to pull it off and ended up screaming out in pain. Observing this, Scott guessed the neck bracelets worked similar to the bracelet Zodi had put on his arm. Once Genin and Zodi were shackled, the goblin placed the third shackle around Scott's neck. He turned to lead them down a long dark corridor, and as he did so the shackle on Scott's neck popped open and fell off. Reacting quickly, Scott caught it before it hit the ground. He was sure the guard would be angry if he found it hadn't fastened correctly, but he wasn't about to tell him. He sidled up next to Genin to show her that his shackle had fallen off. Wanting to remain as quiet as possible, he placed his hand on her neck to bring her ear closer. As he did so, he touched her shackle and it too fell open. Scott quickly caught it to keep it from hitting the ground. His movement had caught Genin by surprise and she whirled around to see what was going on. Not prepared for her reaction, Scott bumped into her, causing a slight commotion.

"Halt!" the guard behind them yelled. "I thought you were told to shackle them, you blundering lug!" he shouted at the guard in front. Surprised, the guard in front looked back to see Zodi still shackled but Scott and Genin standing there without shackles. Scott could tell he was confused, but also angry. The goblin with the scar grabbed two more shackles, not noticing that Scott held the other two in his hand, and carefully placed them around Genin and Scott, making sure they were secure. As he turned to lead once more, Scott's shackle came unclipped. Once again, he caught it before it hit the ground and was now holding three shackles in his hand.

"Halt!" the guard from behind yelled once more. "Confound you, incapable numskull! I told you to shackle all of them!" he shouted even louder. This time, Genin was shackled, but Scott was still free. By now, the scarred goblin was suspicious and he looked around to see where the shackle around Scott's neck had fallen. His gaze fell on the three shackles Scott was holding and his eyes turned yellow with rage. He moved swiftly towards Scott, and sensing his anger, Scott handed one to him before he could grab them away. The goblin took the band and proceeded to put it on Scott's neck.

Without thinking, Scott dropped one of the shackles he was holding and quickly snapped the other around the neck of the guard. The guard let out a howl, crying out in pain, causing him to release the hold he had on Scott. As he let go, Scott's shackle once again fell off and Scott caught it.

Meanwhile, the guard behind the group rushed up to the front to see what the commotion was. Scott whirled around and sent his foot smashing into the goblin's gut. The goblin doubled over and Scott quickly snapped the other shackle around his neck. Immediately this guard began to shriek with pain. It was at this point when Scott realized that Genin and Zodi were also screaming. He quickly moved toward them and touched each of their shackles, hoping he could release them. Sure enough, as he touched their bands, each one fell off and the pain stopped.

Standing there looking at each other, they weren't sure what to do next. They debated finding a way back out of the mountain or continuing deeper into the mine to find their parents. Knowing this was the reason they were here in the first place, they chose the latter and quickly moved away from the screaming guards. Not far down the path, Scott found a little cove where they hid until they could decide their next course of action.

"Wow!" Zodi exclaimed, now that they had a minute to talk. "For not having been trained as a magus, that was pretty powerful magic."

"What do you mean?" Scott asked.

"What do I mean? Those shackles don't come off except by the permission of someone wearing a sender. The way you released them as if it was no effort at all was incredible. I'm not sure even a great magus could have done that so easily."

Scott didn't know how or why the shackles had fallen off, but he decided to let Zodi think what he wanted. "I don't understand," he said. "Why did the shackles hurt so much when I put them on those guards?"

"They were wearing senders. When you put on a receiver while wearing a sender, it automatically sets off the receiver," Zodi replied.

"And that's why both of you started to scream too?" Scott asked.

"Exactly."

"Were all the other slaves hurt?" Scott asked.

"They could have been, but I doubt it. The senders work by thought. The guards were hurt because they were both wearing a sender and a receiver at the same time. We were hurt because their anger was directed towards us." It was at this point that he realized Scott was no longer wearing the receiver bracelet he had put on him. "Where is the bracelet I put on you?"

"I...I...took it off last night."

"How?"

"The same way I took these shackles off."

"Who are you?" Zodi asked, looking at Scott in amazement. "No wonder that magus wanted you. You can hear and understand womvampirs. You can remove security shackles at will. What else can you do?"

"I could tell you, but then I'd have to kill you," Scott replied with a smile on his face. He was quite enjoying all this attention.

"You didn't have to come with us, but you did anyway. How come?" Zodi asked.

"You saved my life. Now shush, I hear someone coming."

They waited for several minutes, knowing eventually someone would notice the screaming guards. Sure enough, the tunnel soon swarmed with goblins.

"You've done it now. They'll kill us for sure," Zodi remarked.

"What do we do now?" Genin asked.

"I'm not sure," Scott answered. "I suppose your parents must be down there where the guards were leading us."

By now, the cries from the guards had stopped and Scott could hear the lead guard yelling out orders to find the three Lumen children.

"I think we should wait here until things die down a little," Zodi suggested.

"Good idea," Scott replied. They waited for several hours while various patrols ran past them in both directions. After a while, when things calmed down, they decided it was time to move out. Quietly, they climbed out of the cove and headed down the corridor. They hadn't gone more than fifty feet when they ran smack into two goblins rounding a corner. Scott didn't wait for any hellos, instead he slammed his fist into the nose of the first one. The second goblin had a club and swung it at Scott's head. Zodi grabbed this goblin from behind, causing his club to miss. Scott kicked the goblin in the gut and then grabbed his head and brought it down hard onto his knee. The goblin buckled and fell to the floor. The first one was now rising and about to strike out when Zodi grabbed its head and smashed it against the cave wall. The two goblins now lay on the cave floor. Scott didn't know whether they were dead or not, but he wasn't about to stick around and find out.

He led Genin and Zodi down the corridor, where they ran into a fork. They paused for a second, debating which way to go when the sound of footsteps coming from the left automatically made the decision for them. They entered the path on the right, and running around a bend came face to face with several large goblins, including the two Scott had shackled. The goblins immediately seized them and brought them before the lead guard.

"They're not worthy of serving us," the lead goblin snarled. "Take them and feed them to the wolves."

The guards pushed the three children forward and led them away, this time accompanied by several other guards making sure they wouldn't escape.

"I sure hope you have another trick to get us out of this mess," Zodi muttered to Scott. The goblins heard him and smacked Zodi across the head, telling him to shut up. Although Zodi didn't understand goblin talk, he got the meaning and didn't say anything else.

They continued down several corridors until they came to a hole in the ground. A guard lifted up a door and shoved Scott down the hole. Scott rolled down a chute and then fell about six feet to the ground. Zodi and Genin came tumbling after him. Frantically looking around, Scott searched for the wolves, but there were none to be seen.

"Perhaps the wolves went out for dinner tonight," Scott said to both of them.

"Wolves?" Genin asked with frightened eyes.

"How do you know they have wolves down here?" Zodi asked.

"The goblins said they were going to feed us to the wolves. I just assumed there would be wolves down here."

"You can understand goblin talk?" Zodi questioned.

"I...uh...sure. Who can't?"

"Not many, that's for sure."

"Maybe we're in luck," Genin commented. "It doesn't look like the wolves are in."

"Think again," Zodi said, pointing to the opposite end of the cave. Scott turned and sure enough, out of the dark, two wolves were making their way slowly towards them. Genin screamed and Zodi jumped in front of her to protect her.

"Oh yum, yum. I'm starving. I'm starving," Scott could hear one of the wolves saying. All Zodi and Genin heard were a bunch of growls and grunts, but to Scott it sounded like plain English. He thought it odd that these wolves could talk.

"Oh yum. Let's eat now. Can we? Can we?" the smaller wolf said. The older wolf ignored the younger one.

Zodi turned to Scott. "They don't look too big, you take the larger one and I'll take the smaller one."

"Gee, thanks," Scott replied.

Just then the smaller wolf lunged for Zodi, but was halted in midair by the larger one, who had his teeth wrapped around its tail. The younger wolf let out a yelp and then snapped at the older wolf. "What did you do that for?"

"We have to wait for Alon. He always eats first," the older one replied.

"Oh, I can't wait. I'm hungry. I want to eat now. Eat now," the first one kept saying.

Meanwhile, Genin was still whimpering, panicked at the sight of the two wolves.

"He's going to make us wait, isn't he? He always makes us wait, and I hate it. I want to eat now. Want to eat them now," the younger wolf repeated.

Just then another wolf appeared from the darkness. Zodi let out a gasp. This wolf was huge! Almost twice as large as the others. It had massive paws and a large muzzle full of white gleaming teeth. It moved very slowly as if it enjoyed watching its victims squirm before eating them.

"Can we now, can we?" the younger one was yapping at Alon, but Alon's eyes were fixed on the children, as though he were pondering something. "I want to eat!" the younger wolf yapped really loud. Finally, the large wolf looked down at the young pup, and a smile crossed his jowls.

The whole scene was getting on Scott's nerves. "Would you shut up!" he finally yelled at the younger wolf. To Scott's surprise, both the wolves and Genin shut up.

Alon's head jerked up in surprise and his narrow eyes focused on Scott. "How do you speak our language?" Scott heard him say.

"I thought you were speaking my language," Scott replied.

"I assure you, we are not."

"I…uhh…I don't know. I guess it just happens."

"Are you of Lumen royalty?" the large wolf asked.

"I think I am, but I'm not sure."

"I have never known any Lumen, except those of Lumen royal blood, to speak our language. But I was told the royal family had been destroyed. They are no more."

"My mother was the High King's daughter," Scott replied. "She escaped where others could not find her."

"Valar still lives?" Alon asked, astounded at this bit of information.

"Yes! You know my mother?" Scott asked, dumbfounded.

"Wolves have always been friends with the royal family. We, along with the unicorns, were chosen to be part of the family crest. My father was a good friend to the High King, and I to Valar."

Now it was Scott's turn to be amazed. "How did you come to be here?" he asked.

Zodi and Genin were looking at Scott in amazement as he seemed to be conversing with the wolves. They could hear his side of the conversation, but not the wolves.

"When the High King was murdered, we retreated back into the forests. We remained loyal to the royal family and feared for our lives because of it. I was young at the time and made the mistake of resting on a goblin door. The rest you can guess. What has brought you here?" the wolf asked.

"I came to rescue their parents," Scott said, pointing at Zodi and Genin. "We think they're slaves to the goblins."

"You were foolish to come."

"Yeah, I guess I'm young too, but I'll find a way out of here. If you will help me, I'll see what I can do to free you also."

The old wolf laughed. "You are going to free yourself, your friends, and us, out of this den crawling with goblins?"

"Yes," Scott replied, now very serious.

"Ha, ha, ha," the wolf laughed. "Nobody has ever escaped that I know of. How do you intend to accomplish this?"

"I'm not sure," Scott admitted, "but if you'll help us get out of here, I promise I'll do all in my power to rescue you or die trying."

The old wolf considered this for several minutes. Finally he spoke. "I believe you are sincere, though I'm skeptical you'll accomplish your goal." He paused a moment and then continued. "The goblins sleep during the day. If you stand on my back, you might be able to climb back up that chute. You'll have to find an entrance, and wait by it until dark. The doors won't open during the day, and by the time they do open, the place will be crawling with goblins. You'll need an army to get out, but who knows? It's always worth a try."

"Yeah, that's what Thomin said also." Scott thought for a second and it came to him, "An army!" Scott whispered to himself.

"What's that you say?" Alon asked.

"You said I'll need an army to get out of here and I know just where to find one," Scott replied.

The old wolf now looked at Scott as if he truly were insane. "And just where do you plan on getting this army?" he asked.

Scott was too deep in thought to answer that question. "Thank you," he finally said to the large wolf.

"Does this mean we can't eat them?" the youngest wolf asked.

"You'll have to wait, my young friend," Alon said. "Although the probability is slim, this boy just may rescue us some day."

"I support you, Alon," the other wolf said, "but I think you are being foolish to believe a lone boy could rescue us from this goblin fortress."

"Maybe, but it's the only hope we have right now."

Scott turned to Zodi and Genin. "They're going to help us escape," he said.

Genin broke down and began crying again while Zodi put his arm around her shoulders and held her.

"Once again, Scott, you surprise me beyond my imagination. From what I know, not even the greatest of magi are able to speak with wolves. My mother told me once that the High King could speak to wolves, but I didn't believe her. Now, I witness it firsthand. You aren't just a boy from across the sea. You are the son of Valar."

Even though Scott knew he was just a normal boy, it was kind of fun having Zodi admire him like this. Still, he wasn't sure how to respond. It would put him in even more danger if they started telling everyone.

"Why do you say that?" Scott finally asked.

"Even though I couldn't understand the wolves, I could understand you, and I heard you say so to the wolves."

"Oh, yeah," Scott said, recalling his conversation with Alon. "But you must not tell anyone or I'll have to kill you."

"What?" Zodi sputtered, taking Scott all too seriously.

"I'm just kidding, Zodi."

"Oh," he replied.

"But I would appreciate it if both of you wouldn't say anything," Scott asked. "It would put me and my mother in terrible danger. Will you promise?"

"We promise," they both said in unison.

They settled down to wait for daybreak. Hours later they noticed the noise in the tunnels above had died down and Alon told Scott it was time.

"Zodi, you go first and help Genin up," Scott instructed. Zodi stood on the large wolf's back and Scott gave him a boost into the chute. Using his arms and legs, he scuttled up the chute and lifted the door.

"Okay, your turn, Genin," Scott said. Before climbing on the large wolf's back, she gave him and the other two wolves a big hug and thanked them.

"I like her," the youngest wolf barked. "And to think I wanted to eat her."

Scott laughed and lifted her up into the chute. She made it up with ease and then it was Scott's turn. He climbed upon the wolf's back, gave a shove, and grabbed Zodi's outstretched arm. With more difficulty than the others, he finally made it up.

"I'll be back, I promise," he yelled back down the hole. He then headed down deeper inside the mountain.

"Scott, you're going the wrong way, the doors are up," Zodi called after him.

Scott turned back around. "The wolf told me the doors won't open until night, so it's no good trying to get out right now. We might as well try to find your parents."

"I'm all for that," Zodi agreed, "but did the wolf tell you how we get out once we find my parents?"

"Yes. He told me I would need an army."

"Very funny—a wolf with a sense of humor. Did he give you any other suggestions?"

"Nope. He didn't need to, because I really am going to raise an army."

"Being down in these caves has turned your brain to mush. How do you plan on raising an army?"

"You'll see. Let's first find your parents."

Zodi and Genin followed Scott down several corridors and ended up retracing their steps several times. They spent the greater part of the day searching tunnel after tunnel, but couldn't find any leading to their parents. "Those mines have got to be around here somewhere, but where?" Scott asked himself.

"We are running out of time, Scott," Zodi interrupted. "I want to find my parents more than anyone, but we really need to get some help. Thomin was right. This is suicide."

Scott was both dumbfounded and angry. "I can't believe it. You were the one who was so adamant about coming here. I didn't have to come. I risked my life to help you out and now that we're here, you want to leave? We still have time and we're not leaving until we find your parents."

"At the door where we entered, there was another tunnel leading straight into the mountain. We haven't tried that one yet," Genin piped in.

"Are you sure, Genin?" Scott asked.

"Positive."

"Alright, let's try that then."

They ran up the tunnel as fast as they could, and found the place where they had originally entered. Sure enough, another tunnel led straight into the mountain. They were about to enter when they spotted a goblin pacing back and forth several yards in.

"I thought they were all asleep," Zodi whispered.

"They must keep some up to guard the slaves," Scott whispered back.

"What should we do?"

Looking around, Scott noticed the hook on the wall that held the shackles. "Put one of these on," he said, handing a shackle to Zodi. Zodi looked at him like he was crazy. "I'll get it off. We just need to make him think you're a slave. Genin and I will hide and when he comes out here to get you, I'll take him by surprise."

"This better work," warned Zodi, putting the shackle around his neck. He knelt down on the ground and pretended to cry. The goblin muttered what Scott figured was some sort of cuss word, and walked out of the tunnel toward Zodi. He was just about to grab Zodi when Scott hit him on the head with a large rock. The goblin fell unconscious to the floor.

"Come on, we may not have much time," he said, urging Genin and Zodi forward after releasing the shackle around Zodi's neck. They ran into the tunnel and found the sleeping quarters of hundreds of slaves. As they approached, they could see figures sleeping in each berth.

"Behold our army," Scott said, turning to Zodi.

"We're going to free them all?" Zodi asked.

"All of them," Scott said, smiling. "Imagine the confusion it will cause. With any luck, most of them will escape. I'll remove their shackles, but I need you guys to keep them calm and lead them to the door. Tell them to grab anything they can find to fight with. Evening can't be too far away so we've got to act quickly."

Scott crept over to the first slave and touched his shackle. It fell off and he quickly moved to the next slave doing the same thing. Zodi and Genin quietly awoke each of the slaves and told them what was happening. Elated, the slaves didn't need much prompting to get ready. They knew better than their rescuers where the doors were located and soon had gathered near them. As they moved out, the slaves grabbed mining tools and whatever else they could use to defend themselves against the goblins. Little by little, Scott was creating a veritable army.

About halfway through the prisoners, Genin let out a yelp. "Mother!"

"Genin?" a woman replied as though she thought she was still dreaming.

"Mother, we found you," Genin sobbed.

"Genin!" her mother said—louder this time, still not believing her eyes. She hugged her daughter as though she would never let her go. Zodi soon came to their side and gave his mother a hug.

"How did you get in here? Where are all the goblins?" their mother frantically asked.

"Never mind that now. Where is Father?" Zodi asked.

"He's somewhere over there," she said, pointing to another area Scott had not reached yet.

"Help us find him. We must move quickly."

They walked over to their father's quarters and quickly located him. "Scott," Zodi hollered, "we found our father. Please come free him."

Scott ran over and quickly removed the shackle. Their father had a reaction similar to their mother's upon seeing his children. Watching the reunion, Scott was glad he had come with his new friends and had not deserted them. He quickly went back to work, freeing the other slaves, but did not get far when an alarm sounded.

"Quickly! Get your parents out of here," he yelled to Zodi and Genin.

"What about you?" Zodi shouted back.

"I'll be right behind you."

Scott moved faster now, freeing each slave and instructing them to prepare to defend themselves against the goblins. It wasn't long before Scott could hear the telltale sounds of an actual battle taking place outside the sleeping quarters and the collars on the remaining slaves started going off, putting them in excruciating pain. The freed slaves were pouring out of their quarters, furiously fighting their way towards the doors to the outside. Scott finally finished freeing the last slave and now waited to get out himself. The tunnel leading to the main entrance was packed with slaves. The hope for freedom gave the slaves incredible strength and they fought with amazing valor. It wasn't long before the goblins actually retreated and the slaves poured out the doors and into the night.

Scott was one of the last people to get out and was amazed to see just how many people had been held prisoner by the goblins. The prisoners had all congregated at the foot of the mountain, and he noticed an older man standing on a large rock, trying to get the attention of the large group. After a moment, the Lumen people quieted down and the man on the rock was able to speak. He began by warning them to stick together until morning to avoid being captured again by the goblins. Apparently, the goblins had expected to control the crowd with the shackles and had not brought weapons when they had come to investigate the alarm. The older man explained that the goblins were most likely preparing to come after them. With this in mind, it wasn't surprising to see the freed prisoners still being cautious.

Next, the man began to separate the people into groups of approximately twenty. They were in the process of doing so when Scott arrived at the bottom of the mountain. At first, no one paid any attention to him because it was still dark and hard to see. However, a Lumen man recognized him as the one who had freed them and he sent up a cry, causing the others to turn and look. All around him, other people also recognized him and descended upon him to give their thanks. Soon, he was surrounded by people hugging and thanking him and expressing their deep appreciation.

Everything the leader had done to organize the people had just been undone. Their leader, whose name was Omnir, made his way over to the crowd and asked Scott to join him on the rock. Scott was a little hesitant, but he soon realized it was the only way to keep the group organized and prepared for any attack the goblins might attempt.

Once Scott was standing on the rock, Omnir made a short speech on behalf of everyone, thanking him for what he had done. Scott, in turn, gave the credit to Zodi and Genin, and explained it was because of them the rescue had occurred. Looking around he could not see them or their parents anywhere. Omnir continued once again to separate the people into groups of twenty, with an assigned leader to each group. When everyone was assigned to a group, Omnir held a council with each of the leaders to plan what they would do if an attack occurred. Scott was impressed with this man's ability to lead and strategically organize the people. He was also amazed at how quickly Omnir had been able to pull his plan together.

Once all was said and done, Omnir ordered the people to move out. He placed several leaders and a group of lookouts at the back of the group to keep an eye out for any sign of goblins. The rest of the leaders stayed with their groups.

The main body of people had just left the foot of the mountain and entered a path on the forest floor, when a cry rang out from one of the lookouts. Scott looked back and felt his stomach tighten as he watched goblins pour out of the mountain with steel swords glinting in the moonlight. These goblins were armed and ready for war. The prisoners, on the other hand, only had mining tools, sticks, and rocks to defend themselves. There was no way to outrun the goblins, and many were sure to be slaughtered or captured again. Scott had not bothered to grab a weapon either, and wasn't sure what to do.

Omnir's wisdom once again became apparent when he began to shout out orders. He ordered the prisoners to hide themselves just off the path on both sides; some gathered rocks and climbed into the trees. Soon they covered both sides of the path several hundred yards down, all the while keeping themselves concealed from the goblins. A group of twenty remained on the path to keep the goblins from becoming suspicious, and Scott realized that in the forest, the goblins wouldn't be able to tell if there were twenty or a hundred up ahead.

To make things more realistic, the people in view all began screaming when the goblins reached the path. Scott was not sure if this was real or just an act, but it sure sounded real. This gave the goblins confidence and they rushed towards the little group, weapons in hand.

Omnir's plan had worked, and the goblins were now surrounded on all sides. Just before the goblins reached the small group, Omnir let out a cry. Rocks, thrown from the people in the trees, began raining down on the goblins. They halted, confused by what was happening. With the goblins distracted by the rocks, the prisoners on the forest floor now stood up and charged, taking them by surprise. They struck at them with anything they could find and the goblins soon fell into a state of chaos, all semblance of order gone. They wildly swung their swords, but the pounding they were getting on all sides soon took its toll. Those who were able, now retreated, fleeing for their lives.

About fifty goblins lay dead and a hundred more were injured. The prisoners picked up their swords in case the main body of goblins came back. Not one prisoner had been killed, although several had been injured. Scott was amazed at how well this ingenious strategy of warfare had worked. At this point, even though Omnir was relatively sure the goblins would not be back, he was adamant about putting as much distance between them and Goblin Mountain as possible.

The trek took the group the greater part of the night, but they soon reached a major road leading to the city of Tonwah. Tonwah was not as large as Lux, but it was still good sized and many of the prisoners were from there. Those who were from other cities would be able to find transportation back to their homes. When they reached the city walls, Scott spotted Zodi, Genin, and their parents coming towards him. He also saw Thomin's MOC and surmised they had taken it once they had gotten out of the mountain.

Zodi explained that they had flown ahead to get help from the citizens. The town's leaders, claiming that the townspeople were not trained soldiers and would be afraid to battle the goblins, had refused their plea for help. However, as the prisoners arrived, the citizens came out to meet them. Numerous citizens brought food and drink, which were badly needed and greatly appreciated by everyone.

Several of the prisoners and their relatives walked over to Scott, expressing their gratitude. Two of the town's magi and prominent town leaders approached him. Scott had never seen the one that spoke to him first, but the other looked familiar. Scott could not place where he had seen this one before, but his gut feeling told him it wasn't good.

"You must be Scott," the magus said, slightly bowing a gesture of greeting.

"Yes," Scott said, trying to sound as natural as possible. The other magus stared at him with a look of hatred on his face.

"I'm Magus Noka and my companion here is Magus Mitle," the first magus continued.

Magus Mitle quickly came forward, his orange and yellow robes flowing behind him. "It's nice to meet you, Scott," he said, also bowing in a gesture of greeting. He was now standing only a foot away from Scott, making him very uncomfortable. Magus Mitle continued, "I understand you are becoming quite famous around these parts. However did you manage to free all these Lumen from the goblins?"

"Leave the boy alone, Mitle," Magus Noka interrupted. "He's been through quite an ordeal. There will be plenty of time for questions later." Then turning to Scott, "Young man, we have been worried sick about you. Magus Polimar will be so glad to hear you're okay. We must take you to him immediately."

Scott had no idea whom he could trust, but his gut told him it would be better to find his own way to Magus Polimar. "Before I go," he said, "I must say good-bye to my friends."

"Very good. I will be over there talking with Omnir," Magus Noka said. "Please don't take too long." With that, he turned to walk away, leaving Scott alone with Magus Mitle.

"Scott," Magus Mitle began, putting his hand on Scott's shoulder.

He then whispered something to himself that Scott could not hear. At the same time, Scott felt a warm sensation on his shoulder at the exact spot where Magus Mitle's hand rested. The older man let out a yelp and quickly removed his hand, shaking it.

"What is wrong?" Magus Noka asked, turning around at the sound of Mitle's yell. Magus Mitle didn't answer right away because of the pain, so Magus Noka turned to Scott.

"I'm not sure," Scott replied.

"It's nothing," Magus Mitle interjected and then quickly left the group and headed into the city. Magus Noka gave Scott a quizzical look, but turned again to speak with Omnir.

Scott touched his shoulder where it had burned a second ago, but now felt perfectly normal. *What did Magus Mitle do to my shoulder?* he asked himself.

"What's going on?" Zodi asked, interrupting Scott's thoughts.

"I'm not sure," Scott answered, still perplexed by what had just happened.

"We are ready to leave. Do you need a lift anywhere?" Zodi asked.

"Actually, I would love it if you could give me a lift back to Cylindhall."

"Cylindhall? The High King's castle?"

"Is that going to be a problem?"

"No, but why there?" Zodi asked, "No one lives there anymore."

Scott didn't think he should tell Zodi the truth, so instead he said, "I have some friends who live nearby. I'd like to visit them, but first I'd like to visit the castle. I've never been there before." He knew it was a lame excuse, but he couldn't think of anything better.

"All right," Zodi replied. They walked over to Thomin's MOC and climbed aboard. Before they left, Scott asked one of the Lumen prisoners to tell Magus Noka that he would find his own way back to Magus Polimar.

The five of them flew off towards Lux. It was a bit crowded on the MOC, but it did the job. They lifted higher into the air and Scott noticed a castle in the distance, which as they drew nearer, he recognized as the castle from his dream. They were just passing by it when a thought occurred to him. He carefully looked for the highest turret. In his dream, the golden sword had been just inside the tip of the cone-shaped turret.

Could it really be there? he thought, and then yelled, "Stop!"

"What's wrong?" Zodi asked.

"I've decided I want to stay here for a while," Scott replied. "Could you set me down by that castle?"

"We can set you down outside the castle boundaries," Zodi said. "The castle is occupied by Magi Noka and Mitle. You can only enter the castle grounds by invitation."

"That's okay. Set me down outside the castle grounds," Scott said. They landed the MOC next to the castle wall and Scott jumped off.

"Do you have any money?" Minone, Zodi's father, asked.

"All I have is this gold coin," Scott said, pulling out the token that Lino had given him.

"Whoa!" Minone said with excitement. The others also stared at it with eyes just as wide.

"Is that what I think it is?" Zodi asked.

"Where did you get that?" Minone asked. Scott was about to answer when he noticed Minone had jumped off the MOC and was heading towards him. Minone's eyes were fixed on the token as if it were a million dollars. Something about his body language made Scott very nervous, causing him to back away. "Give it to me!" Minone said, holding out his hand. Scott wasn't sure what was happening. Minone had become a completely different person. "Give it to me—now!" Minone demanded again, walking towards him even faster. At this point, Scott slipped the coin back into his pocket and prepared himself to fight if it became necessary. He didn't know why the coin was so valuable, but it obviously had some worth and he wasn't about to just give it away.

Minone was about to attack Scott when Zodi tackled him from behind. "Father, stop!" Zodi yelled. "Scott is our friend and the token belongs to him. What has come over you?"

Minone calmed down a bit but was still glaring at Scott. Without waiting for an answer from his father, Zodi ran over to Scott. "You had better get out of here now," he said, "and don't go showing that to people. It could get you in trouble."

Curious now, Scott asked, "Zodi, how do I use it?"

"I've never had one myself," Zodi answered, "but I've been told you simply hold the coin and call the name of the leppy that gave it to you. The leppy will appear and you can ask your wish. The leppy will give it to you as long as it's within its power. The coin then disappears and you're done."

"Thank you, Zodi. It has been a real adventure."

"No, thank you, Scott," Zodi said, bowing deeply before Scott. "I'd tell you to be careful, but you can obviously take care of yourself." He walked back to where his father was still standing. Scott waved and walked towards the castle. He wasn't sure where he was going but he wanted it to appear as though he did.

Once he was out of sight, Scott made his way into a group of trees, where he could sit in the shade and come up with a plan of action. He had to get to the turret, but the only possible way he could figure was to go inside the castle and make his way up to it from the inside, if that were possible. Magus Noka had appeared to be a nice, upstanding magus. He might risk knocking on the castle door and ask to see Magus Noka, but he would be taking a big risk running into Magus Mitle again. He decided to wait until dark, sneak in, and secretly make his way up. In the meantime, the lack of sleep for the past twenty-four hours was starting to affect him, so he decided to take a nap and wait for dark.

Chapter Thirteen

The Sword

Scott awoke to the sound of voices just on the other side of the hedge he was sleeping under. Being careful not to make a noise, Scott peered out to see Magus Mitle and another man whom he could not see.

"Let's get right to the point," he heard a deep voice say. "You have failed me. I send you to take care of a simple task and you come back with nothing. Where is the boy now?"

"I'm not sure. He was supposed to accompany Magus Noka back to the castle, but instead he took off with his friends," Magus Mitle replied in a soft voice.

"Imbecile! How could you let this chance slip through our hands?"

"We have grossly underestimated this boy," Mitle said, trying to defend himself. "He has incredible power."

The unknown man laughed. "Do you actually expect me to believe that?" he asked. "If he had any magi training we would know about it!"

"That's true. But how do you explain his abilities? We sent our best men to retrieve him from Magus Polimar's and he escaped," Mitle pointed out.

"He was lucky."

"Lucky? Was he lucky when he escaped Magus Mordi's death grip?"

"Mordi was hit from behind."

"In the middle of the night?" Now it was Magus Mitle's turn to laugh. "I suppose someone just happened to be waiting, late at night, just at the right time and in the right spot to hit Magus Mordi over the head in case he decided to use the death grip? Don't you find that just a bit coincidental? Magus Mordi woke up approximately fifteen minutes later and the boy was gone. No one could have left under his own power after such an ordeal."

"Exactly my point," said the first man. "There must have been someone there to help him."

"Maybe. But how could a mere boy kill off two womvampirs? And how could a boy walk into the heart of Goblin Mountain and free hundreds of slaves from right under their noses?" Mitle spoke, listing more of Scott's accomplishments.

"I have to admit, that does have me a bit stumped."

"If that isn't enough proof, then listen to this," Mitle continued. "Today, I tried to cast a spell on him when Noka wasn't paying attention. Look at my hand," he said, holding it out. "It's burned. This is what happened when I cast the spell. A searing heat came from his shoulder, which didn't seem to affect him at all. Only the powerful magic of the ancients' could have done this. How do you explain it?"

The magus, who definitely was in charge, held Magus Mitle's hand observing the burns. "Indeed, this is strange. Do you see how the burns are yellow? This type of burn only comes from an ancient magic that combines several types of light, usually to combat dark spells. It was used by our ancestors long ago, but we no longer know how to harness it." The magus paused for a moment. "That is all the more reason why we must find him. Seek out his friends and find out if they know where he is."

The two magi left and Scott lay there—half laughing at the conversation he had just overheard and half in wonderment. He found it funny that Magus Mitle thought he had great power. He wondered about the body suit the old lady had given him. Was it this suit that gave him such powerful protection? He wondered what else it could do for him. As he lay there, he noticed that the token in his pocket had fallen out so he picked it up and began to examine it.

"Lino," he said out loud, reading the inscription on the coin. Suddenly, Lino the leppy appeared next to him.

"What in lepaldi?" the little man asked as he quickly surveyed his surroundings. "You!" he exclaimed, now recognizing Scott.

"Hi, Lino. I thought you'd be glad to see me," Scott joked. "Do you want a plum?" Scott held out a fruit that looked like a plum and tasted like a plum, although he wasn't sure if it was actually called a plum.

Not saying a word about the name of the fruit, Lino replied in a more cheerful voice, "Don't mind if I do." He took the plum in both hands and the two of them ate without saying much for several minutes. Seeing as how Lino was quite small, the plum looked more like a watermelon in his hands, but he still managed to eat most of it. When he was done, he turned to Scott. "All right," he said, "what's your wish? I guess you have one coming."

Scott hadn't really planned on making his wish, but he figured this was as good a time as any since the little leppy was here anyway. He considered wishing for invisibility so he could sneak into the castle, but then it dawned on him: why not just ask for the sword? "Lino, I would like you to give me the Golden Sword," he said.

"You have to say 'I wish' and then ask your question," Lino instructed him.

"All right. I wish to have the Golden Sword."

"Sorry, can't do that. Its magic is much greater than mine. You'll have to wish for something a bit more reasonable."

"Could you make me invisible?"

"You have to say 'I wish' first."

"Right. I wish to be invisible…until I say 'make me visible again,'" he quickly clarified.

"Sorry. There's no magic that can make you invisible," Lino said.

Scott was beginning to get frustrated and didn't know what else to wish for. Then it hit him. "I wish for a pair of winged boots. You can do that, can't you?" he asked.

"What are winged boots?" the leppy asked with a perplexed look on his face.

Scott was flabbergasted. "What are winged boots! You don't know what winged boots are? You are absolutely useless!" he yelled.

"Ha! Ha! I got you on that one," laughed Lino. "Winged boots I can handle, but I feel sorry for the poor soul who loses them."

"What do you mean 'loses' them?" Scott asked.

"I can't make winged boots appear out of thin air," Lino explained. "They're too complicated. But I can ask all the other leppies if they know where I might find a pair. The first leppy to find one will send them to me."

"Well, then ask them to first look in Magus Polimar's castle. I left a pair there more than a week ago."

"Very well," Lino replied. The leppy sat down and his face took on a strange look as though he was meditating. It didn't take long before an orange glow appeared, and soon a pair of winged boots sat next to Scott. They certainly looked like the same boots he had used before, but Scott didn't know for sure. He put the boots on over his shoes and thanked the leppy.

"May I go now?" Lino asked.

"Sure," Scott replied. Lino disappeared in a twinkle, leaving Scott alone. Scott noticed he was still holding the token Lino had given him, which he thought was strange. Zodi had said it would automatically disappear. Shrugging his shoulders, he put it back in his pocket and looked towards the castle.

Once night fell, Scott decided it was time to put his plan into action. "Well, here goes nothing," he said quietly to himself. He shot into the air and quickly approached the highest turret. After he found a footing on top of it, he examined the spire the best he could in the dark. He grabbed hold of it and tugged. At first, nothing happened, but then it slowly gave way until eventually it came completely loose. There, inside the turret, was a sword and sheath just as he had dreamed. He took ahold of the handle and tried to lift it, but nothing happened. The sword wouldn't budge. He pulled again and again, but still nothing happened.

"Why won't it come?" he mumbled to himself. "It must require more, but what? I've got to talk to someone who knows." He thought about flying to Magus Polimar's, but it was too far away. Magus Noka might know but Scott still didn't know if he could trust him, and besides, he might run into Magus Mitle. He tugged a couple more times with the same results. He peered into the darkness, trying to see if anything was holding the sword in place, but as far as he could see there wasn't. He tried pushing it to see if it would budge even a little. This time, the sword moved a little, but it still felt like three hundred pounds. He did this several more times and then tried lifting again, but to no avail.

"Lino!" he whispered as a thought occurred to him. "I still have the coin. Maybe Lino will know." He stuck his hand in his pocket, pulled out the coin, and called out Lino's name. Immediately, Lino appeared. But when he hit the steep roof he began to slide down. Taken off guard, not only by how steep the roof was, but also by how high it was, he started screaming.

Scott quickly flew down and picked him up in his hands. "Quiet!" he whispered. "Do you want to wake up the whole castle?"

"You again?" Lino asked in surprise. "I was beginning to like you until now."

"I'm sorry, but I need your help again," Scott said.

"Didn't I already grant you a wish?"

"Yes, but I need your help again."

"How did you summon me?"

"I still have the coin."

"Ah, that's right. Because of your generosity, I'm obligated to grant ya two wishes."

"What do you mean?" Scott asked.

"Because you gave me your sack of food without me asking for it, per leppy rules, I have to grant you two wishes."

"You mean I still have one more wish coming to me?"

"That's right. Go ahead. Make your wish."

"Actually, I need to remove this sword from this turret. Can you help me?" Scott asked hopefully.

"I told you I can't get the sword for you!" Lino replied grouchily. "Only someone with the gloves on can wield the sword. The gloves give the bearer strength enough to lift it."

"What sort of gloves?" Scott asked.

"What sort of gloves!" he bellowed back. "Gloves you put on your hands! What other kind of gloves are there?"

"Can I wish for the gloves?" Scott asked.

"Nope. They're guarded also. Not even a leppy can get near them."

"Can you help me find these gloves?" Scott asked.

"You are persistent, aren't you?" Lino said with a little smile. "I'll help you, if it will help me get some sleep. But I don't think it will do you much good. The gloves are heavily guarded. You'll never be able to get near them, even with your flying boots. Just the same, head for that hill just north of here."

After replacing the spire back onto the turret, Scott flew off at a rapid rate, still holding Lino in his hands. He was anxious to get there as soon as possible. It took a while, but eventually they arrived.

"Over there," Lino said, pointing to the edge of a cliff. Scott flew over and landed by the edge. The cliff dropped about three hundred feet into a large, very wide hole in the ground.

"Okay. Where are they?" Scott asked.

"Out there," Lino replied, pointing out over the cliff.

"I don't see anything," Scott said.

"Of course you don't. The whole thing is an illusion to make you believe there is a giant hole. In reality, you'll find that it is quite solid. Out in the middle there is a small box with no opening. The gloves are inside, but I'm not sure how you get them out. What I do know is if you walk out over the hole, you will be attacked by nonbies."

"What are nonbies?" Scott asked.

"Nonbies are a type of bird that flies very fast and has a horn on its head," Lino explained. He then added, "They use those horns to jab you and I guarantee it hurts."

Scott flew out over what still appeared to be a hole. Although it was hard to tell, he estimated where he thought the middle was and slowly dropped down until he finally hit something solid that felt like ground. A second later, the hole disappeared and he was standing on what looked like an ordinary hill. About twenty yards away sat a small box, just as Lino had said.

"Ahh!" Lino yelled. "Here they come!" and he disappeared out of Scott's hands. Scott remained standing there, searching the darkness. He couldn't see anything at first, but it didn't take long before he could hear the beating of wings and noticed a dark cloud approaching him.

"This can't be good," Scott whispered. He leapt into the air and took off in the opposite direction of the dark cloud coming straight towards him. Before he knew it, several nonbies had reached him and were stabbing him in the legs. As soon as he reached the edge of the illusion, the nonbies stopped attacking, but several took up guard around the perimeter. Scott landed and examined his legs. Both legs had been pierced below the thigh and were now bleeding. He looked back and found that the illusion had returned, and it once again looked like a hole with the nonbies standing around the edge.

He decided to take a different approach this time. So far he had been able to understand womvampirs and goblins and he was even able to speak with the wolves, so why not these nonbies? He walked as close as he dared to the group of nonbies, hoping he could talk to them. "Hello," he said. Seeming confused, they looked at each other and then back at Scott, but said nothing. "I've come to get my gloves," Scott stated matter-of-factly. "They belong to me, and you must give them to me. I need to get my sword. It's very important."

Once again they looked at each other, and this time one took off and flew out of sight. He soon came back with another nonbie, who was much larger. The big nonbie studied Scott for several minutes and then flew over to him. Scott prepared to fly if the nonbie attacked, but it didn't. Instead, it said, "I am Torrint. Who are you and why do you claim the sword?"

"My name is Scott. I am the son of Valar, who is the daughter..."

"I know who Valar is," Torrint said, interrupting Scott, "but I was told she was dead."

"She is not dead, just in hiding. Certainly you can understand that," Scott replied.

"I suppose so. I have never known anybody except those from the royal family who could speak our language," Torrint reasoned. "The box will not open unless you approach it just right. If approached properly you will be safe, but one mistake and we are under oath to attack."

"How do I approach the box properly?" Scott asked.

"I can't tell you that."

"Why not? Did you take an oath not to tell?"

"No, but it would defeat the purpose of the test. If I told people how to do it, then anyone could get the gloves and they might fall into the wrong hands."

"Not anyone could get them, because not everyone can speak your language," Scott argued. "Did it ever occur to you that the only way a person could get the gloves is to have you show them? And to do that, they would have to speak your language. Furthermore, to speak your language, a person would have to be of the royal bloodline. The sword belongs to the royal family and I am here to claim it."

"Hmm, I'm not sure," Torrint said hesitantly, "but I suppose it makes sense." He sat there pondering for several minutes before speaking again. "Okay, I'll show you, but it would be best to do this in the daylight. You'll have to wait until morning."

"Thank you," Scott replied.

Changing the subject, Torrint said, "You look a lot like your grandfather. How is Valar doing?"

Scott was surprised by this turn in the conversation, but he answered, "She's doing great."

Torrint nodded and then flew away. The other nonbies joined him, leaving Scott alone again. Knowing there was nothing else he could do until the dawn arrived, he settled in to wait. He found a grassy knoll and was about to lie down when he saw something move about thirty yards away. It was only a shadow, but it resembled the shadow of a man, but not quite exact. Something was different, but he just couldn't put his finger on it.

"Hello, who's there?" he called out, but no answer came. Scott could still see the dark shape of whatever it was—or at least he thought so. It was holding so still that it might as well have been a small tree or a rock, but he was sure he had seen it stop there. He lay down on the grass with his eyes still fixed on the shape. He watched it for what must have been at least an hour, but it didn't budge. Although he had taken a nap earlier, he was still exhausted and sleep overtook him.

Scott wasn't sure how long he had slept when he was once again awakened by voices. "Search the perimeter, the intruder may still be around."

Several MOCs covered the perimeter, and fortunately for Scott, he had chosen a spot that was a ways off from the perimeter. Regardless of that, several still flew fairly close. After a few had passed by him,

Scott guessed he must look like a rock amid several other larger rocks close by him. He held as still as he could so as not to be discovered. He looked over where the shape he had spotted earlier had stood, but it was gone.

So it wasn't just my imagination, he pondered, but his thoughts were interrupted by another voice.

"Your Lordship, we have searched the perimeter, but have found nothing," he heard a voice say. "Perhaps the intruder is injured or dead and lying within the illusion where we cannot see him."

"The illusion would not be active if someone were lying within," came the reply.

"The intruder must have escaped then."

"Perhaps. Deactivate the illusion and let's try to communicate with those filthy nonbie. Make sure none of your men fly within the perimeter of the illusion."

The magus, who Scott didn't recognize, walked into the perimeter, his staff held high. The illusion disappeared, and within seconds a cloud of nonbies appeared heading in the direction of the magus. He quickly stepped back to the outside and the nonbies landed just inside the perimeter as they had done with Scott. The magus made a hand signal to one of the nonbies and it flew away. Seconds later, it returned with Torrint, who landed just in front of the magus.

The magus made a few hand gestures, obviously trying to communicate with Torrint, but Torrint simply stared at him as if none of it made any sense. At this point, the magus began to get angry. He began yelling at Torrint, all the while making the same hand gestures over and over again. The magus obviously felt that Torrint knew what he was trying to ask, but Torrint just sat there staring at him. Finally the magus threw up his arms and jumped on his MOC. "Let's go!" he yelled and they all flew away.

Torrint watched as they flew off and waited until they had completely disappeared. Once they were out of sight, Torrint began looking around, searching for something or someone. "Scott?" he yelled.

"I'm right here," Scott called back.

Torrint flew over and landed by him. "I know I said we should wait until morning, but the king's enemies are obviously watching this place. You'll be safer if we do this now. That way if they come back, you'll at least have the cover of darkness to hide you. So listen carefully. Once you enter the ring, you must do exactly what I say. One mistake, and my fellow nonbies will attack. You'll have to move quickly. It's a good thing you have those boots," he observed. "I don't think this would be possible without them. I will fly with you and land next to each stone you should land on. You must touch them in the right order or the box won't open, and my friends over there will be forced to turn you into Swiss cheese. Are you ready?"

"I guess so," Scott replied, wondering how Torrint would know about Swiss cheese. Scott walked over to the edge, rose into the air, and flew to the rock Torrint was standing next to. It was several yards in from the perimeter, and Scott wondered how anyone would be able to reach it without the help of the winged boots, but supposed a MOC would have done just as well. He landed on the rock, all the while keeping an eye on the other nonbies. None moved, but they all watched him, tensed and ready for flight as if they were at the starting line of a race, ready for the start signal.

Torrint flew over to another rock and Scott landed on that one. As he landed on each of the rocks, they turned a light shade of red. Torrint proceeded to the next rock and Scott followed, being very careful to land on it with good footing. They repeated this routine several times and Scott wondered how many rocks he had to touch. He also wondered how anyone would ever figure this out without being shown.

He followed Torrint over to the next rock, but this time the nonbie had landed right between two rocks. "Which one is it?" Scott asked.

With worry in his voice, Torrint replied, "I'm not sure. I don't remember there being two rocks next to each other like this." The two rocks sat right next to the box and Scott was sure this was the last rock he would have to touch. But what if he touched the wrong one?

Torrint looked at Scott gravely and warned, "You have a fifty percent chance. If for some reason you land on the wrong stone, don't head for the side to escape, you'll never make it. Go straight up. The boundary for the ceiling isn't very high."

"Once the nonbies back down, can I come back and hit the right rock to open the box?" Scott asked.

"No, you would then be hitting out of sequence. You would have to go back to that last rock you just landed on and then come over and hit the correct rock. However, you'll never make it. The nonbies will guard the box until the stones reset themselves, and that won't be until tomorrow night, at which point you'll have to do this all over again. But at least you'll know which stone is the correct one," he added as an afterthought.

Scott nodded, looked carefully at both rocks, and decided that he would hit the left one and automatically head for the sky. If the rock turned red he would be okay. If not, he would already have a head start on the nonbies. As he dropped down, the nonbies tensed, ready for flight. He hit the rock and shot skyward. The nonbies also took flight, and Scott knew he had chosen the wrong stone. One hit his shoe, doing no damage, but another managed to prick his calf just before he left the perimeter. The nonbies retreated, but Scott continued to shoot upwards. He wasn't about to take any chances. He finally came to a stop about three hundred feet straight above the box.

"That was close," he said to himself, rubbing his calf. A deep feeling of disappointment stabbed through him. He couldn't afford to wait another day. He needed those gloves now. Looking down, he could see the nonbies gathered around the box, just as Torrint had said they would. He floated in midair, pondering options, when all of a sudden the nonbies raced to the perimeter.

Scott hadn't noticed, but the MOCs were back. One had made the mistake of flying inside the perimeter and the nonbies had quickly reacted. Three MOCs were now outside the perimeter, and Scott guessed the magi were once again trying to find out who had triggered the illusion.

This was fortunate for Scott, because it drew the nonbies away and gave Scott one of his craziest ideas yet. He rocketed downward at full speed until he was right upon the second to last rock. Screeching to a halt, he hit the rock, jetted over to the last rock, and hit the correct rock this time. The top of the box flew open and to Scott's dismay, it looked empty. He thrust his hands into it and to his amazement felt a pair of gloves. He grabbed the gloves and took off, fully expecting any second to be drilled by a thousand nonbies. He shot skyward, and when he thought all was safe turned to look back. What he saw horrified him. The nonbies were still standing around the perimeter. They hadn't budged, but the MOCs had and were headed directly towards him at full speed. Scott aimed for the clouds, hoping to play a little hide-and-seek. Except this time, the stakes were much higher.

Scott was flying as fast as he could, but the MOCs were rapidly gaining on him and he knew they would reach him before he could reach the clouds. As the first MOC approached, Scott screeched to a halt and moved slightly to the right, which sent the first MOC shooting past him. The second MOC, which was right behind the first, also zoomed past, but realizing what had happened, quickly circled around and resumed the chase. Although not as fast, Scott was certainly more nimble than the MOCs and he easily dodged the second. The third one, however, had come up behind him and Scott turned just in time to see a magus with a staff in hand, mumbling some sort of incantation. A flash of light blazed from his staff and Scott barely dodged it, but in doing so, just about ran into another MOC coming up behind him. Then another fell into place next to it. Several others arrived and he found himself surrounded.

"Give up. We have you surrounded and there is no escape," one of the magi said. "If you come willingly, we will not hurt you."

Scott looked around him; there was a magus on every MOC, and each had his staff pointed at him. He wasn't about to give himself up—something told him going with these men wouldn't be good. Earlier he had noticed a small orchard not too far away, and he was determined to head for the orchard where he could hopefully hide.

They saw the hesitation, and the look on Scott's face must have told them he wasn't going to give up. Before Scott could make a break for it, the magus who had spoken earlier uttered a word and a blast of light shot from his staff, hitting Scott square in the chest. Scott waited for the impact, but oddly, nothing happened.

"Grab him!" the lead magus commanded, fully believing he had disabled Scott. One of the MOCs moved up beside him, where the magus standing on it intended to pull his captive onto it. This left a large gap between the MOCs that had him corralled. Scott decided this was his chance and he bolted.

"Impossible!" he heard the magus yell. "After him!"

Scott shot straight for the orchard, figuring the MOCs would have a hard time following him among the trees. Once inside, he flew a little further and then came to a complete stop, hiding in one of the trees and trying to scope out the situation. He could see the MOCs flying over the trees, each one covering a different area. Scott didn't dare move a muscle. The orchard wasn't that large, and he knew any movement at all might attract their attention. He decided the best course of action was to sit for a while and let the men on the MOCs make the first move.

Up to this point, Scott had been carrying the gloves. He took some time now to examine them and discovered they were much like the boots he was wearing. He pulled them on over his hands and they immediately became invisible. Looking at his hands, it appeared as though he wasn't wearing the gloves at all. His hands didn't even feel like there was anything covering them except for the slightest pressure against them.

As he sat there admiring the gloves, one of the MOCs pulled up and parked itself above the tree he was sitting in. He wasn't sure whether they knew he was there or whether it was just coincidence. Either way it made him nervous, and he decided it was time to make his escape. The problem was, he still hadn't figured out what to do. After a minute or two, he wondered if he would be able to trick them the same way he had tricked the womvampirs. He picked a piece of fruit off the tree and threw it as hard as he could to the other end of the orchard. To his amazement, it went much farther. In fact, it went so much farther that Scott didn't hear it hit the ground, and he guessed it must have landed somewhere outside the orchard. He remembered that Lino had said the gloves would give the wearer extra strength. He picked another piece of fruit and gently tossed it. This time it landed about where he had planned. He heard it crash through the tree branches and tumble to the ground. He looked up to see if the MOC had moved, but it simply stayed put. He threw another fruit and another, but still the MOC didn't move. He was about to make a run for it when he saw a nonbie sitting in one of the trees a few yards off. This gave Scott an idea and he cautiously flew over to it, but as he approached, the nonbie took flight.

"Wait!" he yelled in a loud whisper. At the same time, he also noticed the MOC had followed him, indicating they knew where he was. The nonbie stopped on a branch close by and looked back at Scott.

"I need your help," Scott said to the nonbie.

"How do you speak my language?" the nonbie asked.

"Never mind that right now. Do you know Torrint?"

"Of course I do. Everyone knows Torrint."

"I need you to find him and tell him I'm in trouble. Those Lumen on the MOCs above are after me. I need his help right away."

"I'm sorry, but I don't think the others will let me get near him. I'm not exactly welcome among those nonbies."

"Will you please try?" Scott pled. "Tell him that Scott needs his help."

"I will try," the nonbie replied and then flew off.

This whole time Scott had kept his eye on the MOC above. It continued to hover above him and he wondered what they were up to and how long they would wait. Scott tried to slowly move to another tree, but the MOC followed. They could obviously see him, so trying to sneak out was not going to work. His best chance was to wait for the nonbie to return. He waited for about ten minutes, but there was no sign of its return. He was about to give up and make a run for it when another MOC pulled up with four more right behind.

"That's why!" he whispered to himself. "They were waiting for reinforcements to arrive." Outrunning them seemed impossible now.

About that same time, the nonbie returned. "I'm sorry," he said. "I tried to explain to them, but they wouldn't listen."

"It's okay. Thank you for trying," Scott replied, completely at a loss as to what he was going to do now. Just when he didn't think things could get worse, several of the MOCs took up a formation surrounding him while one lowered into the trees. Two magi were standing on the MOC with their staffs held out, ready for battle. Scott turned to make a run for it, but when he turned around he came face to face with something.

It had big round eyes, and he recognized them as the same eyes he had seen looking in his window that night at CastleOne. It was also the creature Scott thought he had seen earlier that night. It looked kind of like a man, but had wings, gray skin, and claws. All of this happened in a matter of seconds and recognition dawned on Scott. "It's a gargoyle," Scott whispered to himself, still amazed that gargoyles were real. He thought he was doomed for sure. The gargoyle leaped into the air, its wings outstretched, heading directly towards him. Scott didn't have time to react and braced himself for the impact. To his surprise, the gargoyle shot over him and began attacking the two magi.

Scott saw this as his exit cue. He sprang forward and upward, getting just outside the circle of MOCs hovering above. It didn't take them long, however, to catch on to what was happening and begin their pursuit. Scott shot straight up, hurtling himself towards the clouds, willing himself to go faster. The MOCs quickly caught up and just as they were upon him, he stopped and dropped like a rock to the ground, causing the MOCs to change course also.

The MOCs started to work together, cutting Scott off each time he darted off in a different direction. Soon, fifty feet in the air, they had him surrounded again. One magus lifted his staff as if to say, 'Make one move and I'll blast.' Scott could see the MOC with the two magi quickly approaching; they had obviously dealt with their attacker. Scott was not about to sit there and wait to see what they were going to do to him. Using the strength of the gloves, he charged one of the MOCs, slamming his fists into the bottom, sending it tipping just enough to slip by. Without waiting to see their reaction, he shot skyward, but he could sense them once again gaining on him. He had to find a way out of this and quick. He was getting very cold and very tired. He continued higher and higher, expecting them to catch him any minute.

After several minutes without experiencing any resistance, he looked back to see where they were. The MOCs were no longer pursuing him. Instead, they were engaged in a battle against several hundred nonbies. Scott was overcome with relief and extreme gratitude. He wished he could thank them, but realized it would be impossible now. Knowing it would be light soon, he sped off towards the castle where the sword was located. By the time he arrived, the sun was just starting to show its face over the mountain range, so he knew he needed to hurry. He quickly removed the top of the turret and yanked on the sword again. To his surprise, it came free just as easily as if he had pulled a pin out of a pincushion. He quickly placed the turret back in its place and headed for the outskirts of the city, towards the same forest that led to Goblin Mountain.

Chapter Fourteen

Dragons

By now, dawn had arrived in full splendor and Scott figured he had better get out of sight. He landed inside a grove of trees, where he could take time to examine the sword. He was surprised at how short it was. It seemed more like a long knife than a sword. The sheath was made of a material that was similar to leather, yet different somehow. It was then he noticed the shoulder straps, and he pushed his arms through and pulled the sword up onto his back. Again, he was surprised at how lightweight and comfortable it felt.

He reached his arm back to pull the sword out, but couldn't reach the handle. *That's dumb,* he thought. *Why put this on your back if you can't even grab it?* He took the sword off his back, and grasping the handle, pulled. At first, Scott thought his eyes had deceived him. The sword slid out quite easily, but it looked like it had slid through the sheath rather than out of the sheath. He tried to slide the sword back in, but as soon as the blade touched the sheath it melted into it—or at least, that's what it looked like. He attempted to pull it out once more, but this time he tried pulling it through the sheath rather than out of the end. Sure enough, the sword blade slid through the sheath as though it was not solid.

Examining the sword closer now, he realized the blade was made of what looked like gold, but was almost transparent and shinier than normal. He swung the sword in an arcing motion and then brought it down again. The blade was only about two feet long, and Scott wondered what good it would do in battle. He swung the blade hard into the trunk of a small tree, expecting it to wedge itself into the trunk like an ax might do. But instead it sliced through the trunk like a knife slicing through butter. The tree began to fall and he had to jump out of the way to keep from getting squashed. The tree crashed to the ground, making all kinds of noise.

"Oops…uh…timber?" he said, looking around to see if anyone was watching. Relieved, he saw no one. His thoughts turned to Azinine, and once again a sense of urgency overwhelmed him. Now that he had the sword, he needed to find the dragons. He returned the sword back into the sheath and was about to put it on his shoulders when an idea struck him. He placed his hand on the handle and spoke, "Hortu." Then he placed the sheath, with the sword in it, back on his shoulders. Reaching back for the handle, he said, "Abtu," and the sword leaped from its sheath and into his hand. Scott smiled, feeling quite proud of himself for figuring that out. Placing the sword back in its sheath, he began to contemplate his next move.

He wasn't sure how to find the dragons, but he was sure Magus Polimar would know. The tricky part would be getting Magus Polimar to tell him without revealing he actually had the sword. Magus Polimar had already told him he would never give the sword up. Another problem would be getting into the castle without letting anyone else know he was there. He didn't want to risk being attacked again.

Approaching Lux at midday, using a pair of winged boots would be a dead giveaway, so he certainly couldn't go that route. He had to find some other way of getting there. Finally, he decided he would find someone in Tonwah who could give him a lift. He still had Lino's token, and judging by the reaction of Zodi's father, he was confident he could use it to purchase a ride. He walked from the grove of trees and soon found a path that led towards town. Just inside the city gates, he found a gentleman peddling a bunch of knickknacks which were placed on a very old-looking MOC.

"You've come to the right spot," the gentleman began.

"I'm not looking to buy anything," Scott interrupted. "I need you to give me a ride. Does that MOC work?"

"Of course it works!" the man replied, looking somewhat offended. "But I'm not a ride service, I sell goods. Now either buy or go away!"

"I'll pay you to give me a ride to Lux," Scott offered.

"Absolutely not! Unless of course, you have two hundred onin to pay?"

"I have no...no onin at all," Scott said, struggling to remember what the man had called it. "But I do have something else you may want instead."

"There is nothing else I want. Either you give me onin or go away."

Scott pulled out the token. "Not even this?" he asked, holding it out.

The man looked at it for a second and then his eyes grew wide as he recognized it for what it was. "For that, I will give you a ride around the whole sphere!" he replied. He quickly pushed his wares off the MOC to make room for Scott. He then held out his hand for payment.

"You can't have it until you've fulfilled your part of the bargain," Scott said, putting the token back in his pocket. The man leapt at him, his hands reaching for Scott's neck.

Scott quickly slid sideways and threw the man to the ground. He reached backwards. "Abtu!" he yelled and the sword flew into his hands. He thrust the sword towards the man's chest, keeping the man at bay. "You will not get paid until you have given me the ride," Scott threatened.

The man eyed him carefully for a few seconds, and then agreed. "Very well, get on."

"That's better. And don't try anything stupid."

The MOC lifted into the air and Scott could feel himself once again being sucked onto the MOC. They flew a bit higher and then headed towards Lux. They hadn't even been in the air more than thirty seconds when Scott spotted smoke rising in the distance. Curious, he strained to see what was happening.

Could it be? he wondered. He watched a bit longer and then finally he saw it. From where he sat it looked like nothing more than a bird. But he knew it was much larger than that to be seen from this distance. "Stop!" he yelled. Then pointing toward the smoke, he instructed, "Head towards that smoke and step on it."

"Your wish is my command," the man replied.

He changed direction and flew towards the smoke. Sure enough, as they got closer, Scott could see that the flying creature was a dragon. It was circling higher and higher into the air. Scott kept his eye on it so he wouldn't lose sight of it. They were only about halfway there when the dragon ceased its circling pattern and started off in a single direction.

"Turn left and follow that bird," Scott ordered the man.

The peddler turned left and squinted to see the bird Scott was talking about. When he saw it, he came to a complete stop. "Are you crazy?" he exclaimed. "That's not a bird, it's a dragon!"

"It's a bird to me," Scott answered. "Now follow it if you want to get paid."

"That would be suicide. That dragon could take us down with one breath."

"Then get me as close as you dare. Is there any way I can jump off this thing in midair?" The man looked at him as though he really was crazy. "As long as you get your money, what do you care?" Scott added, getting desperate. He didn't want to lose the dragon.

The man shook his head but he started to move once again, and it was in the direction of the dragon. He was able to put Scott within a hundred yards of the dragon, but didn't dare go any closer. Scott gave him the token and signaled to let him go. The man spoke a word that Scott didn't hear and he felt the suction release him. He immediately jumped off and flew as fast as he could after the dragon. He hoped to follow the dragon and let it lead him to Azinine.

He'd followed the dragon for about half an hour when suddenly he felt something very hot hit his back. Scott looked back to see two dragons about twenty yards behind him belching fire. Scott immediately dropped downward, plummeting towards the ground feet first. Not more than two seconds went by and he felt the hair on his head catch fire.

"Ouch!" he yelled. He looked skyward and could see one of the dragons rocketing downward after him. He knew the only way he could out-fly this dragon was to turn upside down and fly headfirst towards the trees. This of course scared him to death, but he had no choice. He quickly flipped, but by the time he had accomplished this, the trees were only fifty feet away and rapidly approaching. There was no way he could stop in time. He arched his back, brought the boots around, and with all his might tried his hardest to pull out of the dive, but the force was too much to pull out completely. He hit the tops of the trees, skimming across them. Branches tore at his clothes, cutting him in several places.

The dragon, on the other hand, was not so lucky and crashed through the trees like a plane out of control. When Scott finally gained control he stopped to assess his situation. He looked at the hole the dragon had made in the trees. He listened for any sign of the dragon and waited to see if it would surface, but couldn't hear or see anything. "Is it dead?" Scott asked himself. He decided to creep closer and get a better look. He had to know if the dragon was still alive. He moved slowly and strained to see any sign of it, but could see nothing.

"Now, Chinzar!" he heard a voice come from behind. It wasn't an audible voice, but one that entered into his mind, similar to that of the womvampirs. Scott whirled around to see the other dragon floating right behind him. At the same moment, the first dragon came rocketing from the trees belching fire like there was no tomorrow. The flames skimmed Scott's back and he lurched backward, directly towards the second dragon in an effort to avoid the flames. That dragon caught him in its claws and held him tight.

"So bold and young, what have we here? Who dares to follow our leader so near?" Scott heard the dragon say.

"Why, my friend, can't you tell? A little boy who has no shell," the other replied.

"This is good, no shell indeed. We'll grind him up to make our mead."

"Chinzar, Malmoth, we have no time to play. We must make haste and be on our way." This time, it was the large dragon he had tried to follow in the first place—or so Scott assumed.

"Are you the dragons who have my friend? A beautiful young girl and a good heart to lend," Scott said, interrupting their conversation.

"You speak our language rather fair, but answer your question, we do not dare," Malmoth, the dragon holding him, replied.

"I've brought the sword to pay her ransom. I think you'll find it rather handsome."

At this, the lead dragon moved closer, his eyes blazing, boring into Scott's. "Do not jest with this old lizard. For if you do, I'll rip out your gizzard. But if it's true, my little lory, then show the sword in all its glory."

Scott reached back his hand to grab the sword. "Abtu," he said and the sword leaped into his hand.

Chinzar, the first dragon, flinched and Malmoth immediately released Scott and moved away.

"Volcar, he really has it. Yes, he does. A greater sight to behold there never was," Malmoth said in amazement to the largest of the dragons.

Volcar didn't budge, but continued to stare at Scott. Finally he spoke. "Follow us now and if you obey, we'll get your friend without dismay."

Scott nodded, put the sword back in its sheath, and let the dragons escort him to their lair. It was a good hour before they came to some very dark mountains. The trees, the ground, the rocks—everything about them had a foreboding look. They went a short distance until they came to a large cave in the mountainside. Along with the dragons, Scott landed on the rocky dirt next to the mouth.

"Set the sword upon my stern, and with the girl I shall return," Volcar ordered Scott.

Scott shook his head, saying, "I'll not give it up, but wait by this tree. It will be yours once the girl is free."

The old dragon smiled as only a dragon can do. "Bold and smart, those traits are rare. I'll bring her back. You may remain here."

The three dragons entered the cave and disappeared. Scott waited outside, and before long they returned with Azinine. She looked horrible, but in good health. "Scott!" she screamed out. She ran over to him shaking and sobbing. Putting his arms around her to give her comfort, she reciprocated and hugged him tight. So tight, in fact, that Scott could hardly breathe. But it didn't matter; it felt good to see her and know that she was okay.

"You look horrible," he joked, trying to make her smile. "Are you all right?"

"You don't look so great yourself," Azinine retorted. "What happened to your hair?"

Before Scott could answer, a loud roar and a large flame belching from the old dragon's mouth interrupted them. "You have your friend, now give it here, so he'll remove the curse we fear."

"Do you have your flying boots on?" Scott whispered to Azinine.

"No, he took them from me."

"The dragon?"

"No, Magus Cohar. He has the dragons under a great spell. That's why they kidnapped me. You must not give that sword to him."

"I have to," Scott said. "I gave them my word. If I don't they'll fry me, and this time it'll be more than just my hair."

"Magus Cohar probably gave them orders to fry you anyway once they have the sword."

"Here," Scott said as he took off his pair of winged boots. "You take these and get out of here. Once you are gone, I'll give them the sword. It won't do Magus Cohar any good because I still have the gloves."

"Someone like Magus Cohar may not need the gloves," she informed him. "He might figure out how to use it without them. You can't give it to him. He admitted to me, or more like bragged, that he's the one who killed the High King and that he's the one who is leading the secret rebellion against the council. I can't believe it! He was the High King's cousin and trusted friend and..."

Another roar went up and the dragon stamped the ground impatiently.

"Go now!" Scott said. "Don't worry about me. After everything else I've been through, I'll find a way out of this," Scott told her with more confidence than he actually felt.

Azinine put on the flying boots and was about to take off when Chinzar stepped up to block her way. "Leave she will not, until we've got the sword you've brought."

"Let her go and fly like a bird, and the sword is yours. You have my word," Scott replied.

Chinzar and Volcar looked at each other. They both appeared to be weighing Scott's terms against something else. Scott was sure Magus Cohar had given them instructions regarding the sword and Azinine, possibly even himself. He lifted his arm up over his shoulder, gave the word, and the sword flew into his hands. He pointed the sword at the older dragon's belly, even though Volcar was still a good fifteen feet away. *If ever there was a time for a bluff, it was now*, he reasoned with himself. "Let her go, free of harm, or I'll take this sword and use its charm."

Volcar's eyes blazed with anger and Scott was certain he was going to fry him, but he held his ground. He knew if he showed any sign of fear, the dragon would realize he was bluffing. Volcar roared and blew out a flame at least thirty feet long. But it was aimed at the sky, not at Scott.

Even though Scott didn't fully comprehend the power of the sword, it was obvious the dragon certainly did and didn't dare attack. Volcar gave a nod to Chinzar, who stepped away from Azinine. She glanced back at Scott with concern in her eyes.

"Go!" Scott yelled and she took flight. The three dragons closed in on him like three bullies cornering their victim in a dead-end alley. It was one of the most frightening experiences Scott had ever had. Quickly, he put the sword back in its sheath and held it out to Volcar. "I meant you no harm. I only wanted the girl. I love her, you see, she is my pearl. I thank you, my friends. I bid you farewell. Now take the sword and may all go well." This seemed to surprise them and Scott guessed they'd expected more of a fight. He put the sword on the ground and backed away.

Using his claw, Volcar picked up the sword and placed it in his jaws. "We have the sword, to be terse. We'll hand it over to remove the curse."

The three dragons entered the cave, leaving Scott alone with no way of getting back home. He wasn't even sure he knew the way back home. He was also thinking that if the dragons returned with their curse removed, he'd be a sitting duck. As crazy as it was, he decided to follow them. He had just given up the sword—the one weapon he needed to protect himself. If he could get it back, it would not only keep the sword from getting into the wrong hands, but he'd have a weapon to protect himself while finding his way home.

He entered the cave and the stench was almost enough to make him turn back. He walked as quietly as he could, which actually wasn't very quiet at all, considering the rocks and debris he was stepping on.

As he went further into the cave, the tunnel started to open up, getting bigger and bigger until he came around a corner where it opened up into a huge cavern. The cave was lit with glowing Lumenarty rocks and he could see the dragons, including two other dragons he had never seen, standing before a man in a robe. About twenty feet away from Scott's hiding place was a huge crystal ball sitting on top of a large rock. The magus didn't have a staff and Scott guessed the ball was used to amplify his magic. The sword lay on a rock shelf and the magus was admiring it. He tried several times to pick it up, but it was no use. He was unable to lift the sword. He then tried several different spells, but nothing worked.

"The sword can only be used with the gloves. Go back, find the boy and get the gloves from him," the magus demanded.

"You said nothing about gloves. Now remove the curse," Volcar demanded menacingly.

"All right," the magus conceded. "All of you stand over there against the wall."

The dragons moved against the wall and the magus spoke an incantation. Immediately what looked like a large glass prism sprang up around the dragons, trapping them inside.

"I'll fetch the boy myself," the magus snarled. "I'll remove the curse and replace it with another. The curse of death. I can't leave you alive to take vengeance upon me!"

The dragons started to roar and belch fire against the cage, but it held. Black smoke began to fill the cage, causing the dragons to choke. They threw their large bodies against the walls, but it still held. The scene playing out before Scott horrified him. These were beautiful, majestic creatures, and this magus was going to leave them to die. He crept out from behind the wall and yelled, "Abtu!" The sword flew from the rock shelf and into Scott's hands. The magus whirled around and immediately held out his fist. Scott recognized it as the death grip and he braced himself for the worst. He expected, any second, to feel the crushing feeling in his chest, but it never came. Frustration crept over the magus' face as he realized the death grip had no effect on Scott.

When Scott finally got his wits about him, he ran over to the magus and kicked him in the gut causing him to double over. He grabbed the sheath and strapped it on his back. He turned towards the crystal ball knowing if he could destroy it, it would considerably weaken the magus' power. Meanwhile, realizing the death grip was futile, the magus spoke a few words and another glass prism appeared, this time around Scott. He brought the sword down hard against the glass cage and it shattered into a thousand pieces. Scott glanced over at the dragons and could see they were starting to fall. They were going mad inside the cage trying to get out.

"You're within reach. Use the blade now," Volcar shouted. "Strike now!"

Scott was still a good ten feet away. What did Volcar mean? There was no way he could strike now. He took a step forward, but another cage sprung up around him. Again, he brought the sword down hard, but this time the wall of the cage moved to avoid the sword. To his surprise, the blade grew to meet its target, shattering the cage one more time.

"Now!" Volcar shouted. This time Scott understood. He raised the blade up high and then swung it down hard, as if the blade were ten feet long. His target this time was the crystal ball. The blade grew and grew until it met its target, striking the ball, which was still a good seven or eight feet away. The crystal ball exploded with a blinding light, knocking Scott off his feet and sending him hard to the floor. At the same time, the cage surrounding the dragons shattered and they quickly began making their way out of the cave.

Volcar ran over to Scott, picked him up in his jaws, and proceeded to the exit of the cave. The dragon's teeth were sharp and Scott groaned as Volcar's teeth dug into his side. "Are you trying to rescue me or eat me?" Scott said sarcastically.

Volcar laughed. "I'm sorry, but there isn't enough time to let you climb up on my back. Please be careful where you swing that sword," he added.

Volcar was the last dragon out, and the others were waiting outside when he finally emerged from the cave entrance. He put Scott down and looked at the others. There were only four of them now. Before he could say anything, Chinzar spoke. "Where is Chalin?"

Volcar hesitated. "She…didn't make it, I am truly sorry."

Chinzar let out a roar that must have been heard for miles. Scott knew she must have been something very special to Chinzar. "It's your fault!" Chinzar growled, turning and leaping towards Scott. By this time, Scott had put the sword back in its sheath and there was no time to pull it out again. Volcar jumped in Chinzar's path, stopping him. "It is not his fault," he said. "He did the best he could. If it had not been for him, we would all be dead right now. We owe him our lives."

"That was my sister!" Chinzar roared. "The last one alive and now she is dead also." He let out another roar and shot fire high into the sky. Still fuming he slunk away, mourning his loss.

"I'm sorry about his sister," Scott replied.

"It wasn't your fault," the big dragon assured him. "He lost another sister about a year ago. She left one day to hunt and never returned. We can only assume she is dead. So you can understand his emotion— to lose a second sister is going to tear him apart. We had better get you out of here."

"Are you really going to let this Lumen go?" the fourth dragon asked incredulously. Scott had not met this one, but had seen her in the cave.

Volcar glared at her for a second and then turned to Scott. "You'll have to excuse my mate, Voxna. We normally don't befriend Lumens."

"We usually eat them," Voxna added.

"I understand," Scott replied.

Volcar gave Voxna an angry look and then turned back to Scott. "Thank you for helping us. We owe you a great deal. Is there anything we can do for you?"

"I could use a lift back to Lux, if it's not a bother."

"That's the least we can do," Volcar said.

"May I take him?" Malmoth, the smallest of the dragons, asked. She seemed the best tempered of the lot, so Scott was pleased she had asked.

"It's up to you, Scott," Volcar said, looking at him.

"Have you eaten?" Scott asked, only half-joking. Volcar and Malmoth chuckled, but Voxna still looked at Scott like a mouse being let go by a bunch of cats. "One more question," Scott said. "Why aren't you talking in rhymes anymore?"

This time, Volcar and Malmoth burst out laughing. "A dragon's life is very boring, a real tragedy to hear one snoring. To make life interesting along the way, it's just a little game we play," Volcar replied.

"It's just a game?" Scott asked.

"That's right," Malmoth said. Scott felt a twinge of anger, embarrassment, and stupidity all at once. He had been playing their game all this time without even realizing it.

"I have to admit you played it quite well," Volcar added.

"I feel very stupid," Scott replied. Then wanting to get on his way, he said, "Are you ready to go, Malmoth?"

"Climb on," she replied. She bent down to let Scott climb onto her back.

"What about Magus Cohar? Will he come after you?" Scott asked Volcar.

"I doubt it. If he's still alive, he knows we won't be so easily trapped again. He would risk a lot coming after us."

"What sort of curse did he place on you?" Scott asked out of curiosity

Volcar was about to tell him, but Voxna interrupted him. "No, Volcar. It is not something we should talk about, even to our…our friends." She looked at Scott. "No offense, but we don't know if you really are a friend or if you'll remain our friend. It would not be wise for us to divulge such things."

"Voxna is right," Volcar said to Scott.

Scott nodded and bid farewell to them all. Malmoth lifted into the sky, heading towards Lux.

"Do you mind if we take a short detour?" Scott asked.

"No. What do you have in mind?" Malmoth asked.

"I have three friends I need to rescue from the goblins," Scott explained. "In fact, I could really use your help."

"Nasty creatures lean and tall. They do not taste so good at all. But I would really like to help, for I really love to hear them yelp."

Scott laughed. "Then let's go!" he yelled.

When Malmoth and Scott landed on Goblin Mountain they still had a few hours before nightfall. It took Scott sometime to find the spot where he, Zodi, and Genin had entered last time. When he finally did, he knelt down on the grass and turned to Malmoth. "The tunnels will be smaller than you're used to, but you should still fit. Once we get deeper in the mountain, there's a room that opens up quite wide, where you should be more comfortable. I need you to keep the goblins away while I rescue my friends." Malmoth nodded and the two waited now in silence, but didn't have much longer to wait. As soon as the sun went down, the door opened and in Scott fell. Immediately two large goblins reached for him. Knowing what to expect this time, Scott was quick to react. He grabbed one of the goblins and threw him across the hallway. He was surprised how easily he had been able to do that, but then he remembered the gloves. Meanwhile, the other goblin, seeing Scott's strength, immediately sounded an alarm calling for other goblins.

By this time Malmoth had managed to climb into the cavern, which sent the goblins screaming and running back down the tunnel. Soon, Scott could hear several goblins coming up the tunnel, but as they rounded the corner, they froze at the sight of Malmoth.

"Let'em have it, Malmoth!" Scott yelled.

Malmoth blew a large flame, burning several goblins and sending the others into a retreat back down the tunnel.

"That was fun," Malmoth exclaimed, as she and Scott continued down into the depths of the cave. The two of them cautiously made their way down the tunnel for some time without meeting any resistance. Their luck soon ran out, though, when they came around a bend and were met with a shower of arrows. Luckily, Scott was on the inside of the bend and was able to duck backwards. Malmoth, on the other hand, was hit by several of them. Normally, arrows would simply bounce off her thick scales, but at such close range, one of her scales shattered, leaving her vulnerable in that spot.

Scott pulled the sword from its sheath, and sticking just his arm around the corner, swung down with all his might. The sword grew to meet its target and Scott heard several howls from the goblins. He struck again and again, sending off more cries. Malmoth let out a roar and sent a long stream of fire shooting down the hallway, sending the goblins scurrying away. Scott led Malmoth down the right fork, away from the cave the goblins had attacked from. They met no further resistance until they came to the prison entrance. There they met several guards who looked as though they were hiding from the action. They sat shaking, eyes wide with fright at the sight of the fire-breathing dragon.

Scott pointed the sword at them. "We have come for the wolves in your prison. Go tell the rest of your friends to leave us alone and no one else will get hurt. Do you understand?" Giving a nod, they hustled off up the tunnel. "I don't know that I trust them so we had better hurry," Scott said as he grabbed one of several ropes hanging on the wall.

"Malmoth, may I tie this rope around your tail and have you pull them up when it's time?" he asked. Malmoth nodded in agreement and Scott proceeded with his plan. She had a large spike on her tail, which made for a great place to secure the rope.

Scott opened the hatch and slid down the hole leading into the prison. "Alon!" Scott barked out. The three wolves appeared, looking very tired and obviously very hungry. "Alon," Scott said with concern, "you don't look so well."

"Scott, it is good to see you, my friend," the old wolf answered. "They haven't fed us so we are all very weak."

Scott gave him a sympathetic smile. "I have come to free you, just as I promised. I have a rope I can tie around each of you. Malmoth will pull you up."

"Who is Malmoth?"

"She's a dragon."

Alon lifted an eyebrow in surprise. "A dragon?" he asked. "You brought a dragon with you?"

"Don't worry," Scott reassured him, "she's a friend."

"I've never known a dragon to befriend anyone but their own kind."

"Maybe so, but nevertheless she's a friend and she's waiting. We must hurry before any goblins come back."

"Okay. Carakaz, you go first," Alon growled, turning to the youngest wolf.

Carakaz hesitated; he didn't want to be the first one to meet the dragon, but the alternative of staying in this pit was not appealing either. He knew he had to get out. He walked over and Scott tied the rope around him.

"When you get to the top, pull on this piece of the rope and it will come loose," Scott instructed him. "Once you are untied, drop the rope back down."

Scott gave Malmoth the signal and she slowly lifted her tail, which in turn lifted the wolf. Carakaz was soon at the top, and seconds later, the rope came back down. Scott tied the rope around Balton next. Balton was only halfway up when they heard Malmoth growl. Something up above was bothering Malmoth and she quickly jerked her tail upwards, sending Balton crashing to the ceiling where he hit his head hard before he managed to slip through the hole and up to the top.

"Malmoth, what is going on up there?" Scott asked.

"More goblins! We must hurry and get out of here. I'm starting to get a bad feeling about this place."

"Balton, throw the rope back down," Scott hollered, but no rope came. "Balton, let the rope back down!" he yelled, but again no answer came. Scott yelled to the dragon, "Malmoth, is Balton up there?"

"I'm afraid your other wolf friend is badly injured," Malmoth replied.

"Carakaz, can you get the rope off of Balton?"

"I'm trying, but he's lying on it," Carakaz replied.

Malmoth saw what was happening and rolled Balton over. Carakaz pulled on the rope and the knot came loose. He quickly grabbed the end and let it down.

"All right, Alon, it's your turn." Scott took the rope, tied it around Alon, and gave Malmoth the signal. Malmoth pulled him safely to the top. Alon loosed the rope and let it down for Scott, who went to grab it. But before he could, it lifted out of the hole again, leaving Scott alone in the pit. He could hear Malmoth roaring and belching fire, and knew the goblins were attacking again, and this time they seemed to be having more success. After about ten minutes, the rope finally came back down. Scott tied it around himself and gave Malmoth the word. Malmoth lifted Scott up, but not as easily as she had the wolves. When he finally got out, Scott could see blood oozing from her side where several arrows had hit her.

"You're injured," Scott said with concern.

"It's just a scratch, but we must get out of here," Malmoth replied.

Scott glanced at Alon, who was licking Balton, trying to get him to wake up. Balton was alive, but was still unconscious. Scott walked over, picked up the wolf, and walked over to Malmoth. "I know you are injured, my friend, but do you have enough strength to carry Balton?"

"Of course! It takes more than a few arrows to pull this dragon down," Malmoth replied. Scott smiled and placed the wolf over Malmoth so that his legs straddled her back.

"Okay, let's go," Scott said. He pulled the sword from his back and held it ready. They walked up the tunnel, meeting no resistance at all, which made Scott even more anxious. Where were the goblins? It was harder not knowing where they were. They came to the point where the two forks joined and opened up into the large room, when Scott stopped in his tracks.

"Azinine?" he whispered. There in the middle of the room was Azinine, standing very still with her eyes glued to Scott. Meanwhile, Carakaz let out a growl and then leaped forward. Malmoth knocked him to the ground and held him down so he couldn't get up. At this point, the other two wolves started to growl.

"There's a deer! Let's eat!" Balton, who had just woken up, barked out.

"Tell them to stay back," Malmoth said to Scott. "It's a trap!"

"Alon, stay back. It's a trap," Scott relayed to the wolves.

"Are you sure?" Alon asked. "We are very hungry and need food."

"Yes, you see a deer, but I see a girl. It must be some sort of spell that causes us to see what we want to see. They must be trying to lure us over there." Scott turned to Malmoth. "Malmoth, how did you know it wasn't real?"

"This is very simple magic," she explained. "And simple magic doesn't work on dragons. In fact, I see Voxna standing on the same spot. It's actually quite funny if you could see her. The illusion shows Voxna as a much younger and smaller dragon. As you know, Voxna is much older and would never fit in this cave."

"It's obviously a trap, but what kind?" Scott asked.

"Knowing goblin magic, it's probably another trapdoor, just like those on the mountainside. On the outside they use soft grass to lure Lumen, or deer, or what have you, to capture it. This must be the same thing. They are trying to lure us over to it."

"Then we should avoid walking over there," Scott cautioned, "but how do we know how large the door is? How do we know where not to walk?"

"We don't, so therefore, we won't," Malmoth replied.

"I don't think we have any other choice," Scott pointed out.

"Ah, my young friend, but we do. And they'll be gnashing their teeth when they find out we flew."

"Malmoth, you are the only one that can fly and I'm pretty sure your wings won't fit in this tunnel."

"I use my wings strictly for propulsion and steering. I get my lift from a gas that my body produces. I have thousands of tiny air sacs under my scales. When I fill these air sacs with gas, I start to rise."

"Are you suggesting we all climb aboard and float over the ground?" Scott asked with wonder in his voice.

"Exactly. However, since I don't have the use of my wings, someone will need to give me a shove."

"I guess I'm best equipped to do that," Scott replied. He told Alon, Balton, and Carakaz what Malmoth had said about the illusion and told them the plan. With Scott's help they all managed to straddle Malmoth's back.

"Are you ready, Malmoth?" Scott asked.

"I think so, but you'll need to be patient. I am not used to flying in such close quarters. I will need to slowly regulate the flow."

Scott could see Malmoth concentrating, but after about five

minutes, they were still waiting.

"Nothing's happening," Scott said, wondering if Malmoth had fallen asleep.

"I told you to be patient," she said. "If I put too much in, we'll slam into the ceiling of this cave."

Scott waited for another five minutes and was just beginning to wonder if this was going to work when Malmoth simply lifted her legs off the ground. Her body stayed right where it was.

"That's a way cool trick," Scott said as he began to push.

"Be sure to hold onto my tail, just in case you're on the ground when it gives way," Malmoth warned Scott.

Scott gave Malmoth a shove, and the dragon started floating across the floor. However, instead of heading for the tunnel entrance at the other end, they veered off course and bumped into a wall. Malmoth cushioned the collision with her claws, but the force caused them to drift backwards and now they were directly over the exact spot where they didn't want to be. Floating the way they were, they would be sitting ducks if the goblins attacked.

"Sorry, Scott," Malmoth said, "but it was the only thing I could do."

"No, it's not your fault. I should have aimed better when I pushed you."

"Scott, I can't use my legs to push us. If I do, I risk pushing us upwards and hitting the ceiling, and that would be even more catastrophic, especially for your wolf friends.

"I guess I'll just have to do it. I should have a few seconds before the trap doors open."

"Be careful," Malmoth warned. "It may give way as soon as you hit the ground. Make sure you have a good hold on my tail."

"Okay, here goes nothing. Hold on," he said to the wolves. Holding tight to Malmoth's tail, he jumped off and gave her a push. She shot forward, this time in the right direction, but Scott was left hanging from her tail as the door opened.

Below he could see hundreds of goblins with swords, scimitars, and other weapons. When they saw their prey escaping, they began to yell and scream. It was the most horrifying sound Scott had ever heard. Since their plan didn't work, the goblins started to make their way back into the tunnel and Scott could hear them getting closer; they weren't going to let them get away so easily.

When they reached the other side, Malmoth raised her tail, lifting Scott out of the hole. He jumped back onto her tail. She released the gas in her body and took off running with everyone still aboard her back. Scott was amazed at how quickly she was able to maneuver in the tunnel. It was a good thing too, because they would not have been able to move as quickly had they all been running on their own. Even now, the goblins were gaining on them. They still had a good hundred yards to go when several goblins caught up to them with swords ready.

"Malmoth, unless you can go faster, you are about to lose your tail and me along with it," Scott yelled.

"I'm going as fast as I can," she answered back. "Can't you use that sword to fend them off?"

"Sure. No problem," Scott replied, embarrassed that he hadn't thought about that. He reached back, gave the command, and the sword flew into his hand. He swung the blade at the first goblin and it leaped out, hitting the goblin's sword, slicing it in half. Now weapon-less, the goblin slowed, causing several goblins behind him to bump into him and each other. This, in turn, resulted in a domino effect and several others behind them tripped. Soon, the whole goblin clan—with the exception of the two still close on their heels—were tripping over each other, causing a very large bottleneck.

Concerned about the two goblins still giving chase, Scott swung at them with the sword. Once again the blade leapt forward, slicing off several fingers of one of the goblins, causing it to drop its weapon. He struck out again at the second goblin, slicing its hand completely off. The two goblins stopped running, now howling out in pain. Further back down the tunnel, Scott could see the mass of goblins regrouping. He looked forward to see the door to the outside just up ahead.

"Once again I slip through your greasy hands, you filthy animals!" Scott yelled out to the goblins and then stuck out his tongue, taunting them.

Reaching the door, Malmoth didn't wait to let anyone off her back. She leapt into the air and shot upwards through the door. The wolves had the sense to see what was coming and held on the best they could, but Scott, on the other hand, was still taunting the goblins. The force of the leap loosened his grip and sent him falling to the cave floor.

The fall dazed Scott and just about broke his left arm. The sword was jarred from his grip and lay about five feet away. When he finally got his wits about him, several goblins were almost upon him. He tried to grab the sword, but a searing pain shot through his arm. Panic set in as a host of goblins approached. Then, as had happened twice before, his fear left, and a surge of strength coursed throughout his body. He wasn't sure if it was pure adrenaline or part of the magic of Lumen, but he was grateful for it. With the help of the gloves, he tossed a nearby barrel of water and then a second one into the oncoming mob, sending them sprawling to the ground. Scott quickly picked up the sword with his right arm and ran up the stairs. He had only taken two steps when a goblin leapt forward and grabbed his leg, pulling him back down. Without even looking Scott swung the sword backwards, severing the goblin's arm and freeing himself from his grasp. He took a couple more steps and then a second goblin grabbed his other leg. Once again he jabbed backwards, but the goblin dodged the swing. The goblin now grabbed him by his other leg and proceeded to drag him down the stairs. With all the strength he could muster, Scott brought the handle of the sword down hard upon its head. The goblin howled out in pain, releasing its grip on Scott.

Another goblin took its place, but this time Scott pointed the sword directly at it and the blade sprung forward, but stopped less than an inch from its chest. Although Scott didn't like the goblins, for some reason he also didn't like killing them.

"Halt," he yelled, "or I'll run you through!"

The goblin stopped, not daring to move any further. Out of the corner of Scott's eye, he caught sight of another goblin flexing a bow with an arrow aimed directly at him. The goblin released and Scott lifted the sword out of reflex as though he was going to block it. To his utter amazement, the blade of the sword fanned out and formed into the shape of a round shield. The arrow struck the sword and disintegrated.

"Whoa, that was awesome!" he exclaimed to himself, half forgetting the goblins.

Scott dropped the sword once again to the chest of the goblin standing near him and the sword turned back into its original form. He slowly backed up, holding the goblins at bay.

He made it out the door and began running down the mountain, his arm throbbing. The goblins were also pouring out in droves, screaming and yelling in pursuit. Still running, Scott managed to put the sword back in its sheath, which allowed him to run a little faster, but not enough. The goblins were gaining on him. They had the advantage of being able to see in the dark better than he did. He kept running in spite of the pain. Seconds later, an arrow from one of the goblins struck him in the leg, causing him to stumble. He fell and his head hit a rock, knocking him unconscious. His body rolled down the mountain into a clump of small trees, where he lay motionless.

Chapter Fifteen
Surprises

Scott woke up to a searing hot pain penetrating his entire body. The pain was so excruciating, he felt as though he would die. In fact, he almost wished he would die to escape from it. Eventually, he recognized it as the same searing pain he had felt the last time he had been given unicorn serum. It continued only a few more minutes and then it was gone. He looked around and discovered he was in a beautiful room and lying in a comfortable bed. He could hear birds singing just outside the window, where he noticed the sun was beginning to disappear behind a mountain in the distance. There was a slight breeze blowing through the room, and Scott could smell the wonderful evening air. For a moment he wondered if he had died and gone to heaven—it was all just too perfect.

He lay there, trying to remember what had happened, but all he could recall were the goblins chasing him. He tried to sit up, but the pain returned with a searing jolt and he immediately lay back down. It felt like every part of his body was injured. Glancing down, he noticed several bandages on his arms and legs and could feel one on his head.

As he lay there, the door opened and in walked Magus Noka. Scott's heart skipped a beat and he tried to remain calm. He had no idea what side this magus was on, and it scared him to think he was possibly being held a prisoner in Noka's castle.

"Hello, Scott. How are you feeling?" he asked with a warm smile.

"I've felt better," Scott replied.

Magus Noka laughed. "I'm sure you have. I just applied some unicorn serum to your wounds, as I'm sure you are well aware. You should be feeling better soon. I have a surprise for you...," he continued, but before he could finish, Azinine came bursting through the doorway.

"Scott," she exclaimed, "you're alive! I was so worried about you." She bent over and put her arms around him, hugging him tightly.

"Ouch!" he cried, wincing in pain. "I may be alive, but just barely."

She drew back, her eyes glistening with tears. "I'm sorry," she apologized, "but I am so happy to see you. I was so worried you would never come back."

"I wasn't so sure I'd come back either," he replied.

"Thank you for coming for me. I knew you would."

"Someone else would've come if I hadn't," Scott replied.

"Maybe, but I had my doubts. Everyone else would think it was too dangerous. But you, you're the only one crazy enough to try such a thing, and for that, I thank you." At that, Scott's spirits soared. He didn't care how bad he was hurting—it was all worth it.

"Azinine," Magus Noka began, "can we leave Scott alone long enough for his surprise?"

Scott gave him a curious look; he had thought Azinine was the surprise. Magus Noka looked over to the door and gave a clap. The door opened and in walked his mother and father. His mother rushed over to his side and gave him a big hug.

"Ouch!" Scott whimpered.

"Oh, honey, I'm so sorry. I was just so worried about you, and I'm so relieved to know you're okay."

"It's all right, Mom. Maybe you could do it again, but just a little softer," he suggested. She gave him a soft hug and kissed him on the forehead.

His father walked over and sat down next to them. "How are you doing, Son?" he asked.

"I'm a little banged up, but grateful to be alive. Although, I have to admit, there were times when I wasn't sure I would make it. What are you guys doing here? Mom, isn't it dangerous for you to be here?" Scott asked, concerned.

"Well, yes, I suppose, but you've been missing for so long, even Lumen wasn't going to keep me away."

Just then, Eric and Ned poked their heads through the doorway, hesitating just a little to come in. They didn't wait long, however, and quickly walked over and sat next to Mr. Frontier. "Hey, guy," Ned spoke softly. "I told you she was nothing but trouble. Maybe next time you'll listen to me." Grinning, he gave Scott a soft slug on the shoulder. Ned was speaking in English, so only Scott, Eric, and his parents understood what was being said.

"'Trouble' is putting it lightly," Scott replied. Then Scott looked at Eric. "What do you think of this place?"

"I have to admit, I thought Mom was a little off her rocker when she first told me, but being here is proof," Eric replied.

"Where's Josh?" Scott asked.

"We didn't dare bring him," Hollie said. "We didn't think Lumen was ready for Josh yet." The grouped laughed.

They talked for several hours listening to Scott recount his adventure. Finally, Magus Noka reminded them that he needed his rest.

They started to leave, promising to return. "Wait," Scott said, raising himself up on one arm. They all turned around, but Scott was looking at Azinine.

"I'm so sorry about your mother. I feel like I'm to blame. If I hadn't come to your place, she would still be alive." Azinine looked confused.

"What are you talking about?" Azinine asked.

"I saw those men turn your mother to stone," Scott replied.

"Oh that," said Azinine. "That was just a stone spell. Though it's very uncomfortable, it's not deadly. It can either be reversed by someone else or it wears off over time. She's fine now."

"Oh, that's good," Scott said with relief.

They all left the room, leaving Scott and Magus Noka alone. The older man was on his way out when Scott asked him to wait. "How did I get here?" he questioned.

"As incredible as it sounds, the stableman thinks a dragon dropped you off," Magus Noka replied. "He saw one flying away from our front door, and when he came to investigate, he found you lying there. That's all we know, though I find that very hard to believe."

"When you found me, was there a sword there also?" Scott asked.

Magus Noka studied Scott's face, seriously contemplating something. After a moment's hesitation, he replied gravely, "No sword, Scott."

Scott was aware that Magus Noka knew about the Golden Sword. By now, every magi must know the gloves have been taken. With that thought, Scott felt to see if the gloves were still on his hands and was relieved to find they were.

"You sleep now and we'll talk more in the morning," Magus Noka said, smiling at him before he walked out.

The next morning Scott was feeling much better. He was still a little sore, but was able to get out of bed. He ate breakfast with his family and they talked some more about the things Scott had experienced. With the exception of his mother, they were amazed to hear Scott's stories. Dragons and goblins were fairy-tale creatures. It was hard for them to imagine their actual existence. Eric's father wanted to know more about the leppy, and Eric kept asking questions about the dragons.

"Someday, I'll introduce you to one," Scott promised Eric. "We might even be able to go for a ride on one."

"Scott," Magus Noka broke in, "you and your mother are still in danger. We must get both of you home as soon as possible."

"That's fine by me," Scott said. "Where is Azinine? I'd like to say good-bye."

"She is out on the terrace, but please make it quick. We need to get going."

Scott walked down the hall towards the terrace. As he approached the doorway, he noticed Azinine holding hands with another boy. A jolt of jealousy coursed through him, followed by a sense of sadness, which was soon replaced with anger when he realized the boy was Ned. Scott watched them for a long moment, not knowing whether he should confront them or simply walk away. Either way, it was an awkward situation. Ned knew his feelings for Azinine, and yet, there he was with her. Standing there, he watched as Azinine put her arms around Ned and gave him a hug and it nearly broke his heart. He quickly turned around and walked back to where his family was waiting for him.

"That was much quicker than I had expected," Magus Noka remarked.

"You said to make it fast, didn't you?" Scott growled back. "Let's go, I don't want to be here any longer than I have to."

His anger was obvious, so no one said anything more about it. They hopped onto the MOC and took off. As they did, Scott looked back to see both Azinine and Ned looking up at them. Azinine was waving both arms and shouting for them to wait, but Scott just looked away.

How could she do this to me after all I did for her? Scott wondered. *She told me she liked me, and now this. And Ned—my best friend! How could he do this to me?* The anger welled up inside of him along with a few tears. He did his best to hide them from everybody, but he was sure his mother must have seen. To his great relief, she didn't say a word.

The MOC finally came to a stop, but Scott was surprised to discover they were not at Cylindhall. Instead, they had landed on a field surrounded by trees growing in an almost perfect circle. In the middle of the field was a circular stone structure, reminding him of the one he had seen in England called Stonehenge.

There were several tall, thin stones standing in a vertical position. Lying across the top of them were more stones, creating what looked like several doorways. Finally, in the middle of the circle stood a single stone structure, or doorway. This one was in much better shape than those at Stonehenge, but the likeness was uncanny.

"Is that how we're getting home?" Scott asked, pointing to the rock structure.

"Didn't you and Azinine come this way?" Magus Noka asked curiously.

This surprised Scott. Magus Polimar knew they had come through the portal at Cylindhall. Didn't Noka know? Scott was surprised that Magus Noka was not aware of which way he had come. Then another thought struck him. Azinine had been very careful not to let anyone see her enter Cylindhall, as though it was a secret. Thinking quickly, he said, "Sure, but aren't there other ways to pass between our worlds?"

"There used to be, but we believe they have all been destroyed. This is the only door left that we know of," Magus Noka answered.

Scott wasn't sure how this worked so he hung back, letting the others go before him so he could observe what they did. Instead of walking to the center of the structure, as he had assumed they would, each person stepped under one of the "stone doorways" on the perimeter. Once everyone was in place, Magus Noka walked to the middle and stood under the doorway in the center.

"CastleOne," he spoke. A bright light lit up from inside each of the stone doorways and grew so intense that Scott had to close his eyes. He felt his feet leave the ground for only a second, and then they were once again back on a solid surface. The brightness subsided and Scott found himself in the forest just outside of CastleOne.

Wow! That was a lot easier than using the chair, Scott thought. Just like the forest on Lumen, he found himself in a circle of stones on a meadow surrounded by a perfect circle of trees. He wondered why he had never seen this before and why the other students hadn't found it either. It was a peculiar enough sight that it certainly could not go unnoticed.

The family said their good-byes to Magus Noka and walked towards the castle. As soon as they stepped into the perimeter of the trees, the meadow and the stones disappeared and it looked as though it was simply a forest with several trees crowded together.

"I don't know if I'll ever get used to that," Scott's father remarked.

"I think it's cool!" Eric replied.

"Whatever you do, don't show it to Joshua!" commented their mother. "He'd play with it all day and night. And knowing him, he'd also try to find a way to replicate it for one of his magic shows."

The others laughed and resumed their walk to the castle. They met Headmaster McDougal on their way, where he cheerfully greeted them. Accompanying them back to CastleOne, he asked if he could meet with Scott and his parents in his office before they left.

The headmaster didn't say much about Scott's adventures—only that because of his absence, Scott would have to remain at school during the summer to make up his classes. If he would agree to that, the headmaster would allow him to take part in the War Games and other events coming up next week. Scott agreed, but wasn't happy about it.

Scott said good-bye to his parents, and his mother ordered him to stay away from Lumen and concentrate on school. Scott said he would certainly try. At the mention of Lumen, his thoughts went back to Azinine and his heart sank. Eric asked him if he wanted to play some basketball, but he declined, pretending to be tired and still quite sore. In reality, he was a bit sore, but really he just wanted to be alone.

On his way up to his room, he passed several students who gave him curious looks. Luckily he didn't run into anyone he really knew. He wasn't in the mood to explain his absence. It was then he realized he didn't know what day it was. He figured it had to be either Saturday or Sunday because classes weren't in session. He opened the door to find his room just as it always had been. It was strange to be back in this world, where everything seemed so normal. It felt like he had just woken up from a bad dream. He lay down on his bed and it wasn't long before he fell asleep.

The next morning he woke up to Ned shaking him. "Wake up, Scott. You'll be late for breakfast."

Scott opened his eyes, trying to focus them. "What time is it?" he asked.

"It's almost eight o'clock," Ned replied.

"What day is it?"

"Wow, you have been out of it. Today is Monday. Hurry and get dressed, we don't want to miss drill today. They'll be posting the match-ups for the tournaments."

Still a little groggy, Scott climbed out of bed and headed for the showers. When he returned, Ned was sitting at his desk reading something. Scott had not bothered to take off the gloves the night before, so he quickly removed them now while Ned wasn't looking. He placed them in the drawer next to the bracelet Azinine had given him. Seeing the bracelet reminded him of what he had witnessed back on Lumen, and his anger flared up again.

While Scott was dressing, Ned turned around and asked, "Hey, how come you didn't say good-bye yesterday before you left? Azinine was really disappointed."

"Yeah, I'll bet," Scott muttered under his breath.

"What did you say?"

"I left because Magus Noka reminded me of the danger that still existed. I was going to say good-bye, but then I saw a couple of back-stabbers and decided it was time to go," Scott replied grumpily.

"What do you mean by 'backstabbers'?" Ned asked.

"You know. People who are nice to your face, but the minute you turn your back on them, they stab you!"

"Oh yeah. I know what you mean. The High King was killed by one of those. How do you know they were backstabbers?"

"I just know!" Scott growled.

"How come you didn't report them to Magus Noka?"

"Because he wouldn't have cared. All right?"

"Scott, what is wrong? Why are you so angry?" Ned asked, now seeing there was more to this than Scott was letting on.

"Never mind. I don't want to discuss it right now. I'll see you at class," he said as he headed for the door, not waiting for Ned. Ned decided not to follow. He had already eaten breakfast and he didn't want to be around Scott while he was in such a foul mood.

Scott walked down to the cafeteria and jumped in line. There were only two other students in front of him. Most of the others had already eaten. While he was standing there, Turner and Slim walked by and stopped when they saw him.

"So, Frontier, you decided to come out of hiding. What's wrong? Did Mommy make you come back to school?" Slim said in a baby voice. "Well, it's a good thing. I was starting to get worried you wouldn't be there when we humiliate you and the rest of your division."

Scott chose to ignore him. He was already so wound up that he was sure he was going to snap any minute.

"Ohhh, what's wrong, little Scotty? Does that make you feel sad?" Slim teased, but this time sticking his face in Scott's. This was too much for Scott. He picked up the pudding he had just placed on his tray and slammed it into Slim's face. With lightning speed, Slim brushed the pudding out of his eyes and sent his fist flying. Scott quickly placed the breakfast tray between his face and Slim's fist and Slim broke the tray in two. He was in the process of throwing another punch when Turner tackled him to the ground.

"What are you doing?" Slim roared at Turner.

"If you hit him, you'll be thrown out of the competition," Turner replied. He then looked up and winked at Scott with a smile. This took Scott by surprise. Although he and Turner had been on better terms, he would never have thought Turner would stick up for him.

"Well, I gotta go," Scott said calmly, as if they had just played a game of checkers or something. "I'll see ya at the competition, Slim." Then he walked away.

By this time, several teachers had arrived, including Buzz. After surveying the mess and seeing Scott walk away, he pretty much guessed what had happened.

"Frontier!" he yelled. "I want to see you in my office right away."

Without even looking at Buzz, Scott drew in a deep breath and changed course, now heading towards the drill teacher's office. Buzz commenced with his usual yelling and then informed Scott he would be unable to participate in the tournament activities.

"What about Slim? Does he get to still participate?" Scott asked.

"Slim isn't the one who started it!" Buzz replied angrily.

"But..," Scott started to say, but was cut off.

"But nothing," Buzz said. "You've got to learn a little more self-control. I know Slim taunted you. I get that. But you didn't have to throw the pudding, you could have just ignored him."

Scott sat there fuming. He knew arguing wasn't going to help things, but he was still so angry.

"Not even the War Games?" Scott questioned with as much self-control as he could possibly muster.

"You may still take part in the War Games," Buzz replied.

"Thanks," Scott replied gratefully, and then followed up with, "Why?"

"Why what?" Buzz replied.

"Why not eliminate me from the War Games too? The headmaster would have."

"Let's just say I'm curious."

"Curious about what?"

"Though I don't approve of your actions, I do admire your courage. I guess I'm curious to see how you'll do in the War Games."

"It may take us three or four hours, but we'll get their flag," Scott stated.

Buzz let out a laugh. "Maybe I should keep you out," he said.

"Why do you say that?"

"Because nobody has ever taken the other team's flag in less than eight hours. Usually it takes anywhere from twelve to twenty-four."

"Well, I'm going to pretend I didn't hear that," Scott retorted.

Still chuckling a bit, Buzz said, "Good for you. That's the kind of attitude everyone should have. You may go now. Tell the other students I'll be there shortly."

Scott nodded and walked out of the room. When he approached the drill range, several Falcons converged on him, including Ned, along with Nancy.

"Don't tell me you got disqualified from the tournament?" Ned asked.

Letting out a deep breath, Scott sighed. "Unfortunately, I did."

Scott spent the rest of the week in solitude. He didn't want to be with Ned and he didn't have any other real friends to hang out with. Ned was pretty miserable too. He had lost his best friend and he didn't even know why. Several times he had tried to get it out of Scott, but Scott just kept ignoring him. Finally, he decided it was time for desperate measures. On Saturday night Ned found Scott outside sitting alone in the gardens.

"Hi," he said as he approached.

"Hi," Scott grumbled back.

Taking a deep breath, Ned began the speech he had rehearsed. "Scott, I don't know why you have been so angry lately and why I'm bearing the brunt of it, but I brought you a surprise to cheer you up."

Scott looked at him curiously, wondering what he was up to. Ned gave a whistle and from up above, Azinine fell into his lap.

"Surprise!" she yelled.

"What are you doing here?" Scott asked in his same grumpy voice.

Azinine jumped off and barked right back at him. "Wow, Ned wasn't kidding. You are being a jerk."

"Jerk? I'm being the jerk?" Scott asked, getting angrier by the minute. "I spend weeks looking for you. I risk my life to rescue you. You tell me you like me. And then you run off with my best friend when my back is turned? And after all that, he has the gall to bring you here as a surprise! All that, and you're calling me a jerk? Well, maybe I am, but at least I would never stab my friend in the back as you two have done."

"Stab in the back?" Ned asked, not quite understanding.

"What do you mean by 'stab in the back'?" Azinine asked.

"The day I left, I went to say good-bye to you, and I found you two holding hands and hugging. That's the kind of affection that goes beyond just being friends."

Azinine's eyes were blazing with anger. Ned, on the other hand, was beginning to laugh, and it wasn't long until he couldn't control it any longer and was rolling on the ground. Scott was confused by Ned's reaction to his outburst.

"You mean to tell me," Azinine said, her face getting redder by the minute, "that you didn't say good-bye because you thought Ned and I..." She was cut off by another chortle of laughter from Ned. "I can't believe you would accuse me of such a thing. Don't you think I have more integrity than that?" she yelled. And then as an afterthought, she slapped him across the cheek. This was more than Ned could handle; he was now laughing so hysterically that tears were streaming down his face and his stomach was aching.

"What is so funny?" Scott yelled, even more irritated by Ned's behavior.

"She...she...," he began, but couldn't get it out because another fit of laughter overcame him.

"Scott," Azinine broke in, "Ned is my brother!"

Scott's eyes grew wide. He looked over at Ned, then to Azinine, and then back to Ned again. Finally a big grin spread across his face. Looking at them both, he said rather sheepishly, "you're brother and sister?" he said in amazement.

"Yes," she replied.

"I'm...sorry. I had no idea. Ned, why didn't you say something?"

Through his laughter, Ned said, "Azinine is not supposed to be here except to bring word to Magus McDougal. You weren't supposed to know I was from Lumen. After you found out, I didn't want to be caught between the two of you, so I never mentioned it."

"Wow! I really apologize for being so mean, but it's your own fault. If you had told me, none of this would have ever happened." Scott then turned to Azinine. "And I'm sorry for accusing you of backstabbing. I would never have thought it, except I saw you with my own two eyes. I guess I shouldn't have jumped to conclusions, but what was I supposed to think?" Azinine sat down next to him and put her arm around him.

"Hey," Scott said, another thought coming to him, "how come I've never met your brother Neil?"

"Neil?" Azinine replied with a questioning look. "We don't have a brother named Neil."

Scott looked over at Ned. "You told me that your brother Neil went to school here last year."

"You told him we have a brother?" Azinine asked.

Ned looked a little embarrassed. "I...I...I was just trying to find a way to spook Scott. How was I supposed to know he'd become so familiar with our family?"

"So there never were any floating chairs?" Scott asked.

Ned shook his head in embarrassment. "Nope."

Azinine was about to say something when they were interrupted by Headmaster McDougal. "Ned, Azinine, I need to speak with you two right away," he said in an urgent tone. "Will you please excuse us, Scott?"

"Sure," Scott replied.

As they left to follow Headmaster McDougal, Scott grabbed Azinine's arm. "I want to see you again," he said.

"You will," she replied with a smile.

Scott stood up, elated to find out that Azinine and Ned were brother and sister. He was about to enter the school when he heard that voice again. "Funny legs, funny legs." He turned around and looked upwards in the direction he had heard the voice. There, right above him, on a tree branch, was a fairly large black-and-white bird.

"Hello, bird," Scott shot back. "If you're going to taunt me like that you should at least introduce yourself."

The bird just about fell off the branch. No one had ever spoken to it except for other birds. "You can talk, you can talk," the bird replied.

"Yes, now please introduce yourself."

"I'm Birchbeak, I'm Birchbeak."

"I'm Scott, I'm Scott," Scott replied, following the same speech pattern as the bird.

"Pleased to meet you, pleased to meet you."

"Before I leave, is there anything I can do for you?" Scott asked, still in a good mood.

"Got food, got food?" the bird asked.

"I could probably drum up some bread."

"Love bread, love bread."

"Then I'll get you some."

He entered the building, glad to know that he wasn't going crazy.

Scott didn't see Ned or Azinine the rest of the evening, nor did he see them all the next day. In fact, Ned didn't show up until Monday morning, the first day of competition. Scott was dressing when Ned walked in the room.

"Ned, where have you been?" he asked.

"I've been on Lumen, discussing things with my father," answered Ned.

"Is everything all right?"

"Sort of. Now is probably not a good time to discuss it. I need to get ready for the competition, but I'll explain later. Guess what?" he asked, changing the subject. "I met Tina in the hall on my way up here. She told me the little incident between you and Slim was planned. Slim purposely tried to antagonize you just so you would react as you did and get yourself thrown out."

"Why me?" Scott asked skeptically. "Certainly there are other Falcons that are more of a threat than I am."

Ned answered with a rueful grin. "Sure. You weren't the only one he tried it on, but you were the only one to fall for it."

"I guess I'll never learn," Scott sighed.

"Still, it was a pretty dirty thing to do," Ned said.

"I guess all is fair in love and war." Then, wanting to get off this subject, Scott said, "You had better get ready. I'll see you down at breakfast."

"Okay," Ned agreed.

Chapter Sixteen

War Games

That afternoon the competition started off with a speech by Headmaster McDougal. He talked about the significance of the games, and of course, the importance of good sportsmanship. Buzz stood up next and reiterated that each member of a division must take part in at least one event, but no more than two events. He then announced the order of the competition. Marksmanship would begin first, followed by the endurance course, and last of all combat. Once all of the events were completed, the points would be tallied and posted for all to review.

The points earned during the competition were important because they played a large role in the strategy each division used during the War Games being held the next day. If a team had a large lead from the events, they could afford to be more aggressive and take more chances than the other team. However, when it was all over, the points from both the competition and the War Games were added together to determine the winner.

For the sake of those who had never participated in the competition before, mainly the freshmen, Buzz went over the rules one more time. "For the marksmanship competition," he began, "each team selects three persons from each grade for a total of twelve shooters from each division. Each person is given a total of twenty seconds to fire off one round, consisting of ten bullets per round. Each target consists of five circles, and each competitor is required to place two bullets in each circle. Points are awarded based on the number of circles hit. The team with the most points wins.

"The endurance course consists of fifteen runners from each division. In competition, only two runners compete at a time instead of the four we have used all year. Points are based on the collective team time and the best individual time.

"Combat requires four competitors from each grade, for a total of sixteen from each division. Freshmen fight against freshmen, sophomores against sophomores, and so on. In addition, there's a wildcard where one student from each division is randomly picked to compete against each other. This keeps the competition interesting, since it's possible for a freshman or a sophomore to be paired up against a junior or a senior." After explaining the rules and answering questions, Buzz called out the names of each division's competitors for the marksmanship tournament. The two divisions lined up and Buzz handed a gun to each of the division leaders, asking them to sight their gun to start off the competition. Ian took his time with his division's gun, shooting off almost twice as many practice shots as Slim had. He wanted to make sure their gun's sight was accurate, but he also knew it would annoy Slim.

When Ian was finally ready, Buzz blew his whistle and the two began to shoot. Slim hit eight out of the ten, while Ian only hit seven. They each handed their guns to the next person in line while Buzz recorded the shots and set up new targets. He then blew his whistle, signaling the next two competitors to begin shooting. This went on until the last two people had taken their turn. At the end of the competition, Buzz announced that the Badgers were ahead seventy-eight to seventy. This, of course, spurred on all sorts of cheers and jeering from the Badger division.

Next, the students moved over to the endurance course, where several students were warming up. Buzz gave those students who were competing in the endurance course about a half hour to get warmed up. Once everyone was ready, they lined up and Buzz squeezed the trigger, signaling the start. The Falcons got a good start with Zack Madsen, who put the falcons ahead by about thirty seconds. After that, both sides didn't gain on each other much until about midway through, when a boy named Charlie Ruegger, from the Falcon division, twisted his foot while racing through the tires. The rules stated that a student must finish, no matter what. Charlie did the best he could, but he had an extremely hard time climbing the wall. He ended up using his sprained foot, causing him excruciating pain. This, along with another superior run by Turner towards the end, gave the Badgers an additional fifty points.

Finally, for the last competition of the day, the students gathered inside the combat building and settled into the bleachers. The Badgers had a good combat team, and there was little hope for the Falcons of making up many points here. Before the competition began, Buzz announced the wildcard drawing. Each division was responsible for providing two judges for this competition, and Buzz now asked for one judge from each division to draw a name for their respective divisions. Buzz held up his hand for everyone to be quiet, and once it calmed down, motioned for the Badger judge to draw. The judge drew a name out and gave it to Buzz.

"Marcus Bryner," Buzz yelled out. A stir of voices shot through the crowd.

"Do you know him?" Scott asked Nancy, who was sitting next to him.

"Sort of," she replied. "He's a junior this year. Not really the best pick for us. He's really quiet and doesn't strike me as the fighting kind, but he might surprise us."

By this time, the Falcon judge had pulled a name out for the Falcons and handed it to Buzz.

"Ned Niedermeier," Buzz yelled out.

"What?" Ned exclaimed, his mouth hanging wide open. "Did he

really call out my name?" he said, turning to Scott.

"Yep," Scott said, just as surprised. "You better start getting warmed up. I'll come with and help you."

"You're going to miss the other fights," Nancy said, hoping Scott would hang around. Without Tina, who was fighting for the Badgers, Nancy had no one to sit by.

"I'll watch them from the warm-up area," Scott said.

The two of them stood up and headed for the dorms. "I can't believe this," Ned said. "Do you think I can beat him?"

"Absolutely!" Scott replied. "Just remember the element of surprise."

"Right, element of surprise. Oh boy, what am I doing?"

"Listen, Ned, you'll do fine," Scott said, trying to reassure him. "There's no reason for us both to go back to the dorm, so I'll wait for you over by the mats. I'd like to watch this first match."

"Okay," Ned responded, still in a bit of a daze as he walked off alone. Scott headed over to the mats and sat down on the corner where the Badgers were warming up. He wanted to see if he could get a look at Marcus Bryner.

"Excuse me," Scott said, tapping one of the Badgers on the shoulder, "which one is Marcus Bryner?"

"He's not here right now, but you can't miss him. He's short with broad shoulders and curly red hair."

"Thanks," Scott replied.

Scott sat there, watching another Badger warm up. Slim was with this one giving him advice—some of it not so nice. "What a slime-ball," Scott muttered to himself.

The first match began and the crowd went wild, cheering up a storm. The first two competitors were freshmen—Dale Young for the Badgers and Lyle Sandberg for the Falcons. Scott knew both of them. They were pretty evenly matched and he was curious to see how they would do against each other. Neither seemed to get the advantage over the other, although they were both trying very hard.

After some time, Scott heard Slim yell, "Dale, quit being such a fairy, you can do better than that," and then a minute later, "You call yourself a Badger!" Scott felt bad for Dale. Not only were those words bad for his self-esteem, but they also distracted him. Lyle, on the other hand, took advantage of it, and he attacked hard each time Slim yelled out. As a result, Lyle won the match with a score of fifteen to five.

As the second match started, Ned walked in and began warming up. Scott headed over to him and sat down. "How are you feeling?" he asked.

"I have butterflies," Ned admitted, "but I'm also excited. Just listen to the crowd. It must be awesome to have them cheering for you."

"Yeah, unless you're losing," Scott said.

"That's what I like about you, Frontier. You have a way of instilling confidence in people."

"Sorry."

Ned continued to warm up. When Scott could help, he did. When he couldn't, he continued to watch the matches. The sophomore round ended and the juniors were getting ready for their matches. So far, the Badgers were down by five points. There was about a ten-minute break between the rounds, and Ned took this time to ask Scott a favor.

"Scott, I left my headband in our room. Would you mind getting it?" he asked.

"No problem." Scott took off and headed towards the dorms. When he got to his room, he grabbed Ned's headband and then started back down the stairs. When he got to the bottom, however, he stopped. He heard hushed voices coming from around the corner and he paused to listen.

"Listen, Chuck." Scott recognized Slim's voice. "In about fifteen minutes, Marcus is going to come down with a very bad stomachache. That means you'll have to draw another name. It's time we taught little Niedermeier he can't mess with us Badgers and get away with it. I've created another name ticket with my name on it. When you draw the name, drop it on the ground. On your way up, switch it with my name ticket. Got it?"

"If they find out, I could get in a lot of trouble, Slim," Chuck responded.

"They won't find out, but if they do, I'll take the blame. Got it?"

"Got…it," Chuck replied hesitantly.

Scott couldn't believe his ears. He knew Slim wasn't playing fair, but he couldn't believe he would stoop this low. He decided it was time Slim learned a lesson or two. He returned to his dorm for a moment, and then headed back to the combat building to find Ned practicing on the kicking bag. On the other side of the room, he noticed several students crouched around a short red-headed kid who was doubled up on the floor. Scott didn't know exactly what had happened, but he knew Slim was behind it.

"Looks like you won't be fighting Marcus," he commented to Ned.

"Yeah. He was over there practicing one moment and the next he was on the ground, holding his gut. I think he must have eaten something bad."

"Whatever it was, Slim was behind it," Scott informed Ned.

"Oh, come on, Scott. He wouldn't hurt his own man," Ned argued.

"I heard him and Chuck talking."

"Who's Chuck?"

"Chuck's the judge who drew the wild-card name for the Badgers."

"Oooh," Ned said.

Scott continued telling Ned what he had overheard. "Slim told him that Marcus was going to get a stomachache and that a new name would need to be drawn. He's rigged it so that his name will be drawn.

Just so he can 'teach little Niedermeier a lesson.' Those were his exact words."

Ned's face went pale. "He'll tear me to pieces and it'll all be legal. Maybe I should come up with a stomachache."

"You could do that, or we could even the odds a little. And at the same time, we could teach Slim a lesson in front of his whole division."

Not liking the sound of this, Ned replied rather hesitantly, "You're scaring me, Scott. Every time you start talking like this, I seem to get in trouble. But keep talking. I'm curious."

"The rules say you are required to wear combat gloves. Right?"

"Yes."

"Well, they don't say what kind of combat gloves. I'll simply let you borrow mine."

"Huh? Why would your combat gloves be any better than mine?" Ned questioned.

"Hello! Earth to Ned. I mean the combat gloves I obtained on Lumen."

"You mean *the* gloves? You have those? Here? With you?" Ned asked, astonished.

"Yep," Scott said with a huge grin.

"And you'll let me wear them?" Ned asked almost reverently.

"Of course!"

"Yes! I've heard about those gloves my whole life, but I never thought I would see them, let alone wear them."

"Well, you're going to get your chance. There are only four more matches and then you're up. Here, put these on." Scott pulled the almost transparent gloves out of his pocket. Ned pulled his gloves off and then with almost a sort of reverence, he slipped on the gloves Scott was holding. He then pulled his own combat gloves back on, over Scott's. Wanting to try them out, he walked over to the kicking bag and slammed a fist into it. The bag shot forward, knocking into a student behind it and sending him to the floor.

"Oops, Sorry," Ned said, offering his hand to the kid. Ned pulled him off the floor with surprising ease. Ned gave the student a smile and walked away. "These are awesome!" he whispered into Scott's ear.

The two of them waited for the last match of the senior round to end. When it finally did, Buzz announced that Marcus was sick and that a new name needed to be drawn. Just as Slim had planned, Chuck picked out a name and dropped it. Watching very closely, Scott thought he saw him switch them, but he did it so quickly that it was hard to tell.

"Slim Johnson!" Chuck yelled out. A gasp went out from the Falcons' side and a large cheer from the Badgers'. Buzz looked down at Slim, asking if he was all right fighting a second time. Slim had already fought in the senior round and had won with ease. It was mostly because of him that the Badgers only trailed by two points now in the combat event. Meeting Buzz's gaze, Slim nodded his approval with a smile.

Ian Karding walked over to Ned. "Ned, just do your best. Try and stay away from him as long as you can until the time runs out. Whatever you do, make sure you protect your head and stomach. Got it?"

"Got it!" Ned said with a big grin on his face.

Ian turned to Trevor, who had just finished his match. "Well, he sure is happy for someone who is about to get the crap kicked out of him."

Trevor laughed. "We all have to learn some time."

Because Slim was already warmed up, no break was called. The referees motioned for the two contestants to join them in the ring. Ned jumped into the ring, all the while throwing fake punches at an imaginary opponent.

"Ned Niedermeier looks surprisingly perky, considering the odds," the announcer spoke.

Ned hopped over to the announcer and grabbed the microphone out of his hands. "I fly like a butterfly and sting like a bee!" he yelled. The crowd roared with laughter, especially the Badger side.

Scott shook his head in amazement at Ned's new attitude. "Did you tell him the gloves won't make his opponent's hits and kicks any less painful?" a voice next to him said. Scott looked over to see the headmaster standing next to him.

"Uhhh...Nope," he answered. "But I'm sure he's about to find out."

"Does it disappoint you not to be able to participate?" the head-master asked.

"A little, but I'll get my chance tomorrow," Scott replied.

"I look forward to it."

Just then the bell rang and Ned began to dance around the ring, still throwing punches at an imaginary opponent. Slim, on the other hand, stood in one spot with his hands and feet slightly swaying, like a cobra ready to strike its prey. "Now, Niedermeier, you are going to find out what happens to little rats who mess with the cats," Slim hissed to Ned.

"Ooooh, I'm scared," Ned replied, feeling confident with the gloves on his hands.

As Ned danced around, he made the mistake of getting a little too close and Slim struck out, slamming a fist directly into Ned's fore-head. The impact sent Ned to the floor. A roar went up from the Badgers' side and the referee awarded Slim two points.

Ned stood up, but this time Slim didn't wait. He jumped forward, now slamming a foot into Ned's gut. Next, with a roundhouse, Slim sent another foot smashing into Ned's head, once again sending him to the floor. Gasps went up from the Falcons' side, while the Badgers kept up their cheers. Another four points were awarded to Slim.

Ned, with amazing resiliency, stood up again. But no sooner had he done so than Slim sent a foot whirling into his legs, knocking him off his feet and sending him once again to the mat. Two more points were awarded to Slim.

The bell rang and Ned teetered over to his corner. "Keep it up, Ned, you're doing great," Ian said, trying to give him some encouragement.

Scott jumped up and gave him some water. "You're not using the gloves, Ned!" he whispered. "They only work when they come in contact with something else. You have to connect with him!"

"Now you tell me," Ned replied, out of breath.

The bell rang again and the two came out of their corners, staring at each other. It looked like David and Goliath, but this time Goliath was winning. Ned had lost his bounce, but he was bound and determined to connect this time. The problem was, to connect, he would have to get close enough to Slim and risk being hit again.

"Element of surprise! Element of surprise!" he could hear Scott yelling at him.

"Element of surprise," he repeated to himself.

Just then, Slim leapt forward, posturing for another strike. Ned screamed out, "Haaaaaa!" and shot forward towards Slim. This tactic took Slim off guard, but only slightly. His punch still had enough power in it to connect with Ned's head, knocking him off balance. Once again Ned hit the floor, this time landing about a foot away from Slim. "Connect," Ned said to himself and swung his glove into Slim's feet. The blow hit Slim with amazing force and knocked his feet out from under him, landing him on his back.

The Falcons' bench went wild and the referee awarded two points to Ned. Slim was quick to get to his feet, annoyed that this little punk actually scored some points off of him. Ned leaped forward, again yelling, "Haaaaa!" Slim kicked a foot directly at Ned's chest and Ned stuck out his gloves in defense. Slim's foot hit hard, but to his surprise his body was thrown backwards into the ropes.

"You're dead meat, Niedermeier," Slim yelled out, enraged. He shot towards Ned with all his might, throwing himself at Ned. His foot caught Ned square in the chest, slamming him hard to the ground. Ned groaned inside, but got up as quickly as he could and charged. Slim stood his ground, welcoming Ned's attack. Just as Ned approached Slim, he quickly stopped, causing Slim to miscalculate his thrust. Ned leaped towards Slim with gloves outstretched, hitting him in the gut and knocking him once again onto his back.

Both student benches were now screaming and yelling, and Ned was dancing in the ring with his arms in the air like he had already won. Slim had fire in his eyes. If looks could kill, Ned would be dead. Slim swung himself around on his back and caught the unsuspecting Ned with his leg, knocking Ned to the floor. As soon as Ned stood up, Slim was right on him throwing another punch. Ned held out his hand and blocked the punch. Slim threw another punch, and Ned blocked that one. He sent a kick and then another punch and another kick, but each time Ned blocked them with his hands.

"You can't keep this up forever, Niedermeier," Slim yelled, and he was right. Ned blocked the next punch, but he was too slow to block the roundhouse with the foot and he crumpled to the floor.

The referee pushed Slim away while he assessed Ned's situation. Ned slowly started to raise himself off the floor, and when he turned around there was fire in his eyes. Ned was mad.

"Attack!" he screamed, and charged with such ferocity that even Slim backed up a bit, but Ned was on him before he could do much of anything else. Ned swung wildly, and it was Slim's turn to go on the defensive and try to block Ned's punches. He blocked the first three or four, but even when he blocked Ned's punches, it felt like Ned was hitting him with a 100 pound barbell. He tried to block the next one, but his arms were bruised and his body ached. Ned struck out and Slim was too slow. It caught Slim square on the head, and he went down hard. Slim's head was swimming; he had never been hit that hard, but he managed to stagger to his feet. Ned, still enraged, grabbed Slim with both hands and lifted him high above his head. The crowd, which had been screaming on both sides, gasped and went suddenly quiet. What they were witnessing was impossible. It was like a kid picking up his dad and lifting him above his head.

Whooping out a Tarzan-like cry, Ned slammed Slim onto the mat with a thunderous thud. The Falcons exploded and everyone was now on their feet. The judges awarded Ned five points for the move, making the score just about even.

Slim looked up at Ned, shock registering on his face and shaken by what had just happened, his body racked with pain. Staring him down, Ned flexed his muscles and let out a growl: "Raaaaaaa!" Slim tried to get up, but his body just wouldn't let him and he fell back to the mat and lay limp. Slim lay there, motionless. Stunned, the crowd once again went quiet. The referee counted to ten and then awarded the win to Ned. The Falcons went nuts, knowing this pulled their team back into the running since a knockout granted the winner twenty-five points and removed any points won by the other opponent. Once all the points were tallied up, the final score was now one hundred seventy-three for the Badgers and one hundred thirty-five for the Falcons.

The Falcons were now flowing out of the stands and jumping into the ring. Several seniors, including Ian Karding, were already there and had placed Ned up on their shoulders. Ned searched for Scott, wanting to share his victory with the person who had made it possible, but he couldn't see him anywhere. Curious about where he might have gone, Ned scanned the crowd but to no avail. Scott had disappeared. Meanwhile, the Falcons were still parading Ned around on their shoulders, and wrapped up in the cheers, Ned soon forgot about Scott. Whooping and hollering, his teammates carried him back to their dorms, where they spent most of the afternoon and evening celebrating.

Around eight o'clock that night, Ian invited his division leaders, and any other interested Falcons, to gather together to discuss their final strategy for the next day. They were just getting started when Scott quietly slipped in and sat down next to Ned.

"Where have you been?" Ned whispered.

Scott didn't answer, but instead put a finger to his lips as Ian stood up to speak.

"All right, people," he began, "we are an unfortunate thirty-eight points behind the Badgers. In order to beat them, we will have to capture at least seven more men than they capture of ours and capture their flag. The Badgers have beaten us the last five years in a row now, by digging a large pit, covering it with a sturdy roof, and then camouflaging it, making it difficult to capture them or shoot them for that matter. Then, they patiently wait for easy pickings to come along, and slowly capture or terminate our numbers. Eventually, they're able to overpower us and take our flag. It's a slow, drawn out process, but it seems to work well for them. This year, I think we should use their strategy against them. It may be a very long battle, but maybe if they sit there long enough, they'll be tempted to come looking for us, especially since they're ahead. I'm hoping they'll feel like they can take more risks. Now that you've heard my thoughts, the floor is now open for other suggestions."

No one spoke for some time. Then Scott hesitantly, slowly, raised his hand.

"Yes, Scott? Do you have an idea?"

"Yes, but my idea is more centered around capturing their flag in record time. Don't we get extra bonus points for doing that?"

"Yes, but the fastest time is eight hours I believe. Considering their strategy, it would be very difficult to beat that. But, let's hear your plan," said Ian.

Scott stood up and walked to the marker board, where a map of the castle grounds was laid out. He drew a circle in the southwest corner of the grounds. "This is where the Badgers' home base is located."

"Whoa, whoa, whoa," Ian said, butting in. "How do you know where their home base is located?"

"Well, let's just say a little birdie told me," Scott said, winking at Ned.

"Are you sure about this?" Ian asked.

"Positive."

"This is great! This will help us a ton. There are a number of things we could do now. In fact, we…"

"Ian, let the kid finish," one of the members said, cutting him off.

"Of course. Please continue, Scott."

"Well, Slim will expect us to send out scouts to try and locate their base camp. It is also logical that you will send out expendable freshmen for this task. Last of all, Slim hates mine and Ned's guts, and we'll use that against him also. So here's my plan. Ned and I will take a band of freshmen out on a scouting excursion. We'll call them Crow squad. We'll purposely roam about a hundred yards from their base, but won't acknowledge that we know where they are. In fact, we'll act like we're lost. We'll fight and quarrel with each other.

"I'm betting Slim won't be able to resist the temptation to either capture or eliminate us. When they do come after us, we'll lead them back in this direction and through this small gully," he said, pointing to a spot on the map. "This gully has steep ledges on both sides and is surrounded by trees. The only way to get out is to go back the way they came or to continue forward. Ian, you'll hide some of your men, we'll call them Tiger squad, in the trees that surround the gully and in front. Once the Badgers chasing us enter the gully, Tiger squad will come from the rear and the front and surround them. If they fight, we'll eliminate them. However, my guess is they'll surrender and let us capture them. That way, we get fewer points.

"We'll quickly strip them of their head gear and put them on Tiger squad. Tiger squad will then take Crow squad back to the Badger base, posing as Badgers. The Badgers will think their men captured us and are bringing us back as prisoners. This will allow us to get close enough to their base without them firing on us. If they let us in, Tiger squad will give our guns back to us and then we'll have them surrounded. We either fire on them or they surrender. What do you think?"

"It's a good plan, but disguising ourselves as the enemy is against the Geneva Convention," Jason West said, very proud of himself for knowing that.

"It's not against the Geneva Convention," Ian countered. "The Geneva Convention is for prisoners of war. However, it does state that if you are caught wearing an enemy uniform or disguised so that the enemy can't tell which side you're on, you can be treated as a spy and aren't subject to the prisoner-of-war rules. In other words, they can shoot you on the spot or treat you however they want. In any case, the school rules don't say anything about wearing the other team's uniform, except that if we are caught or even shot disguised as a Badger, they get double the points."

"So are you suggesting we try Scott's plan?" Jason asked.

"It's risky and even a bit sneaky," Ian replied, "but it just might work. We are far enough behind that we really don't have too much to lose. Even if they do shoot a couple of our guys, it will be worth it if we're able to capture their flag in record time. That would give us an additional twenty-five bonus points, and I would really love to do that. We may even capture enough Badgers to offset any casualties. How do the rest of you feel? All in favor, raise your hand."

No one else had a better idea, so everybody raised their hand and Ian began working out the details of exactly how they would execute this plan, discussing things such as how to act so as to make everything more believable. Believability and surprise were crucial for this to work. However, in the event that something went wrong, Ian selected Trevor and about ten men, who he called Cobra squad. He instructed them to conceal themselves on the opposite side of the Badgers' head-quarters. This way, if Crow squad or Tiger squad were discovered, Trevor's men could start firing from behind and cause some confusion, giving the other Falcons a chance to stay alive.

"The best time to position yourselves is when their men start after Crow squad," Ian instructed Trevor. "They'll be distracted, so there will be less chance of them noticing you. Move quietly and whatever you do, do not let them see you."

The next morning the students eagerly gathered inside the combat building, where they waited for Buzz to arrive. The Badgers were obviously confident they would win with such a large lead.

"We got points, yes we do. We got points, how about you?" they yelled.

Some of the Falcons put their heads together and yelled back, "You have points, you have more. By the end of today, we'll settle the score!"

The yelling went on for about ten minutes before Buzz entered the building. He picked up the microphone and began to speak. "Welcome to the final day of competition. Today begins our War Games. For your information, the longest running contest ran twenty-seven hours and the shortest only eight hours. The average is about twelve hours, so we need to begin if we want to get some sleep tonight. First, I would like to go over the rules for those who haven't participated before and for those of you who seem to easily forget. Each team will be assigned three referees to ensure the rules are followed. Points will be deducted for any rules broken, so please pay attention.

"Every division member will dress in padded military fatigues, helmets, and protective eyeglasses. Each member is also given a semi-automatic gun, along with ammunition. The pellets are filled with paint and each team is assigned a color of paint. This helps identify who shot who. The Falcons are assigned Yellow and the Badgers are assigned red.

"If you are shot anywhere from the waist up, you are considered dead; you must immediately drop your weapon and lie on the ground. The one exception to this rule is the helmet. If you are shot on the helmet, not only are you not dead, but extra points will be awarded to your team. This is done to discourage any of you from shooting your opponent in the head. If you shoot anyone, once you've been hit above the waist, points will be deducted. A referee will tell you when you can get up and return to what is referred to as the graveyard. You can take up to three shots anywhere below the waist before being sent to the graveyard.

"The object is to capture your opponent's flag, which of course is located at their home base. The game will end when a flag has been captured. However, the team with the most points will win. So it is possible to capture the flag and still lose the overall competition. Points are awarded for each team member still alive and for the number of prisoners you have taken. If an opponent surrenders by dropping their weapons, you may not shoot them. You must accept their surrender. If you do shoot, points will be deducted.

"Capturing your opponent's flag is worth fifteen points. Five points will be awarded for each person still alive, whether or not they have been captured. Each prisoner is worth three points. Last of all, there is a twenty-five point bonus for capturing your opponent's flag in record time.

"Awards are given for best military leader, best strategic direction, and outstanding valor. However, as you all know, the best reward of all is the school cannonball, which the winning team will keep in their dormitory for the entire next year. In addition, the losing team has to sing the winner's victory song. Are there any questions?"

He waited for anyone to ask questions, but no one did. "All right then, since the Falcons are behind, we will let them move out first and take up position at their home base. Falcons, you must remain there until you hear the cannon. That will indicate that both sides are ready. Let the games begin!"

The students cheered as they headed over to the lockers containing the War Games gear. Both sides used the same guns and same color of fatigues, but the Badgers wore red helmets and the Falcons wore yellow ones.

Once everyone had their gear on, the Badgers were instructed to stay behind while the Falcons took off into the woods hooting and hollering the whole time. Finally, Ian silenced everyone, reminding them they didn't want to give the Badgers any indication of where their home base was located. Once they arrived, they went over their plan one more time while they waited for the cannon to go off.

"Remember, guys," Ian cautioned them, "execution is everything here. A little bit of good acting wouldn't hurt either. Once Crow squad lures the Badgers into the ravine, assuming they surrender, we have to act quickly. Grab their helmets, swap them with your own, and get back to their home base as quickly as possible. The longer their men are gone, the more suspicious they'll be when we return." Ian then turned to Trevor. "Trevor, you and your squad will need to pay attention. Once you hear gunfire, you've got to attack. If all goes according to plan, the Badgers will retreat in your direction. You will need to head them off. Leave one of your men behind, though. If something goes wrong, we'll need someone to run back to headquarters and let Eric know. Eric, if that happens, your best bet is to take up a defensive position and try and hold out."

They waited for another thirty minutes before the cannon went off. When they heard the roar of the cannon echoing through the forest, everybody got butterflies. Scott, too, felt them deep in his gut, but he was also beginning to feel that odd sensation of courage he had experienced several times while on Lumen.

"Okay, Scott, it's time to move," Ian ordered. "I'll move my men into place and hopefully we'll see you in about an hour."

Scott nodded and then faced his unit. "All right, men," Scott yelled, "let's move out!"

It took Scott and his men about fifty-five minutes to get into position. They had taken a roundabout way in order to position themselves correctly. As they came upon the Badgers' home base, Scott called his men to order. "All right, guys, Ned and I have already worked out a little act to make them think we're lost. What I need from the rest of you is to act discouraged, but not overdo it. Whatever you do, don't look in the direction of their base. That may tip them off that they've been discovered and they won't take the bait. Okay, let's look natural."

The group moved out around some trees and climbed down a small hill. As they rounded a bend, they came into view of the Badgers' base. Scott had warned his men this would be the place the Badgers would spot them.

They walked about fifteen paces further and then Ned tapped Scott on the shoulder. "Scott, I think we should go that way," he said, pointing in another direction. They both took off their helmets to ensure that Slim would know who they were. Scott pulled out a map of the castle grounds and began to study it.

"Be alert, men," he whispered.

"Uhh, Scott? They're coming," one of the members said. Scott looked back, and sure enough about twenty to thirty Badgers were running towards them while being uncommonly silent. Scott and Ned quickly put their helmets back on.

"Let's go!" Scott ordered. "We have to beat them to the ravine. Go, go, go!"

They took off running the shortest way back to the ravine. The ravine was only about a twenty-minute run from where they were, but that was still long enough for the Badgers to catch them if they weren't quick enough. Scott had warned them not to sprint and tire themselves out, so they ran at a steady pace for about three minutes.

However, the Badgers were gaining on them.

"Roger's down!" someone from behind yelled, indicating that Mike Rogers had been hit.

"Pick it up, men!" Scott yelled. "They're gaining on us."

They ran for about another thirty seconds before another member was hit. "Crawly's down!" another voice yelled.

"Ned, they're gaining on us too quickly," Scott yelled over at Ned. "Can you slow them down? Try not to hit them, though. We need as many alive as we can get."

"I'll do my best," Ned replied. He fell out of line, dropped to his belly, and started firing. *Pop! Pop! Pop!* His gun fired off one bullet after another. He hadn't tried to hit them, but one of his bullets met a Badger square in the chest. This sent several other Badgers dropping to the ground while others took cover in the trees. Ned continued to pop off bullets, giving Scott and the others time to cover more ground. As he did so, it hit him that he could hear others crashing through the trees up ahead.

"They're coming through the trees," he said to himself. "Time to go." He jumped up and ran quickly towards the ravine where Scott and his troop were headed. *Smack!* A bullet hit Ned square in the back of the helmet, and seconds later another grazed his pant leg. "Forget this," he muttered to himself and then took off at a pace even the fastest of the Badgers couldn't keep up with. Even so, he ran in a zigzag pattern to make a more difficult target.

"I slowed them down, but they are still right behind us," he said as he ran up beside Scott. Surprised that Ned had caught up so quickly, Scott eyed him suspiciously. "So, did you sprout wings on your feet?" he asked.

"Who, me?" Ned said with a big grin on his face.

Crow squad was getting tired, but the Badgers must have been getting tired also, because their pace seemed to be slowing. Crow squad had just entered the ravine when another man dropped. Watching the action from behind a tree, Ian wanted to fire now. He didn't want to risk losing any more men. On the other hand, he knew all would be lost if he fired on the Badgers before they entered the ravine, so he kept still.

Scott knew his men were getting tired and wouldn't last much longer. "Just a little bit further, guys, keep going!" he yelled. He also knew the Badgers chasing them were getting tired, and he figured it was most likely their pride that kept them going.

Crow squad hit the hill and climbed out of the ravine just as the Badgers entered it. "Now!" Ian yelled. Quickly, Tiger squad entered the ravine from behind, lined the ridge on both sides, and blocked any further progress in front. Stunned, the Badgers screeched to a halt. They were surrounded on all sides with virtually no chance of escape and they knew it.

"Throw down your weapons or we'll fire!" Ian demanded. Knowing there was no way out of this, the Badgers dropped their guns and took off their helmets. Ian scanned the group and was disappointed that Slim was not among them. But it was still a small victory.

"Rudy, take them prisoner," he yelled to one of his men. Rudy and six other men took the Badgers prisoner. Technically, they really needed only one man to do the job. The rules made it clear that prisoners were not allowed to fight back once they were captured. Not taking any chances, Ian wanted to have a few men with Rudy in case they encountered any other Badgers on their way back to their own headquarters.

"Tiger squad, let's finish this thing," Ian yelled out. Tiger squad picked up their opponents' helmets and put them on.

"Augh!" several men yelled as they put them on.

"Oh, I was going to remind you guys to wipe them out first. I'm sure they're pretty sweaty," Ian commented, half-laughing. Tiger squad removed the helmets and wiped them out. When they were ready to move out, Ian said, "Okay, men, when we round the corner and come into view, put your hands in the air and give a victory cheer. We want them to think we are Badgers and have successfully captured the Falcons." Then, as an afterthought, Ian turned to Scott. "Scott, we are going to leave your helmets on. This isn't normal procedure, but you guys can't fight unless you have them on. This may cause some suspicion, but we'll have to chance it. Does everybody understand?"

Everyone nodded and so, once again, Scott and his men headed back towards the Badgers' base with Ian and his men disguised as Badgers. They needed their energy when they arrived, so they walked and it took them some time to get there. When they rounded the final bend, Ian looked but couldn't see the headquarters. What he saw was an unnatural-looking pile of bushes. "Is that it?" he asked Scott.

"Yep."

"All right, men. When we get close, be sure to spread out a bit. I don't want us all clumped together if we have to fight." Ian then whistled and raised his hand in celebration. Others in his group followed his lead and began to cheer and yell. Soon they could hear other Badgers cheering from inside their base.

"So far, so good," Scott whispered.

"Yeah, cross your fingers," Ian breathed out.

They continued to walk forward and soon several Badgers left their base, running towards them. Scott counted ten of them.

"I didn't anticipate this. Got any ideas?" Ian asked Scott.

"Don't take your helmet off. Act happy to see them and try not to talk."

Everyone tried to act as normal as possible. As the men approached, most of them were congratulating their supposed division members, but they stopped about five feet away at the signal of their lead person. He stepped forward, the others remaining behind him.

"Good going, Jim. What's the password?" the lead guy asked. Ian froze. He recognized Dan Henry's voice and he knew Dan wouldn't easily be fooled. This was something he hadn't anticipated at all. Without the password they would be found out for sure, and they were too far away from the base to start a fight now. He tried to think, but his mind was blank.

Suddenly, Scott grabbed Ian's gun and started firing. His first bullet hit Dan square in the chest, and he knocked four others out before they got their wits about them and shot him. Scott had been hit about five times and it hurt, even with protective gear. He fell to the ground, as the rules dictated, and lay silent. For a moment both sides didn't know what to do and just stood there.

Then Dan, even though he was dead, turned to Ian, who he thought was Jim Fox. "You idiot," he yelled. "Why didn't you remove their helmets?"

One of the judges, who was standing nearby, immediately told him to be quiet and deducted five points from his team.

Another Badger stepped forward. "Give the password," he said.

At this point, Ian figured his only option was to shoot the man and hope for the best. But before he could react, the sound of gunfire erupted back at the base. Everyone turned to look. Guns were popping from the opposite side of the base.

Trevor's men! They heard Scott's firing and took that as the signal, Ian thought. "Attack!" he yelled out loud. "Back to the base." The five remaining Badgers also yelled and headed back to the base with Ian and his men right on their tail. Meanwhile, the other freshmen had been given their guns back and they too headed into the fight. As they arrived at the base entrance, Slim beckoned them in. The real Badgers took up a position and started firing. Ian signaled his men to surround them. Two of his men grabbed the flag and hauled it towards the back of the battle, as if they were making more room. No one took much notice with all the commotion of the battle going on. When they were sure no one was looking, the disguised Falcons hoisted the flag out of the base and quietly headed back to one of the judges with it.

Slim had not seen them grab the flag, but he did see them leaving. "Where are you going? I didn't tell you to leave! You'll get shot out there. Come back!" he yelled. Ian quickly grabbed Slim and pulled him to the rear.

"What are you doing?" Slim demanded.

"It's Ian!" the Falcon leader yelled. "We have your men surrounded. Tell them to put down their weapons or I'll shoot you at point-blank range."

Looking around, Slim could see several men with red helmets on and several others with yellow helmets, all pointing their guns at him. Panic welled up inside of him, followed by anger. He wasn't going to give up this easily. His men still outnumbered the Falcons and he wasn't going down without a fight.

"Halt! Slim yelled out. The Badgers stopped shooting and several took cover as bullets were still flying from Cobra squad outside the base. They turned around in surprise, looking at Slim. Without waiting for Slim to speak, Ian announced who he was and informed them they were surrounded. Meanwhile, Cobra squad had sensed what was happening and had ceased firing.

"Drop your weapons slowly or your leader gets it right in the gut. Do it now!" Ian yelled. Shocked and confused, they all just stood there waiting for Slim to give them a command.

"Tell them to drop their weapons," Ian once again demanded of Slim.

"You better do as he asks," Slim said. But as he did so, he quickly knocked Ian's legs out from underneath him, grabbed his gun, and pointed it at his chest. With the tables turned, the Badger leader said with a sneer, "Falcons, surrender now or you'll all be shot. Your leader being the first."

Now it was the Falcons who didn't know what to do. They waited for Ian to give a command. Instead, the Falcon leader addressed his opponents. "Badgers, we have already won the war. Notice that your flag is gone, most likely already turned in. My men have orders to fight if I'm shot. You are surrounded, so you can either surrender with dignity or die uselessly. The choice is yours."

Slim glared at Ian. "We would rather die than be taken prisoner...," he started to say, but was interrupted by the roar of the cannon, signifying that a flag had been captured and the War Games were over. A cheer went up from the Falcons as they celebrated. The flag had been captured in what Ian estimated to be approximately three hours. Less than half the time of the current school record.

Thirty days later, an awards banquet was held. Parents had been invited and Scott sat on a stone wall in front of the castle anxiously anticipating the arrival of his. As he waited, Ned joined him.

"Hey, Scott. Waiting for your parents?"

"Yeah, they should be here pretty soon."

"What a year it's been," Ned said.

"Yeah, pretty crazy," Scott replied.

"What do you plan on doing this summer?"

"Summer school, remember? The good news is, it's only four weeks long. How about you? What will you do this summer?"

"I'm afraid my summer won't be much fun either. Things on Lumen will be getting worse before they get better. We had hoped that Magus Cohar had been killed in the dragons' lair, but he's been spotted in the Great Forest. He's a sick man. Who knows what he'll do next. And now that the sword is missing, those magi pressing for a new king will be pushing harder than ever. They're telling everyone that the sword was stolen by an evil, conspiring magus who will use the sword to unite the forces of evil against our people and bring them into bondage. They claim a new king will bring harmony and unite the people so they can fight and win against this 'so-called' magus. Of course you and I know better."

"I guess I've stirred up a hornet's nest, haven't I?"

"Yes, but it was bound to happen sooner or later. You just caused it to happen sooner. Do you have any idea where the sword is? If we could find it, we might be able to stop this madness, or at least postpone it long enough to find a better resolution."

"I dropped it running from the goblins. As far as I know, they probably have it."

"Let's hope that's not true." Ned was about to ask another question when Scott's parents pulled up. Scott jumped up and ran over to their car.

"Hi, Mom!" he said, helping her out of the car and giving her a hug. When they released their embrace, Scott's mother reached in the car and handed him a package.

"What's this for?"

"Since you'll be staying longer, I thought you might need something to keep you busy."

"Thanks. What is it?"

"It's a surprise, you can open it later."

Just then Scott's dad came over. "Hi, Dad. Thanks for coming," he said, giving his dad a hug.

The three of them headed toward the front entrance when they spotted Ned still sitting on the rock wall where Scott had left him. "Hi, Ned, how are you?" Scott's mother asked.

"I'm doing well, thank you."

"Are your parents coming?"

"Probably not. My mother hates coming here so she avoids it at all cost."

"Really? How come?"

"She doesn't like the clothes. She says they make her look funny. And she can't wear her own clothes because everyone here will think she looks funny, so she prefers to stay home." Scott's mother smiled and nodded. They all walked inside and headed for the largest banquet hall.

"Mom, I'll meet you and Dad there. I'm going to take this package upstairs to my dorm," Scott said as he headed toward his room. Once inside he opened a large drawer and placed the package next to his gloves and body suit. As he closed the drawer, he heard the ringing from the bracelet Azinine had given him. He opened the top drawer and sure enough, the stones were lit.

"She's here!" he said to himself. He closed the drawer and quickly ran down the stairs and headed in the direction of the administrative offices. He was halfway there when he ran, not only into Azinine, but also her parents, Magus Polimar and Oline.

"Scott!" she yelled. "Are you wearing the bracelet?"

"No, but I just happened to be in my room when you signaled."

"I was hoping to find you before the meeting. My dad and I speak a little English, but my mother doesn't speak any at all. We were hoping you would help Ned translate for us."

"I would be happy to," he replied. As they walked down the hall, Scott could tell that Oline, who was wearing a very attractive and normal-looking dress, was walking very slowly.

"Mother, it's going to be fine," Azinine said, putting her arm around her mother. "Scott, do you like our dresses?" she asked, hoping to put her mother's fears to rest.

"They're quite odd looking, but if we sneak in the back door, I'm sure no one will notice."

Oline came to a complete stop and Magus Polimar, who had seemed deep in thought, also looked up, quite astonished at Scott's comment. Azinine, on the other hand, started laughing hysterically at her mom's reaction.

"Mrs. Polimar, I'm just teasing you," Scott said with a smile. "You look really great and as normal as anyone else. My mother is wearing a dress just like yours, so please don't worry."

She smiled. "I should have known. No wonder you and Azinine get along so well."

They continued down the hall until they came to the banquet room. It took him a few seconds, but Scott finally located the table his parents and Ned were sitting at.

"Ned is over there sitting with my parents," Scott pointed, already heading in their direction. They followed him and soon Scott reached a very glum-looking Ned.

"Hey, guess what the cat dragged in?"

"Huh?" Ned mumbled, looking at Scott quizzically.

"Your par..."

But before Scott could finish, Ned spotted his family and jumped up to greet them. "Mom! Dad!" he exclaimed. "You came!" He gave them each a hug and asked them to sit down, pointing to two chairs next to his. They sat down and in their own language talked for several minutes, getting strange looks from people passing by. However, the room soon filled up and Headmaster McDougal approached the podium.

He stood there for about thirty seconds while everyone slowly quieted. "Thank you all for coming," he began. "It's wonderful to look out and see all of you dressed so nice. We've had a great time this year. The students have worked very hard and fought very hard. I know you've all been waiting for the results of our year-end War Games competition. Well, due to some extraordinary efforts, for the first time in five years, we will now have the privilege of hearing from the symphonic Badger choir! They will be singing the Falcon victory song." The Falcons erupted in cheers and clapping. There were some boos from the Badgers, but surprisingly there were a lot of Badgers who were also standing up clapping for the Falcons. The headmaster let them yell for a moment and then held up his hand signaling everyone to quiet down.

"Tonight, we will be giving out awards to the best of the best. But I know you're all very hungry so let's eat first. Welcome!" Everyone clapped and went back to chatting while dinner was served.

Once dinner was over, Headmaster McDougal stood again at the podium to begin handing out the awards. He invited the English department to give their awards and the math department to give their awards and so forth, until it was Buzz's turn to give the awards for the competition.

"Thank you," Buzz said, as everyone stopped clapping. "Most of the years I've been teaching here have been pretty much the same. But every once in a while a year comes around that is most unusual. This is one of those years. I think you'll agree as the evening progresses. In the past, the award for Best Marksman has usually gone to a team member on the winning side of the shooting contest. However, this year the award for Best Marksman goes to a Falcon, even though the Badgers won the shooting competition. This award goes to Amy Hayes, a junior. Amy shot a perfect score. I'd hate to meet her in a dark alley." The crowd clapped and cheered as Amy walked up to receive her award.

"The next award is not surprising since he won this award last year. However, what's odd is that this student was beat earlier this year by a Falcon who also broke the school record. Unfortunately this student was disqualified to compete in the competitions this year. So, for fastest time running the obstacle course, this award goes to Badger Tyson Turner!" The Badger division members erupted in cheers.

"This next award is one of the most surprising," Buzz continued. "In fact, I don't think this has ever happened in the history of this school, but results can't be denied. The award for best combat soldier goes to a Falcon freshman, who, to earn this award, defeated a Badger senior. Ned Niedermeier!" At this, the Falcons went crazy, hooting and hollering, with even some of the Badgers joining in on the clapping. At first Ned couldn't believe it and he just sat there, not daring to get up.

Ned's father turned to Scott. "Did I hear that right? Ned defeated a senior in combat?"

"Yes," Scott replied, "and he beat him pretty good." Ned's father looked puzzled.

"Go get your award, Ned," Scott yelled.

"Scott, I can't accept that award," he whispered out of the corner of his mouth.

"Oh, yes you can! Slim rigged that fight and he is twice your size in more ways than one. Without those gloves it wouldn't have been a fight, it would have been a slaughter. The gloves simply evened the score."

"Well, when you put it that way, I guess I could accept it." Ned jumped out of his chair and started punching an imaginary opponent as he ran up to the stage.

"By the way, Ned," Buzz said as he handed Ned the award, "it's *float* like a butterfly, not *fly* like a butterfly." Most of the students, and some of the parents, didn't understand what he was talking about, but a few did and laughed.

"Okay, now for the award of Outstanding Valor. This award goes to Trevor Carson for leading his small band of men against the whole Badger division and thus allowing the Falcons the opportunity to advance and take the flag."

Trevor approached the podium as everyone clapped, but he seemed to do so hesitantly. He accepted the award and went back to his chair.

"The last award goes to Best Military Leader. Again, the results here leave no doubt, this award goes to Ian Karding who led his division to capture the Badger flag in record time." Once again the audience cheered and clapped as Ian approached the podium to receive his award. As he turned to go back to his seat, Buzz grabbed him and asked him to stay.

"Before you go, there is one last award that you and the rest of the Falcons have earned. Slim," he addressed the Badger division leader, "gather your men together and get ready to sing." Buzz walked over, picked up the school cannonball, and brought it back over to Ian. As he did so, Trevor approached Ian and whispered something in his ear. Ian nodded. Ian took the cannonball and walked over to the microphone.

"I can't even describe how good it feels to receive this award. For the last five years the Badgers have done an admirable job of defeating the Falcons. I have always dreamed of beating the Badgers as division leader, and this year my dream has come true. But my good friend Trevor Carson has reminded me that this battle was not won because of my leadership and not because of his and his men's valor. This battle was won because of the great military mind, military intelligence and sacrificial valor of one very fine soldier. A soldier, I might remind you, who sacrificed himself so that the team might go on to win. I hope all Falcons will agree that this cannonball, though awarded to us all, should be dedicated to Scott Frontier."

All the Falcons stood as they cheered and clapped. Ian beckoned Scott to come forward and receive the cannonball. Scott hesitantly walked forward and Ian presented him with the ball. Together they stood there as the Badgers sang the Falcons' victory song.

With the banquet finished and school over, most of the students headed home with their parents. Scott, of course, would stay and spend four more weeks. He said good-bye to Eric and his parents. He also said good-bye to Azinine and Ned, asking them to visit him while he was still at the castle. Once everyone had left, he headed back to his dorm and got ready for bed. He lay there thinking about everything he had been through. It seemed almost unbelievable, yet it had all happened. He took in a deep breath and let it out slowly. As he did so, his mind drifted off to Lumen and the experiences he had gone through. *Would things ever change there? Would he ever be able to go back to Lumen without having to be afraid for his life?* He hoped so, but was sure his parents, Magus Polimar, Headmaster McDougal, and others would do whatever they could to keep him on Earth until things were safe. He knew they didn't want him on Lumen. He, on the other hand, was determined to go back, danger or not. Though he might not have been so eager had he known the future of Lumen and the part he would play in it. Little did he realize the battle for Lumen was just beginning.

The End...for now

The author would love to hear from his readers.
To provide any comments or questions, please e-mail the author at

TheAncientCastle@gmail.com.

Made in the USA
San Bernardino, CA
08 December 2016